The Tree of Heaven

May Sinclair

BRITISH LIBRARY

First published in 1917

This edition published in 2020 by
The British Library
96 Euston Road
London NW1 2DB

Cataloguing in Publication Data
A catalogue record for this publication is available from the British Library

ISBN 978 0 7123 5307 6
e-ISBN 978 0 7123 6746 2

Text design and typesetting by JCS Publishing Services Ltd
Printed in England by CPI Group (UK), Croydon, CR0 4YY

Series consultant **Simon Thomas** created the middlebrow blog Stuck in a Book in 2007. He is also the co-host of the popular podcast Tea or Books? Simon has a PhD from Oxford University in Interwar Literature.

Contents

The 1910s

- **1910 (May):** Edward VII dies and George V ascends to the throne. He is king until his death in 1936.
- **1912 (April):** The sinking of the *Titanic*.
- **1913 (June):** Emily Davison is killed at the Epsom Derby after stepping in front of the King's horse.
- **1914 (August):** Great Britain declares war on Germany.
- **1916 (January):** After a year and a half of war, the Military Service Act introduces conscription for unmarried men aged 18–41, with some occupational, conscientious, or health exceptions.
- **1916 (May):** Conscription is extended to married men in May 1916.
- **1917:** *The Tree of Heaven* is published.
- **1918 (February):** The Representation of the People Act gave the vote to women aged 30 and over (with a property qualification) and to men aged 21 and over (without a property qualification). About 8.4 million women were enfranchised.
- **1918 (November):** The Parliament (Qualification of Women) Act passes, allowing women to become MPs.
- **1918 (December):** The first UK general election is held in which women can vote. David Lloyd George's coalition government wins a landslide victory. Seventeen women stand for election, one of whom is successful: Constance Markievicz (Sinn Féin).

May Sinclair (1863–1946)

To many literature scholars, May Sinclair is best remembered for having first used the term 'stream of consciousness', which she did in a review of Dorothy Richardson's *Pilgrimage* in 1918, probably borrowing the term from contemporary psychology. While this might have earned her a footnote in literary history, her own work was broad and prolific.

Born Mary Amelia St Clair Sinclair in 1863, she was the youngest of six children and the only daughter. Four of her brothers suffered from a fatal congenital heart disease, and she had to leave Cheltenham Ladies College after a year to help look after them. Her father suffered from alcoholism and died in 1881. Sinclair's first book came out four years later; a volume of poetry published under the name Julian Sinclair.

Over the next 45 years, Sinclair would publish widely – novels, philosophy, criticism, poetry, and biography (she wrote *The Three Brontës* in 1912, which was followed up two years later with a similar set of fictional women in *The Three Sisters*). Her first real success came with *The Divine Fire* in 1904, which concerns the moral lives of a group of artists.

By 1907, Sinclair was living alone and beginning to get involved with the women's suffrage movement. She joined the Women's Freedom League the following year, and later the Women Writer's Suffrage League, which published her 1912 pro-suffrage pamphlet *Feminism*.

Sinclair was interested in Freud's theories and worked at a London psychiatric clinic during the 1910s. While many writers of the period rejected or satirised Freud's work (see, for instance, Rose Macaulay's 1921 novel *Dangerous Ages*), Sinclair took it seriously if not unquestioningly. She was eager to help with the war effort, and travelled to Belgium in 1914 with an ambulance unit – though was only able to stay for a dozen or so days.

She never married, and one of her best-remembered works is a 1922 novella about an unmarried woman, *Life and Death of Harriett Frean*. Parkinson's disease contributed both to the decline in her writing output and to isolation from friends. She died in 1946, having lived with her companion and housekeeper Florence Bartrop for 14 years.

Preface

It's hard to think of a better choice for the first book in the British Library's Women Writers series than *The Tree of Heaven* by May Sinclair. Sinclair is an underrated writer who is perhaps now best known for her ghost stories, in which she used her personal interests in psychology and psychical research to great effect. She was also an early feminist. Both these aspects are important to this novel.

In some ways *The Tree of Heaven* is in keeping with the middlebrow novels of the period, in that it focuses in detail on the emotions and lives of the Harrisons, a fairly ordinary British family. However, its scope is surprisingly wide and varied. In the novel, Sinclair does an impressive job of identifying many of the forces that would shape the twentieth century. These included women's rights; Irish nationalism; changes to marriage and relationships; interest in psychology; the modernist literary scene; attitudes to war; and the pursuit of warfare through increasingly mechanised means. Sinclair contrasts this new age with that of the Victorians through her juxtaposition of the shining hair and strong constitutions of the Harrison children, with her depiction of the odd and incompetent spinster aunts and disreputable Uncle Morrie with his 'sodden body'.

There are two recurring motifs in the novel. The image of a vortex is used repeatedly. At once chaotic and ordered, it whirls the Harrisons inexorably into the future, while they fight to keep their freedom and sense of self. More complex is the image of the tree of heaven itself. Although the tree in the Harrison's garden is identified as actually being an ordinary ash tree at the start of the book, the narrative continues to refer to it as an exotic, non-native tree of heaven until almost the very end, when the war has stripped away family lore and imagination. The tree becomes an icon of the triumph of realism over the sentimentality of the Victorians.

The 1910s changed Europe forever. This book is an unjustly forgotten chronicler of that period.

Tanya Kirk
Lead Curator, Printed Heritage Collections 1601–1900
British Library

PART I

Peace

I

Frances Harrison was sitting out in the garden under the tree that her husband called an ash-tree, and that the people down in her part of the country called a tree of Heaven.

It was warm under the tree, and Frances might have gone to sleep there and wasted an hour out of the afternoon, if it hadn't been for the children.

Dorothy, Michael and Nicholas were going to a party, and Nicky was excited. She could hear Old Nanna talking to Michael and telling him to be a good boy. She could hear young Mary-Nanna singing to Baby John. Baby John was too young himself to go to parties; so to make up for that he was riding furiously on Mary-Nanna's knee to the tune of the "Bumpetty-Bumpetty Major!"

It was Nicky's first party. That was why he was excited.

He had asked her for the third time what it would be like; and for the third time she had told him. There would be dancing and a Magic Lantern, and a Funny Man, and a Big White Cake covered with sugar icing and Rosalind's name on it in pink sugar letters and eight little pink wax candles burning on the top for Rosalind's birthday. Nicky's eyes shone as she told him.

Dorothy, who was nine years old, laughed at Nicky.

"Look at Nicky," she said, "how excited he is!"

And every time she laughed at him his mother kissed him.

"I don't care," said Nicky. "I don't care if I am becited!"

And for the fifth time he asked, "When will it be time to go?"

"Not for another hour and a half, my sweetheart."

"How long," said Nicky, "is an hour and a half?"

Frances had a tranquil nature and she never worried. But as she sat under her tree of Heaven a thought came that made a faint illusion of worry for her mind. She had forgotten to ask Grannie and Auntie Louie and Auntie Emmeline and Auntie Edie to tea.

She had come to think of them like that in relation to her children rather than to her or to each other.

It was a Tuesday, and they had not been there since Friday. Perhaps, she thought, I'd better send over for them now. Especially as it's such a beautiful afternoon. Supposing I sent Michael?

And yet, supposing Anthony came home early? He was always kind to her people, but that was the very reason why she oughtn't to let them spoil a beautiful afternoon for him. It could not be said that any of them was amusing.

She could still hear Mary-Nanna singing her song about the Bumpetty-Bumpetty Major. She could still hear Old Nanna talking to Michael and telling him to be a good boy. That could only end in Michael being naughty. To avert naughtiness or any other disaster from her children was the end of Frances's existence.

So she called Michael to come to her. He came, running like a little dog, obediently.

Michael was glad that he had been sent across the Heath to Grannie's house with a message. It made him feel big and brave. Besides, it would put off the moment when Mary-Nanna would come for him, to make him ready for the party. He was not sure that he wanted to go to it.

Michael did not much like going to Grannie's house either. In all the rooms there was a queer dark-greenness and creepiness. It smelt of bird-cages and elder bushes and of Grandpapa's funeral. And when you had seen Auntie Edie's Senegal wax-bills, and the stuffed fish, and the inside of Auntie Louie's type-writer there was nothing else to see.

His mother said that Grandpapa's funeral was all over, and that the green creepiness came from the green creepers. But Michael knew it didn't. She only said things like that to make you feel nice and comfy when you were going to bed. Michael knew very well that they had put Grandpapa into the drawing-room and locked the door so that the funeral men shouldn't get at him and take him away too soon. And Auntie Louie had kept the key in her pocket.

Funerals meant taking people away.

Old Nanna wouldn't let him talk about it; but Mary-Nanna had told him that was what funerals meant. All the same, as he went up the flagged path, he took care not to look through the black panes of the window where the elder bush was, lest he should see Grandpapa's coffin standing in the place where the big table used to be, and Grandpapa lying inside it wrapped in a white sheet.

Michael's message was that Mummy sent her love, and would Grannie and Auntie Louie and Auntie Emmeline and Auntie Edie come to tea? She was going to have tea in the garden, and would they please come early? As early as possible. That was the part he was not to forget.

The queer thing was that when Michael went to see Grannie and the Aunties in Grannie's house he saw four old women. They wore black dresses that smelt sometimes of something sweet and sometimes like your fingers when you get ink on them. The Aunties looked cross; and Auntie Emmeline smelt as if she had been crying. He thought that perhaps they had not been able to stop crying since Grandpapa's funeral. He thought that was why Auntie Louie's nose was red and shiny and Auntie Edie's eyelids had pink edges instead of lashes. In Grannie's house they never let you do anything. They never did anything themselves. They never wanted to do anything; not even to talk. He thought it was because they knew that Grandpapa was still there all the time.

But outside it the Aunties were not so very old. They rode bicycles. And when they came to Michael's father's house they forgot all about Grandpapa's funeral and ran about and played tennis like Michael's mother and Mrs. Jervis, and they talked a lot.

Michael's mother was Grannie's child. To see how she could be a child you had only to think of her in her nightgown with her long brown hair plaited in a pigtail hanging down her back and tied with a blue ribbon. But he couldn't see how the three Aunties could be Grannie's other children. They were bigger than Grannie and they had grey hair. Grannie was a little thing; she was white and dry; and she had hair like hay. Besides, she hardly ever took any notice of them except to make a face at Auntie Emmeline or Auntie Edie now and then. She did it with her head a little on one side, pushing out her underlip and drawing it back again.

Grannie interested Michael; but more when he thought about her than when she was actually there. She stood for him as the mark and measure of past time. To understand how old Grannie was you had to think backwards; this way: Once there was a time when there was no Michael; but there was Mummy and there was Daddy. And once there was a time when there was no Mummy and no Daddy; but there was Grannie and there was Grandpapa. Now there was no Grandpapa. But he couldn't think back far enough to get to the time when there was no Grannie.

Michael thought that being Grannie must feel like being God.

Before he came to the black window pane and the elder bush he had to run down the slopes and jump the gullies on his side of the Heath, and cross the West Road, and climb the other slope to Grannie's side. And it was not till you got to the row of elms on Judges' Walk that you had to go carefully because of the funeral.

He stood there on the ridge of the Walk and looked back to his own side. There were other houses there; but he knew his father's house by the tree of Heaven in the garden.

The garden stood on a high, flat promontory jutting out into the Heath. A brown brick wall with buttresses, strong like fortifications on a breastwork, enclosed it on three sides. From the flagged terrace at the bottom of the garden you looked down, through the tops of the birch-trees that rose against the rampart, over the wild places of the Heath. There was another flagged terrace at the other end of the garden. The house rose sheer from its pavement, brown brick like the wall, and flat-fronted, with the white wings of its storm shutters spread open, row on row. It barred the promontory from the mainland. And at the back of it, beyond its kitchen garden and its courtyard, a fringe of Heath still parted it from the hill road that went from "Jack Straw's Castle" to "The Bull and Bush." You reached it by a lane that led from the road to the Heath.

The house belonged to the Heath and the open country. It was aware of nothing but the Heath and the open country between it and Harrow on the Hill. It had the air of all the old houses of Hampstead, the wonderful air of not acknowledging the existence of Bank Holidays. It was lifted up high above the town; shut in; utterly secluded.

Anthony Harrison considered that he had done well when he acquired West End House for his wife Frances, and for his children, Dorothea, Michael, Nicholas and John.

Frances had said that, if he was thinking of her, he needn't buy a big place, because she didn't want one. But he might buy it for the children if he liked. Anthony had said that she had no idea of what she mightn't want, once she began to give her mind to it, and that he would like to think of her living in it after he was gone. Not that he had any intention of going; he was only thirty-six (not much older than Frances) and incurably healthy. But since his wife's attention had become absorbed in the children—to the exclusion of every other interest—he was always trying to harrow her by the suggestion. And Frances only laughed at him and told him that he was a silly old thing, and that he needn't think he was going to get round her that way.

There was no other way open for Anthony; unless he were to go bankrupt or get pneumonia or peritonitis. Frances would have been the first to acknowledge that illness or misfortune constituted a claim. And the only things he ever did get were loud, explosive colds in his head which made him a mark for derision. His business was so sound that not even a revolution or a European war could shake it. And his appearance was incompatible with his pretensions to pathos.

It would have paid him better to have been small and weedy, or lamentably fat, or to have had a bald place coming, or crow's feet pointing to grey hairs; for then there might have been a chance for him. But Anthony's body was well made, slender and tall. He had blue eyes and black-brown hair, and the look of an amiable hawk, alert, fiercely benevolent. Frances couldn't see any pathos in the kind of figure she happened to admire most, the only kind she would have tolerated in a husband. And if she *had* seen any pathos in it she wouldn't have married it. Pathos, she said, was all very well in a father, or a brother, or a friend, but in choosing a husband you had to think of your children; and she had wanted boys that would look like Michael and Nicholas and John.

"Don't you mean," Anthony had said, "boys that will look like me?"

"I mean," she had answered, "exactly what I say. You needn't be so arrogant."

Her arrogance had been beyond all bearing since John, the third son, had been born.

And it was Frances, after all, who had made him buy West End House for her own reasons. Both the day nursery and the night nursery had windows to the south. It was the kind of house she had always dreamed of living in, and of Michael, or Nicky living in after she and Anthony were gone. It was not more than seven minutes' walk from the bottom of the lane to the house where her people lived. She had to think about the old people when the poor dears had come up to London in order to be thought about. And it had white storm shutters and a tree of Heaven in the garden.

And, because they had both decided that they would have that house whatever happened, they began to argue and to tease each other. Anthony had said it was all right, only the tree of Heaven wasn't a tree of Heaven;

it was a common ash. He was one of the biggest timber merchants in the country and he ought to know. Frances said she mightn't know much, but she did know that was the kind of tree the people down in her part of the country called a tree of Heaven. Anthony said he couldn't help that. It didn't matter what they called it. It was a common ash.

Then she told him he had no poetry in his composition. She had always dreamed of having a tree of Heaven in her garden; and he was destroying her dream. He replied that he didn't want to destroy her dream, but the tree really *was* an ash. You could tell by the bark, and by the leaves and by the number and the shape of the leaflets. And anyhow, that was the first he'd heard about her dream.

"You don't know," said Frances, "what goes on inside me."

She said that if any of the children developed an imagination he needn't think *he* had anything to do with it.

"I shan't," said Anthony. "I wouldn't have anything to do with it if I could. Facts are good enough for me. The children must be brought up to realize facts."

An ash-tree was a fact and a tree of Heaven was a fancy; unless by any chance she meant *Ailanthus glandulosa*. (He knew she didn't.) If she wanted to know, the buds of the ash were black like ebony. The buds of the tree of Heaven were rose-red, like—like bad mahogany. Wait till the spring and look at the buds.

Frances waited till the spring and looked at the buds, and, sure enough, they were black like ebony.

Anthony also said that if they were choosing a house for the children, it was no earthly use to think about the old people. For the old people would go and the children would remain.

As if to show how right he was, Grandpapa had died early in that summer of 'ninety-five, one month after they had moved into West End House. That still left Grannie and Auntie Louie and Auntie Emmeline and Auntie Edie for Anthony to look after.

She was thinking of them now. She hoped that they would come early in time to see the children. She also hoped that they would go early, so that she and Anthony might have their three sets of tennis before dinner in peace.

There would be no peace if Louie and Edie wanted to play too. The one thing that Anthony could not stand was people wanting to do things they couldn't do, and spoiling them for those who could. He used to say that the sight of Louie anywhere near the tennis court put him off his stroke.

Again, the faint illusion of worry was created by the thought that this dreadful thing might happen, that Louie and Edie might want to play and that Anthony would be put off his stroke and be annoyed, and that his annoyance, his just and legitimate annoyance, would spoil the perfection of the afternoon. And as she played with the illusion it made more real her tranquillity, her incredible content.

Her hands were busy now putting decorative stitches into a frock for John. She had pushed aside a novel by George Moore and a volume of Ibsen's plays. She disliked Ibsen and disapproved of George Moore. Her firm, tight little character defended itself against every form of intellectual disturbance. A copy of the *Times* had fallen from her lap to her feet. Jane, the cat, had found it there, and, purring loudly, had trodden it down into a bed, and now lay on it, asleep. Frances had informed herself of the affairs of the nation.

At the bottom of her mind was the conviction (profound, because unconscious) that the affairs of the nation were not to be compared for interest with her own affairs, and an attitude of condescension, as if she honoured the *Times* by reading it and the nation by informing herself of its affairs; also the very distinct impression that evening papers were more attractive than morning papers. She would have admitted that they owed their attraction to the circumstance that Anthony brought them home with him in his pocket, and that in the evening she was not obliged to inform herself of what might be happening. Anthony was certain to inform her.

Not that anything ever did happen. Except strikes; and even then, no sooner did the features of the strike begin to get dramatic than they were instantly submerged in the flood of conversation that was let loose over them. Mrs. Anthony pitied the poor editors and reporters while Parliament was sitting. She saw them as rather silly, violent and desperate men, yet pathetic in their silliness, violence and desperation, snatching at divorces, and breach of promise cases, and fires in paraffin shops, as drowning men snatch at straws.

Her imagination refused to picture any end to this state of things. There would just be more speeches and more strikes, and still more speeches, going on for ever and ever at home; while foreign affairs and the British Empire went on for ever and ever too, with no connection between the two lines of sequence, and no likeness, except that both somehow went on and on.

That was Anthony's view of England's parliament and of her imperial policy; and it was Mrs. Anthony's. Politics, Anthony said, had become static; and he assured Frances that there was no likelihood that they would ever become dynamic again—ever.

Anthony's view of politics was Mrs. Anthony's view of life.

Nothing ever really happened. Things did not change; they endured; they went on. At least everything that really mattered endured and went on. So that everything that really mattered could—if you were given to looking forward—be foreseen. A strike—a really bad one—might conceivably affect Anthony's business, for a time; but not all the strikes in the world, not all the silly speeches, not all the meddling and muddling of politicians could ever touch one of those enduring things.

Frances believed in permanence because, in secret, she abhorred the thought of change. And she abhorred the thought of change because, at thirty-three, she had got all the things she wanted. But only for the last ten years out of the thirty-three. Before that (before she was Mrs. Anthony), wanting things, letting it be known that you wanted them, had meant not getting them. So that it was incredible how she had contrived to get them all. She had not yet left off being surprised at her own happiness. It was not like things you take for granted and are not aware of. Frances was profoundly aware of it. Her happiness was a solid, tangible thing. She knew where it resided, and what it was made of, and what terms she held it on. It depended on *her*; on her truth, her love, her loyalty; it was of the nature of a trust. But there was no illusion about it. It was *the* reality.

She denied that she was arrogant, for she had not taken one of them for granted, not even Dorothy; though a little arrogance might have been excusable in a woman who had borne three sons and only one daughter before she was thirty-two. Whereas Grannie's achievement had been four daughters, four superfluous women, of whom Anthony had married one and supported three.

To be sure there was Maurice. But he was worse than superfluous, considering that most of the time Anthony was supporting Maurice, too.

She had only known one serious anxiety—lest her flesh and blood should harbour any of the blood and flesh left over after Morrie was made. She had married Anthony to drive out Morrie from the bodies and souls of her children. She meant that, through her and Anthony, Morrie should go, and Dorothea, Michael, Nicholas and John should remain.

❧

As Frances looked at the four children, her mouth tightened itself so as to undo the ruinous adoration of her eyes. She loved their slender bodies, their pure, candid faces, their thick, straight hair that parted solidly from the brush, clean-cut and shining like sheets of polished metal, brown for Dorothy, black-brown for Nicholas, red gold for Michael and white gold for John. She was glad that they were all made like that; slender and clear and hard, and that their very hair was a thing of clean surfaces and definite edges. She disliked the blurred outlines of fatness and fuzziness and fluffiness. The bright solidity of their forms helped her to her adored illusion, the illusion of their childhood as going on, lasting for ever and ever.

They would be the nicest-looking children at Mrs. Jervis's party. They would stand out solid from the fluffiness and fuzziness and fatness of the others. She saw people looking at them. She heard them saying: "Who are the two little boys in brown linen?"—"They are Michael and Nicholas Harrison." The Funny Man came and said: "Hello! I didn't expect to see you here!" It was Michael and Nicholas he didn't expect to see; and the noise in the room was Nicky's darling laughter.

Music played. Michael and Nicholas danced to the music. It was Michael's body and Nicky's that kept for her the pattern of the dance, their feet that beat out its measure. Sitting under the tree of Heaven Frances could see Mrs. Jervis's party. It shimmered and clustered in a visionary space between the tree and the border of blue larkspurs on the other side of the lawn. The firm figures of Michael and Nicholas and Dorothy held it together, kept it from being shattered amongst the steep blue spires of the larkspurs. When it was all over they would still hold it together, so that people would know that it had really happened and remember having been there. They might even remember that Rosalind had had a birthday.

Frances had just bestowed this life after death on Mrs. Jervis's party when she heard Michael saying he didn't want to go to it.

He had no idea why he didn't want to go except that he didn't.

"What?" said Frances. "Not when Nicky and Dorothy are going?"

He shook his head. He was mournful and serious.

"And there's going to be a Magic Lantern"—

"I know."

"And a Funny Man"—

"I know."

"And a Big White Cake with sugar icing and Rosalind's name on it in pink letters, and eight candles"—

"I know, Mummy." Michael's under lip began to shake.

"I thought it was only little baby boys that were silly and shy."

Michael was not prepared to contest the statement. He saw it was the sort of thing that in the circumstances she was bound to say. All the same his under lip would have gone on shaking if he hadn't stopped it.

"I thought you were a big boy," said Frances.

"So I *was*, yesterday. To-day isn't yesterday, Mummy."

"If John-John was asked to a beautiful party *he* wouldn't be afraid to go."

As soon as Michael's under lip had stopped shaking his eyelids began. You couldn't stop your eyelids.

"It's not *afraid*, exactly," he said.

"What is it, then?"

"It's sort—sort of forgetting things."

"What things?"

"I don't know, Mummy. I think—it's pieces of me that I want to remember. At a party I can't feel all of myself at once—like I do now."

She loved his strange thoughts as she loved his strange beauty, his reddish yellow hair, his light hazel eyes that were not hers and not Anthony's.

"What will you do, sweetheart, all afternoon, without Nicky and Dorothy and Mary-Nanna?"

"I don't want Nicky and Dorothy and Mary-Nanna. I want Myself. I want to play with Myself."

She thought: "Why shouldn't he? What right have I to say these things to him and make him cry, and send him to stupid parties that he doesn't want to go to? After all, he's only a little boy."

She thought of Michael, who was seven, as if he were younger than Nicholas, who was only five.

Nicky was different. You could never tell what Michael would take it into his head to think. You could never tell what Nicky would take it into his head to do. There was no guile in Michael. But sometimes there was guile in Nicky. Frances was always on the look out for Nicky's guile.

So when Michael remarked that Grannie and the Aunties would be there immediately and Nicky said, "Mummy, I think my ear is going to ache," her answer was—"You won't have to stay more than a minute, darling."

For Nicky lived in perpetual fear that his Auntie Louie might kiss at him.

Dorothy saw her mother's profound misapprehension and she hastened to put it right.

"It isn't Auntie Louie, Mummy. His ear is really aching."

And still Frances went on smiling. She knew, and Nicky knew that, if a little boy could establish the fact of earache, he was absolved from all social and family obligations for as long as his affliction lasted. He wouldn't have to stand still and pretend he liked it while he was being kissed at.

Frances kept her mouth shut when she smiled, as if she were trying not to. It was her upper lip that got the better of her. The fine, thin edges of it quivered and twitched and curled. You would have said the very down was sensitive to her thought's secret and iniquitous play. Her smile mocked other people's solemnities, her husband's solemnity, and the solemnity (no doubt inherited) of her son Michael; it mocked the demureness and the gravity of her face.

She had brought her face close to Nicky's; and it was as if her mouth had eyes in it to see if there were guile in him.

"Are you a little humbug?" she said.

Nicky loved his mother's face. It never got excited or did silly things like other people's faces. It never got red and shiny like Auntie Louie's face, or hot and rough like Auntie Emmeline's, or wet and mizzly like Auntie Edie's. The softness and whiteness and dryness of his mother's face were delightful to Nicky. So was her hair. It was cold, with a funny sort of coldness that made your fingers tingle when you touched it; and it smelt like the taste of Brazil nuts.

Frances saw the likeness of her smile quiver on Nicky's upper lip. It broke and became Nicky's smile that bared his little teeth and curled up the corners of his blue eyes. (His blue eyes and black-brown hair were Anthony's.) It wasn't reasonable to suppose that Nicky had earache when he could smile like that.

"I'm afraid," she said, "you're a little humbug. Run to the terrace and see if Grannie and the Aunties are coming."

He ran. It was half a child's run and half a full-grown boy's.

Then Mrs. Anthony addressed her daughter.

"Why did you say his ear's aching when it isn't?"

"Because," said Dorothy, "it *is* aching."

She was polite and exquisite and obstinate, like Anthony.

"Nicky ought to know his own ear best. Go and tell him he's not to stand on the top of the wall. And if they're coming wave to them, to show you're glad to see them."

"But—Mummy—I'm not."

She knew it was dreadful before she said it. But she had warded off reproof by nuzzling against her mother's cheek as it tried to turn away from her. She saw her mother's upper lip moving, twitching. The sensitive down stirred on it like a dark smudge, a dust that quivered. Her own mouth, pushed forward, searching, the mouth of a nuzzling puppy, remained grave and tender. She was earnest and imperturbable in her truthfulness.

"Whether you're glad or not you must go," said Frances. She meant to be obeyed.

Dorothy went. Her body was obedient. For as yet she had her mother's body and her face, her blunted oval, the straight nose with the fine, tilted nostrils, her brown eyes, her solid hair, brown on the top and light underneath, and on the curve of the roll above her little ears. Frances had watched the appearance of those details with an anxiety that would have surprised her if she had been aware of it. She wanted to see herself in the bodies of her sons and in the mind of her daughter. But Dorothy had her father's mind. You couldn't move it. What she had said once she stuck to for ever, like Anthony to his ash-tree. As if sticking to a thing for ever could make it right once. And Dorothy had formed the habit of actually being right, like Anthony, nine times out of ten. Frances foresaw that this persistence, this unreasoning rectitude, might, in time, become annoying in a daughter. There were moments when she was almost perturbed by the presence of this small, mysterious organism, mixed up of her body and her husband's mind.

But in secret she admired her daughter's candour, her downrightness and straightforwardness, her disdain of conventions and hypocrisies. Frances was not glad, she knew she was not glad, any more than Dorothy was glad, to see her mother and her sisters. She only pretended. In secret she was afraid of every moment she would have to live with them. She had lived with them too long. She foresaw what would happen this afternoon, how they would look, what they would say and do, and with what gestures. It would be like the telling, for the thirteenth time, of a dull story that you know every word of.

She thought she had sent them a kind message. But she knew she had only asked them to come early in order that they might go early and leave her to her happiness.

She went down to the terrace wall where Michael and Nicky and Dorothy were watching for them. She was impatient, and she thought that she wanted to see them coming. But she only wanted to see if they were coming early. It struck her that this was sad.

Small and distant, the four black figures moved on the slope under the Judges' Walk; four spots of black that crawled on the sallow grass and the yellow clay of the Heath.

"How little they look!" Michael said.

Their littleness and their distance made them harmless, made them pathetic. Frances was sorry that she was not glad. That was the difference between her and Dorothy, that she was sorry and always would be sorry for not being what she ought to be; and Dorothy never would be sorry for being what she was. She seemed to be saying, already, in her clearness and hardness, "What I am I am, and you can't change me." The utmost you could wring from her was that she couldn't help it.

Frances's sorrow was almost unbearable when the four women in black came nearer, when she saw them climbing the slope below the garden and the lane.

II

Grannie took a long time crossing the lawn from the door in the lane to the tree of Heaven.

She came first. Her daughters followed, forced to her slow pace, advancing with an air of imperfect cohesion, of not really belonging to each other, as if they had been strangers associated by some accident. It had grown on them in their efforts to carry off the embarrassment of appearing as an eternal trio. Auntie Louie carried it off best. Sharp and rigid, Auntie Louie's figure never lent itself to any group. But for her black gown she really might not have belonged.

Mrs. Fleming went slowly, not because she was old, for she was only sixty, but because, though she said, and thought, that she was wrapped up in Frances and her children, she was still absorbed, fascinated by her sacred sense of bereavement. She moved as if hypnotized by her own sorrow.

To her three unmarried daughters she behaved with a sort of mystic hostility, a holy detachment and displeasure, as if she suspected them of getting over it, or of wanting to get over it if they could. But to her one married daughter and to her grandchildren she was soft and gentle. So that, when they happened to be all together, her moods changed so rapidly that she seemed a creature of unaccountable caprice. One minute her small, white, dry face quivered with softness and gentleness, and the next it stiffened, or twitched with the inimical, disapproving look it had for Louie and Emmeline and Edith.

The children lifted up their pure, impassive faces to be kissed at. Old Nanna brought Baby John and put him on his grandmother's knee. Dorothy and Nicholas went off with Mary-Nanna to the party. Michael forgot all about playing with himself. He stayed where he was, drawn by the spectacle of Grannie and the Aunties. Grannie was clucking and chuckling to Baby John as she had clucked and chuckled to her own babies long ago. Her under lip made itself wide and full; it worked with an in and out movement very funny and interesting to Michael. The movement meant that Grannie chuckled under protest of memories that were sacred to Grandpapa.

"Tchoo—tchoo—tchoo—tchoo! Chuckaboo! Beautiful boy!" said Grannie.

Auntie Louie looked at her youngest nephew. She smiled her downward, sagging smile, wrung from a virginity sadder than Grannie's grief. She spoke to Baby John.

"You really are rather a nice boy," Auntie Louie said.

But Edie, the youngest Auntie, was kneeling on the grass before him, bringing her face close to his. Baby John's new and flawless face was cruel to Auntie Edie's. So was his look of dignity and wisdom.

"Oh, she says you're only rather nice," said Auntie Edie. "And you're the beautifullest, sweetest, darlingest that ever was. Wasn't she a nasty Auntie Louie? Ten little pink toes. And *there* he goes. Five little tootsies to each of his footsies."

She hid herself behind the *Times* disturbing Jane.

"Where's John-John?" she cried. "Where's he gone to? Can anybody tell me where to find John-John? Where's John-John? Peep-*bo*—there he is! John-John, look at Auntie Edie. Oh, he won't pay any attention to poor me."

Baby John was playing earnestly with Grannie's watch-chain.

"You might leave the child alone," said Grannie. "Can't you see he doesn't want you?"

Auntie Edie made a little pouting face, like a scolded, pathetic child. Nobody ever did want Auntie Edie.

And all the time Auntie Emmy was talking to Frances very loud and fast.

"Frances, I do think your garden's too beautiful for words. How clever of you to think of clearing away the old flower-beds. I hate flower-beds on a lawn. Yet I don't suppose I should have had the strength of mind to get rid of them if it had been me."

As she talked Auntie Emmy opened her eyes very wide; her eyebrows jerked, the left one leaping up above the right; she thrust out her chin at you and her long, inquiring nose. Her thin face was the play of agitated nerve-strings that pulled it thus into perpetual, restless movements; and she made vague gestures with her large, bony hands. Her tongue went tick-tack, like a clock. Anthony said you-could hear Emmy's tongue striking the roof of her-mouth all the time.

"And putting those delphiniums all together like that—Massing the blues. Anthony? I *do* think Anthony has perfect taste. I adore delphiniums."

Auntie Emmy was behaving as if neither Michael nor Baby John was there.

"Don't you think John-John's too beautiful for words?" said Frances. "Don't you like him a little bit too?"

Auntie Emmy winced as if Frances had flicked something in her face.

"Of course I like him too. Why shouldn't I?"

"I don't think you *do*, Auntie Emmy," Michael said.

Auntie Emmy considered him as for the first time.

"What do you know about it?" she said.

"I can tell by the funny things your face does."

"I thought," said Frances, "you wanted to play by yourself."

"So I do," said Michael.

"Well then, go and play."

He went and to a heavenly place that he knew of. But as he played with himself there he thought: "Auntie Emmy doesn't tell the truth. I think it is because she isn't happy."

Michael kept his best things to himself.

"I suppose you're happy," said Grannie, "now you've got the poor child sent away."

Auntie Emmy raised her eyebrows and spread out her hands, as much as to say she was helpless under her mother's stupidity.

"He'd have been sent away anyhow," said Frances. "It isn't good for him to hang about listening to grown-up conversation."

It was her part to keep the peace between her mother and her sisters.

"It seems to me," said Auntie Louie, "that you began it yourself."

When a situation became uncomfortable, Auntie Louie always put her word in and made it worse. She never would let Frances keep the peace.

Frances knew what Louie meant—that she was always flinging her babies in Emmy's face at those moments when the sight of other people's babies was too much for Emmy. She could never be prepared for Emmy's moments.

"It's all very well," Auntie Louie went on; "but I should like to hear of somebody admiring Dorothy. I don't see where Dorothy comes in."

Dorothy was supposed, by the two Nannas, to be Auntie Louie's favourite. If you taxed her with it she was indignant and declared that she was sure she wasn't.

And again Frances knew what Louie meant—that she loved her three sons, Michael and Nicholas and John, with passion, and her one daughter, Dorothea, with critical affection. That was the sort of thing that Louie was always saying and thinking about people, and nobody ever paid the slightest attention to what Louie said or thought. Frances told herself that if there was one emotion that she was more free from than another it was sex jealousy.

The proof of it, which she offered now, was that she had given up Dorothy to Anthony. It was natural that he should care most for the little girl.

Louie said that was easy—when she knew perfectly well that Anthony didn't. Like Frances he cared most for his three sons. She was leaving Dorothy to Anthony so that Anthony might leave Michael and Nicholas to her.

"You might just as well say," Frances said, "that I'm in love with John-John. Poor little Don-Don!"

"I might," said Louie, "just as well."

Grannie said she was sure she didn't understand what they were talking about and that Louie had some very queer ideas in her head.

"Louie," she said, "knows more than I do."

Frances thought: Was Grannie really stupid? Was she really innocent? Was she not, rather, clever, chock-full of the secret wisdom and the secret cruelty of sex?

Frances was afraid of her thoughts. They came to her not like thoughts, but like quick rushes of her blood, partly confusing her. She did not like that.

She thought: Supposing Grannie knew all the time that Emmy was unhappy, and took a perverse pleasure in her knowledge? Supposing she was not really soft and gentle? She could be soft and gentle to her, because of her children and because of Anthony. She respected Anthony because he was well-off and efficient and successful, and had supported her ever since Grandpapa had gone bankrupt. She was proud of Frances because she was Anthony's wife, who had had three sons and only one daughter.

Grannie behaved as if her grandchildren were her own children, as if she had borne three sons and only one daughter, instead of four daughters and only one son. Still, Frances was the vehicle of flesh and blood that carried on her flesh and blood in Michael and Nicholas and John. She respected Frances.

But Frances could remember a time when she had been unmarried like her sisters, and when Grannie had turned on her, too, that look that was half contempt and half hostility or displeasure. Grannie had not wanted her to marry Anthony, any more than she would have wanted Louie or Emmeline or Edith to marry anybody, supposing anybody had wanted to marry them. And Frances and Anthony had defied her. They had insisted on marrying each other. Frances knew that if there had been no Anthony, her mother would have despised her in secret, as in secret she despised Emmeline and Edith. She despised them more than Louie, because, poor things, they wanted, palpably, to be married, whereas Louie didn't, or said she didn't. In her own way, Louie had defied her mother. She had bought a type-writer and a bicycle with her own earnings, and by partially supporting herself she had defied Anthony, the male benefactor. Louie's manner intimated that there was nothing Frances had that she wanted. She had resources in herself, and Frances had none.

Frances persuaded herself that she admired and respected Louie. She knew that she, Frances, was only admired and respected because she had succeeded where her three sisters had failed. She was even afraid that, in moments of exasperation, Grannie used her and Anthony and the children to punish Emmy and Edie for their failure. The least she could do was to stand between them and Grannie.

It was possible that if Grannie had been allowed to ignore them and give her whole attention to Frances or Michael or Baby John, she could have contrived to be soft and gentle for an afternoon. But neither Louie nor Emmeline, nor even Edith, would consent to be ignored. They refused to knuckle under, to give in. Theirs was a perpetual struggle to achieve an individuality in the teeth of circumstances that had denied them any. Frances acknowledged that they were right, that in the same circumstances she would have done the same.

In their different ways and by different methods they claimed attention. They claimed it incessantly, Louie, the eldest, by an attitude of assurance and superiority so stiff and hard that it seemed invulnerable; Emmy by sudden jerky enthusiasms, exaltations, intensities; Edie by an exaggerated animation, a false excitement. Edie would drop from a childish merriment to a childish pathos, when she would call herself "Poor me," and demand pity for being tired, for missing a train, for cold feet, for hair coming down.

There would be still more animation, and still more enthusiasm when Anthony came home.

Frances prided herself on her power of foreseeing things. She foresaw that Anthony would come home early for his game. She foresaw the funny, nervous agony of his face when he appeared on the terrace and caught sight of Grannie and the three Aunties, and the elaborate and exquisite politeness with which he would conceal from them his emotion. She foresaw that she would say to Annie, "When the master comes tell him we're having tea in the garden, under the tree of—under the ash-tree" (for after all, he was the master, and discipline must be maintained). She foresaw the very gestures of his entrance, the ironically solemn bow that he would make to her, far-off, from the terrace; she even foresaw the kind of joke that, for the life of him, he would not be able to help making. She was so made that she could live happily in this world of small, foreseen things.

III

And it all happened as she had foreseen.

Anthony came home early, because it was a fine afternoon. He made the kind of joke that calamity always forced from him, by some perversion of his instincts.

"When is an ash-tree not an ash-tree? When it's a tree of Heaven."

He was exquisitely polite to Grannie and the Aunties, and his manner to Frances, which she openly complained of, was, he said, what a woman brought on herself when she reserved her passion for her children, her sentiment for trees of Heaven, and her mockery for her devoted husband.

"I suppose we can have some tennis *now*," said Auntie Louie.

"Certainly," said Anthony, "we can, and we shall." He tried not to look at Frances.

And Auntie Edie became automatically animated.

"I can't serve for nuts, but I can run. Who's going to play with *me*?"

"I am," said Anthony. He was perfect.

The game of tennis had an unholy and terrible attraction for Auntie Louie and Auntie Edie. Neither of them could play. But, whereas Auntie Louie thought that she could play and took tennis seriously, Auntie Edie knew that she couldn't and took it as a joke.

Auntie Louie stood tall and rigid and immovable. She planted herself, like a man, close up to the net, where Anthony wanted to be, and where he should have been; but Auntie Louie said she was no good if you put her to play back; she couldn't be expected to take every ball he missed.

When Auntie Louie called out "Play!" she meant to send a nervous shudder through her opponents, shattering their morale. She went through all the gestures of an annihilating service that for some reason never happened. She said the net was too low and that spoiled her eye. And when she missed her return it was because Anthony had looked at her and put her off. Still Aunt Louie's attitude had this advantage that it kept her quiet in one place where Anthony could dance round and round her.

But Auntie Edie played in little nervous runs and slides and rushes; she flung herself, with screams of excitement, against the ball, her partner and the net; and she brandished her racket in a dangerous manner. The oftener she missed the funnier it was to Auntie Edie. She had been pretty when she was young, and seventeen years ago her cries and tumbles and collisions had been judged amusing; and Auntie Edie thought they were amusing still. Anthony had never had the heart to undeceive her. So that when Anthony was there Auntie Edie still went about setting a standard of gaiety for other people to live up to; and still she was astonished that they never did, that other people had no sense of humour.

Therefore Frances was glad when Anthony told her that he had asked Mr. Parsons, the children's tutor, and young Norris and young Vereker from the office to come round for tennis at six, and that dinner must be put off till half-past eight.

All was well. The evening would be sacred to Anthony and the young men. The illusion of worry passed, and Frances's real world of happiness stood firm.

And as Frances's mind, being a thoroughly healthy mind, refused to entertain any dreary possibility for long together, so it was simply unable to foresee downright calamity, even when it had been pointed out to her. For instance, that Nicky should really have chosen the day of the party for an earache, the worst earache he had ever had.

He appeared at tea-time, carried in Mary-Nanna's arms, and with his head tied up in one of Mr. Jervis's cricket scarves. As he approached his family he tried hard not to look pathetic.

And at the sight of her little son her whole brilliant world of happiness was shattered around Frances.

"Nicky darling," she said, "why *didn't* you tell me it was really aching?"

"I didn't know," said Nicky.

He never did know the precise degree of pain that distinguished the beginning of a genuine earache from that of a sham one, and he felt that to palm off a sham earache on his mother for a real one, was somehow a sneaky thing to do. And while his ear went on stabbing him, Nicky did his best to explain.

"You see, I never know whether it's aching or whether it's only going to ache. It began a little, teeny bit when the Funny Man made me laugh. And I didn't see the Magic Lantern, and I didn't have any of Rosalind's cake. It came on when I was biting the sugar off. And it was aching in both ears at once. It was," said Nicky, "a jolly sell for me."

At that moment Nicky's earache jabbed upwards at his eyelids and cut them, and shook tears out of them. But Nicky's mouth refused to take any part in the performance, though he let his father carry him upstairs. And, as he lay on the big bed in his mother's room, he said he thought he could bear it if he had Jane-Pussy to lie beside him, and his steam-engine.

Anthony went back into the garden to fetch Jane. He spent an hour looking for her, wandering in utter misery through the house and through the courtyard and stables and the kitchen garden. He looked for Jane in the hothouse and the cucumber frames, and under the rhubarb, and on the scullery roof, and in the water-butt. It was just possible that on a day of complete calamity Jane should have slithered off the scullery roof into the water-butt. The least he could do was to find Jane, since Nicky wanted her.

And in the end it turned out that Jane had been captured in her sleep, treacherously, by Auntie Emmy. And she had escaped, maddened with terror of the large, nervous, incessantly caressing hands. She had climbed into the highest branch of the tree of Heaven, and crouched there, glaring, unhappy.

"Damn the cat!" said Anthony to himself. (It was not Jane he meant.)

He was distressed, irritated, absurdly upset, because he would have to go back to Nicky without Jane, because he couldn't get Nicky what he wanted.

In that moment Anthony loved Nicky more than any of them. He loved him almost more than Frances. Nicky's earache ruined the fine day.

He confided in young Vereker. "I wouldn't bother," he said, "if the little chap wasn't so plucky about it."

"Quite so, sir," said young Vereker.

It was young Mr. Vereker who found Jane, who eventually recaptured her. Young Mr. Vereker made himself glorious by climbing up, at the risk of his neck and in his new white flannels, into the high branches of the tree of Heaven, to bring Jane down.

And when Anthony thanked him he said, "Don't mention it, sir. It's only a trifle," though it was, as Mr. Norris said, palpable that the flannels were ruined. Still, if he hadn't found that confounded cat, they would never, humanly speaking, have had their tennis.

The Aunties did not see Mr. Vereker climbing into the tree of Heaven. They did not see him playing with Mr. Parsons and Anthony and Mr. Norris. For as soon as the three young men appeared, and Emmeline and Edith began to be interested and emphatic, Grannie said that as they wouldn't see anything more of Frances and the children, it was no good staying any longer, and they'd better be getting back. It was as if she knew that they were going to enjoy themselves and was determined to prevent it.

Frances went with them to the bottom of the lane. She stood there till the black figures had passed, one by one, through the white posts on to the Heath, till, in the distance, they became small again and harmless and pathetic.

Then she went back to her room where Nicky lay in the big bed.

Nicky lay in the big bed with Jane on one side of him and his steam-engine on the other, and a bag of hot salt against each ear. Now and then a thin wall of sleep slid between him and his earache.

Frances sat by the open window and looked out into the garden where Anthony and Norris played, quietly yet fiercely, against Vereker and Parsons. Frances loved the smell of fresh grass that the balls and the men's feet struck from the lawn; she loved the men's voices subdued to Nicky's sleep, and the sound of their padding feet, the thud of the balls on the turf, the smacking and thwacking of the rackets. She loved every movement of Anthony's handsome, energetic body; she loved the quick, supple bodies of the young men, the tense poise and earnest activity of their adolescence. But it was not Vereker or Parsons or Norris that she loved or that she saw. It was Michael, Nicholas and John whose adolescence was foreshadowed in those athletic forms wearing white flannels; Michael, Nicky and John, in white flannels, playing fiercely. When young Vereker drew himself to his full height, when his young body showed lean and slender as he raised his arms for his smashing service, it was not young Vereker, but Michael, serious and beautiful. When young Parsons leaped high into the air and thus returned Anthony's facetious sky-scraper on the volley, that was Nicky. When young Norris turned and ran at the top of his speed, and overtook the ball on its rebound from the base line where young Vereker had planted it, when, as by a miracle, he sent it backwards over his own head, paralysing Vereker and Parsons with sheer astonishment, that was John.

Her vision passed. She was leaning over Nicky now, Nicky so small in the big bed. Nicky had moaned.

"Does it count if I make that little noise, Mummy? It sort of lets the pain out."

"No, my lamb, it doesn't count. Is the pain very bad?"

"Yes, Mummy, awful. It's going faster and faster. And it bizzes. And when it doesn't bizz, it thumps." He paused. "I think—p'raps—I could bear it better if I sat on your knee."

Frances thought she could bear it better too. It would be good for Nicky that he should grow into beautiful adolescence and a perfect manhood; but it was better for her that he should be a baby still, that she should have him on her knee and hold him close to her; that she should feel his adorable body press quivering against her body, and the heat of his earache penetrating her cool flesh. For now she was lost to herself and utterly absorbed in Nicky. And her agony became a sort of ecstasy, as if, actually, she bore his pain.

It was Anthony who could not stand it. Anthony had come in on his way to his dressing-room. As he looked at Nicky his handsome, hawk-like face was drawn with a dreadful, yearning, ineffectual pity. Frances had discovered that her husband could both be and look pathetic. He had wanted her to be sorry for him and she was sorry for him, because his male pity was all agony; there was no ecstasy in it of any sort at all. Nicky was far more her flesh and blood than he was Anthony's.

Nicky stirred in his mother's lap. He raised his head. And when he saw that queer look on his father's face he smiled at it. He had to make the smile himself, for it refused to come of its own accord. He made it carefully, so that it shouldn't hurt him. But he made it so well that it hurt Frances and Anthony.

"I never saw a child bear pain as Nicky does," Frances said in her pride.

"If he can bear it, *I* can't," said Anthony. And he stalked into his dressing-room and shut the door on himself.

"Daddy minds more than you do," said Frances.

At that Nicky sat up. His eyes glittered and his cheeks burned with the fever of his earache.

"I don't mind," he said. "Really and truly I don't mind. I don't care if my ear *does* ache.

"It's my eyes is crying, not me."

At nine o'clock, when they were all sitting down to dinner, Nicky sent for his father and mother. Something had happened.

Crackers, he said, had been going off in his ears, and they hurt most awfully. And when it had done cracking his earache had gone away. And Dorothy had brought him a trumpet from Rosalind's party and Michael a tin train. And Michael had given him the train and he wouldn't take the trumpet instead. Oughtn't Michael to have had the trumpet?

And when they left him, tucked up in his cot in the night nursery, he called them back again.

"It was a jolly sell for me, wasn't it?" said Nicky. And he laughed.

IV

It seemed that Nicky would always be like that. Whatever happened, and something was generally happening to him, he didn't care. When he scaled the plaster flower-pot on the terrace, and it gave way under his assault and threw him down the steps on to the gravel walk, he picked himself up, displaying a forehead that was a red abrasion filled in with yellow gravel and the grey dust of the smashed flower-pot, and said, "I don't care. I liked it," before anybody had time to pity him. When Mary-Nanna stepped on his train and broke the tender, he said, "It's all right. I don't care. I shall make another." It was no use Grannie saying, "Don't care came to a bad end"; Nicky made it evident that a bad end would be life's last challenge not to care. No accident, however unforeseen, would ever take him at a disadvantage.

Two years passed and he was just the same.

Frances and Anthony agreed behind his back that Nicky was adorable.

But his peculiar attitude to misfortune became embarrassing when you had to punish him. Nicky could break the back of any punishment by first admitting that it was a good idea and then thinking of a better one when it was too late. It was a good idea not letting him have any cake for tea after he had tested the resilience of the new tyres on his father's bicycle with a penknife; but, Nicky said, it would have been more to the purpose if they had taken his steam-engine from him for a week.

"You didn't think of that, did you, Mummy? I thought of it," said Nicky.

Once he ran away over the West Heath, and got into the Leg of Mutton Pond, and would have been drowned if a total stranger hadn't gone in after him and pulled him out. That time Nicky was sent to bed at four o'clock in the afternoon. At seven, when his mother came to tuck him up and say Good-night, she found him sitting up, smiling and ready.

"Mummy," he said, "I think I ought to tell you. It isn't a bit of good sending me to bed."

"I should have thought it was, myself," said Frances. She almost suspected Nicky of insincerity.

"So it would have been," he assented, "if I didn't 'vent things. You see, I just lie still 'venting things all the time. I've 'vented three things since tea: a thing to make Daddy's bikesickle stand still with Daddy on it; a thing to squeeze corks out of bottles; and a thing to make my steam-engine go faster. That isn't a punishment, is it, Mummy?"

They said that Nicky would grow out of it. But two more years passed and Nicky was still the same.

And yet he was not the same. And Dorothy, and Michael and John were not the same.

For the awful thing about your children was that they were always dying. Yes, dying. The baby Nicky was dead. The child Dorothy was dead and in her place was a strange big girl. The child Michael was dead and in his place was a strange big boy. And Frances mourned over the passing of each age. You could no more bring back that unique loveliness of two years old, of five years old, of seven, than you could bring back the dead. Even John-John was not a baby any more; he spoke another language and had other feelings; he had no particular affection for his mother's knee. Frances knew that all this dying was to give place to a more wonderful and a stronger life. But it was not the same life; and she wanted to have all their lives about her, enduring, going on, at the same time. She did not yet know that the mother of babies and the mother of boys and girls must die if the mother of men and women is to be born.

Thoughts came to Frances now that troubled her tranquillity.

Supposing, after all, the children shouldn't grow up as she wanted them to?

There was Nicky. She could do nothing with him; she could make no impression on him.

There was Michael. She couldn't make him out. He loved them, and showed that he loved them; but it was by caresses, by beautiful words, by rare, extravagant acts of renunciation, inconsistent with his self-will; not by anything solid and continuous. There was a softness in Michael that distressed and a hardness that perplexed her. You could make an impression on Michael—far too easily—and the impression stayed. You couldn't obliterate it. Michael's memory was terrible. And he had secret ways. He was growing more and more sensitive, more and more wrapped up in Himself. Supposing Michael became a morbid egoist, like Anthony's brother, Bartholomew?

And there was Dorothy. She went her own way more than ever, with the absolute conviction that it was the right way. Nothing could turn her. At thirteen her body was no longer obedient. Dorothy was not going to be her mother's companion, or her father's, either; she was Rosalind Jervis's companion. She seemed to care more about little fat, fluffy Rosalind than about any of them except Nicky. Dorothy was interested in Michael; she respected his queer thoughts. It was as if she recognized some power in him that could beat her somewhere some day, and was humble before a thing her cleverness had failed to understand. But it was Nicky that she adored, not Michael; and she was bad for Nicky. She encouraged his naughtiness because it amused her.

Frances foresaw that a time would come, a little later, when Nicky and Dorothy would be companions, not Nicky and his mother.

In the evenings, coming home from the golf-links, Frances and Anthony discussed their children.

Frances said, "You can't make any impression on Nicky. There seems to be no way that you can get at him."

Anthony thought there was a way. It was a way he had not tried yet, that he did not want to try. But, if he could only bring himself to it, he judged that he could make a distinct impression.

"What the young rascal wants is a thorough good spanking," said Anthony.

Nicky said so too.

The first time he got it Nicky's criticism was that it wasn't a bad idea if his father could have pulled it off all right. But he said, "It's no good if you do it through the cloth. And it's no good unless you *want* to hurt me, Daddy. And you don't want. And even if you did want, badly enough to try and hurt, supposing you spanked ever so hard, you couldn't hurt as much as my earache. And I can bear that."

"He's top dog again, you see," said Frances, not without a secret satisfaction.

"Oh, is he?" said Anthony. "I don't propose to be downed by Nicky."

Every instinct in him revolted against spanking Nicky. But when Williams, the groom, showed him a graze on each knee of the pony he had bought for Frances and the children, Anthony determined that, this time, Nicky should have a serious spanking.

"Which of them took Roger out?"

"I'm sure I don't know, sir," said Williams.

But Anthony knew. He lay in wait for Nicky by the door that led from the stable yard into the kitchen garden.

Nicky was in the strawberry bed.

"Was it you who took Roger out this afternoon?"

Nicky did not answer promptly. His mouth was still full of strawberries.

"What if I did?" he said at last, after manifest reflection.

"If you did? Why, you let him down on Golders Hill and cut his knees."

"Holly Mount," said Nicky.

"Holly Mount or Golders Hill, it's all the same to you, you young monkey."

"It isn't, Daddy. Holly Mount's much the worst. It's an awful hill."

"That," said Anthony, "is why you're forbidden to ride down it. You've *got* to be spanked for this, Nicky."

"Have I? All right. Don't look so unhappy, Daddy."

Anthony did much better this time. Nicky (though he shook with laughter) owned it very handsomely. And Anthony had handicapped himself again by doing it through the cloth. He drew the line at shaming Nicky. (Yet—*could* you have shamed his indomitable impudence?)

But he had done it. He had done it ruthlessly, while the strawberries were still wet on Nicky's mouth.

And when it was all over Michael, looking for his father, came into the schoolroom where these things happened. He said he was awfully sorry, but he'd taken Roger out, and Roger had gone down on his knees and cut himself.

No, it wasn't on Holly Mount, it was at the turn of the road on the hill past the "Spaniards."

Anthony paid no attention to Michael. He turned on Michael's brother.

"Nicky, what did you do it for?"

"For a rag, of course. I knew you'd feel such a jolly fool when you found it wasn't me."

"You see, Daddy," he explained later, "you might have known I wouldn't have let Roger down. But wasn't it a ripping sell?"

"What are you to do," said Anthony, "with a boy like that?"

Frances had an inspiration. "Do nothing," she said.

Her tranquillity refused to be troubled for long together.

"Nicky's right. It's no good trying to punish him. After all, *why* punish Nicky? It isn't as if he was really naughty. He never does unkind things, or mean things. And he's truthful."

"Horribly truthful. They all are," said Anthony.

"Well, then, what does Nicky do?"

"He does dangerous things."

"He forgets."

"Nothing more dangerous than forgetting. We must punish him to make him remember."

"But it doesn't make him remember. It only makes him think us fools."

"You know what it means?" said Anthony. "We shall have to send him to school."

"Not yet," said Frances.

School was the thing in the future that she dreaded. Nicky was only nine, and they were all getting on well with Mr. Parsons. Anthony knew that to send Nicky to school now would be punishing Frances, not Nicky. The little fiend would only grin in their faces if they told him he was going to school.

It was no use trying to make impressions on Nicky. He was as hard as nails. He would never feel things.

Perhaps, Frances thought, it was just as well.

V

"I do think it was nice of Jane," said Nicky, "to have Jerry."

"And I do think it was nice of me," said Dorothy, "to give him to you."

Jane was Dorothy's cat; therefore her kittens were Dorothy's.

"I wouldn't have given him to just anybody."

"I know," said Nicky.

"I might have kept him. He's the nicest kitten Jane ever had."

"I know," said Nicky. "It *was* nice of you."

"I might want him back again."

"I—know."

Nicky was quiet and serious, almost humble, as if he went in the fear of losing Jerry. Nobody but Jerry and Dorothy saw Nicky in that mood.

Not that he was really afraid. Nothing could take Jerry from him. If Dorothy could have taken him back again she wouldn't have, not even if she had really wanted him. Dorothy wasn't cruel, and she was only ragging.

But certainly he was Jane's nicest kitten. Jane was half-Persian, white with untidy tabby patterns on her. Jerry was black all over. Whatever attitude he took, his tight, short fur kept the outlines of his figure firm and clear, whether he arched his back and jumped sideways, or rolled himself into a cushion, or squatted with haunches spread and paws doubled in under his breast, or sat bolt upright with his four legs straight like pillars, and his tail curled about his feet. Jerry's coat shone like black looking-glass, and the top of his head smelt sweet, like a dove's breast.

And he had yellow eyes. Mary-Nanna said they would turn green some day. But Nicky didn't believe it. Mary-Nanna was only ragging. Jerry's eyes would always be yellow.

Mr. Parsons declared that Nicky sat for whole hours meditating on Jerry, as if in this way he could make him last longer.

Jerry's life was wonderful to Nicky. Once he was so small that his body covered hardly the palm of your hand; you could see his skin; it felt soft and weak through the thin fur, sleeked flat and wet where Jane had licked it. His eyes were buttoned up tight. Then they opened. He crawled feebly on the floor after Jane, or hung on to her little breasts, pressing out the milk with his clever paws. Then Jerry got older. Sometimes he went mad and became a bat or a bird, and flew up the drawing-room curtains as if his legs were wings.

Nicky said that Jerry could turn himself into anything he pleased; a hawk, an owl, a dove, a Himalayan bear, a snake, a flying squirrel, a monkey, a rabbit, a panther, and a little black lamb of God.

Jerry was a cat now; he was two years old.

Jerry's fixed idea seemed to be that he was a very young cat, and that he must be nursed continually, and that nobody but Nicky must nurse him. Mr. Parsons found that Nicky made surprising progress in his Latin and Greek that year. What had baffled Mr. Parsons up till now had been Nicky's incapacity for sitting still. But he would sit still enough when Jerry was on his knee, pressed tight between the edge of the desk and Nicky's stomach, so that knowledge entered into Nicky through Jerry when there was no other way.

Nicky would even sit still in the open air to watch Jerry as he stalked bees in the grass, or played by himself, over and over again, his own enchanted game. He always played it in the same way. He started from the same clump in the border, to run in one long careening curve across the grass; at the same spot in the lawn he bounded sideways and gave the same little barking grunt and dashed off into the bushes. When you tried to catch him midway he stood on his hind legs and bowed to you slantwise, waving his forepaws, or rushed like lightning up the tree of Heaven, and climbed into the highest branches and clung there, looking down at you. His yellow eyes shone through the green leaves; they quivered; they played; they mocked you with some challenge, some charm, secret and divine and savage.

"The soul of Nicky is in that cat," Frances said.

Jerry knew that he was Nicky's cat. When other people caught him he scrabbled over their shoulders with his claws and got away from them. When Nicky caught him he lay quiet and heavy in his arms, pressing down and spreading his soft body. Nicky's sense of touch had been hardened by violent impacts and collisions, by experiments with jack-knives and saws and chisels and gouges, and by struggling with the material of his everlasting inventions. Through communion with Jerry it became tender and sensitive again. It delighted in the cat's throbbing purr and the thrill of his feet, as Jerry, serious and earnest, padded down his bed on Nicky's knee.

"I like him best, though," said Nicky, "when he's sleepy and at the same time bitesome."

"You mustn't let him bite you," Frances said.

"I don't mind," said Nicky. "He wouldn't do it if he didn't like me."

Jerry had dropped off to sleep with his jaws closing drowsily on Nicky's arm. When it moved his hind legs kicked at it and tore.

"He's dreaming when he does that," said Nicky. "He thinks he's a panther and I'm buffaloes."

Mr. Parsons laughed at him. "Nicky and his cat!" he said. Nicky didn't care. Mr. Parsons was always ragging him.

The tutor preferred dogs himself. He couldn't afford any of the expensive breeds; but that summer he was taking care of a Russian wolfhound for a friend of his. When Mr. Parsons ran with Michael and Nicky round the Heath, the great borzoi ran before them with long leaps, head downwards, setting an impossible pace. Michael and Dorothy adored Boris openly. Nicky, out of loyalty to Jerry, stifled a secret admiration. For Mr. Parsons held that a devotion to a cat was incompatible with a proper feeling for a dog, whence Nicky had inferred that any feeling for a dog must do violence to the nobler passion.

Mr. Parsons tried to wean Nicky from what he pretended to regard as his unmanly weakness. "Wait, Nicky," he said, "till you've got a dog of your own."

"I don't want a dog of my own," said Nicky. "I don't want anything but Jerry." Boris, he said, was not clever, like Jerry. He had a silly face.

"Think so?" said Mr. Parsons. "Look at his jaws. They could break Jerry's back with one snap."

"*Could* he, Daddy?"

They were at tea on the lawn, and Boris had gone to sleep under Mr. Parsons' legs with his long muzzle on his forepaws.

"He could," said Anthony, "if he caught him."

"But he couldn't catch him. Jerry'd be up a tree before Boris could look at him."

"If you want Jerry to shin up trees you must keep his weight down."

Nicky laughed. He knew that Boris could never catch Jerry. His father was only ragging him.

Nicky was in the schoolroom, bowed over his desk. He was doing an imposition, the second aorist of the abominable verb ἔρχομαι, written out five-and-twenty times. (Luckily he could do the last fifteen times from memory.)

Nicky had been arguing with Mr. Parsons. Mr. Parsons had said that the second aorist of ἔρχομαι was not ἦρχον.

Nicky had said, "I can't help it. If it's not ἦρχον it ought to be."

Mr. Parsons had replied: "The verb ἔρχομαι is irregular." And Nicky had retorted, in effect, that no verb had any business to be as irregular as all that. Mr. Parsons had then suggested that Nicky might know more about the business of irregular verbs if he wrote out the second aorist of ἔρχομαι five-and-twenty times after tea.

As it was a particularly fine afternoon, an imposition was, Nicky admitted, a score for Mr. Parsons and a jolly good sell for *him*.

Mr. Parsons had not allowed him to have Jerry on his knee, or even in the room; and this, Nicky owned further, was but just. It wouldn't have been nearly so good a punishment if he had had Jerry with him.

Nicky, bowed over his desk, struggled for the perfect legibility which Mr. Parsons had insisted on, as otherwise the imposition would do him more harm than good. He was in for it, and the thing must be done honourably if it was done at all. He had only looked out of the windows twice to make sure that Boris was asleep under Mr. Parsons' legs. And once he had left the room to see where Jerry was. He had found him in the kitchen garden, sitting on a bed of fresh-grown mustard and cress, ruining it. He sat like a lamb, his forepaws crossed, his head tilted slightly backwards. His yellow eyes gazed at Nicky with a sweet and mournful innocence.

Nicky did not hear the voices in the garden.

"I'm awfully sorry, sir," Mr. Parsons was saying. "I can't think how it could have happened." Mr. Parsons' voice was thick and his face was very red. "I could have sworn the door was shut."

"Johnnie opened it," said Anthony. He seemed to have caught, suddenly, one of his bad colds and to be giving it to Mr. Parsons. They were both in their shirtsleeves, and Anthony carried something in his arms which he had covered with his coat.

The borzoi stood in front of them. His face had a look of foolish ecstasy. He stared at Mr. Parsons, and as he stared he panted. There was a red smear on his white breast; his open jaws still dripped a pink slaver. It sprayed the ground in front of them, jerked out with his panting.

"Get away, you damned brute," said Mr. Parsons.

Boris abashed himself; he stretched out his fore legs towards Mr. Parsons, shook his raised haunches, lifted up his great saw-like muzzle, and rolled into one monstrous cry a bark, a howl, a yawn.

Nicky heard it, and he looked out of the schoolroom window. He saw the red smear on the white curly breast. He saw his father in his shirtsleeves, carrying something in his arms that he had covered with his coat.

Under the tree of Heaven Dorothy and Michael, crouching close against their mother, cried quietly. Frances was crying, too; for it was she who would have to tell Nicky.

Dorothy tried to console him.

"Jerry's eyes would have turned green, if he had lived, Nicky. They would, really."

"I wouldn't have minded. They'd have been Jerry's eyes."

"But he wouldn't have looked like Jerry."

"I wouldn't have cared what he looked like. He'd have *been* Jerry."

"I'll give you Jane, Nicky, and all the kittens she ever has, if that would make up."

"It wouldn't. You don't seem to understand that it's Jerry I want. I wish you wouldn't talk about him."

"Very well," said Dorothy, "I won't."

Then Grannie tried. She recommended a holy resignation. God, she said, had given Jerry to Nicky, and God had taken him away.

"He didn't give him me, and he'd no right to take him. Dorothy wouldn't have done it. She was only ragging. But when God does things," said Nicky savagely, "it isn't a rag."

He hated Grannie, and he hated Mr. Parsons, and he hated God. But he loved Dorothy who had given him Jerry.

Night after night Frances held him in her arms at bed-time while Nicky said the same thing. "If—if I could stop seeing him. But I keep on seeing him. When he sat on the mustard and cress. And when he bit me with his sleep-bites. And when he looked at me out of the tree of Heaven. Then I hear that little barking grunt he used to make when he was playing with himself—when he dashed off into the bushes.

"And I can't *bear* it."

Night after night Nicky cried himself to sleep.

For the awful thing was that it had been all his fault. If he had kept Jerry's weight down Boris *couldn't* have caught him.

"Daddy said so, Mummy."

Over and over again Frances said, "It *wasn't* your fault. It was Don-Don's. He left the door open. Surely you can forgive Don-Don?" Over and over again Nicky said, "I do forgive him."

But it was no good. Nicky became first supernaturally subdued and gentle, then ill. They had to take him away from home, away from the sight of the garden, and away from Mr. Parsons, forestalling the midsummer holidays by two months.

Nicky at the seaside was troublesome and happy, and they thought he had forgotten. But on the first evening at Hampstead, as Frances kissed him Good-night, he said: "Shall I have to see Mr. Parsons to-morrow?"

Frances said: "Yes. Of course."

"I'd rather not."

"Nonsense, you must get over that."

"I—can't, Mummy."

"Oh, Nicky, can't you forgive poor Mr. Parsons? When he was so unhappy?"

Nicky meditated.

"Do you think," he said at last, "he really minded?"

"I'm sure he did."

"As much as you and Daddy?"

"Quite as much."

"Then," said Nicky, "I'll forgive him."

But, though he forgave John and Mr. Parsons and even God, who, to do him justice, did not seem to have been able to help it, Nicky did not forgive himself.

Yet Frances never could think why the sight of mustard and cress made Nicky sick. Neither did Mr. Parsons, nor any schoolmaster who came after him understand why, when Nicky knew all the rest of the verb ἔρχομαι by heart he was unable to remember the second aorist.

He had an excellent memory, but there was always a gap in it just there.

VI

In that peace and tranquillity where nothing ever happened, Jerry's violent death would have counted as an event, a date to reckon by; but for three memorable things that happened, one after another, in the summer and autumn of 'ninety-nine: the return of Frances's brother, Maurice Fleming, from Australia where Anthony had sent him two years ago, on the express understanding that he was to stay there; the simultaneous arrival of Anthony's brother, Bartholomew, and his family; and the outbreak of the Boer War.

The return of Morrie was not altogether unforeseen, and Bartholomew had announced his coming well beforehand, but who could have dreamed that at the end of the nineteenth century England would be engaged in a War that really *was* a War? Frances, with the *Times* in her hands, supposed that that meant more meddling and muddling of stupid politicians, and that it would mean more silly speeches in Parliament, and copy, at last, for foolish violent, pathetic and desperate editors, and breach of promise cases, divorces and fires in paraffin shops reduced to momentary insignificance.

But as yet there was no war, nor any appearance that sensible people interpreted as a sign of war at the time of Morrie's return. It stood alone, as other past returns, the return from Bombay, the return from Canada, the return from Cape Colony, had stood, in its sheer awfulness. To Frances it represented the extremity of disaster.

They might have known what was coming by Grannie's behaviour. One day, the day when the Australian mail arrived, she had subsided suddenly into a state of softness and gentleness. She approached her son-in-law with an air of sorrowful deprecation; she showed a certain deference to her daughter Louie; she was soft and gentle even with Emmeline and Edith.

Mrs. Fleming broke the news to Louie who broke it to Frances who in her turn broke it to Anthony. That was the procedure they invariably adopted.

"I wonder," Grannie said, "what he can be coming back for!" Each time she affected astonishment and incredulity, as if Morrie's coming back were, not a recurrence that crushed you with its flatness and staleness, but a thing that must interest Louie because of its utter unlikeliness.

"I wonder," said Louie, "why he hasn't come before. What else did you expect?"

"I'm sure I don't know," said Grannie helplessly. "Go and tell Frances."

Louie went. And because she knew that the burden of Morrie would fall again on Frances's husband she was disagreeable with Frances.

"It's all very well for you," she said. "You haven't got to live with him. You haven't got to sleep in the room next to him. You don't know what it's like."

"I do know," said Frances. "I remember. You'll have to bear it."

"You haven't had to bear it for fourteen years."

"You'll have to bear it," Frances repeated, "till Anthony sends him out again. That's all it amounts to."

She waited till the children were in bed and she was alone with Anthony.

"Something awful's happened," she said, and paused hoping he would guess.

"I don't know how to tell you."

"Don't tell me if it's that Nicky's been taking my new bike to pieces."

"It isn't Nicky. It's Maurice."

Anthony got up and cleared his pipe, thoroughly and deliberately. She wondered whether he had heard.

"I'd no business to have married you—to have let you in for him."

"Why? What's he been up to now?"

"He's coming home."

"So," said Anthony, "is Bartholomew. I'd no business to have let you in for *him*."

"Don't worry, Frances. If Morrie comes home he'll be sent out again, that's all."

"At your expense."

"I don't grudge any expense in sending Morrie out. Nor in keeping him out."

"Yes. But this time it's different. It's worse."

"Why worse?"

"Because of the children. They're older now than they were last time. They'll understand."

"What if they do? They must learn," Anthony said, "to realize facts."

They realized them rather sooner than he had expected. Nobody but Louie had allowed for the possibility of Morrie's sailing by the same steamer as his letter; and Louie had argued that, if he had done so, he was bound either to have arrived before the letter or to have sent a wire. Therefore they had at least a clear five days of peace before them. Anthony thought he had shown wisdom when, the next morning which was a Wednesday, he sent Grannie and the Aunties to Eastbourne for a week, so that they shouldn't worry Frances, and when on Thursday he made her go with him for a long day in the country, to take her mind off Morrie.

They came back at nine in the evening and found Dorothy, Michael and Nicholas sitting up for them. Michael and Nicky were excited, but Dorothy looked grown-up and important.

"Uncle Morrie's come," they said.

"Dorothy saw him first—"

"Nicky let him in—"

"He hadn't got a hat on."

"We kept him in the schoolroom till Nanna could come and put him to bed."

"He was crying because he'd been to Grannie's house and there wasn't anybody there—"

"And because he'd lost the love-birds he'd brought for Auntie Emmy—"

"And because he couldn't remember which of us was dead."

"No, Mummy, nobody's seen him but us and Nanna."

"Nanna's with him now."

Uncle Morrie never accounted, even to himself, for the time he had spent between the arrival of his ship at Tilbury on Sunday morning and that Saturday afternoon. Neither could he remember what had become of his luggage or whether he had ever had any. Only the County Council man, going his last rounds in the farthest places of the Heath, came upon a small bundle tied in a blue handkerchief, a cap belonging to E.D. Boulger, of the S.S. *Arizona*, a cage of love-birds, and a distinct impression of a recumbent human form, on the grass together, under a young birch tree.

In the stuffy little house behind the Judges' Walk the four women lived now under male protection. When they crossed the Heath they had no longer any need to borrow Anthony from Frances; they had a man of their own. To make room for him Auntie Louie and her type-writer were turned out of their own place, and Auntie Louie had to sleep in Grannie's bed, a thing she hated. To make room for the type-writer the grey parrot was turned out of the dining-room into the drawing-room. And as Maurice couldn't stand either the noise of the type-writer or the noises of the parrot he found both the dining-room and the drawing-room uninhabitable.

Day after day Dorothy and Michael and Nicky, on the terrace, looked out for his coming. (Only extreme distance made Uncle Morrie's figure small and harmless and pathetic.) Day after day he presented himself with an air of distinction and assurance, flushed, and a little battered, but still handsome, wearing a spruce grey suit and a panama hat bought with Anthony's money. Sheep-farming in Australia—he had infinitely preferred the Cape Mounted Police—had ruined Maurice's nerves. He was good for nothing but to lounge in Anthony's garden, to ride his horses—it was his riding that had got him into the Cape Mounted Police—to sit at his table and drink his wines, and, when there was no more wine for him, to turn into "Jack Straw's Castle" for a pick-me-up on his way home.

And before July was out three others were added to the garden group: Bartholomew and Vera and Veronica. And after them a fourth, Vera's friend, Captain Ferdinand Cameron, home on sick leave before anybody expected him.

Frances's tree of Heaven sheltered them all.

VII

Bartholomew, Anthony's brother, lived in Bombay and looked after his business for him in the East. He had something the matter with him, and he had come home to look after his own health. At least, Bartholomew's health was what he was supposed to be looking after; but Dorothy had heard her father say that Bartie had come home to look after Vera.

Vera was Bartie's wife and Veronica's mother. Before she became Mrs. Bartholomew Harrison she had been Frances's schoolfellow and her dearest friend. Frances Fleming had been her bridesmaid and had met Anthony for the first time at Vera's wedding, when he had fallen in love with her; and she had fallen in love with him when they stayed together in Bartholomew's house, before Bartholomew took Vera to Bombay.

Bartie had not been married ten months before he wanted to get Vera out of England; and Vera had not been in India for ten weeks before he wanted her to go back. They were always coming backwards and forwards, but they never came together. Vera would be sent home first, and then Bartie would come over in a great hurry and take her out again.

Twelve years after their marriage Veronica was born at Simla, and the coming and going ceased for three years. Then Bartie sent them both home. That time Vera had refused to travel farther westward than Marseilles. She was afraid of damp and cold, and she had got the ship's doctor to order her to the Riviera. She and Veronica had been living for two years in a small villa at Agaye.

This summer she had come to England. She was no longer afraid of damp and cold. And Bartie followed her.

Dorothy and Michael had no difficulty in remembering Vera, though it was more than six years since they had seen her; for Vera looked the same. Her hair still shone like copper-beech leaves; her face had still the same colour and the same sweet, powdery smell. And if these things had changed Frances would still have known her by her forehead that looked so broad because her eyebrows and her eyes were so long, and by her fine, unfinished, passionate mouth, by her pointed chin and by her ways.

But though her brother-in-law's ways had always been more or less disagreeable, Frances was not prepared for the shock of the renewed encounter with Bartholomew. Bartie was long and grey, and lean even when you allowed for the thickness of his cholera belt. He wore a white scarf about his throat, for his idea was that he had cancer in it. Cancer made you look grey. He, too, had the face of a hawk, of a tired and irritable hawk. It drooped between his hunched shoulders, his chin hanging above the scarf as if he were too tired or too irritable to hold it up. He behaved to Vera and Veronica as if it was they who had worried him into cancer of the throat, they who tired and irritated him.

Vera talked to him as you might talk to a sick child whose peevishness prolongs, unreasonably, its pain. Bartie's manner almost amounted to a public repudiation of her. The whole house vibrated to the shutting of his door at Good-night time. Yet when Bartie came down in the morning, late, and more morose than ever, Vera's mouth made as if it kissed some visionary image of the poor thing's absurdity. She didn't believe for one minute in his cancer. It was an excuse for the shutting of his door.

She kept out of his way as much as possible; yet, when they were together they watched each other. They watched; Bartie openly with sudden dartings and swoopings of his hawk's eyes; Vera furtively. Her eyes were so large and long that, without turning her head, or any visible movement, they could hold his image.

But for Captain Cameron Vera's eyes had a full, open gaze. Spread wide apart under her wide forehead they were like dark moth's wings; they hovered, rested, flickering, vibrating to the fine tips of their corners.

Whatever had been the matter with him in India, Captain Cameron had recovered. His keen, fair, Highland face made Bartie's face look terrible. Ferdie was charming; not more charming to Bartie's wife than he was to Frances; not more charming to Frances than to her sisters; so that even Louie unbent, and Emmeline and Edith fell in love with him. He flirted with Frances under Anthony's nose; and with the Aunties under Grannie's nose. The corners of Vera's mouth followed the tilt of her long eyes' corners as she saw him do it.

You could not think of Vera as the children's Auntie, or as Bartie's wife, or as Veronica's mother.

Veronica was a very little girl who sang songs and was afraid of ghosts.

She slept in her mother's room, and so never could be put to bed till half-past seven, or till her mother was dressed to the last hook of her gown, the last hairpin, the last touch of powder (adhesive without bismuth), and the last shadow drawn fine about her eyelashes. When Vera beautiful in a beautiful gown, came trailing into the room where everybody waited for her, Veronica hid herself behind Uncle Anthony's big chair. When her father told her to come out of that and say Good-night and be quick about it, she came slowly (she was not in the least afraid of Bartie), showing herself bit by bit, honey-coloured hair, eyebrows dark under her gold, very dark against her white; sorrowful, transparent, lucid eyes. A little girl with a straight white face. A little, slender girl in a straight white frock. She stood by Anthony's chair, spinning out the time, smiling at him with her childish wavering mouth, a smile that would not spread, that never went higher than the tip of her white nose, that left her lucid, transparent eyes still sorrowful.

She knew that Anthony would take her on his knee, and that she could sit there with her head tucked under his chin, smiling at him, prolonging her caresses, till Vera told him to put her down and let her go.

Bartie growled: "Did you hear your mother telling you to say Good-night?"

"Yes. But I must kiss Uncle Anthony first. Properly. Once on his mouth. Once—on his nose. And once—on—his—eyes. And—once—on—his dear little—ears."

After that, Veronica went slowly from chair to chair, lingering at each, sitting first on Frances's lap, then on Vera's, spinning out her caresses, that spun out the time and stretched it farther and farther between her and the unearthly hour ahead of her.

But at her father's chair she did not linger for a single instant. She slipped her hand into his hand that dropped it as if it had hurt him; she touched his forehead with her small mouth, pushed out, absurdly, to keep her face as far as possible from his. For, though she was not afraid of Bartie, he was not nice either to sit on or to kiss.

Half-way across the room she lingered.

"I haven't sung 'London Bridge is broken down.' Don't you want me to sing it?"

"No, darling. We want you to go to bed."

"I'm going, Mummy."

And at the door she turned and looked at them with her sorrowful, lucid, transparent eyes.

Then she went, leaving the door open behind her. She left it open on purpose, so that she might hear their voices, and look down into the room on her way upstairs. Besides, she always hoped that somebody would call her back again.

She lingered at the foot of the stairs till Bartie got up and shut the door on her. She lingered at the turn of the stairs and on the landing. But nobody ever called her back again.

And nobody but Nicky knew what she was afraid of.

Veronica was sitting up in the cot that used to be Nicky's when he was little. Nicky, rather cold in his pyjamas, sat on the edge of it beside her. A big, yellow, tremendous moon hung in the sky outside the window, behind a branch of the tree of Heaven, and looked at them.

Veronica crouched sideways on her pillow in a corner of the cot, her legs doubled up tight under her tiny body, her shoulders hunched together, and her thin arms hanging before her straight to her lap. Her honey-coloured hair was parted and gathered into two funny plaits, that stuck out behind her ear. Her head was tilted slightly backwards to rest against the rail of the cot. She looked at Nicky and her look reminded him of something, he couldn't remember what.

"Were *you* ever afraid, Nicky?" she said.

Nicky searched his memory for some image encircled by an atmosphere of terror, and found there a white hound with red smears on his breast and a muzzle like two saws.

"Yes," he said, "I was once."

A lamb—a white lamb—was what Veronica looked like. And Jerry bad looked at him like that when he found him sitting on the mustard and cress the day Boris killed him.

"Afraid—what of?"

"I don't know that it was 'of' exactly."

"Would you be afraid of a ghost, now, if you saw one?"

"I expect I jolly well should, if I *really* saw one."

"Being afraid of ghosts doesn't count, does it?"

"No, of course it doesn't. You aren't afraid as long as I'm here, are you?"

"No."

"I shall stay, then, till you go to sleep."

Night after night he heard her calling to him, "Nicky, I'm frightened." Nobody but Veronica and Nicky were ever in bed on that floor before midnight. Night after night he got up and came to her and stayed beside her till she went to sleep.

Once he said, "If it was Michael he could tell you stories."

"I don't *want* Michael. I want you."

In the day-time she went about looking for him. "Where's Nicky?" she said. "I want him."

"Nicky's in the schoolroom. You can't have him."

"But—I *want* him."

"Can't be helped. You must do without him."

"Will he be very long?"

"Yes, ever so long. Run away like a good little girl and play with Don-Don."

She knew that they told her to play with Don-Don, because she was a little girl. If only she could grow big quick and be the same age as Nicky.

Instead of running away and playing with Don-Don, Ronny went away by herself into the apple-tree house, to wait for Nicky.

The apple-tree house stood on the grass-plot at the far end of the kitchen garden. The apple-tree had had no apples on it for years. It was so old that it leaned over at a slant; it stretched out two great boughs like twisted arms, and was propped up by a wooden post under each armpit. The breast of its trunk rested on a cross-beam. The posts and the cross-beam were the doorway of the house, and the branches were its roof and walls. Anthony had given it to Veronica to live in, and Veronica had given it to Nicky. It was Nicky's and Ronny's house. The others were only visitors who were not expected to stay. There was room enough for them both to stand up inside the doorway, to sit down in the middle, and to lie flat at the far end.

"What more," said Nicky, "do you want?"

He thought that everybody would be sure to laugh at him when he played with Ronny in the apple-tree house.

"I don't care a ram if they do," he said. But nobody ever did, not even Mr. Parsons.

Only Frances, when she passed by that way and saw Nicky and Ronny sitting cramped and close under their roof-tree, smiled unwillingly. But her smile had in it no sort of mockery at all. Nicky wondered why.

"Is it," said Dorothy one morning, "that Ronny doesn't look as if she was Uncle Bartie's daughter, or that Uncle Bartie looks as if he wasn't Ronny's father?"

However suddenly and wantonly an idea struck Dorothy, she brought it out as if it had been the result of long and mature consideration.

"Or is it," said Vera, "that I don't look as if I were Ronny's mother?"

Her eyes had opened all their length to take in Dorothy.

"No. I think it is that Uncle Bartie looks—"

Frances rushed in. "It doesn't matter, my dear, what you think."

"It will some day," said Dorothy.

It was perhaps the best thing she could have said, as showing that she was more interested in the effect she would produce some day than in the sensation she had created there and then.

"May I go round to Rosalind's after lessons?"

"You may."

"And may I stay to lunch if they ask me?"

"You may stay as long as they care to have you. Stay to tea, stay to dinner, if you like."

Dorothy knew by the behaviour of her mother's face that she had scored somewhere, somehow. She also knew that she was in disgrace and yet not in disgrace; which, if you came to think of it, was a funny thing.

About this time Frances began to notice a symptom in herself. She was apt to resent it when Vera discussed her children with her. One late afternoon she and Anthony were alone with Vera. Captain Cameron had not come round that day, and Bartie had gone into town to consult either his solicitor or a specialist. He was always consulting one or the other.

"You're wrong, you two," said Vera. "You think Michael's tender and Nicky's hard and unimpressionable. Michael's hard. You won't have to bother about Michael's feelings."

"Michael's feelings," said Frances, "are probably what I shall have to bother about more than anything."

"You needn't. For one thing, they'll be so unlike your feelings that you won't know whether they're feelings at all. You won't even know whether he's having them or not. Nicky's the one you'll have to look out for. He'll go all the howlers."

"I don't think that Nicky'll be very susceptible. He hasn't shown any great signs so far."

"Hasn't he! Nicky's susceptibility is something awful."

"My dear Vera, you say yourself you don't care about children and that you don't understand them."

"No more I do," said Vera. "But I understand men."

"Do you understand Veronica?"

"Of course I don't. I said men. Veronica's a girl. Besides, I'm Veronica's mother."

"Nicky," said Anthony, "is not much more than nine."

"You keep on thinking of him as a child—a child—nothing but a child. Wait till Nicky has children of his own. Then you'll know."

"They would be rather darlings, Nicky's children," Frances said.

"So would Veronica's."

"Ver-onica?"

You needn't be frightened. Nicky's affection for Ronny is purely paternal."

"I'm not frightened," said Frances. But she left the room. She did not care for the turn the talk had taken. Besides, she wanted Vera to see that she was not afraid to leave her alone with Anthony.

"I'm glad Frances has gone," said Vera, "because I want to talk to you. You'd never have known each other if it hadn't been for me. She couldn't have married you. It was I who saw you both through."

He assented.

"And you said if there was ever anything you could do for me—You haven't by any chance forgotten?"

"I have not."

"Well, if anything should happen to me—"

"But, my dear girl, what *should* happen to you?"

"Things *do* happen, Anthony."

"Yes, but how about Bartie?"

"That's it. Supposing we separated."

"Good Heavens, you're not contemplating *that*, are you?"

"I'm not contemplating anything. But Bartie isn't very easy to live with, is he?"

"No, he's not. He never was. All the same—"

Bartie was impossible. Between the diseases he had and thought he hadn't and the diseases he hadn't and thought he had, he made life miserable for himself and other people. He was a jealous egoist; he had the morbid coldness of the neurotic, and Vera was passionate. She ought never to have married him. All the same—

"All the same I shall stick to Bartie as long as it's possible. And as long as it's possible Bartie'll stick to me. But, if anything happens I want you to promise that you'll take Ronny."

"You must get Frances to promise."

"She'll do anything you ask her to, Anthony."

When Frances came into the room again Vera was crying.

And so Frances promised.

London Bridge is broken down
(*Ride over, My Lady Leigh!*)
Build it up with stones so strong—
Build it up with gold so fine—

It was twenty to eight and Ronny had not so much as begun to say Good-night. She was singing her sons to spin out the time.

London Bridge—

"That'll do, Ronny, it's time you were in bed."

There was no need for her to linger and draw out her caresses, no need to be afraid of going to bed alone. Frances, at Vera's request, had had her cot moved up into the night nursery.

VIII

Anthony had begun to wonder where on earth he should send Morrie out to this time, when the Boer War came and solved his problem.

Maurice, joyous and adventurous again, sent himself to South Africa, to enlist in the Imperial Light Horse.

Ferdie Cameron went out also with the Second Gordon Highlanders, solving, perhaps, another problem.

"It's no use trying to be sorry, Mummy," Dorothy said.

Frances knew what Anthony was thinking, and Anthony knew it was what Frances thought herself: Supposing this time Morrie didn't come back? Then that problem would be solved for ever. Frances hated problems when they worried Anthony. Anthony detested problems when they bothered Frances.

And the children knew what they were thinking. Dorothy went on:

"It's all rot pretending that we want him to come back."

"It was jolly decent of him to enlist," said Nicky.

Dorothy admitted that it was jolly decent. "But," she said, "what else could he do? His only chance was to go away and do something so jolly plucky that *we*'re ashamed of ourselves, and never to come back again to spoil it. You don't want him to spoil it, Mummy ducky, do you?"

Anthony and Frances tried, conscientiously and patriotically, to realize the Boer War. They said it was terrible to have it hanging over them, morning, noon and night. But it didn't really hang over them. It hung over a country that, except once when it had conveniently swallowed up Morrie, they had never thought about and could not care for, a landscape that they could not see. The war was not even part of that landscape; it refused to move over it in any traceable course. It simply hung, or lay as one photographic film might lie upon another. It was not their fault. They tried to see it. They bought the special editions of the evening papers; they read the military dispatches and the stories of the war correspondents from beginning to end; they stared blankly at the printed columns that recorded the disasters of Nicholson's Nek, and Colenso and Spion Kop. But the forms were grey and insubstantial; it was all flat and grey like the pictures in the illustrated papers; the very blood of it ran grey.

It wasn't real. For Frances the brown walls of the house, the open wings of its white shutters, the green garden and tree of Heaven were real; so were "Jack Straw's Castle" and Harrow on the Hill; morning and noon and night were real, and getting up and dressing and going to bed; most real of all the sight and sound and touch of her husband and her children.

Only now and then the vision grew solid and stood firm. Frances carried about with her distinct images of Maurice, to which she could attach the rest. Thus she had an image of Long Tom, an immense slender muzzle, tilted up over a high ridge, nosing out Maurice.

Maurice was shut up in Ladysmith.

"Don't worry, Mummy. That'll keep him out of mischief. Daddy said he ought to be shut up somewhere."

"He's starving, Dorothy. He won't have anything to eat."

"Or drink, ducky."

"Oh, you're cruel! Don't be cruel!"

"I'm not cruel. If I didn't care so awfully for you, Mummy, I shouldn't mind whether he came back or didn't. *You*'re cruel. You ought to think of Grannie and Auntie Louie and Auntie Emmy and Auntie Edie."

"At the moment," said Frances, "I am thinking of Uncle Morrie."

She was thinking of him, not as he actually was, but as he had been, as a big boy like Michael, as a little boy like John, two years younger than she; a little boy by turns spoiled and thwarted, who contrived, nevertheless, to get most things that he happened to want by crying for them, though everybody else went without. And in the grown-up Morrie's place, under the shells of Ladysmith, she saw Nicky.

For Nicky had declared his intention of going into the Army.

"And *I'm* thinking of Morrie," Dorothy said. "I don't want him to miss it."

Frances and Anthony had hung out flags for Mafeking; Dorothy and Nicky, mounted on bicycles, had been careering through the High Street with flags flying from their handlebars. Michael was a Pro-Boer and flew no flags. All these things irritated Maurice.

He had come back again. He had missed it, as he had missed all the chances that were ever given him. A slight wound kept him in hospital throughout the greater part of the siege, and he had missed the sortie of his squadron and the taking of the guns for which Ferdie Cameron got his promotion and his D.S.O. He had come back in the middle of the war with nothing but a bullet wound in his left leg to prove that he had taken part in it.

The part he had taken had not sobered Maurice. It had only depressed him. And depression after prolonged, brutal abstinence broke down the sheer strength by which sometimes he stretched a period of sobriety beyond its natural limits.

For there were two kinds of drinking: great drinking that came seldom and was the only thing that counted, and ordinary drinking that, though it went on most of the time, brought no satisfaction and didn't count at all. And there were two states of drunkenness to correspond: one intense and vivid, without memory, transcending all other states; and one that was no more remarkable than any other. Before the war Morrie's great drinking came seldom, by fits and bursts and splendid unlasting uprushes; after the war the two states tended to approach till they merged in one continual sickly soaking. And while other important and outstanding things, and things that he really wanted to remember, disappeared in the poisonous flood let loose in Morrie's memory, he never for one moment lost sight of the fact that it was he and not Anthony, his brother-in-law, who had enlisted and was wounded.

He was furious with his mother and sisters for not realizing the war. He was furious with Frances and Anthony. Not realizing the war meant not realizing what he had been through. He swore by some queer God of his that he would make them realize it. The least they could do for him was to listen to what he had to say.

"You people here don't know what war is. You think it's all glory and pluck, and dashing out and blowing up the enemy's guns, and the British flag flying, and wounded pipers piping all the time and not caring a damn. Nobody caring a damn.

"And it isn't. It's dirt and funk and stinks and more funk all the time. It's lying out all night on the beastly veldt, and going to sleep and getting frozen, and waking up and finding you've got warm again because your neighbour's inside's been fired out on the top of you. You get wounded when the stretcher-bearers aren't anywhere about, and you crawl over to the next poor devil and lie back to back with him to keep warm. And just when you've dropped off to sleep you wake up shivering, because he's died of a wound he didn't know he'd got.

"You'll find a chap lying on his back all nice and comfy, and when you start to pick him up you can't lift him because his head's glued to the ground. You try a bit, gently, and the flesh gives way like rotten fruit, and the bone like a cup you've broken and stuck together without any seccotine, and you heave up a body with half a head on it. And all the brains are in the other half, the one that's glued down. That's war.

"Huh!" He threw out his breath with a jerk of contempt. It seemed to him that neither Frances nor Anthony was listening to him. They were not looking at him. They didn't want to listen; they didn't want to look at him. He couldn't touch them; he couldn't evoke one single clear image in their minds; there was no horror he could name that would sting them to vision, to realization. They had not been there.

Dorothy and Michael and Nicky were listening. The three kids had imagination; they could take it in. They stared as if he had brought those horrors into the room. But even they missed the reality of it. They saw everything he meant them to see, except him. It was as if they were in the conspiracy to keep him out of it.

He glared at Frances and Anthony. What was the good of telling them, of trying to make them realize it? If they'd only given some sign, made some noise or some gesture, or looked at him, he might have spared them. But the stiff, averted faces of Frances and Anthony annoyed him.

"And if you're a poor wretched Tommy like me, you'll have to sweat in a brutal sun, hauling up cases of fizz from the railway up country to Headquarters, with a thirst on you that frizzles your throat. You see the stuff shining and spluttering, and you go mad. You could kill the man if you were to see him drink it, when you know there's nothing for *you* but a bucket of green water with typhoid germs swimming about in it. That's war.

"You think you're lucky if you're wounded and get bumped down in a bullock wagon thirty miles to the base hospital. But the best thing you can do then is to pop off. For if you get better they make you hospital orderly. And the hospital orderly has to clean up all the muck of the butcher's shop from morning to night. When you're so sick you can't stand you get your supper, dry bread and bully beef. The bully beef reminds you of things, and the bread—well, the bread's all nice and white on the top. But when you turn it over on the other side—it's red. That's war."

Frances looked at him. He thought: "At last she's turned; at last I've touched her; she can realize that."

"Morrie dear, it must have been awful," she said. "It's *too* awful. I don't mind your telling me and Anthony about it; but I'd rather you did it when the children aren't in the room."

"Is that all you think about? The children? The children. You don't care a tinker's cuss about the war. You don't care a damn what happens to me or anybody else. What does it matter who's wounded or who's killed, as long as it isn't one of your own kids?

"I'm simply trying to tell you what war *is*. It's dirt and stink and funk. That's all it is. And there's precious little glory in it, Nicky."

"If the Boers won there would be glory," Michael said.

"Not even if the Boers won," said Maurice.

"Certainly not if the Boers won," said Anthony.

"You'll say next there'd be no glory if there was war between England and Ireland and the Irish won. And yet there would be glory."

"Would there? Go and read history and don't talk rot."

"I have read it," said Michael.

Frances thought: "He doesn't know what he's talking about. Why should he? He's barely thirteen. I can't think where he gets these ideas from. But he'll grow out of them."

It was not Maurice that she saw in Maurice's war-pictures. But he had made them realize what war was; and they vowed that as long as they lived not one of their sons should have anything to do with it.

In the spring of nineteen-one Anthony sent Maurice out to California. The Boer War was ended.

Another year, and the vision of war passed from Frances as if it had never been.

IX

Michael was unhappy.

The almond trees flowered in front of the white houses in the strange white streets.

White squares, white terraces, white crescents; at the turn of the roads the startling beauty of the trees covered with pink blossoms, hot against the hot white walls.

After the pink blossoms, green leaves and a strange white heat everywhere. You went, from pavements burning white, down long avenues grey-white under the shadows of the limes.

A great Promenade going down like a long green tunnel, from the big white Hotel at the top to the High Street at the bottom of the basin where the very dregs of the heat sank and thickened.

Promenade forbidden for no earthly reason that Michael could see, except that it was beautiful. Hotel where his father gave him dinner on his last day of blessed life, telling him to choose what he liked best, as the condemned criminal chooses his last meal on the day they hang him.

Cleeve Hill and Battledown and Birdlip, and the long rampart of Leckhampton, a thin, curling bristle of small trees on the edge of it; forms that made an everlasting pattern on his mind; forms that haunted him at night and tempted and tormented him all day. Memory which it would have been better for him if he had not had, of the raking open country over the top, of broad white light and luminous blue shadows, of white roads switchbacking through the sheep pastures; fields of bright yellow mustard in flower on the lower hills; then, rectangular fir plantations and copses of slender beech trees in the hollows. Somewhere, far-off, the Severn, faint and still, like a river in a dream.

Memory of the round white town in the round pit of the valley, shining, smoking through the thick air and the white orchard blossoms; memory saturated by a smell that is like no other smell on earth, the delicate smell of the Midland limestone country, the smell of clean white dust, and of grass drying in the sun and of mustard flowers.

Michael was in Cheltenham.

It was a matter of many unhappinesses, not one unhappiness. A sudden intolerable unhappiness, the flash and stab of the beauty of the almond-flowers, seen in passing and never seized, beauty which it would have been better for him if he had not seen; the knowledge, which he ought never to have had, that this beauty had to die, was killed because he had not seized it, when, if he could but have held it for one minute, it would have been immortal. A vague, light unhappiness that came sometimes, could not for the life of him think why, from the sight of his own body stripped, and from the feeling of his own muscles. There was sadness for him in his very strength. A long, aching unhappiness that came with his memory of the open country over the tops of the hills, which, in their incredible stupidity and cruelty, they had let him see. A quick, lacerating unhappiness when he thought of his mother, and of the garden on the Heath, and the high ridge of the Spaniards' Road, and London below it, immense and beautiful.

The unhappiness of never being by himself.

He was afraid of the herd. It was with him night and day. He was afraid of the thoughts, the emotions that seized it, swaying, moving the multitude of undeveloped souls as if they had been one monstrous, dominating soul. He was afraid of their voices, when they chanted, sang and shouted together. He loathed their slang even when he used it. He disliked the collective, male odour of the herd, the brushing against him of bodies inflamed with running, the steam of their speed rising through their hot sweaters; and the smell of dust and ink and india-rubber and resinous wood in the warm class-rooms.

Michael was at school.

The thing he had dreaded, that had hung over him, threatening him for years before it happened, had happened. Nothing could have prevented it; their names had been down for Cheltenham long ago; first his, then Nicky's. Cheltenham, because Bartie and Vera lived there, and because it had a college for girls, and Dorothy, who wanted to go to Roedean, had been sent to Cheltenham, because of Bartie and Vera and for no other reason. First Dorothy; then, he, Michael; then, the next term, Nicky. And Nicky had been sent (a whole year before his time) because of Michael, in the hope that Michael would settle down better if he had his brother with him. It didn't seem reasonable.

Not that either Dorothy or Nicky minded when they got there. All that Nicky minded was not being at Hampstead. Being at Cheltenham he did not mind at all. He rather liked it, since Major Cameron had come to stay just outside it—on purpose to annoy Bartie—and took them out riding. Even Michael did not mind Cheltenham more than any other place his people might have chosen. He was not unreasonable. All he asked was to be let alone, and to have room to breathe and get ahead in. As it was, he had either to go with the school mass, or waste energy in resisting its poisonous impact.

He had chosen resistance.

TUDOR HOUSE.
CHELTENHAM,
Sunday.

DEAREST MOTHER,

I've put Sunday on this letter, though it's really Friday, because I'm supposed to be writing it on Sunday when the other fellows are writing. That's the beastly thing about this place, you're expected to do everything when the other fellows are doing it, whether you want to or not, as if the very fact that they're doing it too didn't make you hate it.

I'm writing now because I simply must. If I waited till Sunday I mightn't want to, and anyhow I shouldn't remember a single thing I meant to say. Even now Johnson minor's digging his skinny elbows into one side of me, and Hartley major's biting the feathers off his pen and spitting them out again on the other. But they're only supposed to be doing Latin verse, so it doesn't matter so much. What I mean is it's as if their beastly minds kept on leaking into yours till you're all mixed up with them. That's why I asked Daddy to take me away next term. You see—it's more serious than he thinks—it is, really. You've no idea what it's like. You've got to swot every blessed thing the other fellows swot even if you can't do it, and whether it's going to be any good to you or not. Why, you're expected to sleep when they're sleeping, even if the chap next you snores. Daddy *might* remember that it's Nicky who likes mathematics, not me. It's all very well for Nicky when he wants to go into the Army all the time. There are things *I* want to do. I want to write and I'm going to write. Daddy can't keep me off it. And I don't believe he'd want to if he understood. There's nothing else in the world I'll ever be any good at.

And there are things I want to know. I want to know Greek and Latin and French and German and Italian and Spanish, and Old French and Russian and Chinese and Japanese, oh, and Provençal, and every blessed language that has or has had a literature. I can learn languages quite fast. Do you suppose I've got a chance of knowing one of them—really knowing—even if I had the time? Not much. And that's where being here's so rotten. They waste your time as if it was theirs, not yours. They've simply no notion of the value of it. They seem to think time doesn't matter because you're young. Fancy taking three months over a Greek play you can read in three hours. That'll give you some idea.

It all comes of being in a beastly form and having to go with the other fellows. Say they're thirty fellows in your form, and twenty-nine stick; you've got to stick with them, if it's terms and terms. They can't do it any other way. It's *because* I'm young, Mummy, that I mind so awfully. Supposing I died in ten years' time, or even fifteen? It simply makes me hate everybody.

Love to Daddy and Don.

Your loving MICK.

P.S.—I don't mean that Hartley major isn't good at Latin verse. He is. He can lick me into fits when he's bitten *all* the feathers off.

TUDOR HOUSE.
CHELTENHAM,
Tuesday.

DARLING MUMMY,

Daddy *doesn't* understand. You only think he does because you like him. It's all rot what he says about esprit de corps, the putridest rot, though I know he doesn't mean it.

And he's wrong about gym, and drill and games and all that. I don't mind gym, and I don't mind drill, and I like games. I'm fairly good at most of them—except footer. All the fellows say I'm fairly good—otherwise I don't suppose they'd stick me for a minute. I don't even mind Chapel. You see, when it's only your body doing what the other chaps do, it doesn't seem to matter. If esprit de corps *was* esprit de corps it would be all right. But it's esprit d'esprit. And it's absolutely sickening the things they can do to your mind. I can't stand another term of it.

Always your loving
MICK.

P.S.—How do you know I shan't be dead in ten or fifteen years' time? It's enough to make me.

P.P.S.—It's all very well for Daddy to talk—*he* doesn't want to learn Chinese.

TUDOR HOUSE.
CHELTENHAM,
Thursday.

DEAR FATHER,

All right. Have it your own way. Only I shall kill myself. You needn't tell Mother that—though it won't matter so much as she'll very likely think. And perhaps then you won't try and stop Nicky going into the Army as you've stopped me.

I don't care a 'ram', as Nicky would say, whether you bury me or cremate me; only you might give my Theocritus to old Parsons, and my revolver to Nicky if it doesn't burst. He'd like it.

MICHAEL.

P.S.—If Parsons would rather have my Æschylus he can, or both.

TUDOR HOUSE.
CHELTENHAM,
Sunday.

DARLING MUMMY,

It's your turn for a letter. Do you think Daddy'd let me turn the hen-house into a workshop next holidays, as there aren't any hens? And would he give me a proper lathe for turning steel and brass and stuff for my next birthday? I'm afraid it'll cost an awful lot; but he could take it out of my other birthdays, I don't mind how many so long as I can have the lathe this one.

This place isn't half bad once you get used to it. I like the fellows, and all the masters are really jolly decent, though I wish we had old Parsons here instead of the one we have to do Greek for. He's an awful chap to make you swot.

I don't know what you mean about Mick being seedy. He's as fit as fit. You should see him when he's stripped. But he hates the place like poison half the time. He can't stand being with a lot of fellows. He's a rum chap because they all like him no end, the masters and the fellows, though they think he's funny, all except Hartley major, but he's such a measly little blighter that he doesn't count.

We had a ripping time last Saturday. Bartie went up to town, and Major Cameron took Dorothy and Ronny and Vera and me and Mick to Birdlip in his dog-cart, only Mick and me had to bike because there wasn't room enough. However we grabbed the chains behind and the dog-cart pulled us up the hills like anything, and we could talk to Dorothy and Ronny without having to yell at each other. He did us jolly well at tea afterwards.

Dorothy rode my bike stridelegs coming back, so that I could sit in the dog-cart. She said she'd get a jolly wigging if she was seen. We shan't know till Monday.

You know, Mummy, that kid Ronny's having a rotten time, what with Bartie being such a beast and Vera chumming up with Ferdie and going off to country houses where he is. I really think she'd better come to us for the holidays. Then I could teach her to ride. Bartie won't let her learn here, though Ferdie'd gone and bought a pony for her. That was to spite Ferdie. He's worse than ever, if you can imagine that, and he's got three more things the matter with him.

I must stop now.

Love to Dad and Don and Nanna. Next year I'm to go into physics and stinks—that's chemistry.

Your loving NICKY.

THE LEAS. PARABOLA ROAD.
CHELTENHAM,
Sunday.

DEAREST MUMMY,

I'm awfully sorry you don't like my last term's school report. I know it wasn't what it ought to have been. I have to hold myself in so as to keep in the same class with Rosalind when we're moved up after Midsummer. But as she's promised me faithfully she'll let herself rip next term, you'll see it'll be all right at Xmas. We'll both be in I A the Midsummer after, and we can go in for our matric. together. I wish you'd arrange with Mrs. Jervis for both of us to be at Newnham at the same time. Tell her Rosalind's an awful slacker if I'm not there to keep her up to the mark. No—don't tell her that. Tell her *I'm* a slacker if she isn't there.

I was amused by your saying it was decent of Bartie to have us so often. He only does it because things are getting so tight between him and Vera that he's glad of anything that relaxes the strain a bit. Even us. He's snappier than ever with Ronny. I can't think how the poor kid stands it.

You know that ripping white serge coat and skirt you sent me? Well, the skirt's not nearly long enough. It doesn't matter a bit though, because I can keep it for hockey. It's nice having a mother who *can* choose clothes. You should see the last blouse Mrs. Jervis got for Rosalind. She's burst out of *all* the seams already. You could have heard her doing it.

Much love to you and Daddy and Don-Don. I can't send any to Mr. Parsons now my hair's up. But you might tell him I'm going in strong for Sociology and Economics.—

Your loving
DOROTHY.

P.S.—Vera asked me if I thought you'd take her and Ronny in at Midsummer. I said of course you would—like a shot.

LANSDOWN LODGE.
CHELTENHAM,
Friday.

MY DEAREST FRANCES,

I hope you got my two wires in time. You needn't come down, either of you. And you needn't worry about Mick. Ferdie went round and talked to him like a fa—I mean a big brother, and the revolver (bless his heart!) is at present reposing at the bottom of my glove-box.

All the same we both think you'd better take him away at Midsummer. He says he can stick it till then, but not a day longer. Poor Mick! He has the most mysterious troubles.

I daresay it's the Cheltenham climate as much as anything. It doesn't suit me or Ronny either, and it's simply killing Ferdie by inches. I suppose that's why Bartie makes us stay here—in the hope—

Oh! my dear, I'm worried out of my life about him. He's never got over that fever he had in South Africa. He's looking ghastly.

And the awful thing is that I can't do a thing for him. Not a thing. Unless—

You haven't forgotten the promise you made me two years ago, have you?

Dorothy seemed to think you could put Ronny and me up—again!—at Midsummer. Can you? And if poor Ferdie wants to come and see us, you won't turn him off your door-mat, will you?

Your lovingest
VERA.

Frances said, "Poor Vera! She even makes poor Mick an excuse for seeing Ferdie."

X

Three more years passed and Frances had fulfilled her promise. She had taken Veronica.

The situation had become definite. Bartie had delivered his ultimatum. Either Vera must give up Major Cameron, signing a written pledge in the presence of three witnesses, Frances, Anthony and Bartie's solicitor, that she would neither see him nor write to him, nor hold any sort or manner of communication with him, direct or indirect, or he would obtain a judicial separation. It was to be clearly understood by both of them that he would not, in any circumstances, divorce her. Bartie knew that a divorce was what they wanted, what they had been playing for, and he was not going to make things easy for them; he was going to make things hard and bitter and shameful He had based his ultimatum on the calculation that Vera would not have the courage of her emotions; that even her passion would surrender when she found that it had no longer the protection of her husband's house and name. Besides Vera was expensive, and Cameron was a spendthrift on an insufficient income; he could not possibly afford her. If Bartie's suspicions were correct, the thing had been going on for the last twelve years, and if in twelve years' time they had not forced his hand that was because they had counted the cost, and decided that, as Frances had put it, the "game was not worth the scandal."

For when suspicion became unendurable he had consulted Anthony who assured him that Frances, who ought to know, was convinced that there was nothing in it except incompatibility, for which Bartie was superlatively responsible.

Anthony's manner did not encourage confidence, and he gathered that his own more sinister interpretation would be dismissed with contemptuous incredulity. Anthony was under his wife's thumb and Frances had been completely bamboozled by her dearest friend. Still, when once their eyes were opened, he reckoned on the support of Anthony and Frances. It was inconceivable, that, faced with a public scandal, his brother and his sister-in-law would side with Vera.

It was a game where Bartie apparently held all the cards. And his trump card was Veronica.

He was not going to keep Veronica without Vera. That had been tacitly understood between them long ago. If Vera went to Cameron she could not take Veronica with her without openly confirming Bartie's worst suspicion.

And yet all these things, so inconceivable to Bartie, happened. When it came to the stabbing point the courage of Vera's emotions was such that she defied her husband and his ultimatum, and went to Cameron. By that time Ferdie was so ill that she would have been ashamed of herself if she had not gone. And though Anthony's house was not open to the unhappy lovers, Frances and Anthony had taken Veronica.

Grannie and Auntie Louie and Auntie Emmeline and Auntie Edie came over to West End House when they heard that it had been decided. It was time, they said, that somebody should protest, that somebody should advise Frances for her own good and for the good of her children.

They had always detested and distrusted Vera Harrison; they had always known what would happen. The wonder was it had not happened before. But why Frances should make it easy for her, why Frances should shoulder Vera Harrison's responsibilities, and burden herself with that child, and why Anthony should give his consent to such a proceeding, was more than they could imagine.

Once Frances had stood up for the three Aunties, against Grannie; now Grannie and the three Aunties were united against Frances.

"Frances, you're a foolish woman."

"My folly is my own affair and Anthony's."

"You'll have to pay for it some day."

"You might have thought of your own children first."

"I did. I thought, How would I like *them* to be forsaken like poor Ronny?"

"You should have thought of the boys. Michael's growing up; so is Nicky."

"Nicky is fifteen; Ronny is eleven, if you call that growing up."

"That's all very well, but when Nicky is twenty-one and Ronny is seventeen what are you going to do?"

"I'm not going to turn Ronny out of doors for fear Nicky should fall in love with her, if that's what you mean."

"It *is* what I mean, now you've mentioned it."

"He's less likely to fall in love with her if I bring them up as brother and sister."

"You might think of Anthony. Bartholomew's wife leaves him for another man, and you aid and abet her by taking her child, relieving her of her one responsibility."

"Bartie's wife leaves him, and we help Bartie by taking care of his child—who is *our* niece, not yours."

"My dear Frances, that attitude isn't going to deceive anybody. If you don't think of Anthony and your children, you might think of us. We don't want to be mixed up in this perfectly horrible affair."

"How are you mixed up in it?"

"Well, after all, Frances, we are the family. We are your sisters and your mother and your children's grandmother and aunts."

"Then," said Frances with decision, "you must try to bear it. You must take the rough with the smooth, as Anthony and I do."

And as soon as she had said it she was sorry. It struck her for the first time that her sisters were getting old. It was no use for Auntie Louie, more red and more rigid than ever, to defy the imminence of her forty-ninth birthday. Auntie Emmy's gestures, her mouthings and excitement, only drew attention to the fact that she was forty-seven. And Edie, why, even poor little Auntie Edie was forty-five. Grannie, dry and wiry, hardly looked older than Auntie Edie.

They left her, going stiffly, in offence. And again the unbearable pathos of them smote her. The poor Aunties. She was a brute to hurt them. She still thought of them as Auntie Louie, Auntie Emmy, Auntie Edie. It seemed kinder; for thus she bestowed upon them a colour and vitality that, but for her and for her children, they would not have had. They were helpless, tiresome, utterly inefficient. In all their lives they had never done anything vigorous or memorable. They were doomed to go out before her children; when they were gone they would be gone altogether. Neither Auntie Louie, nor Auntie Emmy, nor Auntie Edie would leave any mark or sign of herself. But her children gave them titles by which they would be remembered after they were gone. It was as if she had bestowed on them a little of her own enduring life.

It was absurd and pathetic that they should think that they were the Family.

But however sorry she was for them she could not allow them to dictate to her in matters that concerned her and Anthony alone. If they were so worried about the scandal, why hadn't they the sense to see that the only way to meet it was to give it the lie by taking Ronny, by behaving as if Ronny were unquestionably Bartie's daughter and their niece? They were bound to do it, if not for Vera's sake, for the dear little girl's sake. And that was what Vera had been thinking of; that was why she had trusted them.

But her three sisters had always disliked Vera. They disliked her because, while they went unmarried, Vera, not content with the one man who was her just and legal portion, had taken another man whom she had no right to. And Auntie Emmeline had been in love with Ferdie.

Still, there was a certain dreadful truth in their reproaches; and it stung. Frances said to herself that she had not been wise. She had done a risky thing in taking Ronny. It was not fair to her children, to Michael and Nicholas and John. She was afraid. She had been afraid when Vera had talked to her about Nicky and Veronica; and when she had seen Veronica and Nicky playing together in the apple-tree house; and when she had heard Ronny's voice outside the schoolroom door crying, "Where's Nicky? I want him. Will he be very long?"

Supposing Veronica should go on wanting Nicky, and supposing Nicky—

Frances was so worried that, when Dorothy came striding across the lawn to ask her what the matter was, and what on earth Grannie and the Aunties had been gassing about all that time, she told her.

Dorothy was nineteen. And Dorothy at nineteen, tall and upright, was Anthony's daughter. Her face and her whole body had changed; they were Anthony's face and body made feminine. Her little straight nose had now a short high bridge; her brown eyes were keen and alert; she had his hawk's look. She put her arm in Frances's, protecting her, and they walked up and down the terrace path, discussing it. In the distance Grannie and the Aunties could be seen climbing the slope of the Heath to Judges' Walk. They were not, Dorothy protested, pathetic; they were simply beastly. She hated them for worrying her mother.

"They think I oughtn't to have taken Ronny. They think Nicky'll want to marry her."

"But Ronny's a kid—"

"When she's not a kid."

"He won't, Mummy ducky, he won't. She'll be a kid for ages. Nicky'll have married somebody else before she's got her hair up."

"Then Ronny'll fall in love with *him*, and get her little heart broken."

"She won't, Mummy, she won't. They only talk like that because they think Ferdie's Ronny's father."

"Dorothy!"

Frances, in horror, released herself from that protecting arm. The horror came, not from the fact, but from her daughter's knowledge of it.

"Poor Mummy, didn't you know? That's why Bartie hates her."

"It isn't true."

"What's the good of that as long as Bartie thinks it is?" said Dorothy.

London Bridge is broken down
(*Ride over my Lady Leigh!*)

Veronica was in the drawing-room, singing "London Bridge."

Michael, in all the beauty of his adolescence, lay stretched out on the sofa, watching her. Her small, exquisite, childish face between the plaits of honey-coloured hair, her small, childish face thrilled him with a singular delight and sadness. She was so young and so small, and at the same time so perfect that Michael could think of her as looking like that for ever, not growing up into a tiresome, bouncing, fluffy flapper like Rosalind Jervis.

Aunt Louie and Aunt Emmeline said that Rosalind was in love with him. Michael thought that was beastly of them and he hoped it wasn't true.

Build it up with gold so fine—

Veronica was happy; for she knew herself to be a cause of happiness. Like Frances once, she was profoundly aware of her own happiness, and for the same reason. It was, if you came to think of it, incredible. It had been given to her, suddenly, when she was not looking for it, after she had got used to unhappiness.

As long as she could remember Veronica had been aware of herself. Aware of herself, chiefly, not as a cause of happiness, but as a cause of embarrassment and uncertainty and trouble to three people, her father, her mother and Ferdie, just as they were causes of embarrassment and trouble and uncertainty to her. They lived in a sort of violent mystery that she, incomprehensibly, was mixed up with. As long as she could remember, her delicate, childish soul had quivered with the vibration of their incomprehensible and tiresome passions. You could never tell what any of them really wanted, though among them they managed to create an atmosphere of most devastating want. Only one thing she knew definitely—that they didn't want *her*.

She was altogether out of it except as a meaningless counter in their incomprehensible, grown-up game. Her father didn't want her; her mother didn't want her very much; and though now and then Ferdie (who wasn't any relation at all) behaved as if he wanted her, *his* wanting only made the other two want her less than ever.

There had been no peace or quietness or security in her little life of eleven years. Their places (and they had had so many of them!) had never had any proper place for her. She seemed to have spent most of her time in being turned out of one room because her father had come into it, and out of another because her mother wanted to be alone in it with Ferdie. And nobody, except Ferdie sometimes, when they let him, ever wanted to be alone in any room with her. She was so tired of the rooms where she was obliged to be always alone with herself or with the servants, though the servants were always kind.

Now, in Uncle Anthony's house, there was always peace and quietness and an immense security. She knew that, having taken her, they wouldn't give her up.

She was utterly happy.

And the house, with its long, wainscoted rooms, its whiteness and darkness, with its gay, clean, shining chintzes, the delicate, faded rose stuffs, the deep blue and purple and green stuffs, and the blue and white of the old china, and its furniture of curious woods, the golden, the golden-brown, the black and the wine-coloured, bought by Anthony in many countries, the round concave mirrors, the pictures and the old bronzes, all the things that he had gathered together and laid up as treasure for his sons; and the garden on the promontory, with its buttressed walls and its green lawn, its flower borders, and its tree of Heaven, saturated with memories, became for her, as they had become for Frances, the sanctuary, crowded with visible and tangible symbols, of the Happiness she adored.

"Sing it again, Ronny."

She sang it again.

London Bridge is broken down—

It was funny of Michael to like the silly, childish song; but if he wanted it he should have it. Veronica would have given any of them anything they wanted. There was nothing that she had ever wanted that they had not given to her.

She had wanted to be strong, to be able to run and ride, to play tennis and cricket and hockey, and Nicky had shown her how. She had wanted books of her own, and Auntie Frances, and Uncle Anthony and Dorothy and Michael had given her books, and Nicky had made her a bookcase. Her room (it was all her own) was full of treasures. She had wanted to learn to sing and play properly, and Uncle Anthony had given her masters. She had wanted people to love her music, and they loved it. She had wanted a big, grown-up sister like Dorothy, and they had given her Dorothy; and she had wanted a little brother of her own age, and they had given her John. John had a look of Nicky. His golden-white hair was light brown now; his fine, wide mouth had Nicky's impudence, even when, like Frances, he kept it shut to smile her unwilling, twitching, mocking smile. She had wanted a father and mother like Frances and Anthony; and they had given her themselves.

And she had wanted to live in the same house with Nicky always.

So if Michael wanted her to sing "London Bridge" to him twenty times over, she would sing it, provided Nicky didn't ask her to do anything else at the same time. For she wanted to do most for Nicky, always.

And yet she was aware of something else that was not happiness. It was not a thing you could name or understand, or seize, or see; you were simply aware of it, as you were aware of ghosts in your room at night. Like the ghosts, it was not always there; but when it *was* there you knew.

It felt sometimes as if Auntie Frances was afraid of her; as if she, Veronica, was a ghost.

And Veronica said to herself, "She is afraid I am not good. She thinks I'll worry her. But I shan't."

That was before the holidays. Now that they had come and Nicky was back, "it" seemed to her something to do with Nicky; and Veronica said to herself, "She is afraid I'll get in his way and worry him, because he's older. But I shan't."

As if she had not been taught and trained not to get in older people's ways and worry them. And as if she wasn't growing older every minute herself!

> Build it up with gold so fine—
> (*Ride over my Lady Leigh!*)
> Build it up with stones so strong—

She had her back to the door and to the mirror that reflected it, yet she knew that Nicky had come in.

"That's the song you used to sing at bed-time when you were frightened," he said.

She was sitting now in the old hen-house that was Nicky's workshop, watching him as he turned square bars of brass into round bars with his lathe. She had plates of steel to polish, and pieces of wood to rub smooth with glass-paper. There were sheets of brass and copper, and bars and lumps of steel, and great poles and planks of timber reared up round the walls of the workshop. The metal filings fell from Nicky's lathe into sawdust that smelt deliciously.

The workshop was nicer than the old apple-tree house, because there were always lots of things to do in it for Nicky.

"Nicky," she said suddenly, "do you believe in ghosts?"

"Well—" Nicky caught his bar as it fell from the lathe and examined it critically.

"You remember when I was afraid of ghosts, and you used to come and sit with me till I went to sleep?"

"Rather."

"Well—there *are* ghosts. I saw one last night. It came into the room just after I got into bed."

"You *can* see them," Nicky said. "Ferdie's seen heaps. It runs in his family. He told me."

"He never told *me*."

"Rather not. He was afraid you'd be frightened."

"Well, I wasn't frightened. Not the least little bit."

"I shall tell him that. He wanted most awfully to know whether you saw them too."

"*Me*? But Nicky—it was Ferdie I saw. He stood by the door and looked at me. Like he does, you know."

The next morning Frances had a letter of two lines from Veronica's mother:

> Ferdie died last evening at half-past eight.
> He wants you to keep Ronny.
> VERA.

It was not till years later that Veronica knew that "He wanted most awfully to know whether you saw them too" meant "He wanted most awfully to know whether you really were his daughter."

PART II

The Vortex

XI

Three years passed. It was the autumn of nineteen-ten. Anthony's house was empty for the time being of all its children except Dorothea.

Michael was in the beginning of his last year at Cambridge. Nicholas was in his second year. He had taken up mathematics and theoretical mechanics. In the long vacation, when the others went into the country, he stayed behind to work in the engineering sheds of the Morss Motor Company. John was at Cheltenham. Veronica was in Dresden.

Dorothea had left Newnham a year ago, having taken a first-class in Economics.

As Anthony came home early one evening in October, he found a group of six strange women in the lane, waiting outside his garden door in attitudes of conspiracy.

Four of them, older women, stood together in a close ring. The two others, young girls, hung about near, but a little apart from the ring, as if they desired not to identify themselves with any state of mind outside their own. By their low sibilant voices, the daring sidelong sortie of their bright eyes, their gestures, furtive and irrepressible, you gathered that there was unanimity on one point. All six considered themselves to have been discovered.

At Anthony's approach they moved away, with slow, casual steps, passed through the posts at the bottom of the lane and plunged down the steep path, as if under the impression that the nature of the ground covered their retreat. They bobbed up again, one after the other, when the lane was clear.

The first to appear was a tall, handsome, bad-tempered-looking girl. She spoke first.

"It's a damned shame of them to keep us waiting like this."

She propped herself up against Anthony's wall and smouldered there in her dark, sullen beauty.

"We were here at six sharp."

"When they know we were told not to let on where we meet."

"We're led into a trap," said a grey-haired woman.

"I say, who *is* Dorothea Harrison?"

"She's the girl who roped Rosalind in. She's all right."

"Yes, but are her people all right?"

"Rosalind knows them."

The grey-haired woman spoke again.

"Well, if you think this lane is a good place for a secret meeting, I don't. Are you aware that the yard of 'Jack Straw's Castle' is behind that wall? What's to prevent them bringing up five or six coppers and planting them there? Why, they've only got to post one 'tee at the top of the lane, and another at the bottom, and we're done. Trapped. I call it rotten."

"It's all right. Here they are."

Dorothea Harrison and Rosalind Jervis came down the lane at a leisured stride, their long coats buttoned up to their chins and their hands in their pockets. Their gestures were devoid of secrecy or any guile. Each had a joyous air of being in command, of being able to hold up the whole adventure at her will, or let it rip.

Rosalind Jervis was no longer a bouncing, fluffy flapper. In three years she had shot up into the stature of command. She slouched, stooping a little from the shoulders, and carried her pink face thrust forward, as if leaning from a platform to address an audience. From this salience her small chin retreated delicately into her pink throat.

"Is Miss Maud Blackadder here?" she said, marshalling her six.

The handsome girl detached herself slowly from Anthony's wall.

"What's the point," she said, "of keeping us hanging about like this—"

"Till *all* our faces are known to the police—"

"There's a johnnie gone in there who can swear to *me*. Why didn't you two turn up before?" said the handsome girl.

"Because," said Dorothea, "that johnnie was my father. He was pounding on in front of us all up East Heath Road. If we'd got here sooner I should have had to introduce you."

She looked at the six benevolently, indulgently. They might have been children whose behaviour amused her. It was as if she had said, "I avoided that introduction, not because it would have been dangerous and indiscreet, but because it would have spoiled your fun for you."

She led the way into the garden and the house and through the hall into the schoolroom. There they found eleven young girls who had come much too soon, and mistaking the arrangements, had rung the bell and allowed themselves to be shown in.

The schoolroom had been transformed into a sort of meeting hall. The big oblong table had been drawn across one end of it. Behind it were chairs for the speakers, before it were three rows of chairs where the eleven young girls sat scattered, expectant.

The six stood in the free space in front of the table and looked at Rosalind with significance.

"This," said Rosalind, "is our hostess, Miss Dorothea Harrison. Dorothy, I think you've met Mrs. Eden, our Treasurer. This is our Secretary, Miss Valentina Gilchrist; Miss Ethel Farmer; Miss Winifred Burstall—"

Dorothy greeted in turn Mrs. Eden, a pretty, gentle woman with a face of dreaming tragedy (it was she who had defended Rosalind outside the gate); Miss Valentina Gilchrist, a middle-aged woman who displayed a large grey pompadour above a rosy face with turned-back features which, when she was not excited, had an incredulous quizzical expression (Miss Gilchrist was the one who had said they had been led into a trap); Miss Ethel Farmer, fair, attenuated, scholastic, wearing pince-nez with an air of not seeing you; and Miss Winifred Burstall, weather-beaten, young at fifty, wearing pince-nez with an air of seeing straight through you to the other side.

Rosalind went on. "Miss Maud Blackadder—"

Miss Blackadder's curt bow accused Rosalind of wasting time in meaningless formalities.

"Miss—" Rosalind was at a loss.

The other girl, the youngest of the eight, came forward, holding out a slender, sallow-white hand. She was the one who had hung with Miss Blackadder in the background.

"Desmond," she said. "Phyllis Desmond."

She shrugged her pretty shoulders and smiled slightly, as much as to say, "She forgets what she ought to remember, but it doesn't matter."

Phyllis Desmond was beautiful. But for the moment her beauty was asleep, stilled into hardness. Dorothy saw a long, slender, sallow-white face, between sleek bands of black hair; black eyes, dulled as if by a subtle film, like breath on a black looking-glass; a beautiful slender mouth, pressed tight, holding back the secret of its sensual charm.

Dorothy thought she had seen her before, but she couldn't remember where.

Rosalind Jervis looked at her watch with a businesslike air; paper and pencils were produced; coats were thrown on the little school-desks and benches in the corner where Dorothy and her brothers had sat at their lessons with Mr. Parsons some twelve years ago; and the eight gathered about the big table, Rosalind taking the presidential chair (which had once been Mr. Parsons' chair) in the centre between Miss Gilchrist and Miss Blackadder.

Miss Burstall and Miss Farmer looked at each other and Miss Burstall spoke.

"We understood that this was to be an informal meeting. Before we begin business I should like to ask one question. I should like to know what we are and what we are here for?"

"We, Mrs. Eden, Miss Valentina Gilchrist, Miss Maud Blackadder and myself," said Rosalind in the tone of one dealing reasonably with an unreasonable person, "are the Committee of the North Hampstead Branch of the Women's Franchise Union. Miss Gilchrist is our Secretary, I am the President and Miss Blackadder is—er—the Committee."

"By whom elected? This," said Miss Burstall, "is most irregular."

Rosalind went on: "We are here to appoint a Vice-President, to elect members of the Committee and enlist subscribers to the Union. These things will take time."

"*We* were punctual," said Miss Farmer.

Rosalind did not even look at her. The moment had come to address the meeting.

"I take it that we are all agreed as to the main issue, that we have not come here to convert each other, that we all want Women's Franchise, that we all mean to have it, that we are all prepared to work for it, and, if necessary, to fight for it, to oppose the Government that withholds it by every means in our power—"

"By every constitutional means," Miss Burstall amended, and was told by Miss Gilchrist that, if she desired proceedings to be regular, she must not interrupt the Chairwoman.

"—To oppose the Government that refuses us the vote, whatever Government it may be, regardless of party, by *every means in our power.*"

Rosalind's sentences were punctuated by a rhythmic sound of tapping. Miss Maud Blackadder, twisted sideways on the chair she had pushed farther and farther back from the table, so as to bring herself completely out of line with the other seven, from time to time, rhythmically, twitching with impatience, struck her own leg with her own walking-stick.

Rosalind perorated. "If we differ, we differ, not as to our end, but solely as to the means we, personally and individually, are prepared to employ." She looked round. "Agreed?"

"Not agreed," said Dorothy and Miss Burstall and Miss Farmer all at once.

"I will now call on Miss Maud Blackadder to speak. She will explain to those of you who are strangers" (she glanced comprehensively at the eleven young girls) "the present program of the Union."

"I protest," said Miss Burstall. "There has been confusion."

"There really *has*, Rosalind," said Dorothy. "You *must* get it straight. You can't start all at sixes and sevens. I protest too."

"We all three protest," said Miss Farmer, frowning and blinking in an agony of protest.

"Silence, if you please, for the Chairwoman," said Miss Gilchrist.

"May we not say one word?"

"You may," said Rosalind, "in your turn. I now call on Miss Blackadder to speak."

At the sound of her own name Miss Blackadder jumped to her feet. The walking-stick fell to the floor with a light clatter and crash, preluding her storm. She jerked out her words at a headlong pace, as if to make up for the time the others had wasted in futilities.

"I am not going to say much, I am not going to take up your time. Too much time has been lost already. I am not a speaker, I am not a writer, I am not an intellectual woman, and if you ask me what I am and what I am here for, and what I am doing in the Union, and what the Union is doing with me, and what possible use I, an untrained girl, can be to you clever women" (she looked tempestuously at Miss Burstall and Miss Farmer who did not flinch), "I will tell you. I am a fighter. I am here to enlist volunteers. I am the recruiting sergeant for this district. That is the use my leaders, who should be *your* leaders, are making of *me*."

Her head was thrown back, her body swayed, rocked from side to side with the violent rhythm of her speech.

"If you ask me why they have chosen *me* I will tell you. It's because I know what I want and because I know how to get what I want.

"I know what I want. Oh, yes, you think that's nothing; you all think you know what you want. But do you? *Do* you?"

"Of course we do!"

"We want the vote!"

"Nothing but the vote!"

"*Nothing but?* Are you quite sure of that? Can you even say you want it till you know whether there are things you want more?"

"What are you driving at?"

"You'll soon see what I'm driving at. I drive straight. And I ride straight. And I don't funk my fences.

"Well—say you all want the vote. Do you know how much you want it? Do you know how much you want to pay for it? Do you know what you're prepared to give up for it? Because, if you don't know *that*, you don't know how much you want it."

"We want it as much as you do, I imagine."

"You want it as much as I do? Good. *Then* you're going to pay the price whatever the price is. *Then* you're ready to give up everything else, your homes and your families and your friends and your incomes. Until you're enfranchised you are not going to own any *man* as father, or brother or husband" (her voice rang with a deeper and stronger vibration) "or lover, or friend. And the man who does not agree with you, the man who refuses you the vote, the man who opposes your efforts to get the vote, the man who, whether he agrees with you or not, *will not help you to get it*, you count as your enemy. That is wanting the vote. That is wanting it as much as I do.

"You women—are you prepared to go against your men? To give up your men?"

There were cries of "Rather!" from two of the eleven young girls who had come too soon.

Miss Burstall shook her head and murmured, "Hopeless confusion of thought. If *this* is what it's going to be like, Heaven help us!"

"You really *are* getting a bit mixed," said Dorothy.

"We protest—"

"Protest then; protest as much as you like. Then we shall know where we are; then we shall get things straight; then we can begin. You all want the vote. Some of you don't know how much, but at least you know you want it. Nobody's confused about that. Do you know how you're going to get it? Tell me that."

Lest they should spoil it all by telling her, Miss Blackadder increased her vehement pace. "You don't because you can't and *I* will tell you. You won't get it by talking about it or by writing about it, or by sitting down and thinking about it, you'll get it by coming in with me, coming in with the Women's Franchise Union, and fighting for it. Fighting women, not talkers—not writers—not thinkers are what we want!"

She sat down, heaving a little with the ground-swell of her storm, amid applause in which only Miss Burstall and Miss Farmer did not join. She was now looking extraordinarily handsome.

Rosalind bent over and whispered something in her ear. She rose to her feet again, flushed, smiling at them, triumphant.

"Our Chairwoman has reminded me that I came here to tell you what the program of our Union is. And I can tell you in six words. It's Hell-for-leather, and it's Neck-or-nothing!"

"Now," said Rosalind sweetly, bowing towards Miss Burstall, "it's your turn. We should like to know what you have to say."

Miss Burstall did not rise and in the end Dorothea spoke.

"My friend, Miss Rosalind Jervis, assumed that we were all agreed, not only as to our aims, but as to our policy. She has not yet discriminated between constitutional and unconstitutional means. When we protested, she quashed our protest. We took exception to the phrase 'every means in our power,' because that would commit us to all sorts of unconstitutional things. It is in my power to squirt water into the back of the Prime Minister's neck, or to land a bomb in the small of his back, or in the centre of the platform at his next public meeting. We were left to conclude that the only differences between us would concern our choice of the squirt or the bomb. As some of us here might equally object to using the bomb or the squirt, I submit that either our protest should have been allowed or our agreement should not have been taken for granted at the start.

"Again, Miss Maud Blackadder, in her sporting speech, her heroic speech, has not cleared the question. She has appealed to us to come in, without counting the cost; but she has said nothing to convince us that when our account at our bank is overdrawn, and we have declared war on all our male friends and relations, and have left our comfortable homes, and are all camping out on the open Heath—I repeat, she has said nothing to convince us that the price we shall have paid is going to get us the thing we want.

"She says that fighters are wanted, and not talkers and writers and thinkers. Are we not then to fight with our tongues and with our brains? Is she leaving us anything but our bare fists? She has told us that she rides straight and that she doesn't funk her fences; but she has not told us what sort of country she is going to ride over, nor where the fences are, not what Hell-for-leather and Neck-or-nothing means.

"We want meaning; we want clearness and precision. We have not been given it yet.

"I would let all this pass if Miss Blackadder were not your colour-sergeant. Is it fair to call for volunteers, for raw recruits, and not tell them precisely and clearly what services will be required of them? How many" (Dorothy glanced at the eleven) "realize that the leaders of your Union, Mrs. Palmerston-Swete, and Mrs. Blathwaite, and Miss Angela Blathwaite, demand from its members blind, unquestioning obedience?"

Maud Blackadder jumped up.

"I protest. I, too, have the right to protest. Miss Harrison calls me to order. She tells me to be clear and precise. Will she be good enough to be clear and precise herself? Will she say whether she is with us or against us? If she is not with us she is against us. Let her explain her position."

She sat down; and Rosalind rose.

"Miss Harrison," she said, "will explain her position to the Committee later. This is an open meeting till seven. It is now five minutes to. Will any of you here"—she held the eleven with her eyes—"who were not present at the meeting in the Town Hall last Monday, hold up your hands? No hands. Then you must all be aware of the object and the policy and the rules of the Women's Franchise Union. Its members pledge themselves to help, as far as they can, the object of the Union; to support the decisions of their leaders; to abstain from public and private criticism of those decisions and of any words or actions of their leaders; and to obey orders—not blindly or unquestioningly, but within the terms of their undertakings.

"Those of you who wish to join us will please write your names and addresses on the slips of white paper, stating what kind of work you are willing to do and the amount of your subscription, if you subscribe, and hand your slips to the Secretary at the door, as you go out."

Miss Burstall and Miss Farmer went out. Miss Blackadder counted—"One—two—"

Eight of the eleven young girls signed and handed in the white slips at the door, and went out.

"Three—four—"

Miss Blackadder reckoned that Dorothea Harrison's speech had cost her five recruits. Her own fighting speech had carried the eleven in a compact body to her side: Dorothea's speech had divided and scattered them again.

Miss Blackadder hurled her personality at the heads of audiences in the certainty that it would hit them hard. That was what she was there for. She knew that the Women's Franchise Union relied on her to wring from herself the utmost spectacular effect. And she did it every time. She never once missed fire. And Dorothea Harrison had come down on the top of her triumph and destroyed the effect of all her fire. She had corrupted five recruits. And, supposing there was a secret program, she had betrayed the women of the Union to fourteen outsiders, by giving it away. Treachery or no treachery, Dorothea Harrison would have to pay for it.

Everybody had gone except the members of the Committee and Phyllis Desmond who waited for her friend, Maud Blackadder.

Dorothy remembered Phyllis Desmond now; she was that art-student girl that Vera knew. She had seen her at Vera's house.

They had drawn round the table again. Miss Blackadder and Miss Gilchrist conferred in whispers.

"Before we go," said Rosalind, "I propose that we ask Miss Dorothea Harrison to be our Vice-President."

Miss Gilchrist nodded to Miss Blackadder who rose. It was her moment.

"And *I* propose," she said, "that before we invite Miss Harrison to be anything we ask her to define her position—clearly and precisely."

She made a sign, and the Secretary was on her feet.

"And first we must ask Miss Harrison to explain *how* she became possessed of the secret policy of the Union which has never been discussed at any open meeting and is unknown to members of the General Committee."

"Then," said Dorothy, "there *is* a secret policy?"

"You seem to know it. We have the right to ask *how* you know? Unless you invented it."

Dorothy faced them. It was inconceivable that it should have happened, that she should be standing there, in the old schoolroom of her father's house, while two strange women worried her. She knew that her back was to the wall and that the Blackadder girl had been on the watch for the last half-hour to get her knife into her. (Odd, for she had admired the Blackadder girl and her fighting gestures.) It was inconceivable that she should have to answer to that absurd committee for her honour. It was inconceivable that Rosalind, her friend, should not help her.

Yet it had happened. With all her platform eloquence Rosalind couldn't, for the life of her, get out one heroic, defending word. From the moment when the Gilchrist woman had pounced, Rosalind had simply sat and stared, like a rabbit, like a fish, her mouth open for the word that would not come. Rosalind was afraid to stand up for her. It was dreadful, and it was funny to see Rosalind looking like that, and to realize the extent of her weakness and her obstinacy.

Yet Rosalind had not changed. She was still the school-girl slacker who could never do a stroke of work until somebody had pushed her into it, who could never leave off working until stopped by the same hand that had set her going. Her power to go, and to let herself rip, and the weakness that made her depend on Dorothy to start her were the qualities that attracted Dorothy to Rosalind from the beginning. But now she was the tool of the fighting Suffrage Women. Or if she wasn't a tool, she was a machine; her brain was a rapid, docile, mechanical apparatus for turning out bad imitations of Mrs. Palmerston-Swete and the two Blathwaites. Her air of casual command, half-swagger, half-slouch, her stoop and the thrusting forward of her face, were copied sedulously from an admired model.

Dorothy found her pitiable. She was hypnotized by the Blathwaites who worked her and would throw her away when she was of no more use. She hadn't the strength to resist the pull and the grip and the drive of other people. She couldn't even hold out against Valentina Gilchrist and Maud Blackadder. Rosalind would always be caught and spun round by any movement that was strong enough. She was foredoomed to the Vortex.

That was Dorothy's fault. It was she who had pushed and pulled the slacker, in spite of her almost whining protest, to the edge of the Vortex; and it was Rosalind, not Dorothy, who had been caught and sucked down into the swirl. She whirled in it now, and would go on whirling, under the impression that her movements made it move.

The Vortex fascinated Dorothy even while she resisted it. She liked the feeling of her own power to resist, to keep her head, to beat up against the rush of the whirlwind, to wheel round and round outside it, and swerve away before the thing got her.

For Dorothy was afraid of the Feminist Vortex, as her brother Michael had been afraid of the little vortex of school. She was afraid of the herded women. She disliked the excited faces, and the high voices skirling their battle-cries, and the silly business of committees, and the platform slang. She was sick and shy before the tremor and the surge of collective feeling; she loathed the gestures and the movements of the collective soul, the swaying and heaving and rushing forward of the many as one. She would not be carried away by it; she would keep the clearness and hardness of her soul. It was her soul they wanted, these women of the Union, the Blathwaites and the Palmerston-Swetes, and Rosalind, and the Blackadder girl and the Gilchrist woman; they ran out after her like a hungry pack yelping for her soul; and she was not going to throw it to them. She would fight for freedom, but not in their way and not at their bidding.

She was her brother Michael, refusing to go to the party; refusing to run with the school herd, holding out for his private soul against other people who kept him from remembering. Only Michael did not hold out. He ran away. She would stay, on the edge of the vortex, fascinated by its danger, and resisting.

But as she looked at them, at Rosalind with her open mouth, at the Blackadder girl who was scowling horribly, and at Valentina Gilchrist, sceptical and quizzical, she laughed. The three had been trying to rush her, and because they couldn't rush her they were questioning her honour. She had asked them plainly for a plain meaning, and their idea of apt repartee was to pretend to question her honour.

Perhaps they really did question it. She didn't care. She loathed their excited, silly, hurrying suspicion; but she didn't care. It was she who had drawn them and led them on to this display of incomparable idiocy. Like her brother Nicholas she found that adversity was extremely funny; and she laughed.

She was no longer Michael, she was Nicky, not caring, delighting in her power to fool them.

"You think," she said, "I'd no business to find out?"

"Your knowledge would certainly have been mysterious," said the Secretary; "unless at least two confidences had been betrayed. Supposing there had been any secret policy."

"Well, you see, I don't know it; and I didn't invent it; and I didn't find it out—precisely. Your secret policy is the logical conclusion of your present policy. I deduced it; that's all. Anybody could have done the same. Does that satisfy you?" (They won't love me any better for making them look fools!)

"Thank you," said Miss Gilchrist. "We only wanted to be sure."

The dinner-bell rang as Dorothy was defining her position.

"I'll work for you; I'll speak for you; I'll write for you; I'll fight for you. I'll make hay of every Government meeting, if I can get in without lying and sneaking for it. I'll go to prison for you, if I can choose my own crime. But I won't give up my liberty of speech and thought and action. I won't pledge myself to obey your orders. I won't pledge myself not to criticize policy I disapprove of. I won't come on your Committee, and I won't join your Union. Is that clear and precise enough?"

Somebody clapped and somebody said, "Hear, Hear!" And somebody said, "Go it, Dorothy!"

It was Anthony and Frances and Captain Drayton, who paused outside the door on their way to the dining-room, and listened, basely.

They were all going now. Dorothy stood at the door, holding it open for them, glad that it was all over.

Only Phyllis Desmond, the art-student, lingered. Dorothy reminded her that they had met at her aunt Vera Harrison's house.

The art-student smiled. "I wondered when you were going to remember."

"I did, but they all called you Desmond. That's what put me out."

"Everybody calls me Desmond. You had a brother or something with you, hadn't you?"

"I might have had two. Which? Michael's got green eyes and yellow hair. Nicky's got blue eyes and black hair."

"It was Nicky—nice name—then."

Desmond's beauty stirred in its sleep. The film of air was lifted from her black eyes.

"I'm dining with Mrs. Harrison to-night," she said.

"You'll be late then."

"It doesn't matter. Lawrence Stephen's never there till after eight. *She won't dine without him.*"

Dorothy stiffened. She did not like that furtive betrayal of Vera and Lawrence Stephen.

"I wish you'd come and see me at my rooms in Chelsea. And bring your brother. Not the green and yellow one. The blue and black one."

Dorothy took the card on which Desmond had scribbled an address. But she did not mean to go and see her. She wasn't sure that she liked Desmond.

Rosalind stayed on to dine with Dorothy's family. She was no longer living with her own family, for Mrs. Jervis was hostile to Women's Franchise. She had rooms off the Strand, not far from the headquarters of the Union.

Frances looked a little careworn. She had been sent for to Grannie's house to see what could be done with Aunt Emmeline, and had found, as usual, that nothing could be done with her. In the last three years the second Miss Fleming had become less and less enthusiastic, and more and more emphatic, till she ceased from enthusiasm altogether and carried emphasis beyond the bounds of sanity. She had become, as Frances put it, extremely tiresome.

It was not accurate to say, as Mrs. Fleming did, that you never knew when Emmeline would start a nervous crisis; for as a matter of fact you could time her to a minute. It was her habit to wait till her family was absorbed in some urgent affair that diverted attention from her case, and then to break out alarmingly. Dorothy was generally sent for to bring her round; but to-day it was Dorothy who had important things on hand. Aunt Emmeline had scented the Suffrage meeting from afar, and had made arrangements beforehand for a supreme crisis that would take all the shine out of Dorothy's affair.

When Frances said that Aunt Emmy had been tiresome again, Dorothy knew what she meant. For Aunt Emmy's idea was that her sisters persecuted her; that Edie was jealous of her and hated her; that Louie had always trampled on her and kept her under; that Frances had used her influence with Grannie to spoil all her chances one after another. It was all Frances's fault that Vera Harrison had come between her and Major Cameron; Frances had encouraged Vera in her infamous intrigue; and between them they had wrecked two lives. And they had killed Major Cameron.

Since Ferdie's death Emmeline Fleming had lived most of the time in a sort of dream in which it seemed to her that these things had really happened.

This afternoon she had been more than usually tiresome. She had simply raved.

"You should have brought her round to the meeting," said Dorothy, "and let her rave there. I'd back Aunt Emmeline against Maud Blackadder. I wish, Rosalind, you'd leave off making faces and kicking my shins. You needn't worry any more, Mummy ducky. I'm going to rope them all into the Suffrage Movement. Aunt Edie can distribute literature, Aunt Louie can interrupt like anything, and Aunt Emmeline can shout and sing."

"I think, Dorothy," said Rosalind with weak bitterness, "that you might have stuck by me."

The two were walking down East Heath Road to the tram-lines where the motor buses started for Charing Cross.

"It was you who dragged me into it, and the least you could do was to stick. Why didn't you keep quiet instead of forcing our hands?"

"I couldn't keep quiet. I'll go with you straight or I won't go with you at all."

"You know what's the matter with you? It's your family. You'll never be any good to us, you'll never be any good to yourself till you've chucked them and got away. For years—ever since you've been born—you've simply been stewing there in the family juice until you're soaked with it. You oughtn't to be living at home. You ought to be on your own—like me."

"You're talking rot, Rosalind. If my people were like yours I'd have to chuck them, I suppose; but they're not. They're angels."

"That's why they're so dangerous. They couldn't influence you if they weren't angels."

"They don't influence me the least little bit. I'd like to see them try. They're much too clever. They know I'd be off like a shot if they did. Why, they let me do every mortal thing I please—turn the schoolroom into a meeting hall for your friends to play the devil in. That Blackadder girl was yelling the house down, yet they didn't say anything. And your people aren't as bad as you make out, you know. You couldn't live on your own if your father didn't give you an allowance. I like Mrs. Jervis."

"Because she likes you."

"Well, that's a reason. It isn't the reason why I like my own mother, because she doesn't like me so very much. That's why she lets me do what I like. She doesn't care enough to stop me. She only really cares for Dad and John and Nicky and Michael."

Rosalind looked fierce and stubborn.

"That's what's the matter with all of you," she said.

"What is?"

"Caring like that. It's all sex. Sex instinct, sex feeling. Maud's right. It's what we're up against all the time."

Dorothy said to herself, "That's what's the matter with Rosalind, if she only knew it."

Rosalind loved Michael and Michael detested her, and Nicky didn't like her very much. She always looked fierce and stubborn when she heard Michael's name.

Rosalind went on. "When it comes to sex you don't revolt. You sit down."

"I do revolt. I'm revolting now. I go much farther than you do. I think the marriage laws are rotten; I think divorce ought to be for incompatibility. I think love isn't love and can't last unless it's free. I think marriage ought to be abolished—not yet, perhaps, but when we've become civilized. It will be. It's bound to be. As it is, I think every woman has a right to have a baby if she wants one. If Emmeline had had a baby, she wouldn't be devastating us now."

"That's what you think, but it isn't what you feel. It's all thinking with you, Dorothy. The revolt goes on in your brain. You'll never do anything. It isn't that you haven't the courage to go against your men. You haven't the will. You don't want to."

"Why should I? What do they do? Father and Michael and Nicky don't interfere with me any more than Mother does."

"You know I'm not thinking of them. They don't really matter."

"Who are you thinking of then? Frank Drayton? You needn't!"

It was mean of Rosalind to hit below the belt like that, when she knew that *she* was safe. Michael had never been brought against her and never would be. It was disgusting of her to imply that Dorothy's state of mind was palpable, when her own (though sufficiently advertised by her behaviour) had received from Michael's sister the consecration of silence as a secret, tragic thing.

They had reached the tram-lines.

At the sight of the Charing Cross 'bus Rosalind assumed an air of rollicking, adventurous travel.

"My hat! What an evening! I shall have a ripping ride down. Don't say there's no room on the top. Cheer up, Dorothy!"

Which showed that Rosalind Jervis was a free woman, suggested that life had richer thrills than marrying Dorothy's brother Michael, and fixed the detested imputation securely on her friend.

Dorothy watched her as she swung herself on to the footboard and up the stair of the motor bus. There was room on the top. Rosalind, in fact, had the top all to herself.

As Dorothy crossed the Heath again in the twilight she saw something white on the terrace of her father's house. Her mother was waiting for her.

She thought at first that Aunt Emmeline had gone off her head and that she had been sent for to keep her quiet. She gloried in their dependence on her. But no, that wasn't likely. Her mother was just watching for her as she used to watch for her and the boys when they were little and had been sent across the Heath to Grannie's house with a message.

And at the sight and memory of her mother Dorothy felt a childish, sick dissatisfaction with herself and with her day, and an absurd longing for the tranquillity and safety of the home whose chief drawback lately had been that it was too tranquil and too safe. She could almost have told her mother how they had all gone for her, and how Rosalind had turned out rotten, and how beastly it had all been. Almost, but not quite. Dorothy had grown up, and she was there to protect and not to be protected. However agreeable it might have been to confide in her mother, it wouldn't have done.

Frances met her at the garden door. She had been crying.

"Nicky's come home," she said.

"Nicky?"

"He's been sent down."

"Whatever for?"

"Darling, I can't possibly tell you."

But in the end she did.

XII

Up till now Frances had taken a quiet interest in Women's Suffrage. It had got itself into the papers and thus become part of the affairs of the nation. The names of Mrs. Palmerston-Swete and Mrs. Blathwaite and Angela Blathwaite had got into the papers, where Frances hoped and prayed that the name of Dorothea Harrison might not follow them. The spectacle of a frantic Government at grips with the Women's Franchise Union had not yet received the head-lines accorded to the reports of divorce and breach of promise cases and fires in paraffin shops; still, it was beginning to figure, and if Frances's *Times* ignored it, there were other papers that Dorothy brought home.

But for Frances the affairs of the nation sank into insignificance beside Nicky's Cambridge affair.

There could be no doubt that Nicky's affair was serious. You could not, Anthony said, get over the letters—the Master's letter and the Professor's letter and Michael's. They had arrived one hour after Nicky, Nicky so changed from his former candour that he refused to give any account of himself beyond the simple statement that he had been sent down. They'd know, he had said, soon enough why.

And soon enough they did know.

To be sure no details could be disentangled from the discreet ambiguities of the Master and the Professor. But Michael's letter was more explicit. Nicky had been sent down because old "Booster" had got it into his head that Nicky had been making love to "Booster's" wife when she didn't want to be made love to, and nothing could get it out of "Booster's" head.

Michael was bound to stand up for his brother, and it was clear to Anthony that so grave a charge could hardly have been brought without some reason. The tone of the letters, especially the Professor's, was extraordinarily restrained. That was what made the thing stand out in its sheer awfulness. The Professor, although, according to Michael, he conceived himself to be profoundly injured, wrote sorrowfully, in consideration of Nicky's youth.

There was one redeeming circumstance, the Master and the Professor both laid stress on it: Anthony's son had not attempted to deny it.

"There must," Frances said wildly, "be some terrible mistake."

But Nicky cut the ground from under the theory of the terrible mistake by continuing in his refusal to deny it.

"What sort of woman," said Anthony, "is the Professor's wife?"

"Oh, awfully decent," said Nicky.

"You had no encouragement, then, no provocation?"

"She's awfully fascinating," said Nicky.

Then Frances had another thought. It seemed to her that Nicky was evading.

"Are you sure you're not screening somebody else?"

"Screening somebody else? Do you mean some other fellow?"

"Yes. I'm not asking you to give the name, Nicky."

"I swear I'm not. Why should I be? I can't think why you're all making such a fuss about it. I don't mean poor old 'Booster.' *He's* got some cause, if you like."

"But what was it you did—*really* did, Nicky?"

"You've read the letters, Mother."

Nicky's adolescence seemed to die and pass from him there and then; and she saw a stubborn, hard virility that frightened and repelled her, forcing her to believe that it might have really happened.

To Frances the awfulness of it was beyond belief. And the pathos of her belief in Nicky was unbearable to Anthony. There were the letters.

"I think, dear," Anthony said, "you'd better leave us."

"Mayn't I stay?" It was as if she thought that by staying she could bring Nicky's youth back to life again.

"No," said Anthony.

She went, and Nicky opened the door for her. His hard, tight man's face looked at her as if it had been she who had sinned and he who suffered, intolerably, for her sin. The click of the door as he shut it stabbed her.

"It's a damnable business, father. We'd better not talk about it."

But Anthony would talk about it. And when he had done talking all that Nicky had to say was: "You know as well as I do that these things happen."

❧

For Nicky had thought it out very carefully beforehand in the train. What else could he say? He couldn't tell them that "Booster's" poor little wife had lost her head and made hysterical love to him, and had been so frightened at what she had done that she had made him promise on his word of honour that, whatever happened, he wouldn't give her away to anybody, not even to his own people.

He supposed that either Peggy had given herself away, or that poor old "Booster" had found her out. He supposed that, having found her out, there was no other line that "Booster" could have taken. Anyhow, there was no other line that *he* could take; because, in the world where these things happened, being found out would be fifty times worse for Peggy than it would be for him.

He tried to recall the scene in the back drawing-room where she had asked him so often to have tea with her alone. The most vivid part was the end of it, after he had given his promise. Peggy had broken down and put her head on his shoulder and cried like anything. And it was at that moment that Nicky thought of "Booster," and how awful and yet how funny it would be if he walked into the room and saw him there. He had tried hard not to think what "Booster's" face would look like; he had tried hard not to laugh as long as Peggy's head was on his shoulder, for fear of hurting her feelings; but when she took it off he did give one half-strangled snort; for it really was the rummest thing that had ever happened to him.

He didn't know, and he couldn't possibly have guessed, that as soon as the door had shut on him Peggy's passion had turned to rage and utter detestation of Nicky (for she had heard the snort); and that she had gone straight to her husband's study and put her head on *his* shoulder, and cried, and told him a lie; and that it was Peggy's lie and not the Professor's imagination that had caused him to be sent down. And even if Peggy had not been Lord Somebody's daughter and related to all sorts of influential people she would still have been capable of turning every male head in the University. For she was a small, gentle woman with enchanting manners and the most beautiful and pathetic eyes, and she had not yet been found out. Therefore it was more likely that an undergraduate with a face like Nicky's should lose his head than that a woman with a face like Peggy's should, for no conceivable reason, tell a lie. So that, even if Nicky's word of honour had not been previously pledged to his accuser, it would have had no chance against any statement that she chose to make. And even if he had known that she had lied, he couldn't very well have given it against poor pretty Peggy who had lost her head and got frightened.

As Nicky packed up his clothes and his books he said, "I don't care if I am sent down. It would have been fifty times worse for her than it is for me."

He had no idea how bad it was, nor how much worse it was going to be. For it ended in his going that night from his father's house to the house in St. John's Wood where Vera and Mr. Lawrence Stephen lived.

And it was there that he met Desmond.

Nicky congratulated himself on having pulled it off so well. At the same time he was a little surprised at the ease with which he had taken his father and mother in. He might have understood it if he had known that Vera had been before him, and that she had warned them long ago that this was precisely the sort of thing they would have to look out for. And as no opinion ever uttered on the subject of their children was likely to be forgotten by Frances and Anthony, when this particular disaster came they were more prepared for it than they would have believed possible.

But there were two members of his family whom Nicky had failed altogether to convince, Michael and Dorothy. Michael luckily, Nicky said to himself, was not on the spot, and his letter had no weight against the letters of the Master and the Professor, and on this also Nicky had calculated. He reckoned without Dorothy, judging it hardly likely that she would be allowed to know anything about it. Nobody, not even Frances, was yet aware of Dorothy's importance.

And Dorothy, because of her importance, blamed herself for all that happened afterwards. If she had not had that damned Suffrage meeting, Rosalind would not have stayed to dinner; if Rosalind had not stayed to dinner she would not have gone with her to the tram-lines; if she had not gone with her to the tram-lines she would have been at home to stop Nicky from going to St. John's Wood. As it was, Nicky had reached the main road at the top of the lane just as Dorothy was entering it from the bottom.

At first Frances did not want Dorothy to see her father. He was most horribly upset and must not be disturbed. But Dorothy insisted. Her father had the letters, and she must see the letters.

"I may understand them better than you or Daddy," she said. "You see, Mummy, I know these Cambridge people. They're awful asses, some of them."

And though her mother doubted whether attendance at the Professor's lectures would give Dorothy much insight into the affair, she had her way. Anthony was too weak to resist her. He pushed the letters towards her without a word. He would rather she had been left out of it. And yet somehow the sight of her, coming in, so robust and undismayed and competent, gave him a sort of comfort.

Dorothy did not agree with Michael. There was more in it than the Professor's imagination. The Professor, she said, hadn't got any imagination; you could tell from the way he lectured. But she did not believe one word of the charge against her brother. Something had happened and Nicky was screening somebody.

"I'll bet you anything you like," said Dorothy, "it's 'Booster's' wife. She's made him give his word."

Dorothy was sure that "Booster's" wife was a bad lot.

"Nicky said she was awfully decent."

"He'd *have* to. He couldn't do it by halves."

"They couldn't have sent him down, unless they'd sifted the thing to the bottom."

"I daresay they've sifted all they could, the silly asses."

She could have killed them for making her father suffer. The sight of his drawn face hurt her abominably. She had never seen him like that. She wasn't half so sorry for her mother who was sustained by a secret, ineradicable faith in Nicky. Why couldn't he have faith in Nicky too? Was it because he was a man and knew that these things happened?

"Daddy—being sent down isn't such an awful calamity. It isn't going to blast his career or anything. It's always touch and go. *I* might have been sent down any day. I should have been if they'd known about me half what they don't know about Nicky. Why can't you take it as a rag? You bet *he* does."

Anthony removed himself from her protecting hand. He got up and went to bed.

But he did not sleep there. Neither he nor Frances slept. And he came down in the morning looking worse than ever.

Dorothy thought, "It must be awful to have children if it makes you feel like that." She thought, "It's a lucky thing they're not likely to cut up the same way about me." She thought again, "It must be awful to have children." She thought of the old discussions in her room at Newnham, about the woman's right to the child, and free union, and easy divorce, and the abolition of the family. Her own violent and revolutionary speeches (for which she liked to think she might have been sent down) sounded faint and far-off and irrelevant. She did not really want to abolish Frances and Anthony. And yet, if they had been abolished, as part of the deplorable institution of parentage, it would have been better for them; for then they would not be suffering as they did.

It must be awful to have children. But perhaps they knew that it was worth it.

And as her thoughts travelled that way they were overtaken all of a sudden by an idea. She did not stop to ask herself what business her idea had in that neighbourhood. She went down first thing after breakfast and sent off two wires; one to Captain Drayton at Croft House, Eltham; one to the same person at the Royal Military Academy, Woolwich.

Can I see you? It's about Nicky.
DOROTHY HARRISON.

Wires to show that she was impersonal and businesslike, and that her business was urgent. "Can I see you?" to show that he was not being invited to see *her*. "It's about Nicky" to justify the whole proceeding. "Dorothy Harrison" because "Dorothy" by itself was too much.

As soon as she had sent off her wires Dorothy felt a sense of happiness and well-being. She had no grounds for happiness; far otherwise; her great friendship with Rosalind Jervis was disintegrating bit by bit owing to Rosalind's behaviour; the fiery Suffrage meeting had turned into dust and ashes; her darling Nicky was in a nasty scrape; her father and mother were utterly miserable; yet she was happy.

Half-way home her mind began to ask questions of its own accord.

"Supposing you had to choose between the Suffrage and Frank Drayton?"

"But I haven't got to."

"You might have. You know you might any minute. You know he hates it. And supposing—"

But Dorothy refused to give any answer.

His wire came within the next half-hour.

Coming three sharp. FRANK.

Her sense of well-being increased almost to exaltation.

He arrived with punctuality at three o'clock. (He was in the gunners and had a job at Woolwich.) She found him standing on the hearthrug in the drawing-room. He had blown his nose when he heard her coming, and that meant that he was nervous. She caught him stuffing his pocket-handkerchief (a piece of damning evidence) into his breast-pocket.

With her knowledge of his nervousness her exaltation ceased as if it had not been. At the sight of him it was as if the sentence hidden somewhere in her mind—"You'll have to choose. You know you'll have to"—escaping thought and language, had expressed itself in one suffocating pang. Unless Nicky's affair staved off the dreadful moment.

"Were you frightfully busy?"

"No, thank goodness."

The luck she had had! Of course, if he had been busy he couldn't possibly have come.

She could look at him now without a tightening in her throat. She liked to look at him. He was made all of one piece. She liked his square face and short fine hair, both the colour of light-brown earth; his eyes, the colour of light-brown earth under clear water; eyes that looked small because they were set so deep. She liked their sudden narrowing and their deep wrinkles when he smiled. She liked his jutting chin, and the fine, rather small mouth that jerked his face slightly crooked when he laughed. She liked that slender crookedness that made it a face remarkable and unique among faces. She liked his brains. She liked all that she had ever seen or heard of him.

Vera had told them that once, at an up-country station in India, he had stopped a mutiny in a native battery by laughing in the men's faces. Somebody that Ferdie knew had been with him and saw it happen. The men broke into his office where he was sitting, vulnerably, in his shirtsleeves. They had brought knives with them, beastly native things, and they had their hands on the handles, ready. They screamed and gesticulated with excitement. And Frank Drayton leaned back in his office chair and looked at them, and burst out laughing, because, he said, they made such funny faces. When they got to fingering their knives, he tilted back his chair and rocked with laughter. His sudden, incredible mirth frightened them and stopped the mutiny. She could see him, she could see his face jerked crooked with delight.

That was the sort of thing that Nicky would have done. She loved him for that. She loved him because he was like Nicky.

She was not able to recall the process of the states that flowered in that mysterious sense of well-being and exaltation. A year ago Frank Drayton had been only "that nice man we used to meet at Cheltenham." First of all he had been Ferdie's and Vera's friend. Then he became Nicky's friend; the only one who took a serious interest in his inventions and supported him when he wanted to go into the Army and consoled him when he was frustrated. Then he had become the friend of the family. Now he was recognized as more particularly Dorothea's friend.

At Cheltenham he had been home on leave; and it was not until this year that he had got his job at Woolwich teaching gunnery, while he waited for a bigger job in the Ordnance Department. Ferdie Cameron had always said that Frank Drayton would be worth watching. He would be part of the brains of the Army some day. Nicky watched him. His brains and their familiarity with explosives and the machinery of warfare had been his original attraction for Nicky. But it was Dorothea who watched him most.

She plunged abruptly into Nicky's affair, giving names and lineage. "You know all sorts of people, do you know anything about her?"

He looked at her clearly, without smiling. Then he said, "Yes. I know a good bit about her. Is that what's wrong with Nicky?"

"Not exactly. But he's been sent down."

His wry smile intimated that such things might be.

Then she told him what the Master had written and what the Professor had written and what Michael had written, and what Nicky had said, and what she, Dorothea thought. Drayton smiled over the Master's and the Professor's letters, but when it came to Michael's letter he laughed aloud.

"It's all very well for *us*. But Daddy and Mummy are breaking their hearts. Daddy says he's going down to Cambridge to see what really did happen."

Again that clear look. She gathered that he disapproved of "Booster's" wife. He disapproved of so many things: of Women's Suffrage; of revolutions; of women who revolted; of anybody who revolted; of Mrs. Palmerston-Swete and Mrs. Blathwaite and Angela Blathwaite. It was putting it too mildly to say he disapproved of Rosalind Jervis; he detested her. He disapproved of Vera and of her going to see Vera; she remembered that he had even disapproved, long ago, of poor Ferdie, though he liked him. Evidently he disapproved of "Booster's" wife for the same reason that he disapproved of Vera. That was why he didn't say so.

"I believe you think all the time I'm right," she said. "Would you go down if you were he?"

"No. I wouldn't."

"Why not?"

"Because he won't get anything out of them. They can't give her away any more than Nicky can. Or than *you* can, Dorothy."

"You mean I've done it already—to you. I *had* to, because of Nicky. I can't help it if you *do* think it was beastly of me."

"My dear child—"

He got up vehemently, as if his idea was to take her in his arms and stifle her outbreak that way. But something in her eyes, cold, unready, yet aware of him, repelled him.

He thought: "It's too soon. She's all rigid. She isn't alive yet. That's not what she wired for." He thought: "I wish people wouldn't send their children to Newnham. It retards their development by ten years."

And she thought: "No. I mustn't let him do that. For then he won't be able to go back on me when I tell him my opinions. It would be simply trapping him. Supposing—supposing—"

She did not know that that instinctive renunciation was her answer to the question. Her honour would come first.

"Of course. Of course you had to."

"What would you do about it if you were Daddy?"

"I should send them all to blazes."

"No, but *really* do?"

"I should do nothing. I should leave it. You'll find that before very long there'll be letters of apology and restitution."

"Will you come down to the office with me and tell Daddy that?"

"Yes, if you'll come to tea with me somewhere afterwards." (He really couldn't be expected to do all this for nothing.)

She sent her mother to him while she put on her hat and coat. When she came down Frances was happy again.

"You see, Mummy, I was right, after all."

"You always were right, darling, all the time."

For the life of her she couldn't help giving that little flick at her infallible daughter.

"She *is* right—most of the time," said Drayton. His eyes covered and protected her.

Anthony was in his office, sitting before the open doors of the cabinet where he kept his samples of rare and valuable woods. The polished slabs were laid before him on the table in rows, as he had arranged them to show to a customer: wine-coloured mahogany, and golden satinwood; ebony black as jet; tulip-wood mottled like fine tortoiseshell; coromandel wood, striped black and white like the coat of a civet cat; ghostly basswood, shining white on dead white; woods of clouded grain, and woods of shining grain, grain that showed like the slanting, splintered lines of hewn stone, like moss, like the veins of flowers, the fringes of birds' feathers, the striping and dappling of beasts; woods of exquisite grain where the life of the tree drew its own image in its own heart; woods whose surface was tender to the touch like a fine tissue; and sweet-smelling sandalwood and camphor-wood and cedar.

Anthony loved his shining, polished slabs of wood. If a man must have a business, let it be timber. Timber was a clean and fine and noble thing. He had brought the working of his business to such a pitch of smooth perfection that his two elder sons, Michael and Nicholas, could catch up with it easily and take it in their stride.

Now he was like a sick child that has ranged all its toys in front of it and finds no comfort in them.

And, as he looked at them, the tulip-wood and the scented sandalwood and camphor-wood gave him an idea.

The Master and the Professor had both advised him to send his son Nicholas out of England for a little while. "Let him travel for six months and get the whole miserable business out of his head."

Nicky, when he gave up the Army, had told him flatly that he would rather die than spend his life sitting in a beastly office. Nicky had put it to him that timber meant trees, and trees meant forests; why, lots of the stuff they imported came from the Himalaya and the West Indies and Ceylon. He had reminded him that he was always saying a timber merchant couldn't know enough about the living tree. Why shouldn't he go into the places where the living trees grew and learn all about them? Why shouldn't he be a tree-expert? Since they were specializing in rare and foreign woods, why shouldn't he specialize in rare and foreign trees?

And the slabs of tulip-wood and scented camphor-wood and sandalwood were saying to Anthony, "Why not?" Neither he nor Frances had wanted Nicky to go off to the West Indies and the Himalaya; but now, since clearly he must go off somewhere, why not?

Drayton and Dorothy came in just as Anthony (still profoundly dejected) was saying to himself, "Reinstate him. Give him responsibility—curiosity—healthy interests. Get the whole miserable business out of his head."

It seemed incredible, after what they had gone through, that Drayton should be standing there, telling him that there was nothing in it, that there never had been any miserable business, that it was all a storm in a hysterical woman's teacup. He blew the whole dirty nightmare to nothing with the laughter that was like Nicky's own laughter.

Then Anthony and Drayton and Dorothy sat round the table, drafting letters to the Master and the Professor. Anthony, at Drayton's dictation, informed them that he regretted the step they had seen fit to take; that he knew his own son well enough to be pretty certain that there had been some misunderstanding; therefore, unless he received within three days a written withdrawal of the charge against his son Nicholas, he would be obliged to remove his son Michael from the Master's College.

The idea of removing Michael was Anthony's own inspiration.

Drayton's advice was that he should give Nicky his choice between Oxford and Germany, the big School of Forestry at Aschaffenburg. If he chose Germany, he would be well grounded; he could specialize and travel afterwards.

"Now *that's* all over," Anthony said, "you two had better come and have tea with me somewhere."

But there was something in their faces that made him consult his watch and find that "Oh dear me, no! he was afraid he couldn't." He had an appointment at five.

When they were well out of sight he locked up his toys in his cabinet, left the appointment at five to Mr. Vereker, and went home to tell Frances about the letters he had written to Cambridge and the plans that had been made for Nicky's future.

"He'll choose Germany," Anthony said. "But that can't be helped."

Frances agreed that they could hardly have hit upon a better plan.

So the affair of Nicky and "Booster's" wife was as if it had never been. And for that they thanked the blessed common sense and sanity of Captain Drayton.

And yet Anthony's idea was wrecked by "Booster's" wife. It had come too late. Anthony had overlooked the fact that his son had seventeen hours' start of him. He was unaware of the existence of Nicky's own idea; and he had not allowed for the stiff logic of his position.

When he drove down in his car to St. John's Wood to fetch Nicky, he found that he had left that afternoon for Chelsea, where, Vera told him, he had taken rooms.

She gave him the address. It had no significance for Anthony.

Nicky refused to be fetched back from his rooms in Chelsea. For he had not left his father's house in a huff; he had left it in his wisdom, to avoid the embarrassment of an incredible position. His position, as he pointed out to his father, had not changed. He was as big a blackguard to-day as he was yesterday; the only difference was, that to-morrow or the next day he would be a self-supporting blackguard.

He wouldn't listen to his father's plan. It was a beautiful plan, but it would only mean spending more money on him. He'd be pretty good, he thought, at looking after machinery. He was going to try for a job as a chauffeur or foreman mechanic. He thought he knew where he could get one; but supposing he couldn't get it, if his father cared to take him on at the works for a bit he'd come like a shot; but he couldn't stay there, because it wouldn't be good enough.

He was absolutely serious, and absolutely firm in the logic of his position. For he argued that, if he allowed himself to be taken back as though nothing had happened, this, more than anything he could well think of, would be giving Peggy away.

He sent his love to his mother and Dorothy, and promised to come out and dine with them as soon as he had got his job.

So Anthony drove back without him. But as he drove he smiled. And Frances smiled, too, when he told her.

"There he is, the young monkey, and there he'll stay. It's magnificent, but of course he's an ass."

"If you can't be an ass at twenty," said Frances, "when can you be?"

They said it was so like Nicky. For all he knew to the contrary his career was ruined; but he didn't care. You couldn't make any impression on him. They wondered if anybody ever would.

Dorothy wondered too.

"What sort of rooms has he got, Anthony?" said Frances.

"Very nice rooms, at the top of the house, looking over the river."

"Darling Nicky, I shall go and see him. What are you thinking of, Dorothy?"

Dorothy was thinking that Nicky's address at Chelsea was the address that Desmond had given her yesterday.

XIII

When Frances heard that Nicholas was going about everywhere with the painter girl they called Desmond, she wrote to Vera to come and see her. She could never bring herself to go to the St. John's Wood house that was so much more Mr. Lawrence Stephen's house than it was Vera's.

The three eldest children went now and then, refusing to go back on Vera. Frances did not like it, but she had not interfered with their liberty so far as to forbid it positively; for she judged that frustration might create an appetite for Mr. Stephen's society that otherwise they might not, after all, acquire.

Vera understood that her husband's brother and sister-in-law could hardly be expected to condone her last aberration. Her attachment to Ferdie Cameron had been different. It was inevitable, and in a sense forgivable, seeing that it had been brought about by Bartie's sheer impossibility. Besides, the knowledge of it had dawned on them so gradually and through so many stages of extenuating tragedy, that, even when it became an open certainty, the benefit of the long doubt remained. And there was Veronica. There was still Veronica. Even without Veronica Vera would have had to think of something far worse than Lawrence Stephen before Frances would have cast her off. Frances felt that it was not for her to sit in judgment under the shelter of her tree of Heaven. Supposing she could only have had Anthony as Vera had had Ferdie, could she have lived without him? For Frances nothing in the world had any use or interest or significance but her husband and her children; her children first, and Anthony after them. For Vera nothing in the world counted but her lover.

"If only I were as sure of Lawrence as you are of Anthony!" she would say.

Yet she lived the more intensely, if the more dangerously, through the very risks of her exposed and forbidden love.

Vera was without fidelity to the unreturning dead; but she made up for it by an incorruptible adoration of the living. And she had been made notorious chiefly through Stephen's celebrity, which was, you might say, a pure accident.

Thus Frances made shelter for her friend. Only Vera must be made to understand that, though *she* was accepted Lawrence Stephen was not. He was the point at which toleration ceased.

And Vera did understand. She understood that Frances and Anthony disapproved of her last adventure considerably more on Ferdie's and Veronica's account than on Bartie's. Even family loyalty could not espouse Bartie's cause with any zest. For Bartie showed himself implacable. Over and over again she had implored him to divorce her so that Lawrence might marry her, and over and over again he had refused. His idea was to assert himself by refusals. In that way he could still feel that he had power over her and a sort of possession. It was he who was scandalous. Even now neither Frances nor Anthony had a word to say for him.

So Vera consented to be received surreptitiously, by herself, and without receiving Frances and Anthony in her turn. It had hurt her; but Stephen's celebrity was a dressing to her wound. He was so distinguished that it was unlikely that Frances, or Anthony either, would ever have been received by him without Vera. She came, looking half cynical, half pathetic, her beauty a little blurred, a little beaten after seventeen years of passion and danger, saying that she wasn't going to force Larry down their throats if they didn't like him; and she went away sustained by her sense of his distinction and *his* repudiations.

And she found further support in her knowledge that, if Frances and Anthony could resist Lawrence, their children couldn't. Michael and Dorothy were acquiring a taste for him and for the people he knew; and he knew almost everybody who was worth knowing. To be seen at the parties he and Vera gave in St. John's Wood was itself distinction. Vera had never forgotten and never would forget what Anthony and Frances had done for her and Ferdie when they took Veronica. She wanted to make up, to pay back, to help their children as they had helped her child; to give the best she had, and do what they, poor darlings, couldn't possibly have done. Nicholas was all right; but Michael's case was lamentable. In his family and in the dull round of their acquaintance there was not anybody who was likely to be of the least use to Michael; not anybody that he cared to know. No wonder that he kept up his old attitude of refusing to go to the party. Lawrence Stephen had promised her that he would help Michael.

And Frances was afraid. She saw her children, Michael, Nicholas and Dorothy, swept every day a little farther from the firm, well-ordered sanctities, a little nearer to the unclean moral vortex that to her was the most redoubtable of all. She hid her fear, because in her wisdom she knew that to show fear was not the way to keep her children. She hid her strength because she knew that to show it was not the way. Her strength was in their love of her. She had only used it once when she had stopped Nicky from going into the Army. She had said to herself then, "I will never do that again." It wasn't fair. It was a sort of sacrilege, a treachery. Love was holy; it should never be used, never be bargained with. She tried to hold the balance even between their youth and their maturity.

So Frances fought her fear.

She had known that Ferdie Cameron was good, as she put it, "in spite of everything"; but she had not seen Lawrence Stephen, and she did not know that he had sensibilities and prejudices and scruples like her own, and that he and Vera distinguished very carefully between the people who would be good for Michael and Nicholas and Dorothy, and the people who would not. She did not know that they both drew the line at Desmond.

Vera protested that it was not her fault, it was not Lawrence's fault that Nicky had met Desmond. She had never asked them to meet each other. She did not deny that it was in her house they *had* met; but she had not introduced them. Desmond had introduced herself, on the grounds that she knew Dorothy. Vera suspected that, from the first moment when she had seen him there—by pure accident—she had marked him down. Very likely she had wriggled into Dorothy's Suffrage meeting on purpose. She was capable of anything.

Not that Vera thought there was any need for Frances to worry. It was most unlikely that Desmond's business with Nicky could be serious. For one thing she was too young herself to care for anybody as young as Nicky. For another she happened to be in the beginning, or the middle, certainly nowhere near the end of a tremendous affair with Headley Richards. As she was designing the dresses and the scenery for the new play he was putting on at the Independent Theatre, Vera argued very plausibly that the affair had only just started, and that Frances must allow it a certain time to run.

"I hope to goodness that the Richards man will marry her."

"My dear, how can he? He's married already to a nice little woman that he isn't half tired of yet. Desmond was determined to have him and she's got him; but he's only taken her in his stride, as you may say. I don't suppose he cares very much one way or another. But with Desmond it's a point of honour."

"What's a point of honour?"

"Why, to have him. Not to be left out. Besides, she always said she could take him from poor little Ginny Richards, and she's done it. That was another point of honour."

With a calmness that was horrible to Frances, Vera weighed her friend Desmond's case. To Frances it was as if she had never known Vera. Either Vera had changed or she had never known her. She had never known women, or men either, who discussed such performances with calmness. Vera herself hadn't made her infidelities a point of honour.

These were the passions and the thoughts of Lawrence Stephen's and of Desmond's world; these were the things it took for granted. These people lived in a moral vortex; they whirled round and round with each other; they were powerless to resist the swirl. Not one of them had any other care than to love and to make love after the manner of the Vortex. This was their honour, not to be left out of it, not to be left out of the vortex, but to be carried away, to be sucked in, and whirl round and round with each other and the rest.

The painter girl Desmond was horrible to Frances.

And all the time her mind was busy with one question: "Do you think Nicky knows?"

"I'm perfectly sure he doesn't."

"Perhaps—if he did—"

"No, my dear, that's no good. If you tell him he won't believe it. You'll have all his chivalry up in arms. And you'll be putting into his head what may never come into it if he's left alone. And you'll be putting it into Desmond's head."

Captain Drayton, whom Anthony consulted, said, "Leave him alone." Those painting and writing johnnies were a rum lot. You couldn't take them seriously. The Desmond girl might be everything that Vera Harrison said she was. He didn't think, though, that the idea of making love to her would enter Nicky's head if they left him alone. Nicky's head had more important ideas in it.

So they left him alone.

And at first Nicholas really was too busy to think much of Desmond. Too busy with his assistant manager's job at the Morss Motor Works; too busy with one of the little ideas to which he owed the sudden rise in his position: the little idea of making the Morss cars go faster; too busy with his big Idea which had nothing whatever to do with the Morss Company and their cars.

His big Idea was the idea of the Moving Fortress. The dream of a French engineer, the old, abandoned dream of the *forteresse mobile*, had become Nicky's passion.

He claimed no originality for his idea. It was a composite of the armoured train, the revolving turret, the tractor with caterpillar wheels and the motor-car. These things had welded themselves together gradually in Nicky's mind during his last year at Cambridge. The table in Nicky's sitting-room at the top of the house in Chelsea was now covered with the parts of his model of the Moving Fortress. He made them at the Works, one by one; for the Morss Company were proud of him, and he had leave to use their material and plant now and then for little ideas of his own. The idea of the Moving Fortress was with him all day in the workshops and offices and showrooms, hovering like a formless spiritual presence among the wheeled forms. But in the evening it took shape and sound. It arose and moved, after its fashion, as he had conceived it, beautiful, monstrous, terrible. At night, beside the image of the *forteresse mobile*, the image of Desmond was a thin ghost that stood back, mournful and dumb, in the right-hand corner of the vision.

But the image of Desmond was there.

At first it stood for Nicky's predominant anxiety: "I wonder when Desmond will have finished the drawings."

The model of the Moving Fortress waited upon Desmond's caprice.

The plans of the parts and sections had to be finished before these could be fitted together and the permanent model of the Moving Fortress set up. The Moving Fortress itself waited upon Desmond.

For, though Nicky could make and build his engine, he could not draw his plans properly; and he could not trust anybody who understood engines to draw them. He was haunted, almost insanely, by the fear that somebody else would hit upon the idea of the Moving Fortress; it seemed to him so obvious that no gunner and no engineer could miss it. And the drawings Desmond made for him, the drawings in black and white, the drawings in grey wash, and the coloured drawings were perfect. Nicky, unskilled in everything but the inventing and building up of engines, did not know how perfect the drawings were, any more than he knew the value of the extraordinary pictures that hung on the walls and stood on the easels in her studio; but he did know that, from the moment when he took Desmond into his adventure, he and his Idea were dependent on her.

He didn't care. He liked Desmond. He couldn't help it if Drayton disapproved of her and if Dorothy didn't like her. She was, he said to himself, a ripping good sort. She might be frightfully clever; Nicky rather thought she was; but she never let you feel it; she never talked that revolting rot that Rosalind and Dorothy's other friends talked. She let you think.

It was Desmond who told him that his sister didn't like her and that Frank Drayton disapproved of her.

"They wouldn't," said Nicky, "if they knew you." And he turned again to the subject of his Moving Fortress.

For Desmond's intelligence was perfect, and her sympathy was perfect, and her way of listening was perfect. She sat on the floor, on the orange and blue cushions, in silence and in patience, embracing her knees with her long, slender, sallow-white arms, while Nicky stamped up and down her studio and talked to her, like a monomaniac, about his Moving Fortress. It didn't bore her to listen, because she didn't have to answer; she had only to look at him and smile, and nod her head at him now and then as a sign of enthusiasm. She liked looking at him; she liked his young naïveté and monomania; she liked his face and all his gestures, and the poise and movement of his young body.

And as she looked at him the beauty that slept in her dulled eyes and in her sallow-white face and in her thin body awoke and became alive. It was not dangerous yet; not ready yet to tell the secret held back in its long, subtle, serious, and slender lines. Desmond's sensuality was woven with so fine a web that you would have said it belonged less to her body than to her spirit and her mind.

In nineteen-eleven, on fine days in the late spring and early summer, when the Morss Company lent him a car, or when they sent him motoring about the country on their business, he took Desmond with him and Desmond's painting box and easel. And they rested on the grass borders of the high roads and on the edges of the woods and moors, and Desmond painted her extraordinary pictures while Nicky lay on his back beside her with his face turned up to the sky and dreamed of flying machines.

For he had done with his Moving Fortress. It only waited for Desmond to finish the last drawing.

When he had that he would show the plans and the model to Frank Drayton before he sent them to the War Office.

He lived for that moment of completion.

And from the autumn of nineteen-ten to the spring of nineteen-eleven Desmond's affair with Headley Richards increased and flowered and ripened to its fulfilment. And in the early summer she found that things had happened as she had meant that they should happen.

She had always meant it. She had always said, and she had always thought that women were no good unless they had the courage of their opinions; the only thing to be ashamed of was the cowardice that prevented them from getting what they wanted.

Desmond had no idea that the violence of the Vortex had sucked her in. Being in the movement of her own free will, she thought that by simply spinning round faster and faster she added her own energy to the whirl. It was not Dorothy's vortex, or the vortex of the fighting Suffrage woman. Desmond didn't care very much about the Suffrage; or about any kind of freedom but her own kind; or about anybody's freedom but her own. Maud Blackadder's idea of freedom struck Desmond as sheer moral and physical insanity. Yet each, Desmond and Dorothy and Maud Blackadder and Mrs. Blathwaite and her daughter and Mrs. Palmerston-Swete, had her own particular swirl in the immense Vortex of the young century. If you had youth and life in you, you were in revolt.

Desmond's theories were Dorothy's theories too; only that while Dorothy, as Rosalind had said, thought out her theories in her brain without feeling them, Desmond felt them with her whole being; and with her whole being, secret, subtle and absolutely relentless, she was bent on carrying them out.

And in the summer, in the new season, Headley Richards decided that he had no further use for Desmond. The new play had run its course at the

Independent Theatre, a course so brief that Richards had been disappointed. He put down the failure mainly to the queerness of the dresses and the scenery she had designed for him. Desmond's new art was too new; people weren't ready yet for that sort of thing. At the same time he discovered that he was really very much attached to his own wife Ginny, and when Ginny nobly offered to give him his divorce he had replied nobly that he didn't want one. And he left Desmond to face the music.

Desmond's misery was acute; but it was not so hopeless as it would have been if she could have credited Ginny Richards with any permanent power of attraction for Headley. She knew he would come back to her. She knew the power of her own body. She held him by the tie that was never broken so long as it endured. He would never marry her; yet he would come back.

But in the interval between these acts there was the music.

And the first sound of the music, the changed intonations of her landlady, frightened Desmond; for though she was older than Nicky she was very young. And there were Desmond's people. You may forget that you have people and behave as if they weren't there; but, if they are there, sooner or later they will let you know it. An immense volume of sound and some terrifying orchestral effects were contributed by Desmond's people. So that the music was really very bad to bear.

Desmond couldn't bear it. And in her fright she thought of Nicky.

She knew that she hadn't a chance so long as he was absorbed in the Moving Fortress. But the model was finished and set up and she was at work on the last drawing. And no more ideas for engines were coming into Nicky's head. The Morss Company and Nicky himself were even beginning to wonder whether there ever would be any more.

Then Nicky thought of Desmond. And he showed that he was thinking of her by sitting still and not talking when he was with her. She did not fill that emptiness and spaciousness of Nicky's head, but he couldn't get her out of it.

When Vera noticed the silence of the two she became uneasy, and judged that the time had come for discreet intervention.

"Nicky," she said, "is it true that Desmond's been doing drawings for you?"

"Yes," said Nicky, "she's done any amount."

"My dear boy, have you any idea of the amount you'll have to pay her?"

"I haven't," said Nicky, "I wish I had. I hate asking her, and yet I suppose I'll have to."

"Of course you'll have to. *She* won't hate it. She's got to earn her living as much as you have."

"Has she? You don't mean to say she's hard up?"

He had never thought of Desmond as earning her own living, still less as being hard up.

"I only wish she were," said Vera, "for your sake."

"Why on earth for my sake?"

"Because *then*, my dear Nicky, you wouldn't have to pay so stiff a price."

"I don't care," said Nicky, "how stiff the price is. I shall pay it."

And Vera replied that Desmond, in her own queer way, really was a rather distinguished painter. "Pay her," she said. "Pay her for goodness sake and have done with it. And if she wants to give you things don't let her."

"As if," said Nicky, "I should dream of letting her."

And he went off to Chelsea to pay Desmond then and there.

Vera thought that she had been rather clever. Nicky would dash in and do the thing badly. He would be very proud about it, and he would revolt from his dependence on Desmond, and he would show her—Vera hoped that he would show her—that he did not want to be under any obligation to her. And Desmond would be hurt and lose her temper. The hard look would get into her face and destroy its beauty, and she would say detestable things in a detestable voice, and a dreadful ugliness would come between them, and the impulse of Nicky's yet unborn passion would be checked, and the memory of that abominable half-hour would divide them for ever.

But Vera herself had grown hard and clever. She had forgotten Nicky's tenderness, and she knew nothing at all about Desmond's fright. And, as it happened, neither Nicky nor Desmond did any of the things she thought they would do.

Nicky was not impetuous. He found Desmond in her studio working on the last drawing of the Moving Fortress, with the finished model before her. That gave him his opening, and he approached shyly and tentatively.

Desmond put on an air of complete absorption in her drawing; but she smiled. A pretty smile that lifted the corners of her mouth and made it quiver, and gave Nicky a queer and unexpected desire to kiss her.

He went on wanting to know what his debt was—not that he could ever really pay it.

"Oh, you foolish Nicky," Desmond said.

He repeated himself over and over again, and each time she had an answer, and the answers had a cumulative effect.

"There isn't any debt. You don't pay anything—"

"I didn't do it for *that*, you silly boy."

"What did I do it for? I did it for fun. You couldn't draw a thing like that for anything else. Look at it—"

—"Well, if you want to be horrid and calculating about it, think of the lunches and the dinners and the theatre tickets and the flowers you've given *me*. Oh, and the gallons and gallons of petrol. How am I ever to pay you back again?"

Thus she mocked him.

"Can't you see how you're spoiling it all?"

And then, passionately: "Oh, Nicky, please don't say it again. It hurts."

She turned on him her big black looking-glass eyes washed bright, each with one tear that knew better than to fall just yet. He must see that she was holding herself well in hand. It would be no use letting herself go until he had forgotten his Moving Fortress. He was looking at the beastly thing now, instead of looking at her.

"Are you thinking of another old engine?"

"No," said Nicky. "I'm not thinking of anything."

"Then you don't want me to do any more drawings?"

"No."

"Well then—I wonder whether you'd very much mind going away?"

"Now?"

"No. Not now. But soon. From here. Altogether."

"Go? Altogether? Me? Why?"

He was utterly astonished. He thought that he had offended Desmond past all forgiveness.

"Because I came here to be alone. To work. And I can't work. And I want to be alone again."

"Am I—spoiling it?"

"Yes. You're spoiling it damnably."

"I'm sorry, Desmond. I didn't mean to. I thought—"

But he hadn't the heart to say what he had thought.

She looked at him and knew that the moment was coming.

It had come.

She turned away from the table where the Moving Fortress stood, threatening her with its mimic guns, and reminding Nicky of the things she most wanted him to forget. She withdrew to her crouching place at the other end of the studio, among the cushions.

He followed her there with slow, thoughtful steps, steps full of brooding purpose and of half-unconscious meaning.

"Nicky, I'm so unhappy. I didn't know it was possible for anybody to be so unhappy in this world."

She began to cry quietly.

"Desmond—what is it? What is it? Tell me. Why can't you tell me?"

She thought, "It will be all right if he kisses me once. If he holds me in his arms once. Then I can tell him."

For then he would know that he loved her. He was not quite sure now.

She knew that he was not quite sure. She trusted to the power of her body to make him sure.

Her youth neither understood his youth, nor allowed for it, nor pitied it.

He had kissed her. He had held her in his arms and kissed her more than once while she cried there, hiding her face in the hollow of his arm. She was weak and small. She was like some small, soft, helpless animal and she was hurt. Her sobbing and panting made her ribs feel fragile like the ribs of some small, soft, helpless animal under the pressure of his arms. And she was frightened.

He couldn't stand the sight of suffering. He had never yet resisted the appeal of small, weak, helpless things in fright and pain. He could feel Desmond's heart going thump, thump, under the blue thing he called her pinafore. Her heart hurt him with its thumping.

And through all his painful pity he knew that her skin was smooth and sweet like a sallow-white rose-leaf. And Desmond knew that he knew it. His mouth slid with an exquisite slipperiness over the long, polished bands of her black hair; and he thought that he loved her. Desmond knew that he thought it.

And still she waited. She said to herself, "It's no good his thinking it. I daren't tell him till he says it. Till he asks me to marry him."

He had said it at last. And he had asked her to marry him. And then she had told him.

And all that he said was, "I don't care." He said it to Desmond, and he said it to himself.

The funny thing was that he did not care. He was as miserable as it was well possible to be, but he didn't really care. He was not even surprised. It was as if the knowledge of it had been hiding in the back of his head behind all the ideas.

And yet he couldn't have known it all the time. Either it must have gone away when his ideas went, or he must have been trying not to see it.

She had slipped from his arms and stood before him, dabbing her mouth and eyes now and then with her pocket-handkerchief, controlling herself, crying quietly.

She knew, what had not dawned on Nicky yet, that he didn't love her. If he had loved her he would have cared intolerably. He didn't care about Headley Richards because he didn't care about Desmond any more. He was only puzzled.

"Why did you do it?"

"I can't think why. I must have been off my head. I didn't know what it was like. I didn't know. I thought it would be wonderful and beautiful. I thought he was wonderful and beautiful."

"Poor little Desmond."

"Oh, Nicky, do you think me a beast? Does it make you hate me?"

"No. Of course it doesn't. The only awful thing is—"

"What? Tell me."

"Well—you see—"

"You mean the baby? I know it's awful. You needn't tell me that, Nicky."

He stared at her.

"I mean it's so awful for *it*."

She thought he had been thinking of himself and her.

"Why should it be?"

"Why? There isn't any why. It just is. I *know* it is."

He was thinking of Veronica.

"You see," he said simply, "that's why this sort of thing is such a rotten game. It's so hard on the kiddy. I suppose you didn't think of that. You couldn't have, or else you wouldn't—"

He paused. There was one thing he had to know. He must get it out of her.

"It hasn't made you feel that you don't want it?"

"Oh—I don't know what I want—*now*. I don't know what it makes me feel!"

"Don't let it, Desmond. Don't let it. It'll be all right. You won't feel like that when you've married me. Can't you see that *that's* the wonderful and beautiful part?"

"*What* is?" she said in her tired drawl.

"*It*—the poor kiddy."

Because he remembered Veronica he was going to marry Desmond.

Veronica's mother was the first to hear about it. Desmond told her.

Veronica's mother was determined to stop it for the sake of everybody concerned.

She wrote to Nicholas and asked him to come and dine with her one evening when Lawrence Stephen was dining somewhere else. (Lawrence Stephen made rather a point of not going to houses where Vera was not received; but sometimes, when the occasion was political, or otherwise important, he had to. That was her punishment, as Bartholomew had meant that it should be.)

Nicky knew what he had been sent for, and to all his aunt's assaults and manoeuvres he presented an inexpugnable front.

"You mustn't do it; you simply mustn't."

He intimated that his marriage was his own affair.

"It isn't. It's the affair of everybody who cares for you."

"Their caring isn't my affair," said Nicky.

And then Vera began to say things about Desmond.

"It's absurd of you," she said, "to treat her as if she was an innocent child. She isn't a child, and she isn't innocent. She knew perfectly well what she was about. There's nothing she doesn't know. She meant it to happen, and she made it happen. She said she would. She meant you to marry her, and she's making you marry her. I daresay she said she would. She's as clever and determined as the devil. Neither you nor Headley Richards ever had a chance against her."

"She hasn't got a dog's chance against all you people yelping at her now she's down. I should have thought—"

"You mean *I've* no business to? That was different. I didn't take any other woman's husband, or any other woman's lover, Nicky."

"If you had," said Nicky, "I wouldn't have interfered."

"I wouldn't interfere if I thought you cared *that* for Desmond. But you don't. You know you don't."

"Of course I care for her."

He said it stoutly, but he coloured all the same, and Vera knew that he was vulnerable.

"Oh, Nicky dear, if you'd only waited—"

"What do you mean?"

His young eyes interrogated her austerely; and she flinched. "I don't know what I mean. Unless I mean that you're just a little young to marry anybody."

"I don't care if I am. I don't *feel* young, I can tell you. Anyhow Desmond's years younger."

"Desmond is twenty-three. You're twenty. It's Veronica who's years younger."

"Veronica?"

"She's sixteen. You don't imagine Desmond is as young as that, do you? Wait till she's twenty-five and you're twenty-two."

"It wouldn't do poor Desmond much good if I did. I could kill Headley Richards."

"What for?"

"For leaving her."

Vera smiled. "That shows how much you care. You wouldn't have felt like killing him if he'd stuck to her. Why should you marry Headley Richards' mistress and take on his child? It's preposterous."

"It isn't. If the other fellow's a brute it's all the more reason why I shouldn't be. I want to be some use in this rotten world where people are so damnably cruel to each other. And there's that unhappy kiddy. You've forgotten the kiddy."

"Do you mean to say it's Desmond's child *you*'re thinking of?"

"I can't understand any woman not thinking of it," said Nicky.

He looked at her, and she knew that he remembered Veronica.

Then she gave him back his own with interest, for his good.

"If you care so much, why don't you choose a better mother for your own children?"

It was as if she said: "If you care so much about Veronica, why don't you marry *her*?"

"It's a bit too late to think of that now," said poor Nicky.

Because he had cared so much about Veronica he was going to marry Desmond.

"I couldn't do anything with him," Vera said afterwards. "Nothing I said made the least impression on him."

That however (as both Vera and Nicky were aware), was not strictly true. But, in spite of Nicky's terrible capacity for remembering, she stuck to it that Desmond's affair would have made no impression on him if it had not been for that other absurd affair of the Professor's wife. And it would have been better, Lawrence Stephen said, for Nicky to have made love to all the married women in Cambridge than for him to marry Phyllis Desmond.

These reflections were forced on them by the ironic coincidence of Nicky's engagement with his rehabilitation at the University.

Drayton's forecast was correct; Nicky's brother Michael had not been removed from Nicky's College eight months before letters of apology and restitution came. But both apology and restitution came too late.

For by that time Nicky had married Desmond.

XIV

After Nicholas, Veronica; and after Veronica, Michael.

Anthony and Frances sat in the beautiful drawing-room of their house, one on each side of the fireplace. They had it all to themselves, except for the cats, Tito and Timmy, who crouched on the hearthrug at their feet. Frances's forehead and her upper lip were marked delicately with shallow, tender lines; Anthony's eyes had crow's-feet at their corners, pointing to grey hairs at his temples. To each other their faces were as they had been fifteen years ago. The flight of time was measured for them by the generations of the cats that had succeeded Jane and Jerry. For still in secret they refused to think of their children as grown up.

Dorothy was upstairs in her study writing articles for the Women's Franchise Union. They owed it to her magnanimity that they had one child remaining with them in the house. John was at Cheltenham; Veronica was in Dresden. Michael was in Germany, too, at that School of Forestry at Aschaffenburg which Anthony had meant for Nicky. They couldn't bear to think where Nicky was.

When Frances thought about her children now her mind went backwards. If only they hadn't grown up; if only they could have stayed little for ever! In another four years even Don-Don would be grown up—Don-Don who was such a long time getting older that at fourteen, only two years ago, he had been capable of sitting in her lap, a great long-legged, flumbering puppy, while mother and son rocked dangerously together in each other's arms, like two children, laughing together, mocking each other.

She was going to be wiser with Don-Don than she had been with Nicky. She would be wiser with Michael when he came back from Germany. She would keep them both out of the Vortex, the horrible Vortex that

Lawrence Stephen and Vera had let Nicky in for, the Vortex that seized on youth and forced it into a corrupt maturity. After Desmond's affair Anthony and Frances felt that to them the social circle inhabited by Vera and Lawrence Stephen would never be anything but a dirty hell.

As for Veronica, the longer she stayed in Germany the better.

Yet Frances knew that they had not sent Veronica to Dresden to prevent her mother from getting hold of her. When she remembered the fear she had had of the apple-tree house, she said to herself that Desmond was a judgment on her for sending little Veronica away.

And yet it was the kindest thing they could have done for her. Veronica was happy in Dresden, living with a German family and studying music and the language. She had no idea that music and the language were mere blinds, and that she had been sent to the German family to keep her out of Nicky's way.

They would have them all back again at Christmas. Frances counted the days. From to-night, the seventh of June, to December the twentieth was not much more than six months.

To-night, the seventh of June, was Nicky's wedding-night. But they did not know that. Nicky had kept the knowledge from them, in his mercy, to save them the agony of deciding whether they would recognize the marriage or not. And as neither Frances nor Anthony had ever faced squarely the prospect of disaster to their children, they had turned their backs on Nicky's marriage and supported each other in the hope that at the last minute something would happen to prevent it.

The ten o'clock post, and two letters from Germany. Not from Michael, not from Veronica. One from Frau Schäfer, the mother of the German family. It was all in German, and neither Anthony nor Frances could make out more than a word here and there. "Das süsse, liebe Mädchen" meant Veronica. But certain phrases: "traurige Nachrichten"… "furchtbare Schwächheit" … "… eine entsetzliche Blutleere …" terrified them, and they sent for Dorothy to translate.

Dorothy was a good German scholar, but somehow she was not very fluent. She scowled over the letter.

"What does it mean?" said Frances. "Hæmorhage?"

"No. No. Anæmia. Severe anæmia. Heart and stomach trouble."

"But 'traurige Nachrichten' is 'bad news.' They're breaking it to us that she's dying."

(It was unbearable to think of Nicky marrying Ronny; but it was more unbearable to think of Ronny dying.)

"They don't say they're sending *us* bad news; they say they think Ronny must have had some. To account for her illness. Because they say she's been so happy with them."

"But what bad news could she have had?"

"Perhaps she knows about Nicky."

"But nobody's told her, unless Vera has."

"She hasn't. I know she hasn't. She didn't want her to know."

"Well, then—"

"Mummy, you don't *have* to tell Ronny things. She always knows them."

"How on earth could she know a thing like that?"

"She might. She sort of sees things—like Ferdie. She may have seen him with Desmond. You can't tell."

"Do they say what the doctor thinks?"

"Yes. He thinks it's worry and Heimweh—homesickness. They want us to send for her and take her back. Not let her have another term."

Though Frances loved Veronica she was afraid of her coming back. For she was more than ever convinced that something would happen and that Nicky would not marry Desmond.

The other letter was even more difficult to translate or to understand when translated.

The authorities at Aschaffenburg requested Herr Harrison to remove his son Michael from the School of Forestry. Michael after his first few weeks had done no good at the school. In view of the expense to Herr

Harrison involved in his fees and maintenance, they could not honestly advise his entering upon another term. It would only be a deplorable throwing away of money on a useless scheme. His son Michael had no thoroughness, no practical ability, and no grasp whatever of theoretic detail. From Herr Harrison's point of view this was the more regrettable inasmuch as the young man had colossal decision and persistence and energy of his own. He was an indefatigable dreamer. Very likely—when his dreams had crystallized—a poet. But the idea Herr Harrison had had that his son Michael would make a man of business, or an expert in Forestry, was altogether fantastic and absurd. And from the desperate involutions of the final sentence Dorothy disentangled the clear fact that Michael's personal charm, combined with his hostility to discipline, his complete indifference to the aims of the authorities, and his utter lack of any sense of responsibility, made him a dangerous influence in any school.

That was the end of Anthony's plans for Michael.

The next morning Nicky wired from some village in Sussex: "Married yesterday.—NICKY."

After that nothing seemed to matter. With Nicky gone from them they were glad to have Michael back again. Frances said they might be thankful for one thing—that there wasn't any German Peggy or any German Desmond in Michael's problem.

And since both Michael and Veronica were to be removed at once, the simplest arrangement was that he should return to Dresden and bring her back with him.

Frances had never been afraid for Michael.

Michael knew that he had made havoc of his father's plans. He couldn't help that. His affair was far too desperate. And any other man but his father would have foreseen that the havoc was inevitable and would have made no plans. He knew he had been turned into the tree-travelling scheme that had been meant for Nicky, because, though Nicky had slipped out of it, his father simply couldn't bear to give up his idea. And no wonder, when the dear old thing had so few of them.

He had been honest with his father about it; every bit as honest as Nicky had been. He had wanted to travel if he could go to China and Japan, just as Nicky had wanted to travel if he could go to places like the West Indies and the Himalaya. And he didn't mind trying to get the trees in when he was there. He was even prepared to accept Germany and the School for Forestry if Germany was the only way to China and Japan. But he had told his father not to mind if nothing came of it at the end of all the travelling. And his father had said he would take the risk. He preferred taking the risk to giving up his idea.

And Michael had been honest with himself. He had told himself that he too must take some risks, and the chances were that a year or two in Germany wouldn't really hurt him. Things never did hurt you as much as you thought they would. He had thought that Cambridge would do all sorts of things to him, and Cambridge had not done anything to him at all. As for Oxford, it had given him nearly all the solitude and liberty he wanted, and more companionship than he was ever likely to want. At twenty-two Michael was no longer afraid of dying before he had finished his best work. In spite of both Universities he had done more or less what he had meant to do before he went to Germany. His work had not yet stood the test of time, but to make up for that he himself, in his uneasy passion for perfection, like Time, destroyed almost as much as he created. Still, after some pitiless eliminations, enough of his verse remained for one fine, thin book.

It would be published if Lawrence Stephen approved of the selection.

So, Michael argued, even if he died to-morrow there was no reason why he should not go to Germany to-day.

He was too young to know that he acquiesced so calmly because his soul was for a moment appeased by accomplishment.

He was too young to know that his soul had a delicate, profound and hidden life of its own, and that in secret it approached the crisis of transition. It was passing over from youth to maturity, like a sleep-walker, unconscious, enchanted, seeing its way without seeing it, safe only from the dangers of the passage if nobody touched it, and if it went alone.

Michael had no idea of what Germany could and would do to his soul.

Otherwise he might have listened to what Paris had to say by way of warning.

For his father had given him a fortnight in Paris on his way to Germany, as the reward of acquiescence. That (from Herr Harrison's point of view) was a disastrous blunder. How could the dear old Pater be expected to know that Paris is, spiritually speaking, no sort of way even to South Germany? He should have gone to Brussels, if he was ever, spiritually speaking, to get there at all.

And neither Anthony nor Frances knew that Lawrence Stephen had plans for Michael.

Michael went to Paris with his unpublished poems in his pocket and a letter of introduction from Stephen to Jules Réveillaud. He left it with revolution in his soul and the published poems of Réveillaud and his followers in his suit-case, straining and distending it so that it burst open of its own accord at the frontier.

Lawrence Stephen had said to him: "Before you write another line read Réveillaud and show him what you've written."

Jules Réveillaud was ten years older than Michael, and he recognized the symptoms of the crisis. He could see what was happening and what had happened and would happen in Michael's soul. He said: "One third of each of your poems is good. And there are a few—the three last—which are all good."

"Those," said Michael, "are only experiments."

"Precisely. They are experiments that have succeeded. That is why they are good. Art is always experiment, or it is nothing. Do not publish these poems yet. Wait and see what happens. Make more experiments. And whatever you do, do not go to Germany. That School of Forestry would be very bad for you. Why not," said Réveillaud, "stay where you are?"

Michael would have liked to stay for ever where he was, in Paris with Jules Réveillaud, in the Rue Servandoni. And because his conscience kept on telling him that he would be a coward and a blackguard if he stayed in Paris, he wrenched himself away.

In the train, going into Germany, he read Réveillaud's "Poèmes" and the "Poèmes" of the young men who followed him. He had read in Paris Réveillaud's "Critique de la Poésie Anglaise Contemporaine." And as he read his poems, he saw that, though he, Michael Harrison, had split with "la poésie anglaise contemporaine," he was not, as he had supposed, alone. His idea of being by himself of finding new forms, doing new things by himself to the disgust and annoyance of other people, in a world where only one person, Lawrence Stephen, understood or cared for what he did, it was pure illusion. These young Frenchmen, with Jules Réveillaud at their head, were doing the same thing, making the same experiment, believing in the experiment, caring for nothing but the experiment, and carrying it farther than he had dreamed of carrying it. They were not so far ahead of him in time; Réveillaud himself had only two years' start; but they were all going the same way, and he saw that he must either go with them or collapse in the soft heap of rottenness, "la poésie anglaise contemporaine."

He had made his own experiments in what he called "live verse" before he left England, after he had said he would go to Germany, even after the final arrangements had been made. His father had given him a month to "turn round in," as he put it. And Michael had turned completely round.

He had not shown his experiments to Stephen. He didn't know what to think of them himself. But he could see, when once Réveillaud had pointed it out to him, that they were the stuff that counted.

In the train going into Germany he thought of certain things that Réveillaud had said: "Nous avons trempé la poésie dans la peinture et la musique. Il faut la délivrer par la sculpture. Chaque ligne, chaque vers, chaque poème taillé en bloc, sans couleur, sans decor, sans rime." ... "La sainte pauvresse du style dépouillé." ... "Il faut de la dureté, toujours de la dureté."

He thought of Réveillaud's criticism, and his sudden startled spurt of admiration: "Mais! Vous l'avez trouvée, la beauté de la ligne droite."

And Réveillaud's question: "Vraiment? Vous n'avez jamais lu un seul vers de mes poèmes? Alors, c'est étonnant." And then: "C'est que la réalité est plus forte que nous."

The revolting irony of it! After stumbling and fumbling for years by himself, like an idiot, trying to get it, the clear hard Reality; trying not to collapse into the soft heap of contemporary rottenness; and, suddenly, to get it without knowing that he had got it, so that, but for Réveillaud, he might easily have died in his ignorance; and then, in the incredible moment of realization, to have to let go, to turn his back on Paris, where he wanted to live, and on Réveillaud whom he wanted to know, and to be packed in a damnable train, like a parcel, and sent off to Germany, a country which he did not even wish to see.

He wondered if he could have done it if he had not loved his father? He wondered if his father would ever understand that it was the hardest thing he had ever yet done or could do?

But the trees would be beautiful. He would rather like seeing the trees.

Trees—

He wondered whether he would ever care about a tree again.

Trees—

He wondered whether he would ever see a tree again, ever smell tree-sap, or hear the wind sounding in the ash-trees like a river and in the firs like a sea.

Trees—

He wondered whether any tree would ever come to life for him again.

He looked on at the tree-felling. He saw slaughtered trees, trees that tottered, trees that staggered in each other's branches. He heard the scream and the shriek of wounded boughs, the creaking and crashing of the trunk, and the long hiss of branches falling, trailing through branches to the ground. He smelt the raw juice of broken leaves and the sharp tree dust in the saw pits.

The trees died horrible deaths, in the forests under the axes of the woodmen, and in the schools under the tongues of the Professors, and in Michael's soul. The German Government was determined that he should know all about trees. Its officials, the Professors and instructors, were sorry if he didn't like it, but they were ordered by their Government and paid by their Government to impart this information; they had contracted with

Herr Harrison to impart it to his son Michael for so long as he could endure it, and they imparted it with all their might.

Michael rather liked the Germans of Aschaffenburg. Instead of despising him because he would never make a timber merchant or a tree expert, they admired and respected him because he was a poet. The family he lived with, Herr Henschel and Frau Henschel, and his fellow-boarders, Carl and Otto Kraus, and young Ludwig Henschel, and Hedwig and Löttchen admired and respected him because he was a poet. When he walked with Ludwig in the great forests Michael chanted his poems, both in English and in German, till Ludwig's soul was full of yearning and a delicious sorrow, so that Ludwig actually shed tears in the forest. He said that if he had not done so he would have burst. Ludwig's emotions had nothing whatever to do with the forest or with Michael's poems, but he thought they had.

Michael knew that his only chance of getting out of Germany was to show an unsurpassable incompetence. He showed it. He flourished his incompetence in the faces of all the officials, until some superofficial wrote a letter to his father that gave him his liberty.

The Henschels were sorry when he left. The students, Otto and Carl and Ludwig, implored him not to forget them. Hedwig and Löttchen cried.

Michael was not pleased when he found that he was to go home by Dresden to bring Veronica back. He wanted to be alone on the journey. He wanted to stop in Paris and see Jules Réveillaud. He was afraid that Ronny had grown into a tiresome flapper and that he would have to talk to her.

And he found that Ronny had skipped the tiresome stage and had grown up. Only her school clothes and her girlish door-knocker plait tied up with broad black ribbon reminded him that she was not yet seventeen.

Ronny was tired. She did not want to talk. When he had tucked her up with railway rugs in her corner of the carriage she sat still with her hands in her muff.

"I shall not disturb your thoughts, Michael," she said.

She knew what he had been thinking. Her clear eyes gazed at him out of her dead white face with an awful look of spiritual maturity.

"What can have happened to her?" he wondered.

But she did not disturb his thoughts.

Up till then Michael's thoughts had not done him any good. They had been bitter thoughts of the months he had been compelled to waste in Bavaria when every minute had an incomparable value; worrying, irritating thoughts of the scenes he would have to have with his father, who must be made to understand, once for all, that in future he meant to have every minute of his own life for his own work. He wondered how on earth he was to make his people see that his work justified his giving every minute to it. He had asked Réveillaud to give him a letter that he could show to his father. He was angry with his father beforehand, he was so certain that he wouldn't see.

He had other thoughts now. Thoughts of an almond tree flowering in a white town; of pink blossoms, fragile, without leaves, casting a thin shadow on white stones; the smell of almond-flowers and the sting of white dust in an east wind; a drift of white dust against the wall.

Thoughts of pine trees falling in the forest, glad to fall. He thought: The pine forest makes itself a sea for the land wind, and the young pine tree is mad for the open sea. She gives her slender trunk with passion to the axe; for she thinks that she will be stripped naked, and that she will be planted in the ship's hold, and that she will carry the great main-sail. She thinks that she will rock and strain in the grip of the sea-wind, and that she will be whitened with the salt and the foam of the sea.

"She does not know that she will be sawn into planks and made into a coffin for the wife of the sexton and grave-digger of Aschaffenburg."

Thoughts of Veronica in her incredible maturity, and of her eyes, shining in her dead white face, far back through deep crystal, and of the sense he got of her soul poised, steady and still, with wings vibrating.

He wondered where it would come down.

He thought: "Of course, Veronica's soul will come down like a wild pigeon into the ash-tree in our garden, and she will think that our ash-tree is a tree of Heaven."

Presently he roused himself to talk to her.

"How is your singing getting on, Ronny?"

"My singing voice has gone."

"It'll come back again."

"Not unless—"

But he couldn't make her tell him what would bring it back.

When Michael came to his father and mother to have it out with them his face had a hard, stubborn look. He was ready to fight them. He was so certain that he would have to fight. He had shown them Jules Réveillaud's letter.

He said, "Look here, we've got to get it straight. It isn't any use going on like this. I'm afraid I wasn't very honest about Germany."

"Weren't you?" said Anthony. "Let me see, I think you said you'd take it on your way to China and Japan."

"Did I? I tried to be straight about it. I thought I was giving it a fair chance. But that was before I'd seen Réveillaud."

"Well," said Anthony, "now that you have seen him, what is it exactly that you want to do?"

Michael told him.

"You can make it easy for me. Or you can make it hard. But you can't stop me."

"What makes you think I want to stop you?"

"Well—you want me to go into the business, though I told you years ago there was only one thing I should ever be any good at. And I see your point. I can't earn my living at it. That's where I'm had. Still, I think Lawrence Stephen will give me work, and I can rub along somehow."

"Without my help, you mean?"

"Well, yes. Why *should* you help me? You've wasted tons of money on me as it is. Nicky's earning his own living, and he's got a wife, too. Why not me?"

"Because you can't do it, Michael."

"I can. I don't mind roughing it. I could live on a hundred a year—or less, if I don't marry."

"Well, I don't mean you to try. You needn't bother about what you can live on and what you can't live on. It was all settled last night. Your mother and I talked it over. We don't want you to go into the business. We don't want you to take work from Mr. Stephen. We want you to be absolutely free to do your own work, under the best possible conditions, whether it pays or not. Nothing in the world matters to us but your happiness. You're to have a hundred and fifty a year when you're living at home and two hundred and fifty when you're living abroad. I suppose you'll want to go abroad sometimes. I can't give you a bigger allowance, because I have to help Nicky—"

Michael covered his face with his hands.

"Oh—don't, Daddy. You do make me feel a rotten beast."

"We should feel rottener beasts," said Frances, "if we stood in your way."

"Then," said Michael (he was still incredulous), "you do care?"

"Of course we care," said Anthony.

"I don't mean for me—for *it*?"

"My dear Mick," said Frances, "we care for It almost as much as we care for you. We're sorry about Germany though. Germany was one of your father's bad jokes."

"Germany—a joke?"

"Did you take it seriously? Oh, you silly Michael!"

"But," said Michael, "how about Daddy's idea? He loved it."

"I loved it," said Anthony, "but I've given it up."

They knew that this was defeat, for Michael was top-dog. And it was also victory.

They had lost Nicholas, or thought they had lost Nicholas, by opposing him. But Michael and Michael's affection they would have always.

Besides, Anthony hadn't given up his idea. He had only transferred it—to his youngest son, John.

XV

It was five weeks since Nicholas's wedding-day and Desmond had quarrelled with him three times.

First, because he had taken a flat in Aubrey Walk, with a studio inside it, instead of a house in Campden Hill Square with a studio outside it in the garden.

Then, because he had refused to go into his father's business.

Last of all, because of Captain Drayton and the Moving Fortress.

Nicky had said that his father, who was paying his rent, couldn't afford the house with the studio in the garden; and Desmond said Nicky's father could afford it perfectly well if he liked. He said he had refused to go into his father's business for reasons which didn't concern her. Desmond pointed out that the consequences of his refusal were likely to concern her very much indeed. As for Captain Drayton and the Moving Fortress, nobody but a supreme idiot would have done what Nicky did.

But Nicky absolutely refused to discuss what he had done. Nobody but a cad and a rotter would have done anything else.

In the matter of the Moving Fortress what had happened was this.

The last of the drawings was not finished until Desmond had settled down in the flat in Aubrey Walk. You couldn't hurry Desmond. Nicky hadn't even waited to sign his name in the margins before he had packed the plans in his dispatch-box and taken them to the works, and thence, hidden under a pile of Morss estimates, to Eltham. He couldn't rest till he had shown them to Frank Drayton. He could hardly wait till they had dined, and till Drayton, who thought he was on the track of a new and horrible explosive, had told him as much as he could about it.

Nicky gave his whole mind to Drayton's new explosive in the hope that, when his turn came, Drayton would do as much for him.

"You know," he said at last, "the old idea of the *forteresse mobile*?

"Yes."

He couldn't tell whether Drayton was going to be interested or not. He rather thought he wasn't.

"It hasn't come to anything, *has* it?"

Drayton smiled and his eyes glittered. He knew what that excited gleam in Drayton's eyes meant.

"No," he said. "Not yet."

And Nicky had an awful premonition of his doom.

"Well," he said, "I believe there's something in it."

"So do I, Nicky."

Drayton went on. "I believe there's so much in it that—Look here, I don't know what put it into your head, and I'm not asking, but that idea's a dead secret. For God's sake don't talk about it. You mustn't breathe it, or it'll get into the air. And if it does my five years' work goes for nothing. Besides we don't want Germany to collar it."

And then: "Don't look so scared, old chap. I was going to tell you about it when I'd got the plans drawn."

He told him about it then and there.

"Low on the ground like a racing-car—"

"Yes," said Nicky.

"Revolving turret for the guns—no higher than *that*—"

"Yes," said Nicky.

"Sort of armoured train. Only it mustn't run on rails. It's got to go everywhere, through anything, over anything, if it goes at all. It must turn in its own length. It must wade and burrow and climb, Nicky. It must have caterpillar wheels—"

"By Jove, of course it must," said Nicky, as if the idea had struck him for the first time.

"What have you got there?" said Drayton finally as Nicky rose and picked up his dispatch-box. "Anything interesting?

"No," said Nicky. "Mostly estimates."

For a long time afterwards he loathed the fields between Eltham and Kidbrooke, and the Mid-Kent line, and Charing Cross Station. He felt as a man feels when the woman he loves goes from him to another man. His idea had gone from him to Drayton.

And that, he said to himself, was just like his luck, just like the jolly sells that happened to him when he was a kid.

To be sure, there was such a thing as sharing. He had only to produce his plans and his finished model, and he and Drayton would go partners in the Moving Fortress. There was no reason why he shouldn't do it. Drayton had not even drawn his plans yet; he hadn't thought out the mechanical details.

He thought, "I could go back now and tell him."

But he did not go back. He knew that he would never tell him. If Drayton asked him to help him with the details he would work them out all over again with him; but he would never show his own finished plans or his own model.

He didn't know whether it had been hard or easy for him to give up the Moving Fortress. He did it instinctively. There was—unless he had chosen to be a blackguard—nothing else for him to do.

Besides, the Moving Fortress wasn't his idea. Drayton had had it first. Anybody might have had it. He hadn't spoken of it first; but that was nothing. The point was that he had had it first, and Nicky wasn't going to take it from him.

It meant more to Drayton, who was in the Service, than it could possibly mean to him. He hadn't even got a profession.

As he walked back through the fields to the station, he said to himself that he didn't really care. It was only one more jolly sell. He didn't like giving up his Moving Fortress; but it wouldn't end him. There was something in him that would go on.

He would make another engine.

He didn't care. There was something in him that would go on.

"I can't see," Desmond had said, "why Captain Drayton should be allowed to walk off with your idea."

"He's worked five years on it."

"He hasn't worked it *out* yet, and you have. Can't you see"—her face was dark and hard with anger—"there's money in it?"

"If there is, all the more reason why I shouldn't bag it."

"And where do I come in?"

"Not just here, I'm afraid. It isn't your business."

"Not my business? When I did the drawings? You couldn't possibly have done them yourself."

At that point Nicky refused to discuss the matter farther.

And still Desmond brooded on her grievance. And still at intervals Desmond brought it up again.

"There's stacks of money in your father's business—"

"There's stacks of money in that Moving Fortress—"

"You are a fool, Nicky, to throw it all away."

He never answered her. He said to himself that Desmond was hysterical and had a morbid fancy.

But it didn't end there.

He had taken the drawings and the box that had the model of the Moving Fortress in it and buried them in the locker under the big north window in Desmond's studio.

And there, three weeks later, Desmond found them. And she packed the model of the Moving Fortress and marked it "Urgent with Care," and sent it to the War Office with a letter. She packed the drawings in a portfolio—having signed her own and Nicky's name on the margins—and sent them to Captain Drayton with a letter. She said she had no doubt she was doing an immoral thing; but she did it in fairness to Captain Drayton, for she was sure he would not like Nicky to make so great a sacrifice. Nicky, she said, was wrapped up in his Moving Fortress. It was his sweetheart, his baby. "He will never forgive me," she said, "as long as he lives. But I simply *had* to let you know. It means so much to him."

For she thought, "Because Nicky's a fool, I needn't be one."

Drayton came over the same evening after he had got the letter. He shouted with laughter.

"Nicky," he said, "you filthy rotter, why on earth didn't you tell me? … It *was* Nickyish of you. … What if I did think of it first? I should have had to come to you for the details. It would have been jolly to have worked it out together. … Not a bit of it! Your wife's absolutely right. Good thing, after all, you married her.

"By the way, she says there's a model. I want to see that model. Have you got it here?"

Nicky went up into the studio to look for it. He couldn't find it in the locker where he'd left it. "Wherever is the damned thing?" he said.

"The damned thing," said Desmond, "is where you should have sent it first of all—at the War Office. You're clever, Nicky, but you aren't quite clever enough."

"I'm afraid," he said, "*you've* been a bit too clever, this time."

Drayton agreed with him. It was, he said, about the worst thing that could possibly have happened.

"She shouldn't have done that, Nicky. What on earth could have made her do it?"

"Don't ask me," said Nicky, "what makes her do things."

"It looks," Drayton meditated, "as if she didn't trust me. I'm afraid she's dished us. God knows whether we can ever get it back!"

Desmond had a fit of hysterics when she realized how clever she had been.

Desmond's baby was born late in November of that year, and it died when it was two weeks old. It was as if she had not wanted it enough to give it life for long outside her body.

For though Desmond had been determined to have a child, and had declared that she had a perfect right to have one if she chose, she did not care for it when it came. And when it died Nicky was sorrier than Desmond.

He had not wanted to be a father to Headley Richards' child. And yet it was the baby and nothing but the baby that had let him in for marrying Desmond. So that, when it died, he felt that somehow things had tricked and sold him. As they had turned out he need not have married Desmond after all.

She herself had pointed out the extreme futility of his behaviour, lest he should miss the peculiar irony of it. For when her fright and the cause of her fright were gone Desmond resented Nicky's having married her. She didn't really want anybody to marry her, and nobody but Nicky would have dreamed of doing it.

She lay weak and pathetic in her bed for about a fortnight; and for a little while after she was content to lie stretched out among her cushions on the studio floor, while Nicky waited on her. But, when she got well and came downstairs for good, Nicky saw that Desmond's weakness and pathos had come with the baby and had gone with it. The real Desmond was not weak, she was not pathetic. She was strong and hard and clever with a brutal cleverness. She didn't care how much he saw. He could see to the bottom of her nature, if he liked, and feel how hard it was. She had no more interest in deceiving him.

She had no more interest in him at all.

She was interested in her painting again. She worked in long fits, after long intervals of idleness. She worked with a hard, passionless efficiency. Nicky thought her paintings were hideous and repulsive; but he did not say so. He was not aware of the extent to which Desmond imitated her master, Alfred Orde-Jones. He knew nothing about painting and he had got used to the things. He had got used to Desmond, slouching about the flat, in her sloping, slovenly grace, dressed in her queer square jacket and straight short skirt, showing her long delicate ankles, and her slender feet in their grey stockings and black slippers.

He was used to Desmond when she was lazy; when she sat hunched up on her cushions and smoked one cigarette after another without a word, and watched him sullenly. Her long, slippered feet, thrust out, pointed at him, watching. Her long face watched him between the sleek bands of hair and the big black bosses plaited over her ears.

The beauty of Desmond's face had gone to sleep again, stilled into hardness by the passing of her passion. A sort of ugliness was awake there, and it watched him.

In putting weakness and pathos away from her Desmond had parted with two-thirds of her power. Yet the third part still served to hold him, used with knowledge and a cold and competent economy. He resented it, resisted it over and over again; and over and over again it conquered resentment and resistance. It had something to do with her subtle, sloping lines, with her blackness and her sallow whiteness, with the delicate scent and the smoothness of her skin under the sliding hand. He couldn't touch her without still feeling a sort of pity, a sort of affection.

But she could take and give caresses while she removed her soul from him in stubborn rancour.

He couldn't understand that. It amazed him every time. He thought it horrible. For Nicky's memory was faithful. It still kept the impression of the Desmond he had married, the tender, frightened, helpless Desmond he had thought he loved. The Desmond he remembered reminded him of Veronica.

And Desmond said to herself, "He's impossible. You can't make any impression on him. I might as well be married to a Moving Fortress."

Months passed. The War Office had not yet given up Nicky's model of the Moving Fortress. In the first month it was not aware of any letter or of any parcel or of any Mr. Nicholas Harrison. In the second month inquiries would be made and the results communicated to Captain Drayton. In the third month the War Office knew nothing of the matter referred to by Captain Drayton.

Drayton hadn't a hope. "We can't get it back, Nicky," he said.

"I can," said Nicky, "I can get it back out of my head."

All through the winter of nineteen-eleven and the spring of nineteen-twelve they worked at it together. They owned that they were thus getting better results than either of them could have got alone. There were impossibilities about Nicky's model that a gunner would have seen at once, and there were faults in Drayton's plans that an engineer would not have made. Nicky couldn't draw the plans and Drayton couldn't build the models. They said it was fifty times better fun to work at it together.

Nicky was happy.

Desmond watched them sombrely. She and Alfred Orde-Jones, the painter, laughed at them behind their backs. She said, "How funny they are! Frank wouldn't hurt a fly and Nicky wouldn't say 'Bo!' to a goose if he thought it would frighten the goose, and yet they're only happy when they're inventing some horrible machine that'll kill thousands of people who never did them any harm." He said, "That's because they haven't any imagination."

Nicky got up early and went to bed late to work at the Moving Fortress. The time between had to be given to the Works. The Company had paid him fairly well for all his patents in the hope of getting more of his ideas, and when they found that no ideas were forthcoming they took it out of him in labour. He was too busy and too happy to notice what Desmond was doing.

One day Vera said to him, "Nicky, do you know that Desmond is going about a good deal with Alfred Orde-Jones?"

"Is she? Is there any reason why she shouldn't?"

"Not unless you call Orde-Jones a reason."

"You mean I've got to stop it? How can I?"

"You can't. Nothing can stop Desmond."

"What do you think I ought to do about it?"

"Nothing. She goes about with scores of people. It doesn't follow that there's anything in it."

"Oh, Lord, I should hope not! That beastly bounder. What *could* there be in it?"

"He's a clever painter, Nicky. So's Desmond. There's that in it."

"I've hardly a right to object to that, have I? It's not as if I were a clever painter myself."

But as he walked home between the white-walled gardens of St. John's Wood, and through Regent's Park and Baker Street, and down the north side of Hyde Park and Kensington Gardens, he worried the thing to shreds.

There couldn't be anything in it.

He could see Alfred Orde-Jones—the raking swagger of the tall lean body in the loose trousers, the slouch hat and the flowing tie. He could see his flowing black hair and his haggard, eccentric face with its seven fantastic accents, the black eyebrows, the black moustache, the high, close-clipped side whiskers, the two forks of the black beard.

There couldn't be anything in it.

Orde-Jones's mouth was full of rotten teeth.

And yet he never came home rather later than usual without saying to himself, "Supposing I was to find him there with her?"

He left off coming home late so that he shouldn't have to ask himself that question.

He wondered what—if it really did happen—he would do. He wondered what other men did. It never occurred to him that at twenty-two he was young to be considering this problem.

He rehearsed scenes that were only less fantastic than Orde-Jones's face and figure, or that owed their element of fantasy to Orde-Jones's face and figure. He saw himself assaulting Orde-Jones with violence, dragging him out of Desmond's studio, and throwing him downstairs. He wondered what shapes that body and those legs and arms would take when they got to the bottom. Perhaps they wouldn't get to the bottom all at once. He would hang on to the banisters. He saw himself simply opening the door of the studio and ordering Orde-Jones to walk out of it. Really, there would be nothing else for him to do but to walk out, and he would look an awful ass doing it. He saw himself standing in the room and looking at them, and saying, "I've no intention of interrupting you." Perhaps Desmond would answer, "You're not interrupting us. We've finished all we had to say." And *he* would walk out and leave them there. Not caring.

He wondered if *he* would look an awful ass doing it.

In the end, when it came, he hadn't to do any of these things. It happened very quietly and simply, early on a Sunday evening after he had got back from Eltham. He had dined with Drayton and his people on Saturday, and stayed, for once, overnight, risking it.

Desmond was sitting on a cushion, on the floor, with her thin legs in their grey stockings slanting out in front of her. She propped her chin on her hands. Her thin, long face, between the great black ear-bosses, looked at him thoughtfully, without rancour.

"Nicky," she said, "Alfred Orde-Jones slept with me last night."

And he said, simply and quietly, "Very well, Desmond; then I shall leave you. You can keep the flat, and I or my father will make you an allowance. I shan't divorce you, but I won't live with you."

"Why won't you divorce me?" she said.

"Because I don't want to drag you through the dirt."

She laughed quietly. "Dear Nicky," she said, "how sweet and like you! But don't let's have any more chivalrous idiocy. I don't want it. I never did." (She had forgotten that she had wanted it very badly once. But Nicky did not remind her of that time. No matter. She didn't want it now). "Let's look at the thing sensibly, without any rotten sentiment. We've had some good times together, and we've had some bad times. I'll admit that when you married me you saved me from a very bad time. That's no reason why we should go on giving each other worse times indefinitely. You seem to think I don't want you to divorce me. What else do you imagine Alfred came for last night? Why we've been trying for it for the last three months.

"Of course, if you'll let *me* divorce *you* for desertion, it would be very nice of you. That," said Desmond, "is what decent people do."

He went out and telephoned to his father. Then he left her and went back to his father's house.

Desmond asked the servant to remember particularly that it was the fifteenth of June and that the master was going away and would not come back again.

As Nicky walked up the hill and across the Heath, he wondered why it had happened, and why, now that it had happened, he cared so little. He could have understood it if he hadn't cared at all for Desmond. But he had cared in a sort of way. If she had cared at all for him he thought they might have made something of it, something enduring, perhaps, if they had had children of their own.

He still couldn't think why it had happened. But he knew that, even if he had loved Desmond with passion, it wouldn't have been the end of him. The part of him that didn't care, that hadn't cared much when he lost his Moving Fortress, was the part that Desmond never would have cared for.

He didn't know whether it was outside him and beyond him, bigger and stronger than he was, or whether it was deep inside, the most real part of him. Whatever happened or didn't happen it would go on.

How could he have ended *here*, with poor little Desmond? There was something ahead of him, something that he felt to be tremendous and holy. He had always known it waited for him. He was going out to meet it; and because of it he didn't care.

And after a year of Desmond he was glad to go back to his father's house; even though he knew that the thing that waited for him was not there.

Frances and Anthony were happy again. After all, Heaven had manipulated their happiness with exquisite art and wisdom, letting Michael and Nicholas go from them for a little while that they might have them again more completely, and teaching them the art and wisdom that would keep them.

Some day the children would marry; even Nicky might marry again. They would prepare now, by small daily self-denials, for the big renunciation that must come.

Yet in secret they thought that Michael would never marry; that Nicky, made prudent by disaster, wasn't really likely to marry again. John would marry; and they would be happy in John's happiness and in John's children.

And Nicky had not been home before he offered to his parents the spectacle of an outrageous gaiety. You would have said that life to Nicholas was an amusing game where you might win or lose, but either way it didn't matter. It was a rag, a sell. Even the proceedings, the involved and ridiculous proceedings of his divorce, amused him.

It was undeniably funny that he should be supposed to have deserted Desmond.

Frances wondered, again, whether Nicky really had any feelings, and whether things really made any impression on him.

XVI

It was a quarter past five on a fine morning, early in July. On the stroke of the quarter Captain Frank Drayton's motor-car, after exceeding the speed limit along the forlorn highway of the Caledonian Road, drew up outside the main entrance of Holloway Gaol. Captain Frank Drayton was alone in his motor-car.

He had the street all to himself till twenty past five, when he was joined by another motorist, also conspicuously alone in his car. Drayton tried hard to look as if the other man were not there.

The other man tried even harder to look as if he were not there himself. He was the first to be aware of the absurdity of their competitive pretences. He looked at his watch and spoke.

"I hope they'll be punctual with those doors. I was up at four o'clock."

"I," said Drayton, "was up at three."

"I'm waiting for my wife," said the other man.

"I am *not*," said Drayton, and felt that he had scored.

The other man's smile allowed him the point he made.

"Yes, but my wife happens to be Lady Victoria Threlfall."

The other man laughed as if he had made by far the better joke.

Drayton recognized Mr. Augustin Threlfall, that Cabinet Minister made notorious by his encounters with the Women's Franchise Union. Last year Miss Maud Blackadder had stalked him in the Green Park and lamed him by a blow from her hunting-crop. This year his wife, Lady Victoria Threlfall, had headed the June raid on the House of Commons.

And here he was at twenty minutes past five in the morning waiting to take her out of prison.

And here was Drayton, waiting for Dorothea, who was not his wife yet.

"Anyhow," said the Cabinet Minister, "we've done them out of their Procession."

"What Procession?"

All that Drayton knew about it was that, late last night, a friend he had in the Home Office had telephoned to him that the hour of Miss Dorothea Harrison's release would be five-thirty, not six-thirty as the papers had it.

"The Procession," said the Cabinet Minister, "that was to have met 'em at six-thirty. A Car of Victory for Mrs. Blathwaite, and a bodyguard of thirteen young women on thirteen white horses. The girl who smashed my knee-cap is to be Joan of Arc and ride at the head of 'em. In armour. Fact. There's to be a banquet for 'em at the Imperial at nine. We can't stop *that*. And they'll process down the Embankment and down Pall Mall and Piccadilly at eleven; but they won't process here. We've let 'em out an hour too soon."

A policeman came from the prison-yard. He blew a whistle. Four taxi-cabs crept round the corner furtively, driven by visibly hilarious chauffeurs.

"The triumphant procession from Holloway," said the Cabinet Minister, "is you and me, sir, and those taxi-cabs."

On the other side of the gates a woman laughed. The released prisoners were coming down the prison-yard.

The Cabinet Minister cranked up his engine with an unctuous glee. He was boyishly happy because he and the Home Secretary had done them out of the Car of Victory and the thirteen white horses.

The prison-gates opened. The Cabinet Minister and Drayton raised their caps.

The leaders, Mrs. Blathwaite and Angela Blathwaite and Mrs. Palmerston-Swete came first. Then Lady Victoria Threlfall. Then Dorothea. Then sixteen other women.

Drayton did not look at them. He did not see what happened when the Cabinet Minister met his wife. He did not see the sixteen other women. He saw nothing but Dorothea walking by herself.

She had no hat on. Her clothes were as the great raid had left them, a month ago. Her serge coat was torn at the breast-pocket, the three-cornered flap hung, showing the white lining. Another three-cornered flap hung from her right knee. She carried her small, hawk-like head alert and high. Her face had the incomparable bloom of youth. Her eyes shone. They and her face showed no memory of the prison cell, the plank-bed, and the prison walls; they showed no sense of Drayton's decency in coming to meet her, no sense of anything at all but of the queerness, the greatness and the glory of the world—of him, perhaps, as a part of it. She stepped into the car as if they had met by appointment for a run into the country.

"I shan't hurt your car. I'm quite clean, though you mightn't think it. The cells were all right this time."

He disapproved of her, yet he adored her.

"Dorothy," he said, "do you want to go to that banquet?"

"No, but I've got to. I must go through with it. I swore I'd do the thing completely or not at all."

"It isn't till nine. We've three whole hours before we need start."

"What are you going to do with me?"

"I'm going to take you home first. Then I suppose I shall have to drive you down to that beastly banquet."

"That won't take three and a half hours. It's a heavenly morning. Can't we do something with it?"

"What would you like to do?"

"I'd like to stop at the nearest coffee-stall. I'm hungry. Then—Are you frightfully sleepy?"

"Me? Oh, Lord, no."

"Then let's go off somewhere into the country."

They went.

They pulled up in a green lane near Totteridge to finish the buns they had brought with them from the coffee-stall.

"Did you ever smell anything like this lane? Did you ever eat anything like these buns? Did you ever drink anything like that divine coffee? If epicures had any imagination they'd go out and obstruct policemen and get put in prison for the sake of the sensations they'd have afterwards."

"That reminds me," he said, "that I want to talk to you. No—but seriously."

"I don't mind how seriously you talk if I may go on eating."

"That's what I brought the buns for. So that I mayn't be interrupted. First of all I want to tell you that you haven't taken me in. Other people may be impressed with this Holloway business, but not me. I'm not moved, or touched, or even interested."

"Still," she murmured, "you did get up at three o'clock in the morning."

"If you think I got up at three o'clock in the morning to show my sympathy, you're mistaken."

"Sympathy? I don't need your sympathy. It was worth it, Frank. There isn't anything on earth like coming out of prison. Unless it is going in."

"That won't work, Dorothy, when I know why you went in. It wasn't to prove your principles. Your principles were against that sort of thing. It wasn't to get votes for women. You know as well as I do that you'll never get them that way. It wasn't to annoy Mr. Asquith. You knew Mr. Asquith wouldn't care a hang. It was to annoy me."

"I wonder," she said dreamily, "if I shall *ever* be able to stop eating."

"You can't take me in. I know too much about it. You said you were going to keep out of rows. You weren't going on that deputation because it meant a row. You went because I asked you not to go."

"I did; and I should go again to-morrow for the same reason."

"But it isn't a reason. It's not as if I'd asked you to go against your conscience. Your conscience hadn't anything to do with it."

"Oh, hadn't it! I went because you'd no right to ask me not to."

"If I'd had the right you'd have gone just the same."

"What do you mean by the right?"

"You know perfectly well what I mean."

"Of course I do. You mean, and you meant that if I'd married you you'd have had the right, not just to ask me not to, but to prevent me. That was what I was out against. I'd be out against it to-morrow and the next day, and for as long as you keep up that attitude."

"And yet—you said you loved me."

"So I did. So I do. But I'm out against that too."

"Good Lord, against what?"

"Against your exploiting my love for your purposes."

"My poor dear child, what do you suppose I wanted?"

She had reached the uttermost limit of absurdity, and in that moment she became to him helpless and pathetic.

"I knew there was going to be the most infernal row and I wanted to keep you out of it. Look here, you'd have thought me a rotter if I hadn't, wouldn't you?

"Of course you would. And there's another thing. You weren't straight about it. You never told me you were going."

"I never told you I wasn't."

"I don't care, Dorothy; you weren't straight. You ought to have told me."

"How could I tell you when I knew you'd only go trying to stop me and getting yourself arrested."

"Not me. They wouldn't have touched me."

"How was I to know that? If they had I should have dished you. And I'd have stayed away rather than do that. I didn't tell Michael or Nicky or Father for the same reason."

"You'd have stayed at home rather than have dished me? Do you really mean that?"

"Of course I mean it. And I meant it. It's you," she said, "who don't care."

"How do you make that out?"

He really wanted to know. He really wanted, if it were possible, to understand her.

"I make it out this way. Here have I been through *the* adventure and *the* experience of my life. I was in the thick of the big raid; I was four weeks shut up in a prison cell; and you don't care; you're not interested. You never said to yourself, 'Dorothy was in the big raid, I wonder what happened to her?' or 'Dorothy's in prison, I wonder how she's feeling?' You didn't care; you weren't interested.

"If it had happened to you, I couldn't have thought of anything else, I couldn't have got it out of my head. I should have been wondering all the time what you were feeling; I couldn't have rested till I knew. It would have been as if I was in prison myself. And now, when I've come out, all you think of is how you can rag and score off me."

She was sitting beside him on the green bank of the lane. Her hands were clasped round her knees. One knickerbockered knee protruded through the three-cornered rent in her skirt; she stared across the road, a long, straight stare that took no heed of what she saw, the grey road, and the green bank on the other side, topped by its hedge of trees.

Her voice sounded quiet in the quiet lane; it had no accent of self-pity or reproach. It was as if she were making statements that had no emotional significance whatever.

She did not mean to hurt him, yet every word cut where he was sorest.

"I wanted to tell you about it. I counted the days, the minutes till I could tell you; but you wouldn't listen. You don't want to hear."

"I won't listen if it's about women's suffrage. And I don't want to hear if it's anything awful about you."

"It is about me, but it isn't awful.

"That's what I want to tell you.

"But, first of all—about the raid. I didn't mean to be in it at all, as it happens. I meant to go with the deputation because you told me not to. You're right about that. But I meant to turn back as soon as the police stopped us, because I hate rows with the police, and because I don't believe in them, and because I told Angela Blathwaite I wasn't going in with her crowd any way. You see, she called me a coward before a lot of people and said I funked it. So I did. But I should have been a bigger coward if I'd gone against my own will, just because of what she said. That's how she collars heaps of women. They adore her and they're afraid of her. Sometimes they lie and tell her they're going in when their moment comes, knowing perfectly well that they're not going in at all. I don't adore her, and I'm not afraid of her, and I didn't lie.

"So I went at the tail of the deputation where I could slip out when the row began. I swear I didn't mean to be in it. I funked it far too much. I didn't mind the police and I didn't mind the crowd. But I funked being with the women. When I saw their faces. You would have funked it.

"And anyhow I don't like doing things in a beastly body. Ugh!

"And then they began moving.

"The police tried to stop them. And the crowd tried. The crowd began jeering at them. And still they moved. And the mounted police horses got excited, and danced about and reared a bit, and the crowd was in a funk then and barged into the women. That was rather awful.

"I could have got away then if I'd chosen. There was a man close to me all the time who kept making spaces for me and telling me to slip through. I was just going to when a woman fell. Somewhere in the front of the deputation where the police were getting nasty.

"Then I had to stay. I had to go on with them. I swear I wasn't excited or carried away in the least. Two women near me were yelling at the police. I hated them. But I felt I'd be an utter brute if I left them and got off safe. You see, it was an ugly crowd, and things were beginning to be jolly dangerous, and I'd funked it badly. Only the first minute. It went—the funk I mean—when I saw the woman go down. She fell sort of slanting through the crowd, and it was horrible. I couldn't have left them then any more than I could have left children in a burning house.

"I thought of you."

"You thought of me?"

"Yes. I thought of you—how you'd have hated it. But I didn't care. I was sort of boosted up above caring. The funk had all gone and I was absolutely happy. Not insanely happy like some of the other women, but quietly, comfily happy.

"After all, I didn't do anything you *need* have minded."

"What *did* you do?" he said.

"I just went on and stood still and refused to go back. I stuck my hands in my pockets so that I shouldn't let out at a policeman or anything (I knew you wouldn't like *that*). I may have pushed a bit now and then with my shoulders and my elbows; I can't remember. But I didn't make one sound. I was perfectly lady-like and perfectly dignified."

"I suppose you *know* you haven't got a hat on?"

"It didn't *come* off. I *took* it off and threw it to the crowd when the row began. It doesn't matter about your hair coming down if you haven't got a hat on, but if your hair's down and your hat's bashed in and all crooked you look a perfect idiot.

"It wasn't a bad fight, you know, twenty-one women to I don't know how many policemen, and the front ones got right into the doorway of St. Stephen's. That was where they copped me.

"But that, isn't the end of it.

"The fight was only the first part of the adventure. The wonderful thing was what happened afterwards. In prison.

"I didn't think I'd really *like* prison. That was another thing I funked. I'd heard such awful things about it, about the dirt, you know. And there wasn't any dirt in my cell, anyhow. And after the crowds of women, after the meetings and the speeches, the endless talking and the boredom, that cell was like heaven.

"Thank God, it's always solitary confinement. The Government doesn't know that if they want to make prison a deterrent they'll shut us up together. You won't give the Home Secretary the tip, will you?

"But that isn't what I wanted to tell you about.

"It was something bigger, something tremendous. You'll not believe this part of it, but I was absolutely happy in that cell. It was a sort of deep-down unexcited happiness. I'm not a bit religious, but I *know* how the nuns feel in *their* cells when they've given up everything and shut themselves up with God. The cell was like a convent cell, you know, as narrow as that bit of shadow there is, and it had nice white-washed walls, and a planked-bed in the corner, and a window high, high up. There ought to have been a crucifix on the wall above the plank-bed, but there wasn't a crucifix. There was only a shiny black Bible on the chair.

"Really Frank, if you're to be shut up for a month with just one book, it had better be the Bible. Isaiah's ripping. I can remember heaps of it: 'in the habitation of jackals, where they lay, shall be grass with reeds and rushes. And an highway shall be there … the redeemed shall walk there: and the ransomed of the Lord shall return with singing into Zion' … 'They that wait upon the Lord shall renew their strength; they shall mount up with wings as eagles; they shall run, and not be weary; they shall walk, and not faint.' I used to read like anything; and I thought of things. They sort of came to me.

"That's what I wanted to tell you about. The things that came to me were so much bigger than the thing I went in for. I could see all along we weren't going to get it that way. And I knew we *were* going to get it some other way. I don't in the least know how, but it'll be some big, tremendous way that'll make all this fighting and fussing seem the rottenest game. That was one of the things I used to think about."

"Then," he said, "you've given it up? You're corning out of it?"

She looked at him keenly. "Are those still your conditions?"

He hesitated one second before he answered firmly. "Yes, those are still my conditions. You still won't agree to them?"

"I still won't agree. It's no use talking about it. You don't believe in freedom. We're incompatible. We don't stand for the same ideals."

"Oh, Lord, what *does* that matter?"

"It matters most awfully."

"I should have thought," said Drayton, "it would have mattered more if I'd had revolting manners or an impediment in my speech or something."

"It wouldn't, *really*."

"Well, you seem to have thought about a lot of things. Did you ever once think about me, Dorothy?"

"Yes, I did. Have you ever read the Psalms? There's a jolly one that begins: 'Blessed be the Lord my strength, which teacheth my hands to war and my fingers to fight.' I used to think of you when I read that. I thought of you a lot.

"That's what I was coming to. It was the queerest thing of all. Everything seemed ended when I went to prison. I knew you wouldn't care for me after what I'd done—you must really listen to this, Frank—I knew you couldn't and wouldn't marry me; and it somehow didn't matter. What I'd got hold of was bigger than that. I knew that all this Women's Suffrage business was only a part of it, a small, ridiculous part.

"I sort of saw the redeemed of the Lord. They were men, as well as women, Frank. And they were all free. They were all free because they were redeemed. And the funny thing was that you were part of it. You were mixed up in the whole queer, tremendous business. Everything was ended. And everything was begun; so that I knew you understood even when you didn't understand. It was really as if I'd got you tight, somehow; and I knew you couldn't go, even when you'd gone."

"And yet you don't see that it's a crime to force me to go."

"I see that it would be a worse crime to force you to stay if you mean going.

"What time is it?"

"A quarter to eight."

"And I've got to go home and have a bath. Whatever you do, don't make me late for that infernal banquet. You *are* going to drive me there?"

"I'm going to drive you there, but I'm not going in with you."

"Poor darling! Did I ask you to go in?"

He drove her back to her father's house. She came out of it burnished and beautiful, dressed in clean white linen, with the broad red, white and blue tricolour of the Women's Franchise Union slanting across her breast.

He drove her to the Banquet of the Prisoners, to the Imperial Hotel, Kingsway. They went in silence; for their hearts ached too much for speaking. But in Dorothy's heart, above the aching, there was that queer exaltation that had sustained her in prison.

He left her at the entrance of the hotel, where Michael and Nicholas waited to receive her.

Michael and Nicholas went in with her to the Banquet. They hated it, but they went in.

Veronica was with them. She too wore a white frock, with red, white and blue ribbons.

"Drayton's a bit of a rotter," Michael said, "not to see you through."

"How can he when he feels like that about it?"

"As if we didn't feel!"

Three hundred and thirty women and twenty men waited in the Banquet Hall to receive the prisoners.

The high galleries were festooned with the red, white and blue of the Women's Franchise Union, and hung with flags and blazoned banners. The silk standards and the emblems of the Women's Suffrage Leagues and Societies, supported by their tall poles, stood ranged along three walls. They covered the sham porphyry with gorgeous and heroic colours, purple and blue, sky-blue and sapphire blue and royal blue, black, white and gold, vivid green, pure gold, pure white, dead-black, orange and scarlet and magenta.

From the high table under the windows streamed seven dependent tables decorated with nosegays of red, white and blue flowers. In the centre of the high table three arm-chairs, draped with the tricolour, were set like three thrones for the three leaders. They were flanked by nine other chairs on the right and nine on the left for the eighteen other prisoners.

There was a slight rustling sound at the side door leading to the high table. It was followed by a thicker and more prolonged sound of rustling as the three hundred and fifty turned in their places.

The twenty-one prisoners came in.

A great surge of white, spotted with red and blue, heaved itself up in the hall to meet them as the three hundred and fifty rose to their feet.

And from the three hundred and fifty there went up a strange, a savage and a piercing collective sound, where a clear tinkling as of glass or thin metal, and a tearing as of silk, and a crying as of children and of small, slender-throated animals were held together by ringing, vibrating, overtopping tones as of violins playing in the treble. And now a woman's voice started off on its own note and tore the delicate tissue of this sound with a solitary scream; and now a man's voice filled up a pause in the shrill hurrahing with a solitary boom.

To Dorothea, in her triumphal seat at Angela Blathwaite's right hand, to Michael and Nicholas and Veronica in their places among the crowd, that collective sound was frightful.

From her high place Dorothea could see Michael and Nicholas, one on each side of Veronica, just below her. At the same table, facing them, she saw her three aunts, Louie, Emmeline and Edith.

It was from Emmeline that those lacerating screams arose.

The breakfast and the speeches of the prisoners were over. The crowd was on its feet again, and the prisoners had risen in their high places.

Out of the three hundred and seventy-one, two hundred and seventy-nine women and seven men were singing the Marching Song of the Militant Women.

Shoulder to shoulder, breast to breast,
Our army moves from east to west.
Follow on! Follow on!

With flag and sword from south and north,
The sounding, shining hosts go forth.
Follow on! Follow on!

Do you not hear our marching feet,
From door to door, from street to street?
Follow on! Follow on!

Dorothea was fascinated and horrified by the singing, swaying, excited crowd.

Her three aunts fascinated her. They were all singing at the top of their voices. Aunt Louie stood up straight and rigid. She sang from the back of her throat, through a mouth not quite sufficiently open; she sang with a grim, heroic determination to sing, whatever it might cost her and other people.

Aunt Edie sang inaudibly, her thin shallow voice, doing its utmost, was overpowered by the collective song. Aunt Emmeline sang shrill and loud; her body rocked slightly to the rhythm of a fantastic march. With one large, long hand raised she beat the measure of the music. Her head was thrown back; and on her face there was a look of ecstasy, of a holy rapture, exalted, half savage, not quite sane.

Dorothea was fascinated and horrified by Aunt Emmeline.

The singing had threatened her when it began; so that she felt again her old terror of the collective soul. Its massed emotion threatened her. She longed for her white-washed prison cell, for its hardness, its nakedness, its quiet, its visionary peace. She tried to remember. Her soul, in its danger, tried to get back there. But the soul of the crowd in the hail below her swelled and heaved itself towards her, drawn by the Vortex. She felt the rushing of the whirlwind; it sucked at her breath: the Vortex was drawing her, too; the powerful, abominable thing almost got her. The sight of Emmeline saved her.

She might have been singing and swaying too, carried away in the same awful ecstasy, if she had not seen Emmeline. By looking at Emmeline she saved her soul; it stood firm again; she was clear and hard and sane.

She could look away from Emmeline now. She saw her brothers, Michael and Nicholas. Michael's soul was the prey of its terror of the herd-soul. The shrill voices, fine as whipcord and sharp as needles, tortured him. Michael looked beautiful in his martyrdom. His fair, handsome face was set clear and hard. His yellow hair, with its hard edges, fitted his head like a cap of solid, polished metal. Weariness and disgust made a sort of cloud over his light green eyes. When Nicky looked at him Nicky's face twitched and twinkled. But he hated it almost as much as Michael hated it.

She thought of Michael and Nicholas. They hated it, and yet they stuck it out. They wouldn't go back on her. She and Lady Victoria Threlfall were to march on foot before the Car of Victory from Blackfriars Bridge along the Embankment, through Trafalgar Square and Pall Mall and Piccadilly to Hyde Park Corner. And Michael and Nicholas would march beside them to hold up the poles of the standard which, after all, they were not strong enough to carry.

She thought of Drayton who had not stuck it out. And at the same time she thought of the things that had come to her in her prison cell. She had told him the most real thing that had ever happened to her, and he had not listened. He had not cared. Michael would have listened. Michael would have cared intensely.

She thought, "'I am not come to bring peace, but a sword.'" The sword was between her and her lover.

She had given him up. She had chosen, not between him and the Vortex, but between him and her vision which was more than either of them or than all this.

She looked at Rosalind and Maud Blackadder who sang violently in the hall below her. She had chosen freedom. She had given up her lover. She wondered whether Rosalind or the Blackadder girl could have done as much, supposing they had had a choice?

Then she looked at Veronica.

Veronica was standing between Michael and Nicholas. She was slender and beautiful and pure, like some sacrificial virgin. Presently she would be marching in the Procession. She would carry a thin, tall pole, with a round olive wreath on the top of it, and a white dove sitting in the ring of the olive wreath. And she would look as if she was not in the Procession but in another place.

When Dorothea looked at her she was lifted up above the insane ecstasy and the tumult of the herd-soul. Her soul and the soul of Veronica went alone in utter freedom.

Follow on! Follow on!

For Faith's our spear and Hope's our sword,
And Love's our mighty battle-lord.
Follow on! Follow on!

And Justice is our flag unfurled,
The flaming flag that sweeps the world.
Follow on! Follow on!

And "Freedom!" is our battle-cry;
For Freedom we will fight and die.
Follow on! Follow on!

The Procession was over a mile long.

It stretched all along the Embankment from Blackfriars Bridge to Westminster. The Car of Victory, covered with the tricolour, and the bodyguard on thirteen white horses were drawn up beside Cleopatra's Needle and the Sphinxes.

Before the Car of Victory, from the western Sphinx to Northumberland Avenue, were the long regiments of the Unions and Societies and Leagues, of the trades and the professions and the arts, carrying their banners, the purple and the blue, the black, white and gold, the green, the orange and the scarlet and magenta.

Behind the Car of Victory came the eighteen prisoners with Lady Victoria Threlfall and Dorothea at their head, under the immense tricolour standard that Michael and Nicholas carried for them. Behind the prisoners, closing the Procession, was a double line of young girls dressed in white with tricolour ribbons, each carrying a pole with the olive wreath and dove, symbolizing, with the obviousness of extreme innocence, the peace that follows victory. They were led by Veronica.

She did not know that she had been chosen to lead them because of her youth and her processional, hieratic beauty; she thought that the Union had bestowed this honour on her because she belonged to Dorothea.

From her place at the head of the Procession she could see the big red, white and blue standard held high above Dorothea and Lady Victoria Threlfall. She knew how they would look; Lady Victoria, white and tense, would go like a saint and a martyr, in exaltation, hardly knowing where she was, or what she did; and Dorothea would go in pride, and in disdain for the proceedings in which her honour forced her to take part; she would have an awful knowledge of what she was doing and of where she was; she would drink every drop of the dreadful cup she had poured out for herself, hating it.

Last night Veronica had thought that she too would hate it; she thought that she would rather die than march in the Procession. But she did not hate it or her part in it. The thing was too beautiful and too big to hate, and her part in it was too little.

She was not afraid of the Procession or of the soul of the Procession. She was not afraid of the thick crowd on the pavements, pressing closer and closer, pushed back continually by the police. Her soul was by itself. Like Dorothea's soul it went apart from the soul of the crowd and the soul of the Procession; only it was not proud; it was simply happy.

The band had not yet begun to play; but already she heard the music sounding in her brain; her feet felt the rhythm of the march.

Somewhere on in front the policemen made gestures of release, and the whole Procession began to move. It marched to an unheard music, to the rhythm that was in Veronica's brain.

They went through what were once streets between walls of houses, and were now broad lanes between thick walls of people. The visible aspect of things was slightly changed, slightly distorted. The houses stood farther back behind the walls of people; they were hung with people; a swarm of people clung like bees to the house walls.

All these people were fixed where they stood or hung. In a still and stationary world the Procession was the only thing that moved.

She had a vague, far-off perception that the crowd was friendly.

A mounted policeman rode at her side. When they halted at the cross-streets he looked down at Veronica with an amused and benign expression. She had a vague, far-off perception that the policeman was friendly. Everything seemed to her vague and far-off.

Only now and then it struck her as odd that a revolutionary Procession should be allowed to fill the streets of a great capital, and that a body of the same police that arrested the insurgents should go with it to protect them, to clear their triumphal way before them, holding up the entire traffic of great thoroughfares that their bands and their banners and their regiments should go through.

She said to herself "What a country! It couldn't happen in Germany; it couldn't happen in France, or anywhere in Europe or America. It could only happen in England."

Now they were going up St. James's Street towards Piccadilly. The band was playing the Marseillaise.

And with the first beat of the drum Veronica's soul came down from its place, and took part in the Procession. As long as they played the Marseillaise she felt that she could march with the Procession to the ends of the world; she could march into battle to the Marseillaise; she could fight to that music and die.

The women behind her were singing under their breath. They sang the words of the Women's Marseillaise.

And Veronica, marching in front of them by herself, sang another song. She sang the Marseillaise of Heine and of Schumann.

> Dann reitet mein Kaiser wohl über mein Grab,
> Viel' Schwerter klirren und blitzen;
> Dann steig' ich gewaffnet hervor aus mein Grab,—
> Den Kaiser, den Kaiser zu schützen!

The front of the Procession lifted as it went up Tyburn Hill.

Veronica could not see Michael and Nicholas, but she knew that they were there. She knew it by the unusual steadiness of the standard that they carried. Far away westwards, in the middle and front of the Procession, the purple and the blue, the gold and white, the green, the scarlet and orange and magenta standards rocked and staggered; they bent forwards; they were flung backwards as the west wind took them. But the red, white and blue standard that Michael and Nicholas carried went before her, steady and straight and high.

And Veronica followed, carrying her thin, tall pole with the olive wreath on the top of it, and the white dove sitting in the ring of the wreath. She went with the music of Schumann and Heine sounding in her soul.

XVII

Another year passed.

Frances was afraid for Michael now. Michael was being drawn in. Because of his strange thoughts he was the one of all her children who had most hidden himself from her; who would perhaps hide himself from her to the very end.

Nicholas had settled down. He had left the Morss Company and gone into his father's business for a while, to see whether he could stand it. John was going into the business too when he left Oxford. John was even looking forward to his partnership in what he called "the Pater's old tree-game." He said, "You wait till I get my hand well in. Won't we make it rip!"

John was safe. You could depend on him to keep out of trouble. He had no genius for adventure. He would never strike out for himself any strange or dangerous line. He had settled down at Cheltenham; he had settled down at Oxford.

And Dorothea had settled down.

The Women's Franchise Union was now in the full whirl of its revolution. Under the inspiring leadership of the Blathwaites it ran riot up and down the country. It smashed windows; it hurled stone ginger-beer bottles into the motor-cars of Cabinet Ministers; it poured treacle into pillar-boxes; it invaded the House of Commons by the water-way, in barges, from which women, armed with megaphones, demanded the vote from infamous legislators drinking tea on the Terrace; it went up in balloons and showered down propaganda on the City; now and then, just to show what violence it could accomplish if it liked, it burned down a house or two in a pure and consecrated ecstasy of Feminism. It was bringing to perfection its last great tactical manoeuvre, the massed raid followed by the hunger-strike in prison. And it was considering seriously the very painful but possible necessity of interfering with British sport—say the Eton and Harrow Match at Lord's—in some drastic and terrifying way that would bring the men of England to their senses.

And Dorothea's soul had swung away from the sweep of the whirlwind. It would never suck her in. She worked now in the office of the Social Reform Union, and wrote reconstructive articles for *The New Commonwealth* on Economics and the Marriage Laws.

Frances was not afraid for her daughter. She knew that the revolution was all in Dorothea's brain.

When she said that Michael was being drawn in she meant that he was being drawn into the vortex of revolutionary Art. And since Frances confused this movement with the movements of Phyllis Desmond she judged it to be terrible. She understood from Michael that it was *the* Vortex, the only one that really mattered, and the only one that would ever do anything.

And Michael was not only in it, he was in it with Lawrence Stephen.

Though Frances knew now that Lawrence Stephen had plans for Michael, she did not realize that they depended much more on Michael himself than on him. Stephen had said that if Michael was good enough he meant to help him. If his poems amounted to anything he would publish them in his *Review*. If any book of Michael's poems amounted to anything he would give a whole article to that book in his *Review*. If Michael's prose should ever amount to anything he would give him regular work on the *Review*.

In nineteen-thirteen Michael Harrison was the most promising of the revolutionary young men who surrounded Lawrence Stephen, and his poems were beginning to appear, one after another, in the *Green Review*. He had brought out a volume of his experiments in the spring of that year; they were better than those that Réveillaud had approved of two years ago; and Lawrence Stephen had praised them in the *Green Review*.

Lawrence Stephen was the only editor "out of Ireland," as he said, who would have had the courage either to publish them or to praise them.

And when Frances realized Michael's dependence on Lawrence Stephen she was afraid.

"You wouldn't be, my dear, if you knew Larry," Vera said.

For Frances still refused to recognize the man who had taken Ferdinand Cameron's place.

Lawrence Stephen was one of those Nationalist Irishmen who love Ireland with a passion that satisfies neither the lover nor the beloved. It was a pure and holy passion, a passion so entirely of the spirit as to be compatible with permanent bodily absence from its object. Stephen's body had lived at ease in England (a country that he declared his spirit hated) ever since he had been old enough to choose a habitation for himself.

He justified his predilection on three grounds: Ireland had been taken from him; Ireland had been so ruined and raped by the Scotch and the English that nothing but the soul of Ireland was left for Irishmen to love. He could work and fight for Ireland better in London than in Dublin. And again, the Irishman in England can make havoc in his turn; he can harry the English, he can spite, and irritate and triumph and get his own back in a thousand ways. Living in England he would be a thorn in England's side.

And all this meant that there was no place in Ireland for a man of his talents and his temperament. His enemies called him an opportunist: but he was a opportunist gone wrong, abandoned to an obstinate idealism, one of those damned and solitary souls that only the north of Ireland produces in perfection. For the Protestantism of Ulster breeds rebels like no other rebels on earth, rebels as strong and obstinate and canny as itself. Before he was twenty-one Stephen had revolted against the material comfort and the spiritual tyranny of his father's house.

He was the great-grandson of an immigrant Lancashire cotton spinner settled in Belfast. His western Irish blood was steeled with this mixture, and braced and embittered with the Scottish blood of Antrim where his people married.

Therefore, if he had chosen one career and stuck to it he would have been formidable. But one career alone did not suffice for his inexhaustible energies. As a fisher of opportunities he drew with too wide a net and in too many waters. He had tried parliamentary politics and failed because no party trusted him, least of all his own. And yet few men were more trustworthy. He turned his back on the House of Commons and took to journalism. As a journalistic politician he ran Nationalism for Ireland and Socialism for England. Neither Nationalists nor Socialists believed in him; yet few men were more worthy of belief. In literature he had distinguished himself as a poet, a playwright, a novelist and an essayist. He did everything so well that he was supposed not to do anything quite well enough. Because of his politics other men of letters suspected his artistic sincerity; yet few artists were more sincere. His very distinction was unsatisfying. Without any of the qualities that make even a minor statesman, he was so far contaminated by politics as to be spoiled for the highest purposes of art; yet there was no sense in which he had achieved popularity.

Everywhere he went he was an alien and suspected. Do what he would, he fell between two countries and two courses. Ireland had cast him out and England would none of him. He hated Catholicism and Protestantism alike, and Protestants and Catholics alike disowned him. To every Church and every sect he was a free thinker, destitute of all religion. Yet few men were more religious. His enemies called him a turner and a twister; yet on any one of his lines no man ever steered a straighter course.

A capacity for turning and twisting might have saved him. It would at any rate have made him more intelligible. As it was, he presented to two countries the disconcerting spectacle of a many-sided object moving with violence in a dead straight line. He moved so fast that to a stationary on-looker he was gone before one angle of him had been apprehended. It was for other people to turn and twist if any one of them was to get a complete all-round view of the amazing man.

But taken all round he passed for a man of hard wit and suspicious brilliance.

And he belonged to no generation. In nineteen-thirteen he was not yet forty, too old to count among the young men, and yet too young for men of his own age. So that in all Ireland and all England you could not have found a lonelier man.

The same queer doom pursued him in the most private and sacred relations of his life. To all intents and purposes he was married to Vera Harrison and yet he was not married. He was neither bound nor free.

All this had made him sorrowful and bitter.

And to add to his sorrowfulness and bitterness he had something of the Celt's spiritual abhorrence of the flesh; and though he loved Vera, after his manner, there were moments when Vera's capacity for everlasting passion left him tired and bored and cold.

All his life *his* passions had been at the service of ideas. All his life he had looked for some great experience, some great satisfaction and consummation; and he had not found it.

In nineteen-thirteen, with half his life behind him, the opportunist was still waiting for his supreme opportunity.

❧

Meanwhile his enemies said of him that he snatched.

But he did not snatch. The eyes of his idealism were fixed too steadily on a visionary future. He merely tried, with a bored and weary gesture, to waylay the passing moment while he waited. He had put his political failure behind him and said, "I will be judged as an artist or not at all." They judged him accordingly and their judgment was wrong.

There was not the least resemblance between Lawrence Stephen as he was in himself and Lawrence Stephen as he appeared to the generation just behind him. To conservatives he passed for the leader of the revolution in contemporary art, and yet the revolution in contemporary art was happening without him. He was not the primal energy in the movement of the Vortex. In nineteen-thirteen his primal energies were spent, and he was trusting to the movement of the Vortex to carry him a little farther than he could have gone by his own impetus. He was attracted to the young men of the Vortex because they were not of the generation that had rejected him, and because he hoped thus to prolong indefinitely his own youth. They were attracted to him because of his solitary distinction, his comparative poverty, and his unpopularity. A prosperous, well-established Stephen would have revolted them. He gave the revolutionaries the shelter of his *Review*, the support of his name, and the benefit of his bored and wearied criticism. They brought him in return a certain homage founded on his admirable appreciation of their merits and tempered by their sense of his dealings with the past they abominated.

"Stephen is a bigot," said young Morton Ellis; "he believes in Swinburne."

Stephen smiled at him in bored and weary tolerance.

He believed in too many things for his peace of mind. He knew that the young men distrusted him because of his beliefs, and because of his dealings with the past; because he refused to destroy the old gods when he made place for the new.

Young Morton Ellis lay stretched out at his ease on the couch in Stephen's study.

He blinked and twitched as he looked up at his host with half irritated, half affable affection.

The young men came and went at their ease in and out of that house in St. John's Wood which Lawrence Stephen shared with Vera Harrison. They were at home there. Their books stood in his bookcase; they laid their manuscripts on his writing table and left them there; they claimed his empty spaces for the hanging of their pictures yet unsold.

Every Friday evening they met together in the long, low room at the top of the house, and they talked.

Every Friday evening Michael left his father's house to meet them there, and to listen and to talk.

To-night, round and about Morton Ellis, the young poet, were Austen Mitchell, the young painter, and Paul Monier-Owen, the young sculptor, and George Wadham, the last and youngest of Morton Ellis's disciples.

Lawrence Stephen stood among them like an austere guest in some rendezvous of violent youth, or like the priest of some romantic religion that he has blasphemed yet not quite abjured. He was lean and dark and shaven; his black hair hung forward in two masses, smooth and straight and square; he had sorrowful, bitter eyes, and a bitter, sorrowful mouth, the long Irish upper lip fine and hard drawn, while the lower lip quivered incongruously, pouted and protested and recanted, was sceptical and sensitive and tender. His short, high nose had wide yet fastidious nostrils.

It was at this figure that Morton Ellis continued to gaze with affability and irritation. It was this figure that Vera's eyes followed with anxious, restless passion, as if she felt that at any moment he might escape her, might be off, God knew where.

Lawrence Stephen was ill at ease in that house and in the presence of his mistress and his friends.

"I believe in the past," he said, "because I believe in the future. I want continuity. Therefore I believe in Swinburne; and I believe in Browning and in Tennyson and Wordsworth; I believe in Keats and Shelley and in Milton. But I do not believe, any more than you do, in their imitators. I believe in destroying their imitators. I do not believe in destroying them."

"You can't destroy their imitators unless you destroy them. They breed the disgusting parasites. Their memories harbour them like a stinking suit of old clothes. They must be scrapped and burned if we're to get rid of the stink. Art has got to be made young and new and clean. There isn't any disinfectant that'll do the trick. So long as old masters are kow-towed to as masters people will go on imitating them. When a poet ceases to be a poet and becomes a centre of corruption, he must go."

Michael said, "How about *us* when people imitate us? Have we got to go?"

Morton Ellis looked at him and blinked. "No," he said. "No. We haven't got to go."

"I don't see how you get out of it."

"I get out of it by doing things that can't be imitated."

There was a silence in which everybody thought of Mr. George Wadham. It made Mr. Wadham so uncomfortable that he had to break it.

"I say, how about Shakespeare?" he said.

"Nobody, so far, *has* imitated Shakespeare, any more than they have *succeeded* in imitating me."

There was another silence while everybody thought of Morton Ellis as the imitator of every poetic form under the sun except the forms adopted by his contemporaries.

"That's all very well, Ellis," said Stephen, "but you aren't the Holy Ghost coming down out of heaven. We can trace your sources."

"My dear Stephen, I never said I was the Holy Ghost. Nobody ever does come down out of heaven. You *can* trace my sources, thank God, because they're clean. I haven't gone into every stream that swine like —— and —— and —— and —— and ——" (he named five contemporary distinctions) "have made filthy with their paddling."

He went on. "The very damnable question that you've raised, Harrison, is absurd. You believe in the revolution. Well then, supposing the revolution's coming—you needn't suppose it, because it's come. We *are* the revolution—the revolution means that we've made a clean sweep of the past. In the future no artist will want to imitate anybody. No artist will be allowed to exist unless he's prepared to be buried alive or burned alive rather than corrupt the younger generation with the processes and the products of his own beastly dissolution.

"That's why violence is right.

> O Violenza, sorgi, balena in questo cielo
> Sanguigno, stupra le albe,
> irrompi come incendio nei vesperi,
> fa di tutto il sereno una tempesta,
> fa di tutta la vita una bataglia,
> fa con tutte le anime un odio solo!

"There's no special holiness in violence. Violence is right because it's necessary."

"You mean it's necessary because it's right."

Austen Mitchell spoke. He was a sallow youth with a broad,

flat-featured, British face, but he had achieved an appearance of great strangeness and distinction by letting his hay-coloured hair grow long and cultivating two beards instead of one.

"Violence," he continued, "is not a means; it's an end! Energy must be got for its own sake, if you want to generate more energy instead of standing still. The difference between Pastism and Futurism is the difference between statics and dynamics. Futurist art is simply art that has gone on, that has left off being static and become dynamic. It expresses movement. Owen will tell you better than I can why it expresses movement."

A light darted from the corner of the room where Paul Monier-Owen had curled himself up. His eyes flashed like the eyes of a young wild animal roused in its lair.

Paul Monier-Owen was dark and soft and supple. At a little distance he had the clumsy grace and velvet innocence of a black panther, half cub, half grown. The tips of his ears, the corners of his prominent eyes, his eyebrows and his long nostrils tilted slightly upwards and backwards. Under his slender, mournful nose his restless smile showed the white teeth of a young animal.

Above this primitive, savage base of features that responded incessantly to any childish provocation, the intelligence of Monier-Owen watched in his calm and beautiful forehead and in his eyes.

He said, "It expresses movement, because it presents objects directly as cutting across many planes. To do this you have to break up objects into the lines and masses that compose them, and project those lines and masses into space on any curve, at any angle, according to the planes you mean them to cross, otherwise the movements you mean them to express. The more planes intersected the more movement you get. By decomposing figures you compose movements. By decomposing groups of figures you compose groups of movement. Nothing but a cinema can represent objects as intact and as at the same time moving; and even the cinema only does this by a series of decompositions so minute as to escape the eye.

"You want to draw a battle-piece or the traffic at Hyde Park Corner. It can't be done unless you break up your objects as Mitchell breaks them up. You want to carve figures in the round, wrestling or dancing. It can't be done unless you dislocate their lines and masses as I dislocate them, so as to throw them all at once into those planes that the intact body could only have traversed one after another in a given time.

"By taking time into account as well as space we produce rhythm.

"I know what you're going to say, Stephen. The Dancing Faun and the Frieze of the Parthenon express movements. But they do nothing of the sort. They express movements arrested at a certain point. They are supposed to represent nature, but they do not even do that, because arrested motion is a contradiction in terms, and because the point of arrest is an artificial and arbitrary thing.

"Your medium limits you. You have to choose between the intact body which is stationary and the broken and projected bodies which are in movement. That is why we destroy or suppress symmetry in the figure and in design. Because symmetry is perfect balance which is immobility. If I wanted to present perfect rest I should do it by an absolute symmetry."

"And there's more in it than that," said Austen Mitchell. "We're out against the damnable affectations of naturalism and humanism. If I draw a perfect likeness of a fat, pink woman I've got a fat, pink woman and nothing else but a fat pink woman. And a fat, pink woman is a work of Nature, not a work of art. And I'm lying. I'm presenting as a reality what is only an appearance. The better the likeness the bigger the lie. But movement and rhythm are realities, not appearances. When I present rhythm and movement I've done something. I've made reality appear."

He went on to unfold a scheme for restoring vigour to the exhausted language by destroying its articulations. These he declared to be purely arbitrary, therefore fatal to the development of a spontaneous and individual style. By breaking up the rigid ties of syntax, you do more than create new forms of prose moving in perfect freedom, you deliver the creative spirit itself from the abominable contact with dead ideas. Association, fixed and eternalized by the structure of the language, is the tyranny that keeps down the live idea.

"We've got to restore the innocence of memory, as Gauguin restored the innocence of the eye."

Michael noticed that the talk was not always sustained at this constructive level. And to-night, towards twelve o'clock, it dropped and broke in a welter of vituperation. It was, first, a frenzied assault on the Old Masters, a storming of immortal strongholds, a tearing and scattering of the wing feathers of archangels; then, from this high adventure it sank to a perfunctory skirmishing among living eminences over forty, judged, by reason of their age, to be too contemptible for an attack in force. It rallied again to a bombing and blasting of minute ineptitudes, the slaughter of "swine like —— and —— and —— and —— and ——"; and ended in a furious pursuit of a volatile young poet, Edward Rivers, who had escaped by sheer levity from the tug of the Vortex, and was setting up a small swirl of his own.

Michael was with the revolutionaries heart and soul; he believed in Morton Ellis and Austen Mitchell and Monier-Owen even more than he believed in Lawrence Stephen, and almost as much as he believed in Jules Réveillaud. They stood for all the realities and all the ideas and all the accomplishments to which he himself was devoted. He had no sort of qualms about the wholesale slaughter of the inefficient.

But to-night, as he listened to these voices, he felt again his old horror of the collective soul. The voices spoke with a terrible unanimity. The vortex—*the* Vortex—was like the little vortex of school. The young men, Ellis and Mitchell and Monier-Owen, belonged to a herd like the school-herd, hunting together, crying together, saying the same thing. Their very revolt against the Old Masters was a collective and not an individual revolt. Their chase was hottest when their quarry was one of the pack who had broken through and got away. They hated the fugitive, solitary private soul.

And yet it was only as private souls that Ellis and Mitchell and Monier-Owen counted. Each by himself did good things; each, if he had the courage to break loose and go by himself, might do a great thing some day. Even George Wadham might do something if he could get away from Ellis and the rest. Edward Rivers had had courage.

Michael thought: "It's Rivers now. It'll be my turn next." But he had a great longing to break loose and get away.

He thought: "I don't know where they're all going to end. They think they're beginning something tremendous; but I can't see what's to come of it. And I don't see how they can go on like that for ever. I can't see what's coming. Yet something must come. *They* can't be the end."

He thought: "Their movement is only a small swirl in an immense Vortex. It may suck them all down. But it will clear the air. They will have helped to clear it."

He thought of himself going on, free from the whirl of the Vortex, and of his work as enduring; standing clear and hard in the clean air.

PART III

Victory

XVIII

It was July, nineteen-fourteen, a month remarkable in the British Isles because of the fine weather and the disturbances in the political atmosphere due to the fine weather.

Every other evening in that July Anthony Harrison reminded his family that fine weather is favourable to open-air politics, and that the mere off-chance of sunstroke is enough to bring out the striker. And when Michael asked him contentiously what the weather had to do with Home Rule, he answered that it had everything to do with it by increasing parliamentary blood-pressure.

"Wait," he said, "till we get a good thunderstorm You'll see how long the strike'll last, and what Sir Edward Carson has to say to Mr. Redmond then."

Anthony kept his head. He had seen strikes before, and he knew that Home Rule had never been a part of practical politics and never would be.

And Michael and Dorothea laughed at him. They had their own views about the Home Rule question and the Labour question, and they could have told Anthony what the answers were going to be; only they said it wasn't any good talking to Father; when he got an idea into his dear old head it stuck there.

Now, on Mother, if you talked to her long enough, you could make some impression; you could get ideas into her head and you could get them out.

Frances, no longer preoccupied with the care of young children, had time for the affairs of the nation. She was a more intelligent woman than the Mrs. Anthony Harrison who, nineteen years ago, informed herself of the affairs of the nation from a rapid skimming of the *Times*. In the last four years the affairs of the nation had thrust themselves violently upon her attention. She had even realized the Woman's Suffrage movement as a vivid and vital affair, since Dorothy had taken part in the fighting and had gone to prison.

Frances, sitting out this July under her tree of Heaven with the *Times*, had a sense of things about to happen if other things didn't happen to prevent them. At any rate she had no longer any reason to complain that nothing happened.

It was the Home Rule crisis now. The fact that England and Ireland were on the edge of civil war was brought home to her, not so much by the head-lines in the papers as by the publication of her son Michael's insurgent poem, "Ireland," in the *Green Review*.

For Michael had not grown out of his queer idea. He was hardly thirteen when he had said that civil war between England and Ireland would be glorious if the Irish won, and he was saying it still. His poem was the green flag that he flew in the face of his family and of his country. Neither Frances nor Anthony would have been likely to forget the imminence of civil war (only that they didn't really believe in it), when from morning till night Michael talked and wrote of nothing else. In this Michael was not carried away by collective feeling; his dream of Ireland's freedom was a secret and solitary dream. Nobody he knew shared it but Lawrence Stephen. The passion he brought to it made him hot and restless and intense. Frances expressed her opinion of the Irish crisis when she said, "I wish that Carson man would mind his own business. This excitement is very bad for Michael."

And she thanked Heaven that Ireland was not England, and that none of them lived there. If there was civil war in Ireland for a week or two, Anthony and the boys would be out of it.

Frances was also alive to the war between Capital and Labour. There was, indeed, something very intimate and personal to Frances in this particular affair of the nation; for Anthony's business was being disagreeably affected by the strike in the building trade.

So much so that Anthony had dismissed his chauffeur and given up his idea of turning the stable loft into a billiard-room. He had even thought of trying to let the shooting-box and the cottage on the Yorkshire moors which he had bought, unforeseeingly, in the spring of last year; but Michael and Nicholas had persuaded him that this extreme measure was unnecessary.

And Frances, even with the strike hanging over her, was happy. For the children, at their first sight of possible adversity, were showing what was in them. Their behaviour made her more arrogant than ever. Michael and Dorothea had given up their allowances and declared their complete ability to support themselves. (They earned about fifty pounds a year each on an average.) She had expected this from Dorothy, but not from Michael. Nicholas was doing the chauffeur's work in his absence; and John showed eagerness to offer up his last year at Oxford; he pressed it on his father as his contribution to the family economies.

Veronica brought her minute dividends (paid to her every quarter through Ferdinand Cameron's solicitors), and laid them at Frances's and Anthony's feet. ("As if," Anthony said, "I could have taken her poor little money!") Veronica thought she could go out as a music teacher.

There were moments when Frances positively enjoyed the strike. Her mind refused to grasp the danger of the situation. She suspected Anthony of exaggerating his losses in order to draw out Dorothy and Michael and Nicholas and John, and wallow in their moral beauty. He, too, was arrogant. He was convinced that, though there might be girls like Dorothea, there were no boys like his three sons. As for the strike in the building trade, strikes, as Anthony insisted, had happened before, and none of them had threatened for very long either Frances's peace of mind or Anthony's prosperity.

The present strike was not interfering in the least with Mrs. Anthony Harrison's Day, the last of the season. It fell this year, on the twenty-fifth of July.

Long afterwards she remembered it by what happened at the end of it.

Frances's Day—the fourth Saturday in the month—was one of those slight changes that are profoundly significant. It stood for regeneration and a change of heart. It marked the close of an epoch. Frances's life of exclusive motherhood had ended; she had become, or was at any rate trying to become, a social creature. Her Day had bored her terribly at first, when it didn't frighten her; she was only just beginning to get used to it; and still, at times, she had the air of not taking it seriously. It had been forced on her. Dorothea had decided that she must have a Day, like other people.

She had had it since Michael's first volume of Poems had come out in the spring of the year before, when the young men who met every Friday evening in Lawrence Stephen's study began to meet at Michael's father's house.

Anthony liked to think that his house was the centre of all this palpitating, radiant life; of young men doing all sorts of wonderful, energetic, important, interesting things. They stirred the air about him and kept it clean; he liked the sound of their feet and of their voices, and of their laughter. And when the house was quiet and Anthony had Frances to himself he liked that, too.

But Frances thought: "If only they wouldn't come quite so often—if only I could have my children *sometimes* to myself!"

It was the last rebellion of her flesh that had borne and suckled them.

There was this to be said for Frances's Day that it attracted and diverted, and confined to one time and one place a whole crowd of tiresome people, who, without it, would have spread themselves over the whole month; also that it gave a great deal of innocent happiness to the "Poor dears." Frances meant old Mrs. Fleming, and Louie and Emmeline and Edith Fleming, who figured as essential parts of the social event. She meant Mr. and Mrs. Jervis, who, in the inconceivability of their absence on Frances's Day, wondered more than ever why their daughter Rosalind found them so impossible. She meant Mr. Vereker and Mr. Norris from the office, and their wives and children, and Anthony's secretary, Miss Lathom. If Miss Lathom were not engaged to young George Vereker, she soon would be, to judge by the behaviour of their indiscreet and guileless faces.

Frances also meant her brother-in-law, Bartholomew, home from India for good, and cherishing a new disease, more secret and more dangerous than his cancer; she meant her brother Maurice, who was genuinely invalided, who had come back from California for the last time and would never be sent out anywhere again.

Dorothea had said: "Let's kill them all off in one awful day." Frances had said: "Yes, but we must do it decently. We must be kind to them, poor dears!"

Above all they must be decent to Grannie and the Aunties, and to Uncle Morrie and Uncle Bartie. That was the only burden she had laid on her children. It was a case of *noblesse oblige*; their youth constrained them. They had received so much, and they had been let off so much; not one of them had inherited the taint that made Maurice and Emmeline Fleming and Bartie Harrison creatures diseased and irresponsible. They could afford to be pitiful and merciful.

And now that the children were grown up Frances could afford to be pitiful and merciful herself. She could even afford to be grateful to the poor dears. She looked on Maurice and Emmeline and Bartie as scapegoats, bearers of the hereditary taint, whose affliction left her children clean. She thought of them more and more in this sacred and sacrificial character. At fifty-two Frances could be gentle over the things that had worried and irritated her at thirty-three. Like Anthony she was still young and strong through the youth and strength of her children.

And the poor dears were getting weak and old. Grannie was seventy-nine, and Maurice, the youngest of that generation, was forty-nine, and he looked sixty. Every year Frances was more acutely aware of their pathos, their futility, their mortality. They would be broken and gone so soon and so utterly, leaving no name, no sign or memorial of themselves; only living in the memories of her children who would remain.

And, with an awful sense of mortality surrounding them, her children had learned that they must be kind because the old people would be gone while they endured and remained.

This Saturday being the last of the season, they had all come; not only the Flemings, but the Jervises and Verekers and Norrises, and Uncle Bartie. The fine weather alone would have brought them.

Bartie, more morose and irritable than ever, sat under the tree of Heaven and watched the triumphal progress of the Day. He scowled darkly and sourly at each group in turn; at the young men in white flannels playing tennis; at Mr. and Mr. Jervis and the Verekers and Norrises; at the Flemings, old Mrs. Fleming, and Louie and Emmeline and Edith, and the disgraceful Maurice, all five of them useless pensioners on his brother's bounty; Maurice a thing of battered, sodden flesh hanging loose on brittle bone, a rickety prop for the irreproachable summer suit bought with Anthony's money. He scowled at the tables covered with fine white linen, and at the costly silver and old china, at the sandwiches and cakes and ices, and the piled-up fruits and the claret cup and champagne cup glowing and shining in the tall glass jugs, and at the pretty maidservants going to and fro in their accomplished service.

Bartie wondered how on earth Anthony managed it. His wonder was a savage joy to Bartie.

Mr. Jervis, a heavy, pessimistic man, wondered how they managed it, and Mr. Jervis's wonder had its own voluptuous quality. Mr. Vereker and Mr. Norris, who held that a strike was a downright serious matter, also wondered. But they were sustained by their immense belief in Mr. Anthony. Mr. Anthony knew what he was doing; he always had known. A strike might be serious while it lasted, but it didn't last. And Mr. Nicholas was in the business now, and Mr. John was coming into it next year, and Mr. Nicholas might be married again by that time; and the chances were that the firm of Harrison and Harrison would last long enough to provide for a young Vereker and a still younger Norris.

In spite of the strike, Mr. and Mrs. Vereker and Mr. and Mrs. Norris, like Frances and Anthony, were extraordinarily cheerful that afternoon.

So were young George Vereker and Miss Lathom.

"I can't think why I feel so happy," said Mrs. Vereker to Mrs. Norris. She was looking at her son George.

"Nor I, either," said Miss Lathom, who was trying suddenly to look at nothing in particular.

Miss Lathom lied and Mrs. Vereker lied; they knew perfectly well why they were happy. Each knew that the other lied; each knew that the other knew she knew; and neither of them could have said why she found it so necessary to lie.

And to Frances this happiness of Mrs. Vereker, and of young Vereker and Miss Lathom was significant and delightful, as if she had been personally responsible for it.

A day flashed out of her memory on a trail of blue larkspurs and of something that she had forgotten, something that was mixed up with Mr. and Mrs. Jervis and Rosalind. She stared at the larkspurs as if they held the clue—Nicky's face appeared among the tall blue spires, Nicky's darling face tied up in a scarf, brown stripes and yellow stripes—something to do with a White Cake—it must have been somebody's birthday. Now she had it—Mr. Jervis's cricket scarf. It was the day of Nicky's worst earache, the day when Mr. Vereker climbed the tree of Heaven—was it possible that Mr. Vereker had ever climbed that tree?—the day when Michael wouldn't go to the party—Rosalind's birthday.

Eight candles burning for Rosalind. Why, it was nineteen years ago. Don-Don was a baby then, and Michael and Nicky were only little boys. And look at them now!

She fed her arrogance by gazing on the tall, firmly knit, slender bodies of her sons, in white flannels, playing furiously and well.

"Dorothy is looking very handsome," Mrs. Jervis said.

Yes, certainly Dorothy was looking handsome; but Frances loved before all things the male beauty of her sons. In Michael and Nicholas it had reached perfection, the clean, hard perfection that would last, as Anthony's had lasted.

She thought of their beauty that had passed from her, dying many deaths, each death hurting her; the tender mortal beauty of babyhood, of childhood, of boyhood; but this invulnerable beauty of their young manhood would be with her for a long time. John would have it. John was only a fairer Nicholas; but as yet his beauty had not hardened; his boyhood lingered in the fine tissues of his mouth, and in his eyelids and the soft corners of his eyes; so that in John she could still see what Nicky had been.

She had adored Anthony's body, as if she had foreseen that it would give her such sons as these; and in her children she had adored the small bodies through whose clean, firm beauty she foresaw the beauty of their manhood. These were the same bodies, the same faces that she had loved in them as children; nothing was blurred or twisted or overlaid.

Michael at six-and-twenty was beautiful and serious as she had foreseen him. Frances knew that Michael had genius, and at other moments she was proud of his genius; but at this particular moment, sitting beside her friend and conscious of her jealousy, she was chiefly aware of his body.

Michael's body was quiescent; its beauty gave her a proud, but austere and tranquil satisfaction. It was when she looked at her second son that something caught at her breath and held it. She saw him as the lover and bridegroom of Veronica. Her sense of his virility was terrible to her and delightful.

Perhaps they were engaged already.

And Frances was sorry for Mrs. Jervis, who had borne no sons, who had only borne one unattractive and unsatisfactory daughter. She used to be sorry for her because Rosalind was pink and fat and fluffy; she was sorry for her now because Rosalind was unsatisfactory. She was sorry for Mrs. Norris because her boy could never grow up like Michael or Nicholas or John. She was sorry for Mrs. Vereker because George, though he looked all right when he was by himself, became clumsy and common at once beside Michael and Nicholas and John. George was also in white flannels; he played furiously and well; he played too furiously and too consciously well; he was too damp and too excited; his hair became damp and excited as he played; his cries had a Cockney tang.

Her arrogance nourished itself on these contrasts.

Mrs. Jervis looked wistfully at the young men as they played. She looked still more wistfully at Dorothy.

"What do you do," she said, "to keep your children with you?"

"I do nothing," Frances said. "I don't try to keep them. I've never appealed to their feelings for my own purposes, or taken advantage of their affection, that's all.

"They know that if they want to walk out of the house to-morrow, and stay out, they can. Nobody'll stop them."

There was a challenging, reminiscent glint in Mr. Jervis's eyes, and his wife was significantly silent. Frances knew what they were thinking.

"Nicky," she said, "walked out; but he came back again as soon as he was in trouble. Michael walks out and goes abroad every year; but he comes back again. Dorothy walks out, but she's never dreamed of not coming back again."

"Of course, if you aren't afraid of taking risks," said Mr. Jervis.

"I *am* afraid. But I've never shown it."

"It's very strange that Dorothy hasn't married." Mrs. Jervis spoke. She derived comfort from the thought that Dorothy was eight-and-twenty and not married.

"Dorothy," said Frances, "could marry to-morrow if she wanted to; but she doesn't want."

She was sorry for her friend, but she really could not allow her that consolation.

"Veronica is growing up very good-looking," said Mrs. Jervis then.

But it was no use. Frances was aware that Veronica was grown up, and that she was good-looking, and that Nicky loved her; but Mrs. Jervis's shafts fell wide of all her vulnerable places. Frances was no longer afraid.

"Veronica," she said, "is growing up very good."

It was not the word she would have chosen, yet it was the only one she could think of as likely to convey to Mrs. Jervis what she wanted her to know, though it left her obtuseness without any sense of Veronica's mysterious quality.

She herself had never tried to think of a word for it before; she was only driven to it now because she detected in her friend's tone a challenge and a warning. It was as if Rosalind's mother had said, extensively and with pointed reference to the facts: "Veronica is dangerous. Her mother has had adventures. She is grown-up and she is good-looking, and Nicky is susceptible to that sort of thing. If you don't look out he will be caught again. The only difference between Phyllis Desmond and Veronica is in their skins."

So when Frances said Veronica was good, she meant that Mrs. Jervis should understand, once for all, that she was not in the least like her mother or like Phyllis Desmond.

That was enough for Mrs. Jervis. But it was not enough for Frances, who found her mind wandering off from Rosalind's mother and looking for the word of words that would express her own meaning to her own satisfaction.

Her thoughts went on deep down under the stream of conversation that flowed through her from Mrs. Jervis on her right hand to Mrs. Vereker and Mrs. Norris on her left.

Veronica was good. But she was not wrapped up in other people's lives as Frances was wrapped up. She was wrapped up, not in herself, but in some life of her own that, as Frances made it out, had nothing in the world to do with anybody else's.

And yet Veronica knew what you were feeling and what you were thinking, and what you were going to do, and what was happening to you. (She had really known, in Dresden, what was happening to Nicky when Desmond made him marry her.) It was as if in her the walls that divide every soul from every other soul were made of some thin and porous stuff that let things through. And in this life of yours, for the moments that she shared it, she lived intensely, with uncanny delight and pain that were her own and not her own.

And Frances wanted some hard, tight theory that would reconcile these extremes of penetration and detachment.

She remembered that Ferdinand Cameron had been like that. He saw things. He was a creature of queer, sudden sympathies and insights. She supposed it was the Highland blood in both of them.

Mrs. Vereker on her right expressed the hope that Mr. Bartholomew was better. Frances said he never would be better till chemists were forbidden to advertise and the *British Medical Journal* and *The Lancet* were suppressed. Bartie would read them; and they supplied him with all sorts of extraordinary diseases.

She thought: Seeing things had not made poor Ferdie happy; and Veronica in her innermost life was happy. She had been happy when she came back from Germany, before she could have known that Nicky cared for her, before Nicky knew it himself.

Supposing she had known it all the time? But that, Frances said to herself, was nonsense. If she had known as much as all that, why should she have suffered so horribly that she had nearly died of it? Unless—supposing—it had been his suffering that she had nearly died of?

Mrs. Norris on her left was saying that she was sorry to see Mr. Maurice looking so sadly; and Frances heard herself replying that Morrie hadn't been fit for anything since he was in South Africa.

Between two pop-gun batteries of conversation the serious theme sustained itself. She thought: Then, Nicky *had* suffered. And Veronica was the only one who knew. She knew more about Nicky than Nicky's mother. This thought was disagreeable to Frances.

It was all nonsense. She didn't really believe that these things happened. Yet, why not? Michael said they happened. Even Dorothy, who didn't believe in God and immortality or anything, believed that.

She gave it up; it was beyond her; it bothered her.

"Yes. Seventy-nine her last birthday."

Mrs. Norris had said that Mrs. Fleming was wonderful.

Frances thought: "It's wonderful what Veronica does to them."

❧

The sets had changed. Nicholas and a girl friend of Veronica's played against George Vereker and Miss Lathom; John, with Mr. Jervis for his handicap, played against Anthony and Mr. Norris. The very young Norris fielded. All afternoon he had hoped to distinguish himself by catching some ball in full flight as it went "out." It was a pure and high ambition, for he knew he was so young and unimportant that only the eyes of God and of his mother watched him.

Michael had dropped out of it. He sat beside Dorothy under the tree of Heaven and watched Veronica.

"Veronica's wonderful," he said. "Did you see that?"

Dorothy had seen.

Veronica had kept Aunt Emmeline quiet all afternoon. She had made Bartie eat an ice under the impression that it would be good for him. And now she had gone with Morrie to the table where the drinks were, and had taken his third glass of champagne cup from him and made him drink lemonade instead.

"How does she do it?" said Michael.

"I don't know. She doesn't know herself. I used to think I could manage people, but I'm not in it with Ronny. She ought to be a wardress in a lunatic asylum."

"Now look at that!"

Veronica had returned to the group formed by Grannie and the Aunties and some strangers. The eyes of the four Fleming women had looked after her as she went from them; they looked towards her now as if some great need, some great longing were appeased by her return.

Grannie made a place by her side for the young girl; she took her arm, the young white arm, bare from the elbow in its short sleeve, and made it lie across her knees. From time to time Grannie's yellow, withered hand stroked the smooth, warm white arm, or held it. Emmeline and Edith squatted on the grass at Veronica's feet; their worn faces and the worn face of Louie looked at her. They hung on her, fascinated, curiously tranquillized, as if they drank from her youth.

"It's funny," Dorothy said, "when you think how they used to hate her."

"It's horrible," said Michael.

He got up and took Veronica away.

He was lying at her feet now on the grass in the far corner of the lawn under the terrace.

"Why do you go to them?" he said.

"Because they want me."

"You mustn't go when they want you. You mustn't let them get hold of you."

"They don't get hold of me—nothing gets hold of me. I want to help them. They say it does them good to have me with them."

"I should think it *did* do them good! They feed on you, Ronny. I can see it by the way they look at you. You'll die of them if you don't give it up."

"Give what up?"

"Your game of keeping them going. That is your game, isn't it? Everybody's saying how wonderful Grannie is. They mean she ought to have been dead years ago.

"They were all old, horribly old and done for, ages ago. I can remember them. But they know that if they can get a young virgin sacrificed to them they'll go on. *You're* the young virgin. *You're* making them go on."

"If I could—it wouldn't hurt me. Nothing hurts you, Michael, when you're happy. It's awful to think how they've lived without being happy, without loving.

"They used to hate me because I'm Vera's daughter. They don't hate me now."

"You don't hate what you feed on. You love it. They're vampires. They'll suck your life out of you. I wonder you're not afraid of them.

"*I'm* afraid of them. I always was afraid of them; when I was a kid and Mother used to send me with messages to that beastly spooky house they live in. I used to think it was poor old Grandpapa's ghost I funked. But I know now it wasn't. It was those four terrible women. *They're* ghosts. I thought you were afraid of ghosts."

"I'm much more afraid of you, when you're cruel. Can't you see how awful it must be for them to be ghosts? Ghosts among living people. Everybody afraid of them—not wanting them."

"Michael—it would be better to be dead!"

Towards the end of the afternoon Frances's Day changed its appearance and its character. In the tennis courts Michael's friends played singles with an incomparable fury, frankly rejecting the partners offered them and disdaining inferior antagonists; they played, Ellis against Mitchell and Monier-Owen against Nicholas.

They had arrived late with Vera and Lawrence Stephen.

It had come to that. Anthony and Frances found that they could not go on for ever refusing the acquaintance of the man who had done so much for Michael. Stephen's enthusiastic eulogy of Michael's Poems had made an end of that old animosity a year ago. Practically, they had had to choose between Bartie and Lawrence Stephen as the turning point of honour. Michael had made them see that it was possible to overvalue Bartie; also that it was possible to pay too high a price for a consecrated moral attitude. In all his life the wretched Bartie had never done a thing for any of them, whereas he, Michael, owed his rather extraordinary success absolutely to Lawrence Stephen. If the strike made his father bankrupt he would owe his very means of livelihood to Lawrence Stephen.

Besides, he liked Stephen, and it complicated things most frightfully to go on living in the same house with people who disliked him.

If, Michael said, they chose to dissociate themselves altogether from their eldest son and his career, very well. They could go on ignoring and tacitly insulting Mr. Stephen. He could understand their taking a consistently wrong-headed line like that; but so long as they had any regard, either for him or his career, he didn't see how they could very well keep it up any longer. He was sorry, of course, that his career had let them in for Stephen if they didn't like him; but there it was.

And beyond a doubt it was there.

"You might vindicate Bartie gloriously," Michael said, "by turning me out of the house and disinheriting me. But would it be worth while? I'm not asking you to condone Stephen's conduct—if you can't condone it; I'm asking you either to acknowledge *or* repudiate your son's debts.

"After all, if *he* can condone your beastly treatment of him—I wouldn't like him if he was the swine you think him."

And Anthony had appealed to Michael's mother.

To his "Well, Frances, what do you think? Ought we or oughtn't we?" she had replied: "I think we ought to stand solid behind Michael."

It was Michael's life that counted, for it was going on into a great future. Bartie would pass and Michael would remain.

Their nervous advances had ended in a complete surrender to Stephen's charm.

Vera and Stephen seemed to think that the way to show the sincerity and sweetness of their reconciliation was to turn up as often as possible on Frances's Day. They arrived always at the same hour, a little late; they came by the road and the front door, so that when Bartie saw them coming he could retreat through the garden door and the lane. The Flemings and the Jervises retreated with him; and presently, when it had had a good look at the celebrities, the rest of the party followed.

This Saturday Frances's Day dwindled and melted away and closed, after its manner; only Vera and Stephen lingered. They stayed on talking to Michael long after everybody else had gone.

Stephen said he had come to say good-bye to Michael's people and to make a proposal to Michael himself. He was going to Ireland.

Vera interrupted him with passion.

"He isn't. He hasn't any proposal to make. He hasn't come to say good-bye."

Her restless, unhappy eyes turned to him incessantly, as if, more than ever, she was afraid that he would escape her, that he would go off God knew where.

God knew where he was going, but Vera did not believe that he was going to Ireland. He had talked about going to Ireland for years, and he had never gone.

Stephen looked as if he did not see her; as if he did not even see Michael very distinctly.

"I'm going," he said, "to Ireland on Monday week, the third of August. I mayn't come back for long enough. I may not come back at all."

"That's the sort of thing he keeps on saying."

"I may not come back *at all*. So I want you to take over the *Review* for me. Ellis and my secretary will show you how it stands. You'll know what to do. I can trust you not to let it down."

"He doesn't mean what he says, Michael. He's only saying it to frighten me. He's been holding it over me for years.

"*Say* you'll have nothing to do with it. *Say* you won't touch his old *Review*."

"Could I go to Ireland for you?"

"You couldn't."

"Why not? What do you think you're going to do there?"

"I'm going to pull the Nationalists together, so that if there's civil war in Ireland, the Irish will have a chance to win. Thank God for Carson! He's given us the opportunity we wanted."

"Tell him he's not to go, Michael. He won't listen to me, but he'll mind what you say."

"I want to go instead of him."

"You can't go instead of me. Nobody can go instead of me."

"I can go with you."

"You can't."

"Larry, if you take Michael to Ireland, Anthony and Frances will never forgive you. *I'll* never forgive you."

"I'm not taking Michael to Ireland, I'm telling you. There's no reason why Michael should go to Ireland at all. It isn't *his* country."

"You needn't rub *that* in," said Michael.

"It isn't *yours*," said Vera. "Ireland doesn't want you. The Nationalists don't want you. You said yourself they've turned you out of Ireland. When you've lived in England all these years why should you go back to a place that doesn't want you?"

"Because if Carson gets a free hand I see some chance of Ireland being a free country."

Vera wailed and entreated. She said it showed how much he cared for her. It showed that he was tired of her. Why couldn't he say so and have done with it?

"It's not," she said, "as if you could really do anything. You're a dreamer. Ireland has had enough of dreamers."

And Stephen's eyes looked over her head, into the high branches of the tree of Heaven, as if he saw his dream shining clear through them like a moon.

The opportunist could see nothing but his sublime opportunity.

Michael went back with him to dine and talk it over.

There was to be civil war in Ireland then?

He thought: If only Lawrence would let him go with him. He wanted to go to Ireland. To join the Nationalists and fight for Ireland, fight for the freedom he was always dreaming about—*that* would be a fine thing. It would be a finer thing than writing poems about Ireland.

Lawrence Stephen went soberly and steadily through the affair of the *Review*, explaining things to Michael. He wanted this done, and this. And over and over again Michael's voice broke through his instructions. Why couldn't he go to Ireland instead of Lawrence? Or, if Lawrence wouldn't let him go instead of him, he might at least take him with him. He didn't want to stay at home editing the *Review*. Ellis or Mitchell or Monier-Owen would edit it better than he could. Even the wretched Wadham would edit it just as well. He wanted to go to Ireland and fight.

But Lawrence wouldn't let him go. He wasn't going to have the boy's blood on his hands. His genius and his youth were too precious.

Besides, Ireland was not his country.

It was past ten o'clock. Frances was alone in the drawing-room. She sat by the open window and waited and watched.

The quiet garden lay open to her sight. Only the inner end of the farther terrace, under the orchard wall, was hidden by a high screen of privet.

It seemed hours to Frances since she had seen Nicky and Veronica go down the lawn on to the terrace.

And then Anthony had gone out too. She was vexed with Anthony. She could see him sitting under his ash-tree, her tree of Heaven; his white shirt-front gave out an oblong gleam like phosphorous in the darkness under the tree. She was watching to see that he didn't get up and go on to the terrace.

Anthony had no business in the garden at all. He was catching cold in it. He had sneezed twice. She wanted Nicholas and Veronica to have the garden to themselves to-night, and the perfect stillness of the twilight to themselves, every tree and every little leaf and flower keeping quiet for them; and there was Anthony sneezing.

She was restless and impatient, as if she carried the burden of their passion in her own heart.

Presently she could bear it no longer. She got up and called to Anthony to come in. He came obediently.

"What are you thinking of," she said, "planting yourself out there and sneezing? I could see your shirt-front a mile off. It's indecent of you."

"Why indecent?"

"Because Nicky and Veronica are out there."

"I don't see them."

"Do you suppose they want you to see them?"

She turned the electric light on full, to make darkness of their twilight out there.

Nicky and Veronica talked together in the twilight, sitting on the seat under the orchard wall behind the privet screen. They did not see Anthony sitting under the ash-tree, they did not hear him, they did not hear Frances calling to him to come in. They were utterly unaware of Frances and Anthony.

"Ronny," he said, "did Michael say anything to you?"

"When?"

"This afternoon, when he made you come with him here?"

"How do you mean, 'say anything'?"

"You know what I mean."

"*Mick*?"

"Yes. Did he ask you to marry him?"

"No. He said a lot of funny things, but he didn't say that. He wouldn't."

"Why wouldn't he?"

"Because—he just wouldn't."

"Well, he says he understands you."

"Then," said Veronica conclusively, "of course he wouldn't."

"Yes; but he says *I* don't."

"Dear Nicky, you understand me when nobody else does. You always did."

"Yes, when we were kids. But supposing *now* I ever didn't, would it matter? You see, I'm stupid, and caring—caring awfully—might make me stupider. *Have* people got to understand each other?"

To that she replied astonishingly, "Are you quite sure you understand about Ferdie?"

"Ferdie?"

"Yes." She turned her face full to him. "I don't know whether you know about it. *I* didn't till Mother told me the other day. I'm Ferdie's daughter.

"*Did* you know?"

"Oh, Lord, yes. I've known it for—oh, simply ever so long."

"Who told you?"

"Dorothy, I think. But I guessed it because of something he said once about seeing ghosts."

"I wonder if you know how I feel about it? I want you to understand that. I'm not a bit ashamed of it. I'm proud. I'm *glad* I'm Ferdie's daughter, not Bartie's. … I'd take his name, so that everybody should know I was his daughter, only that I like Uncle Anthony's name best. I'm glad Mother loved him."

"So am I, Ronny. I know I shouldn't have liked Bartie's daughter. Bartie's daughter wouldn't have been you."

He took her in his arms and held her face against his face. And it was as if Desmond had never been.

A little while ago he had hated Desmond because she had come before Veronica; she had taken what belonged to Veronica, the first tremor of his passion, the irrecoverable delight and surprise. And now he knew that, because he had not loved her, she had taken nothing.

"Do you love me?"

"Do you love *me*?"

"You know I love you."

"You know. You know."

What they said was new and wonderful to them as if nobody before them had ever thought of it.

Yet that night, all over the Heath, in hollows under the birch-trees, and on beds of trampled grass, young lovers lay in each other's arms and said the same thing in the same words: "Do you love me?" "You know I love you!" over and over, in voices drowsy and thick with love.

"There's one thing I haven't thought of," said Nicky. "And that's that damned strike. If it hits Daddy badly we may have to wait goodness knows how long. Ages we may have to."

"I'd wait all my life if I could have you in the last five seconds of it. And if I couldn't, I'd still wait."

And presently Veronica remembered Michael.

"Why did you ask me whether Mick had said anything?"

"Because I thought you ought to know about it before you—Besides, if he *had*, we should have had to wait a bit before we told him."

It seemed that there was nothing to prevent them marrying to-morrow if they liked. The strike, Anthony said, couldn't hit him as badly as all that.

He and Frances sat up till long past midnight, talking about their plans, and the children's plans. It was all settled. The first week in August they would go down to Morfe for the shooting. They would stay there till the first week in September. Nicky and Veronica would be married the first week in October. And they would go to France and Belgium and Germany for their honeymoon.

XIX

They did not go down to Morfe the first week in August for the shooting.

Neither did Lawrence Stephen go to Ireland on Monday, the third. At the moment when he should have been receiving the congratulations of the Dublin Nationalists after his impassioned appeal for militant consolidation, Mr. Redmond and Sir Edward Carson were shaking hands dramatically in the House of Commons. Stephen's sublime opportunity, the civil war, had been snatched from him by the unforeseen.

And there was no chance of Nicky and Veronica going to Belgium and France and Germany for their honeymoon.

For within nine days of Frances's Day Germany had declared war on France and Russia, and was marching over the Belgian frontier on her way to Paris.

Frances, aroused at last to realization of the affairs of nations, asked, like several million women, "What does it mean?"

And Anthony, like several million men, answered, "It means Armageddon." Like several million people, they both thought he was saying something as original as it was impressive, something clear and final and descriptive.

"Armageddon!" Stolid, unimaginative people went about saying it to each other. The sound of the word thrilled them, intoxicated them, gave them an awful feeling that was at the same time, in some odd way, agreeable; it stirred them with a solemn and sombre passion. They said, "Armageddon. It means Armageddon." Yet nobody knew and nobody asked or thought of asking what Armageddon meant.

"Shall We come into it?" said Frances. She was thinking of the Royal Navy turning out to the last destroyer to save England from invasion; of the British Army most superfluously prepared to defend England from the invader, who, after all, could not invade; of Indian troops pouring into England if the worst came to the worst. She had the healthy British mind that refuses and always has refused to acknowledge the possibility of disaster. Yet she asked continually, "Would England be drawn in?" She was thankful that none of her sons had gone into the Army or the Navy. Whoever else was in, they would be out of it.

At first Anthony said, "No. Of course England wouldn't be drawn in."

Then, on the morning of England's ultimatum, the closing of the Stock Exchange and the Banks made him thoughtful, and he admitted that it looked as if England might be drawn in after all. The long day, without any business for him and Nicholas, disturbed him. There was a nasty, hovering smell of ruin in the air. But there was no panic. The closing of the Banks was only a wise precaution against panic. And by evening, as the tremendous significance of the ultimatum sank into him, he said definitively that England would not be drawn in.

Then Drayton, whom they had not seen for months (since he had had his promotion) telephoned to Dorothy to come and dine with him at his club in Dover Street. Anthony missed altogether the significance of *that*.

He had actually made for himself an after-dinner peace in which coffee could be drunk and cigarettes smoked as if nothing were happening to Europe.

"England," he said, "will not be drawn in, because her ultimatum will stop the War. There won't *be* any Armageddon."

"Oh, won't there!" said Michael. "And I can tell you there won't be much left of *us* after it's over."

He had been in Germany and he knew. He carried himself with a sort of stern haughtiness, as one who knew better than any of them. And yet his words conveyed no picture to his brain, no definite image of anything at all.

But in Nicholas's brain images gathered fast, one after another; they thickened; clear, vivid images with hard outlines. They came slowly but with order and precision. While the others talked he had been silent and very grave.

"*Some* of us'll be left," he said. "But it'll take us all our time."

Anthony looked thoughtfully at Nicholas. A sudden wave of realization beat up against his consciousness and receded.

"Well," he said, "we shall know at midnight."

An immense restlessness came over them.

At a quarter-past eight Dorothy telephoned from her club in Grafton Street. Frank had had to leave her suddenly. Somebody had sent for him. And if they wanted to see the sight of their lives they were to come into town at once. St. James's was packed with people from Whitehall to Buckingham Palace. It was like nothing on earth, and they mustn't miss it. She'd wait for them in Grafton Street till a quarter to nine, but not a minute later.

Nicky got out his big four-seater Morss car. They packed themselves into it, all six of them somehow, and he drove them into London. They had a sense of doing something strange and memorable and historic.

Dorothy, picked up at her club, showed nothing but a pleasurable excitement. She gave no further information about Frank. He had had to go off and see somebody. What did he think? He thought what he had always thought; only he wouldn't talk about it.

Dorothy was not inclined to talk about it either.

The Morss was caught in a line blocked at the bottom of Albemarle Street by two streams of cars, mixed with two streams of foot passengers, that poured steadily from Piccadilly into St. James's Street.

Michael and Dorothy got out and walked. Nicholas gave up his place to Anthony and followed with Veronica.

Their restlessness had been a part of the immense restlessness of the crowd. They were drawn, as the crowd was drawn; they went as the crowd went, up and down, restlessly, from Trafalgar Square and Whitehall to Buckingham Palace; from Buckingham Palace to Whitehall and Trafalgar Square. They drifted down Parliament Street to Westminster and back again. An hour ago the drifting, nebulous crowd had split, torn asunder between two attractions; its two masses had wheeled away, one to the east and the other to the west; they had gathered themselves together, one at each pole of the space it now traversed. The great meeting in Trafalgar Square balanced the multitude that had gravitated towards Buckingham Palace, to see the King and Queen come out on their balcony and show themselves to their people.

And as the edges of the two masses gave way, each broke and scattered, and was mixed again with the other. Like a flood, confined and shaken, it surged and was driven back and surged again from Whitehall to Buckingham Palace, from Buckingham Palace to Whitehall. It looked for an outlet in the narrow channels of the side-streets, or spread itself over the flats of the Green Park, only to return restlessly upon itself, sucked back by the main current in the Mall.

It was as if half London had met there for Bank Holiday. Part of this crowd was drunk; it was orgiastic; it made strange, fierce noises, like the noises of one enormous, mystically excited beast; here and there, men and women, with inflamed and drunken faces, reeled in each other's arms; they wore pink paper feathers in their hats. Some, only half intoxicated, flicked at each other with long streamers of pink and white paper, carried like scourges on small sticks. These were the inspired.

But the great body of the crowd was sober. It went decorously in a long procession, young men with their sweethearts, friends, brothers and sisters, husbands and wives, fathers and mothers with their children; none, or very few, went alone that night.

It was an endless procession of faces; grave and thoughtful faces; uninterested, respectable faces; faces of unmoved integrity; excited faces; dreaming, wondering, bewildered faces; faces merely curious, or curiously exalted, slightly ecstatic, open-mouthed, fascinated by each other and by the movements and the lights; laughing, frivolous faces, and faces utterly vacant and unseeing.

On every other breast there was a small Union Jack pinned; every other hand held and waggled a Union Jack. The Union Jack flew from the engine of every other automobile. In twelve hours, out of nowhere, thousands and thousands of flags sprang magically into being; as if for years London had been preparing for this day.

And in and out of this crowd the train of automobiles with their flags dashed up and down the Mall for hours, appearing and disappearing. Intoxicated youths with inflamed faces, in full evening dress, squatted on the roofs of taxi-cabs or rode astride on the engines of their cars, waving flags.

All this movement, drunken, orgiastic, somnambulistic, mysteriously restless, streamed up and down between two solemn and processional lines of lights, two solemn and processional lines of trees, lines that stretched straight from Whitehall to Buckingham Palace in a recurrent pattern of trees and lamps, dark trees, twilit trees, a lamp and a tree shining with a metallic unnatural green; and, at the end of the avenue, gilded gates and a golden-white façade.

The crowd was drifting now towards the Palace. Michael and Dorothea, Nicholas and Veronica, went with it. In this eternal perambulation they met people that they knew; Stephen and Vera; Mitchell, Monier-Owen; Uncle Morrie and his sisters. Anthony, looking rather solemn, drove past them in his car. It was like impossible, grotesque encounters in a dream.

Outside the Palace the crowd moved up and down without rest; it drifted and returned; it circled round and round the fountain. In the open spaces the intoxicated motor-cars and taxi-cabs darted and tore with the folly of moths and the fury of destroyers. They stung the air with their hooting. Flags, intoxicated flags, still hung from their engines. They came flying drunkenly out of the dark, like a trumpeting swarm of enormous insects, irresistibly, incessantly drawn to the lights of the Palace, hypnotized by the golden-white façade.

Suddenly, Michael's soul revolted.

"If this demented herd of swine is a great people going into a great war, God help us! Beasts—it's not as if *their* bloated skins were likely to be punctured."

He called back over his shoulders to the others.

"Let's get out of this. If we don't I shall be sick."

He took Dorothy by her arm and shouldered his way out.

The water had ceased playing in the fountain.

Nicholas and Veronica stood by the fountain. The water in the basin was green like foul sea-water. The jetsam of the crowd floated there. A small child leaned over the edge of the basin and fished for Union Jacks in the filthy pool. Its young mother held it safe by the tilted edge of its petticoats. She looked up at them and smiled. They smiled back again and turned away.

It was quiet on the south side by the Barracks. Small, sober groups of twos and threes strolled there, or stood with their faces pressed close against the railings, peering into the barrack yard. Motionless, earnest and attentive, they stared at the men in khaki moving about on the other side of the railings. They were silent, fascinated by the men in khaki. Standing safe behind the railing, they stared at them with an awful, sombre curiosity. And the men in khaki stared back, proud, self-conscious, as men who know that the hour is great and that it is their hour.

"Nicky," Veronica said, "I wish Michael wouldn't say things like that."

"He's dead right, Ronny. That isn't the way to take it, getting drunk and excited, and rushing about making silly asses of themselves. They *are* rather swine, you know."

"Yes; but they're pathetic. Can't you see how pathetic they are? Nicky, I believe I love the swine—even the poor drunken ones with the pink paper feathers—just because they're English; because awful things are going to happen to them, and they don't know it. They're English."

"You think God's made us all like that? He *hasn't*."

They found Anthony in the Mall, driving up and down, looking for them. He had picked up Dorothy and Aunt Emmeline and Uncle Morrie.

"We're going down to the Mansion House," he said, "to hear the Proclamation. Will you come?"

But Veronica and Nicholas were tired of crowds, even of historic crowds. Anthony drove off with his car-load, and they went home.

"I never saw Daddy so excited," Nicky said.

But Anthony was not excited. He had never felt calmer or cooler in his life.

He returned some time after midnight. By that time it had sunk into him. Germany *had* defied the ultimatum and England *had* declared war on Germany.

He said it was only what was to be foreseen. He had known all the time that it would happen—really.

The tension of the day of the ultimatum had this peculiar psychological effect that all over England people who had declared up to the last minute that there would be no War were saying the same thing as Anthony and believing it.

Michael was disgusted with the event that had put an end to the Irish Revolution. It was in this form that he conceived his first grudge against the War.

This emotion of his was like some empty space of horror opened up between him and Nicholas; Nicky being the only one of his family who was as yet aware of its existence.

For the next three days, Nicholas, very serious and earnest, shut himself up in his workshop at the bottom of the orchard and laboured there, putting the last touches to the final, perfect, authoritative form of the Moving Fortress, the joint creation of his brain and Drayton's, the only experiment that had survived the repeated onslaughts of the Major's criticism. The new model was three times the size of the lost original; it was less like a battleship and more like a racing-car and a destroyer. It was his and Drayton's last word on the subject of armaments.

It was going to the War Office, this time, addressed to the right person, and accompanied by all sorts of protective introductions, and Drayton blasting its way before it with his new explosive.

In those three days Nick found an immense distraction in his Moving Fortress. It also served to blind his family to his real intentions. He knew that his real intentions could not be kept from them very long. Meanwhile the idea that he was working on something made them happy. When Frances saw him in his overalls she smiled and said: "Nicky's got *his* job, anyhow." John came and looked at him through the window of the workshop and laughed.

"Good old Nicky," he said. "Doing his bit!"

In those three days John went about with an air of agreeable excitement. Or you came upon him sitting in solitary places like the dining-room, lost in happy thought. Michael said of him that he was unctuous. He exuded a secret joy and satisfaction. John had acquired a sudden remarkable maturity. He shone on each member of his family with benevolence and affection, as if he were its protector and consoler, and about to confer on it some tremendous benefit.

"Look at Don-Don," Michael said. "The bloodthirsty little brute. He's positively enjoying the War."

"You might leave me alone," said Don-Don. "I shan't have it to enjoy for long."

He was one of those who believed that the War would be over in four months.

Michael, pledged to secrecy, came and looked at the Moving Fortress. He was interested and intelligent; he admired that efficiency of Nicky's that was so unlike his own.

Yet, he wondered, after all, was it so unlike? He, too, was aiming at an art as clean and hard and powerful as Nicky's, as naked of all blazonry and decoration, an art which would attain its objective by the simplest, most perfect adjustment of means to ends.

And Anthony was proud of that hidden wonder locked behind the door of the workshop in the orchard. He realized that his son Nicholas had taken part in a great and important thing. He was prouder of Nicholas than he had been of Michael.

And Michael knew it.

Nicky's brains could be used for the service of his country.

But Michael's? Anthony said to himself that there wasn't any sense—any sense that he could endure to contemplate—in which Michael's brains could be of any use to his country. When Anthony thought of the mobilization of his family for national service, Michael and Michael's brains were a problem that he put behind him for the present and refused to contemplate. There would be time enough for Michael later.

Anthony was perfectly well aware of his own one talent, the talent which had made "Harrison and Harrison" the biggest timber-importing firm in England. If there was one thing he understood it was organization. If there was one thing he could not tolerate it was waste of good material, the folly of forcing men and women into places they were not fit for. He had let his eldest son slip out of the business without a pang, or with hardly any pang. He had only taken Nicholas into it as an experiment. It was on John that he relied to inherit it and carry it farther.

As a man of business he approved of the advertised formula: "Business as Usual." He understood it to mean that the duty which England expected every man to do was to stay in the place he was most fitted for and to go where he was most wanted. Nothing but muddle and disaster could follow any departure from this rule.

It was fitting that Frances and Veronica should do Red Cross work. It was fitting that Dorothy should help to organize the relief of the Belgium refugees. It was fitting that John should stay at home and carry on the business, and that he, Anthony, should enlist when he had settled John into his place. It was, above all, fitting that Nicky should devote himself to the invention and manufacture of armaments. He could not conceive anything more wantonly and scandalously wasteful than a system that could make any other use of Nicky's brains. He thanked goodness that, with a European War upon us, such a system, if it existed, would not be allowed to live a day.

As for Michael, it might be fitting later—very much later—perhaps. If Michael wanted to volunteer for the Army then, and if it were necessary, he would have no right to stop him. But it would not be necessary. England was going to win this War on the sea and not on land. Michael was practically safe.

And behind Frances's smile, and John's laughter, and Michael's admiration, and Anthony's pride there was the thought: "Whatever happens, Nicky will be safe."

And the model of the Moving Fortress was packed up—Veronica and Nicky packed it—and it was sent under high protection to the War Office. And Nicky unlocked the door of his workshop and rested restlessly from his labour.

And there was a call for recruits, and for still more recruits.

Westminster Bridge became a highway for regiments marching to battle. The streets were parade-grounds for squad after squad of volunteers in civilian clothes, self-conscious and abashed under the eyes of the men in khaki.

❧

And Michael said: "This is the end of all the arts. Artists will not be allowed to exist except as agents for the recruiting sergeant. *We*'re dished."

That was the second grudge he had against the War. It killed the arts in the very hour of their renaissance. "Eccentricities" by Morton Ellis, with illustrations by Austin Mitchell, and the "New Poems" of Michael Harrison, with illustrations by Austin Mitchell, were to have come out in September. But it was not conceivable that they should come out.

At the first rumour of the ultimatum Michael and Ellis had given themselves up for lost.

❧

Liège fell and Namur was falling.

And the call went on for recruits, and for still more recruits. And Nicky in five seconds had destroyed his mother's illusions and the whole fabric of his father's plans.

It was one evening when they were in the drawing-room, sitting up after Veronica had gone to bed.

"I hope you won't mind, Father," he said; "but I'm going to enlist to-morrow."

He did not look at his father's face. He looked at his mother's. She was sitting opposite him on the couch beside Dorothy. John balanced himself on the head of the couch with his arm round his mother's shoulder. Every now and then he stooped down and rubbed his cheek thoughtfully against her hair.

A slight tremor shook her sensitive, betraying upper lip; then she looked back at Nicholas and smiled.

Dorothy set her mouth hard, unsmiling.

Anthony had said nothing. He stared before him at Michael's foot, thrust out and tilted by the crossing of his knees. Michael's foot, with its long, arched instep, fascinated Anthony. He seemed to be thinking: "If I look at it long enough I may forget what Nicky has said."

"I hope you won't mind, Father; but I'm enlisting too."

John's voice was a light, high echo of Nicky's.

With a great effort Anthony roused himself from his contemplation of Michael's foot.

"I—can't—see—that my minding—or not minding—has anything—to do—with it."

He brought his words out slowly and with separate efforts, as if they weighed heavily on his tongue. "We've got to consider what's best for the country all round, and I doubt if either of you is called upon to go."

"*Some* of us have got to go," said Nicky.

"Quite so. But I don't think it ought to be you, Nicky; or John, either."

"I suppose," said Michael, "you mean it ought to be me."

"I don't mean anything of the sort. One out of four's enough."

"One out of four? Well then—"

"That only leaves me to fight," said Dorothy.

"I wasn't thinking of you, Michael. Or of Dorothy."

They all looked at him where he sat, upright and noble, in his chair, and most absurdly young.

Dorothy said under her breath: "Oh, you darling Daddy."

"*You* won't be allowed to go, anyhow," said John to his father. "You needn't think it."

"Why not?"

"Well—." He hadn't the heart to say: "Because you're too old."

"Nicky's brains will be more use to the country than my old carcass."

Nicky thought: "You're the very last of us that can be spared." But he couldn't say it. The thing was so obvious. All he said was: "It's out of the question, your going."

"Old Nicky's out of the question, if you like," said John. "He's going to be married. He ought to be thinking of his wife and children."

"Of course he ought," said Anthony. "Whoever goes first, it isn't Nicky."

"*You* ought to think of Mummy, Daddy ducky; and you ought to think of *us*," said Dorothy.

"I," said John, "haven't got anybody to think of. I'm not going to be married, and I haven't any children."

"*I* haven't got a wife and children yet," said Nicky.

"You've got Veronica. You ought to think of her."

"I am thinking of her. You don't suppose Veronica'd stop me if I wanted to go? Why, she wouldn't look at me if I didn't want to go."

Suddenly he remembered Michael.

"I mean," he said, "after my *saying* that I was going."

Their eyes met. Michael's flickered. He knew that Nicky was thinking of him.

"Then Ronny knows?" said Frances.

"Of course she knows. *You* aren't going to try to stop me, Mother?"

"No," she said. "I'm not going to try to stop you—this time."

She thought: "If I hadn't stopped him seven years ago, he would be safe now, with the Army in India."

One by one they got up and said "Good-night" to each other.

But Nicholas came to Michael in his room.

He said to him: "I say, Mick, don't you worry about not enlisting. At any rate, *not yet*. Don't worry about Don and Daddy. They won't take Don because he's got a mitral murmur in his heart that he doesn't know about. He's going to be jolly well sold, poor chap. And they won't take the guv'nor because he's too old; though the dear old thing thinks he can bluff them into it because he doesn't look it.

"And look here—don't worry about me. As far as I'm concerned, the War's a blessing in disguise. I always wanted to go into the Army. You know how I loathed it when they went and stopped me. Now I'm going in and nobody—not even mother—really wants to keep me out. Soon they'll all be as pleased as Punch about it.

"And I sort of know how you feel about the War. You don't want to stick bayonets into German tummies, just *because* they're so large and oodgy. You'd think of that first and all the time and afterwards. And I shan't think of it at all.

"Besides, you disapprove of the War for all sorts of reasons that I can't get hold of. But it's like this—you couldn't respect yourself if you went into it; and I couldn't respect myself if I stayed out."

"I wonder," Michael said, "if you really see it."

"Of course I see it. That's the worst of you clever writing chaps. You seem to think nobody can ever see anything except yourselves."

When he had left him Michael thought: "I wonder if he really does see? Or if he made it all up?"

They had not said to each other all that they had really meant. Of Nicky's many words there were only two that he remembered vividly, "Not yet."

Again he felt the horror of the great empty space opened up between him and Nicky, deep and still and soundless, but for the two words: "Not yet."

XX

It was as Nicholas had said. Anthony and John were rejected; Anthony on account of his age, John because of the mitral murmur that he didn't know about.

The guv'nor had lied, John said, like a good 'un; swore he was under thirty-five and stuck to it. He might have had a chance if he'd left it at that, because he looked a jolly sight better than most of 'em when he was stripped. But they'd given him so good an innings that the poor old thing got above himself, and spun them a yarn about his hair having gone grey from a recent shock. That dished him. They said they knew that sort of hair; they'd been seeing a lot of it lately.

Anthony was depressed. He said bitter things about "red tape," and declared that if that was the way things were going to be managed it was a bad look-out for the country. John was furious. He said the man who examined him was a blasted idiot who didn't know his own rotten business. He'd actually had the beastly cheek to tell him they didn't want him dropping down dead when he went into action, or fainting from sheer excitement after they'd been to the trouble and expense of training him. As if he'd be likely to do a damn silly thing like that. He'd never been excited in his life. It was enough to *give* him heart-disease.

So John and Anthony followed the example of their women, and joined the ambulance classes of the Red Cross. And presently they learned to their disgust that, though they might possibly be accepted as volunteers for Home Service, their disabilities would keep them for ever from the Front.

At this point Anthony's attention was diverted to his business by a sudden Government demand for timber. As he believed that the War would be over in four months he did not, at first, realize the personal significance of this. Still, there could be no doubt that its immediate message for him was that business must be attended to. He had not attended to it many days before he saw that his work for his country lay there under his hand—in his offices and his stackyards and factories. He sighed and sat down to it, and turned his back resolutely on the glamour of the Front. The particular business in hand had great issues and a fascination of its own.

And his son John sat down to it beside him, with a devoted body and a brain alive to the great issues, but with an ungovernable and abstracted soul.

And Nicky, a recruit in Kitchener's Army, went rapidly through the first courses of his training; sleeping under canvas; marching in sun and wind and rain; digging trenches, ankle-deep, waist high, breast high in earth, till his clear skin grew clearer, and his young, hard body harder every day.

And every day the empty spiritual space between him and Michael widened.

With the exception of Michael and old Mrs. Fleming, Anthony's entire family had offered itself to its country; it was mobilized from Frances and Anthony down to the very Aunties. In those days there were few Red Cross volunteers who were not sure that sooner or later they would be sent to the Front. Their only fear was that they might not be trained and ready when the moment of the summons came. Strong young girls hustled for the best places at the ambulance classes. Fragile, elderly women, twitching with nervous anxiety, contended with these remorseless ones and were pushed to the rear. Yet they went on contending, sustained by their extraordinary illusion.

Aunt Louie, displaying an unexpected and premature dexterity with bandages, was convinced that she would be sent to the Front if nobody else was. Aunt Emmeline and Aunt Edith, in states of cerebral excitement, while still struggling to find each other's arteries, declared that they were going to the Front. They saw no earthly reason why they should not go there. Uncle Maurice haunted the Emergency class-rooms at the Polytechnic, wearing an Esmarch triangular bandage round his neck, and volunteered as an instructor. He got mixed up with his bandages, and finally consented to the use of his person as a lay-figure for practical demonstrations while he waited for his orders to go to the Front.

They forebore to comment on the palpable absurdity of each other's hopes.

For, with the first outbreak of the War, the three Miss Flemings had ceased from mutual recrimination. They were shocked into a curious gentleness to each other. Every evening the old schoolroom (Michael's study) was turned into a Red Cross demonstration hall, and there the queer sight was to be seen of Louie, placable and tender, showing Edith over and over again how to adjust a scalp bandage on Emmeline's head, and of Emmeline motionless for hours under Edie's little, clumsy, pinching fingers. It was thus, with small vibrations of tenderness and charity, that they responded to the vast rhythm of the War.

And Grannie, immutable in her aged wisdom and malevolence, pushed out her lower lip at them.

"If you three would leave off that folly and sit down and knit, you might be some use," said Grannie. "Kitchener says that if every woman in England knitted from morning till night he wouldn't have enough socks for his Army."

Grannie knitted from morning till night. She knitted conspicuously, as a protest against bandage practice; giving to her soft and gentle action an air of energy inimical to her three unmarried daughters. And not even Louie had the heart to tell her that all her knitting had to be unravelled overnight, to save the wool.

"A set of silly women, getting in Kitchener's way, and wasting khaki!"

Grannie behaved as if the War were her private and personal affair, as if Kitchener were her right-hand man, and all the other women were interfering with them.

Yet it looked as if all the women would be mobilized before all the men. The gates of Holloway were opened, and Mrs. Blathwaite and her followers received a free pardon on their pledge to abstain from violence during the period of the War. And instantly, in the first week of war, the Suffrage Unions and Leagues and Societies (already organized and disciplined by seven years' methodical resistance) presented their late enemy, the Government, with an instrument of national service made to its hand and none the worse because originally devised for its torture and embarrassment.

The little vortex of the Woman's Movement was swept without a sound into the immense vortex of the War. The women rose up all over England and went into uniform.

And Dorothea appeared one day wearing the khaki tunic, breeches and puttees of the Women's Service Corps. She had joined a motor-ambulance as chauffeur, driving the big Morss car that Anthony had given to it. Dorothea really had a chance of being sent to Belgium before the end of the month. Meanwhile she convoyed Belgian refugees from Cannon Street Station.

She saw nothing before her as yet. Her mind was like Cannon Street Station—a dreadful twilit terminus into which all the horror and misery of Belgium poured and was congested.

Cannon Street Station. Presently it was as if she were spending all of her life that counted there; as if for years she had been familiar with the scene.

Arch upon iron arch, and girder after iron girder holding up the blurred transparency of the roof. Iron rails running under the long roof, that was like the roof of a tunnel open at one end. By day a greyish light, filtered through smoke and grit and steam. Lamps, opaque white globes, hanging in the thick air like dead moons. By night a bluish light, and large, white globes grown opalescent like moons, lit again to a ghastly, ruinous life.

The iron breasts of engines, huge and triumphant, advancing under the immense fanlight of the open arch. Long trains of carriages packed tight with packages with, enormous bundles; human heads appearing, here and there, above the swollen curves of the bundles; human bodies emerging in the struggle to bring forth the bundles through the narrow doors.

For the first few weeks the War meant to Dorothea, not bleeding wounds and death, but just these train-loads of refugees—just this one incredible spectacle of Belgium pouring itself into Cannon Street Station. Her clear hard mind tried and failed to grasp the sequences of which the final act was the daily unloading of tons of men, women and children on Cannon Street platform. Yesterday they were staggering under those bundles along their straight, flat roads between the everlasting rows of poplars; their towns and villages flamed and smoked behind them; some of them, goaded like tired cattle, had felt German bayonets at their backs—yesterday. And this morning they were here, brave and gay, smiling at Dorothea as she carried their sick on her stretcher and their small children in her arms.

And they were still proud of themselves.

A little girl tripped along the platform, carrying in one hand a large pasteboard box covered with black oilcloth, and in the other a cage with a goldfinch in it. She looked back at Dorothea and smiled, proud of herself because she had saved her goldfinch. A Belgian boy carried a paralysed old man on his shoulders. He grinned at Dorothea, proud of himself because he had saved his grandfather. A young Flemish peasant woman pushed back the shawl that covered her baby's face to show her how pretty he was; she laughed because she had borne him and saved him.

And there were terrible things significant of yesterday. Women and girls idiotic with outrage and grief. A young man lamed in trying to throw himself into a moving train because he thought his lost mother was in it. The ring screening the agony of a woman giving birth to her child on the platform. A death in the train; stiff, upturned feet at the end of a stretcher that the police-ambulance carried away.

And as Dorothea drove her car-loads of refugees day after day in perfect safety, she sickened with impatience and disgust. Safety was hard and bitter to her. Her hidden self was unsatisfied; it had a monstrous longing. It wanted to go where the guns sounded and the shells burst, and the villages flamed and smoked; to go along the straight, flat roads between the poplars where the refugees had gone, so that her nerves and flesh should know and feel their suffering and their danger. She was not feeling anything now except the shame of her immunity.

She thought: "I can't look at a Belgian woman without wishing I were dead. I shall have no peace till I've gone."

Her surface self was purely practical. She thought: "If I were in Belgium I could get them out of it quicker than they could walk."

Dorothea could bring all her mind to bear on her Belgians, because it was at ease about her own people. They, at any rate, were safe. Her father and poor Don were out of it. Michael was not in it—yet; though of course he would be in it some time. She tried not to think too much about Michael. Nicky was safe for the next six months. And Frank was safe. Frank was training recruits. He had told her he might be kept indefinitely at that infernal job. But for that he would be fighting now. He wanted her to be sorry for him; and she was sorry for him. And she was glad too.

One afternoon, late in August, she had come home, to sleep till dinner-time between her day's work and her night's work, when she found him upstairs in her study. He had been there an hour waiting for her by himself. The others were all at bandage practice in the schoolroom.

"I hope you don't mind," he said. "Your mother told me to wait up here."

She had come in straight from the garage; there was a light fur of dust on her boots and on the shoulders of her tunic, and on her face and hair. Her hands were black with oil and dirt from her car.

He looked at her, taking it all in: the khaki uniform (it was the first time he had seen her in it), the tunic, breeches and puttees, the loose felt hat turned up at one side, its funny, boyish chin-strap, the dust and dirt of her; and he smiled. His smile had none of the cynical derision which had once greeted her appearances as a militant suffragist.

"And yet," she thought, "if he's consistent, he ought to loathe me now."

"Dorothea. Going to the War," he said.

"Not *yet*—worse luck."

"Are you going as part of the Canadian contingent from overseas, or what?"

"I wish I was. Do you think they'd take me if I cut my hair off?"

"They might. They might do anything. This is a most extraordinary war."

"It's a war that makes it detestable to be a woman."

"I thought—" For a moment his old ungovernable devil rose in him.

"What did you think?"

"No matter. That's all ancient history. I say, you look like business. Do you really mean it? Are you really going to Flanders?"

"Do you suppose any woman would go and get herself up like this if she wasn't going *some*where?"

He said (surprisingly), "I don't see what's wrong with it." And then: "It makes you look about eighteen."

"That's because you can't see my face for the dirt."

"For the chin-strap, you mean. Dorothy—do you realize that you're not eighteen? You're eight-and-twenty."

"I do," she said. "But I rather hoped you didn't; or that if you did, you wouldn't say so."

"I realize that I'm thirty-eight, and that between us we've made a pretty mess of each other's lives."

"Have I made a mess of *your* life?'

"A beastly mess."

"I'm sorry. I wouldn't have done it for the world if I'd known. You know I wouldn't.

"But one doesn't know things."

"One doesn't if one's Dorothea. One knows some things awfully well; but not the things that matter."

"Well—but what could I do?" she said.

"You could have done what you can do now. You could have married me. And we would have had three years of each other."

"You mean three centuries. There *was* a reason why we couldn't manage it."

"There wasn't a reason. There isn't any reason now.

"Look here—to-day's Wednesday. Will you marry me on Friday if I get leave and a licence and fix it up to-morrow? We shall have three days."

"Three days." She seemed to be saying to herself that for three days—No, it wasn't worth while.

"Well, three months perhaps. Perhaps six, if my rotten luck doesn't change. Because, I'm doing my level best to make it change. So, you see, it's got to be one thing or another."

And still she seemed to be considering: Was it or was it not worth while?

"For God's sake don't say you're going to make conditions. There really isn't time for it. You can think what you like and say what you like and do what you like, and wear anything—wear a busby—I shan't care if you'll only marry me."

"Yes. That's the way you go on. And yet you don't say you love me. You never have said it. You—you're leaving me to do all that."

"Why—what else have I been doing for seven years? Nine years—ten years?"

"Nothing. Nothing at all. You just seem to think that I can go off and get married to a man without knowing whether he cares for me or not.

"And now it's too late. My hands are all dirty. So's my face—filthy—you mustn't—"

"I don't care. They're your hands. It's your face. I don't care."

The chin-strap, the absurd chin-strap, fretted his mouth. He laughed. He said, "She takes her hat off when she goes into a scrimmage, and she keeps it on *now*!"

She loosened the strap, laughing, and threw her hat, the hat of a Canadian trooper, on to the floor. His mouth moved over her face, over her hair, pressing hard into their softness; his arms clasped her shoulders; they slipped to her waist; he strained her slender body fast to him, straight against his own straightness, till the passion and the youth she had denied and destroyed shook her.

He said to himself, "She *shall* come alive. She *shall* feel. She *shall want* me. I'll make her. I should have thought of this ten years ago."

Her face was smooth; it smiled under the touch of his mouth and hands. And fear came with her passion. She thought, "Supposing something happens before Friday. If I could only give myself to him now—to-night."

Then, very gently and very tenderly, he released her, as if he knew what she was thinking. He was sorry for her and afraid. Poor Dorothy, who had made such a beastly mess of it, who had come alive so late.

She thought, "But—he wouldn't take me that way. He'd loathe me if he knew."

Yet surely there was the same fear in his eyes as he looked at her?

❧

They were sitting beside each other now, talking quietly. Her face and hands were washed clean; as clean, she said, as they ever would be.

"When I think," he said, "of the years we've wasted. I wonder if there was anything that could have prevented it."

"Only your saying what you've said now. That it didn't matter—that it made no difference to you what I did. But, you see, it made all the difference. And there we were."

"It didn't—really."

She shook her head. "We thought it did."

"No. Do you remember that morning I fetched you from Holloway?

"Yes." And she said as he had said then, "I don't want to talk about it. I don't want to think about it—except that it was dear of you."

"And yet it was from that morning—from five-thirty a.m.—that we seemed to go wrong.

"There's something I wanted most awfully to say, if you could stand going back to it for just one second. Do you remember saying that I didn't care? That I never thought of you when you were in prison or wondered what you were feeling? *That's* what put me off. It hurt so atrociously that I couldn't say anything.

"It wasn't true that I didn't think about you. I thought about nothing else when I wasn't working; I nearly went off my head with thinking.

"And you said I didn't listen to what you told me. That wasn't true. I was listening like anything."

"Darling—what did I tell you?"

"Oh—about the thing you called your experience, or your adventure, or something."

"My adventure?"

"That's what you called it. A sort of dream you had in prison. I couldn't say anything because I was stupid. It was beyond me. It's beyond me now."

"Never mind my adventure. What *does* it matter?"

"It matters awfully. Because I could see that it meant something big and important that I couldn't get the hang of. It used to bother me. I kept on trying to get it, and not getting it."

"You poor dear! And I've forgotten it. It did feel frightfully big and important and real at the time. And now it's as if it had happened to somebody else—to Veronica or somebody—not me."

"It was much more like Veronica. I do understand the rest of that business. Now, I mean. I own I didn't at the time."

"It's all over, Frank, and forgotten. Swallowed up in the War."

"*You*'re not swallowed up."

"Perhaps I shall be."

"Well, if you are—if I am—all the more reason why I want you to know that I understand what you were driving at. It was this way, wasn't it? You'd got to fight, just as I've got to fight. You couldn't keep out of it any more than I can keep out of this War."

"You couldn't stay out just for me any more than I can stay out for just you."

"And in a sort of way I'm in it for you. And in a sort of way you were in it—in that damnable suffrage business—for me."

"How clever of you," she said, "to see it!"

"I didn't see it then," he said simply, "because there wasn't a war on. We've both had to pay for my stupidity."

"And mine. And my cowardice. I ought to have trusted you to see, or risked it. We should have had three—no, two—years."

"Well, anyhow, we've got this evening."

"We haven't. I've got to drive Belgians from nine till past midnight."

"We've got Friday. Suppose they'll give me leave to get married in. I say—how about to-morrow evening?"

"I can't. Yes, I can. At least, I shall. There's a girl I know who'll drive for me. They'll have to give me leave to get married in, too."

She thought: "I can't go to Flanders now, unless he's sent out. If he *is*, nothing shall stop me but his coming back again."

It seemed to her only fair and fitting that they should snatch at their happiness and secure it, before their hour came.

She tried to turn her mind from the fact that at Mons the British line was being pressed back and back. It would recover. Of course it would recover. We always began like that. We went back to go forwards faster, when we got into our stride.

The next evening, Thursday, the girl she knew drove for Dorothea.

When Frances was dressing for dinner her daughter came to her with two frocks over her arm.

"Mummy ducky," she said, "I think my head's going. I can't tell whether to wear the white thing or the blue thing. And I feel as if it mattered more than anything. More than anything on earth."

Frances considered it—Dorothea in her uniform, and the white frock and the blue frock.

"It doesn't matter a little bit," she said. "If he could propose to you in that get-up—"

"Can't you see that I want to make up for *that* and for all the things he's missed, the things I haven't given him. If only I was as beautiful as you, Mummy, it wouldn't matter."

"My dear—my dear—"

Dorothy had never been a pathetic child—not half so pathetic as Nicky with his recklessness and his earache—but this grown-up Dorothy in khaki breeches, with her talk about white frocks and blue frocks, made Frances want to cry.

Frank was late. And just before dinner he telephoned to Dorothy that he couldn't be with her before nine and that he would only have one hour to give her.

Frances and Anthony looked at each other. But Dorothy looked at Veronica.

"What's the matter, Ronny? You look simply awful."

"Do I? My head's splitting. I think I'll go and lie down."

"You'd better."

"Go straight to bed," said Frances, "and let Nanna bring you some hot soup."

But Veronica did not want Nanna and hot soup. She only wanted to take herself and her awful look away out of Dorothy's sight.

"Well," said Anthony, "if she's going to worry herself sick about Nicky *now*—"

Frances knew that she was not worrying about Nicky.

❦

It was nine o'clock.

At any minute now Frank might be there. Dorothy thought: "Supposing he hasn't got leave?" But she knew that was not likely. If he hadn't got leave he would have said so when he telephoned.

The hour that was coming had the colour of yesterday. He would hold her in his arms again till she trembled, and then he would be afraid, and she would be afraid, and he would let her go.

The bell rang, the garden gate swung open; his feet were loud and quick on the flagged path of the terrace. He came into the room to them, holding himself rather stiffly and very upright. His eyes shone with excitement. He laughed the laugh she loved, that narrowed his eyes and jerked his mouth slightly crooked.

They all spoke at once. "You've got leave?" "*He's* got it all right." "What kept you?" "You *have* got leave?"

His eyes still shone; his mouth still jerked, laughing.

"Well, no," he said. "That's what I haven't got. In fact, I'm lucky to be here at all."

Nanna came in with the coffee. He took his cup from her and sat down on the sofa beside Frances, stirring his coffee with his spoon, and smiling as if at something pleasant that he knew, something that he would tell them presently when Nanna left the room.

The door closed softly behind her. He seemed to be listening intently for the click of the latch.

"Funny chaps," he said meditatively. "They keep putting you off till you come and tell them you want to get married to-morrow. Then they say they're sorry, but your marching orders are fixed for that day.

"Twelve hours isn't much notice to give a fellow."

He had not looked at Dorothy. He had not spoken to her. He was speaking to Anthony and John and Frances who were asking questions about trains and boats and his kit and his people. He looked as if he were not conscious of Dorothy's eyes fixed on him as he sat, slowly stirring his coffee without drinking it. The vibration of her nerves made his answers sound muffled and far-off.

She knew that her hour was dwindling slowly, wasting, passing from her minute by minute as they talked. She had an intolerable longing to be alone with him, to be taken in his arms; to feel what she had felt yesterday. It was as if her soul stood still there, in yesterday, and refused to move on into to-day.

Yet she was glad of their talking. It put off the end. When they stopped talking and got up and left her alone with him, that would be the end.

Suddenly he looked straight at her. His hands trembled. The cup he had not drunk from rattled in its saucer. It seemed to Dorothea that for a moment the whole room was hushed to listen to that small sound. She saw her mother take the cup from him and set it on the table.

One by one they got up, and slunk out of the room, as if they were guilty, and left her alone with him.

It was not like yesterday. He did not take her in his arms. He sat there, looking at her rather anxiously, keeping his distance. He seemed to be wondering how she was going to take it.

He thought: "I've made a mess of it again. It wasn't fair to make her want me—when I might have known. I ought to have left it."

And suddenly her soul swung round, released from yesterday.

She knew what he had wanted yesterday: that her senses should be ready to follow where her heart led. But that was not the readiness he required from her to-day; rather it was what his anxious eyes implored her to put away from her.

There was something more.

He wasn't going to say the obvious things, the "Well, this is hard luck on both of us. You must be brave. Don't make it too hard for me." (She could have made it intolerable.) It wasn't that. He knew she was brave; he knew she wouldn't make it hard for him; he knew he hadn't got to say the obvious things.

There was something more; something tremendous. It came to her with the power and sweetness of first passion; but without its fear. She no longer wanted him to take her in his arms and hold her as he had held her yesterday. Her swinging soul was steady; it vibrated to an intenser rhythm.

She knew nothing now but that what she saw was real, and that they were seeing it together. It was Reality itself. It was more than they. When realization passed it would endure.

Never as long as they lived would they be able to speak of it, to say to each other what it was they felt and saw.

❦

He said, "I shall have to go soon."

And she said, "I know. Is there anything I can do?"

"I wish you'd go and see my mother some time. She'd like it."

"I should love to go and see her. What else?"

"Well—I've no business to ask you, but I wish you'd give it up."

"I'll give anything up. But what?"

"That ambulance of yours that's going to get into the firing line."

"Oh—"

"I know why you want to get there. You want to tackle the hardest and most dangerous job. Naturally. But it won't make it easier for *us* to win the War. You can't expect us to fight so comfy, and to be killed so comfy, if we know our womenkind are being pounded to bits in the ground we've just cleared. If I thought *you* were knocking about anywhere there—"

"It would make it too hard?"

"It would make me jumpy. The chances are I shouldn't have much time to think about it, but when I did—"

"You'd think 'She might have spared me *that*.'"

"Yes. And you might think of your people. It's bad enough for them, Nicky going."

"It isn't only that I'd have liked to be where you'll be, and where he'll be. That was natural."

"It's also natural that we should like to find you here when we come back."

"I was thinking of those Belgian women, and the babies—and England; so safe, Frank; so disgustingly safe."

"*I* know. Leaving the children in the burning house?"

(She had said that once and he had remembered.)

"You can do more for them by staying in England—I'm asking you to take the hardest job, really."

"It isn't; if it's what you want most."

He had risen. He was going. His hands were on her shoulders, and they were still discussing it as if it were the most momentous thing.

"Of course," she said, "I won't go if you feel like that about it. I want you to fight comfy. You mustn't worry about me."

"Nor you about *me*. I shall be all right. Remember—it's *your* War, too—it's the biggest fight for freedom—"

"I know," she said.

And then: "Have you got all your things?"

"Somebody's got 'em."

"I haven't given you anything. You must have my wrist-watch."

She unstrapped the leather band and put it on him.

"My wrist's a whopper."

"So's mine. It'll just meet—at the last hole. It's phosphorous," she said. "You can see the time by it in the dark."

"I've nothing for *you*. Except—" he fumbled in his pockets—"I say—here's the wedding-ring."

They laughed.

"What more could you want?" she said.

He put it on her finger; she raised her face to him and he stooped and kissed her. He held her for a minute in his arms. But it was not like yesterday.

Suddenly his face stiffened. "Tell them," he said, "that I'm going."

The British were retreating from Mons.

The German attack was not like the advance of an Army but like the travelling of an earthquake, the bursting of a sea-wall. There was no end to the grey battalions, no end to the German Army, no end to the German people. And there was no news of British reinforcements, or rumour of reinforcements.

"They come on like waves. Like waves," said Dorothea, reading from the papers.

"I wouldn't read about it if I were you, darling," said Frances.

"Why not? It isn't going to last long. We'll rally. See if we don't."

Dorothea's clear, hard mind had gone under for the time, given way before that inconceivable advance. She didn't believe in the retreat from Mons. It couldn't go on. Reinforcements had been sent.

Of course they had been sent. If Frank was ordered off at twelve hours' notice that meant reinforcements, or there wouldn't be any sense in it. They would stop the retreat. We were sitting here, safe; and the least we could do for *them* was to trust them, and not believe any tales of their retreating.

And all the time she wondered how news of him would come. By wire? By letter? By telephone? She was glad that she hadn't got to wait at home, listening for the clanging of the garden gate, the knock, the ringing of the bell.

She waited five days. And on the evening of the sixth day the message came from his mother to her mother: "Tell your dear child for me that my son was killed five days ago, in the retreat from Mons. And ask her to come and see me; but not just yet."

She had enclosed copies of the official telegram; and the letter from his Colonel.

After Mons, the siege of Antwerp. The refugees poured into Cannon Street Station.

Dorothea tried hard to drown her grief in the grief of Belgium. But she could not drown it. She could only poison it with thoughts that turned it into something more terrible than grief. They came to her regularly, beginning after midnight, when she lay in bed and should have slept, worn out with her hard day's driving.

She thought: "I could bear it if I hadn't wasted the time we might have had together. All those years—like a fool—over that silly suffrage.

"I could bear it if I hadn't been cruel to him. I talked to him like a brute and an idiot. I told him he didn't care for freedom. And he's died for it. He remembered that. It was one of the last things he remembered. He said, 'It's *your* War—it's the biggest fight for freedom.' And he's killed in it.

"I could bear it if I'd given myself to him that night—even for one night.

"How do you know he'd have loathed it? I ought to have risked it. I was a coward. He got nothing."

His persistent image in her memory tortured her. It was an illusion that prolonged her sense of his material presence, urging it towards a contact that was never reached. Death had no power over this illusion. She could not see Drayton's face, dead among the dead.

Obsessed by her illusion she had lost her hold on the reality that they had seen and felt together. All sense of it was gone, as if she had dreamed it or made it up.

Presently she would not have her work to keep her from thinking. The Ambulance Corps was going out to Flanders at the end of September, and it would take her car with it and a new driver.

Frances's heart ached when she looked at her.

"If I could only help you."

"You can't, Mummy ducky," she would say. And she would get up and leave the room where Frances was. Sometimes she would go to Veronica; but more often she hid away somewhere by herself.

Frances thought: "She is out of my reach. I can't get at her. She'll go to anybody rather than to me. It used to be Rosalind. Now it's Veronica."

But Dorothy could not speak about Drayton to her mother.

Only to Veronica, trying to comfort her, she said, "I could bear it if he'd been killed in an attack. But to go straight, like that, into the retreat. He couldn't have had five hours' fighting.

"And to be killed—Retreating.

"He got nothing out of it but agony."

Veronica said, "How do you know he got nothing out of it? You don't know what he may have got in the last minute of it."

"Ronny, I don't believe I should mind so much if I were going out to Flanders—if there was the least little chance of a bullet getting me. But I gave him my word I wouldn't go.

"Do you think I'm bound by that—now?"

"Now? You're more bound than ever, because he's more near you, more alive."

"You wouldn't say that if you loved him."

❧

One day a package came to her from Eltham. Two notes were enclosed with it, one from Drayton's mother and one from Drayton:

"Frank said I was to send you this if he was killed. I think he must have known that he would not come back."

> My Dear Dorothy,—You will think this is a very singular bequest. But I want you to see that my memory is fairly good.

The very singular bequest was a Bible, with three cigarette-lighters for markers, and a date on the fly-leaf: "July 5th, 1912." The cigarette-lighters referred her to Psalm cxliv., and Isaiah xxxv. and xl., and pencil marks to the verses:

> Blessed be the Lord my strength which teacheth my hands to war and my fingers to fight. …
>
> And an highway shall be there … the redeemed shall walk there, and the ransomed of the Lord shall return …
>
> … They that wait upon the Lord shall renew their strength; they shall mount up with wings as eagles; they shall run and not be weary; they shall walk and not faint.

And their last hour came back to her with its mysterious, sweet and powerful passion that had no fear in it; and she laid hold again on the Reality they had seen and felt together.

The moment passed. She wanted it to come back, for as long as it lasted she was at peace.

But it did not come back. Nothing came back but her anguish of remorse for all that she had wasted.

XXI

After Drayton's death Frances and Anthony were sobered and had ceased to feed on illusions. The Battle of the Marne was fought in vain for them. They did not believe that it had saved Paris.

Then came the fall of Antwerp and the Great Retreat. There was no more Belgium. The fall of Paris and the taking of Calais were only a question of time, of perhaps a very little time. Then there would be no more France. They were face to face with the further possibility of there being no more England.

In those months of September and October Anthony and Frances were changed utterly to themselves and to each other. If, before the War, Frances had been asked whether she loved England, she would, after careful consideration, have replied truthfully, "I like England. But I dislike the English people. They are narrow and hypocritical and conceited. They are snobbish; and I hate snobs." At the time of the Boer War, beyond thinking that the British ought to win, and that they would win, and feeling a little spurt as of personal satisfaction when they did win, she had had no consciousness of her country whatsoever. As for loving it, she loved her children and her husband, and she had a sort of mild, cat-like affection for her garden and her tree of Heaven and her house; but the idea of loving England was absurd; you might just as well talk of loving the Archbishopric of Canterbury. She who once sat in peace under the tree of Heaven with her *Times* newspaper, and flicked the affairs of the nation from her as less important than the stitching on her baby's frock, now talked and thought and dreamed of nothing else. She was sad, not because her son Nicholas's time of safety was dwindling week by week, but because England was in danger; she was worried, not because Lord

Kitchener was practically asking her to give up her son Michael, but because she had found that the race was to the swift and the battle to the strong, and that she was classed with her incompetent sisters as too old to wait on wounded soldiers. Every morning she left her household to old Nanna's care and went down to the City with Anthony, and worked till evening in a room behind his office, receiving, packing, and sending off great cases of food and clothing to the Belgian soldiers.

Anthony was sad and worried, not because he had three sons, all well under twenty-seven, but simply and solely because the Government persisted in buying the wrong kind of timber—timber that swelled and shrank again—for rifles and gun-carriages, and because officials wouldn't listen to him when he tried to tell them what he knew about timber, and because the head of a department had talked to *him* about private firms and profiteering. As if any man with three sons under twenty-seven would want to make a profit out of the War; and as if they couldn't cut down everybody's profits if they took the trouble. They might cut his to the last cent so long as we had gun-carriages that would carry guns and rifles that would shoot. He knew what he was talking about and they didn't.

And Frances said he was right. He always had been right. She who had once been impatient over his invariable, irritating rightness, loved it now. She thought and said that if there were a few men like Anthony at the head of departments we should win the War. We were losing it for want of precisely that specialized knowledge and that power of organization in which Anthony excelled. She was proud of him, not because he was her husband and the father of her children, but because he was a man who could help England. They were both proud of Michael and Nicholas and John, not because they were their sons, but because they were men who could fight for England.

They found that they loved England with a secret, religious, instinctive love. Two feet of English earth, the ground that a man might stand and fight for, became, mysteriously and magically, dearer to them than their home. They loved England more than their own life or the lives of their children. Long ago they had realized that fathers do not beget children nor mothers bear them merely to gratify themselves. Now, in September and October, they were realizing that children are not begotten and born for their own profit and pleasure either.

When they sat together after the day's work they found themselves saying the most amazing things to each other.

Anthony said, "Downham thinks John's heart is decidedly better. I shouldn't wonder if he'd have to go." Almost as if the idea had been pleasant to him.

And Frances: "Well, I suppose if we had thirteen sons instead of three, we ought to send them all."

"Positively," said Anthony. "I believe I'd let Dorothy go out now if she insisted."

"Oh, no, I think we might be allowed to keep Dorothy."

She pondered. "I suppose one will get used to it in time. I grudged giving Nicky at first. I don't grudge him now. I believe if he went out to-morrow, and was killed, I should only feel how splendid it was of him."

"I wish poor Dorothy could feel that way about Drayton."

"She does—really. But that's different. Frank had to go. It was his profession. Nicky's gone in of his own free will."

He did not remind her that Frank's free will had counted in his choice of a profession.

"Once," said Frances, "volunteers didn't count. Now they count more than the whole Army put together."

They were silent, each thinking the same thing; each knowing that sooner or later they must speak of it.

Frances was the braver of the two. She spoke first.

"There's Michael. I don't know what to make of him. He doesn't seem to want to go."

That was the vulnerable place; there they had ached unbearably in secret. It was no use trying to hide it any longer. Something must be done about Michael.

"I wish you'd say something to him, Anthony."

"I would if I were going myself. But how can I?"

"When he knows that you'd have gone before any of them if you were young enough."

"I can't say anything. You'll have to."

"No, Anthony. I can't ask him to go any more than you can. Nicky is the only one of us who has any right to."

"Or Dorothy. Dorothy'd be in the trenches now if she had her way."

"I can't think how he can bear to look at Dorothy."

But in the end she did say something.

She went to him in his room upstairs where he worked now, hiding himself away every evening out of their sight. "Almost," she thought, "as if he were ashamed of himself."

Her heart ached as she looked at him; at the fair, serious beauty of his young face; at the thick masses of his hair that would not stay as they were brushed back, but fell over his forehead; it was still yellow, and shining as it shone when he was a little boy.

He was writing. She could see the short, irregular lines of verse on the white paper. He covered them with his hand as she came in lest she should see them. That hurt her.

"Michael," she said, "I wonder if you *ever* realize that we are at war."

"The War isn't a positive obsession to me, if that's what you mean."

"It isn't what I mean. Only—that when other people are doing so much—

"George Vereker enlisted yesterday."

"I don't care what other people are doing. I never did. If George Vereker chooses to enlist it is no reason why I should."

"My darling Mick, I'm not so sure. Isn't it all the more reason, when so much more has been done for you than was ever done for him?"

"It's no use trying to get at me."

"England's fighting for her life," said Frances.

"So's Germany.

"You see, I can't feel it like other people. George Vereker hates Germany; I don't. I've lived there. I don't want to make dear old Frau Henschel a widow, and stick a bayonet into Ludwig and Carl, and make Hedwig and Löttchen cry."

"I see. You'd rather Carl and Ludwig stuck bayonets into George and Nicky, and that Ronny and Dorothy and Alice Lathom cried."

"Bayonetting isn't my business."

"Your own safety is. How can you bear to let other men fight for you?"

"They're not fighting for *me*, Mother. You ask them if they are, and see what they'll say to you. They're fighting for God knows what; but they're no more fighting for me than they're fighting for Aunt Emmeline."

"They *are* fighting for Aunt Emmeline. They're fighting for everything that's weak and defenceless."

"Well, then, they're not fighting for me. I'm not weak and defenceless," said Michael.

"All the more shame for you, then."

He smiled, acknowledging her score.

"You don't mean that, really, Mummy. You couldn't resist the opening for a repartee. It was quite a nice one."

"If," she said, "you were only *doing* something. But you go on with your own things as though nothing had happened."

"I *am* doing something. I'm keeping sane. And I'm keeping sanity alive in other people."

"Much you care for other people," said Frances as she left the room.

But when she had shut the door on him her heart turned to him again. She went down to Anthony where he waited for her in his room.

"Well?" he said.

"It's no use. He won't go."

And Frances, quite suddenly and to her own surprise, burst into tears.

He drew her to him, and she clung to him, sobbing softly.

"My dear—my dear. You mustn't take it to heart like this. He's as obstinate as the devil; but he'll come round."

He pressed her tighter to him. He loved her in her unfamiliar weakness, crying and clinging to him.

"It's not that," she said, recovering herself with dignity. "I'm glad he didn't give in. If he went out, and anything happened to him, I couldn't bear to be the one who made him go."

After all, she didn't love England more than Michael.

They were silent.

"We must leave it to his own feeling," she said presently.

But Anthony's heart was hard against Michael.

"He must know that *public* feeling's pretty strong against him. To say nothing of *my* feeling and *your* feeling."

He did know it. He knew that they were all against him; his father and his mother, and John and Dorothy. Because he couldn't bear to look at Dorothy, and couldn't bear Dorothy to look at him, he kept out of her way as much as possible.

As for public opinion, it had always been against him, and he against it.

But Anthony was mistaken when he thought that the pressure of these antagonisms would move Michael an inch from the way he meant to go. Rather, it drew out that resistance which Michael's mind had always offered to the loathsome violences of the collective soul. From his very first encounters with the collective soul and its emotions they had seemed to Michael as dangerous as they were loathsome. Collective emotion might be on the side of the archangels or on the side of devils and of swine; its mass was what made it dangerous, a thing that challenged the resistance of the private soul. But in his worst dreams of what it could do to him Michael had never imagined anything more appalling than the collective patriotism of the British and their Allies, this rushing together of the souls of four countries to make one monstrous soul.

And neither Anthony nor Frances realized that Michael, at this moment, was afraid, not of the War so much as of the emotions of the War, the awful, terrifying flood that carried him away from his real self and from everything it cared for most. Patriotism was, no doubt, a fine emotion; but the finer the thing was, the more it got you; it got you and you were done for. He was determined that it shouldn't get him. They couldn't see—and that was Michael's grievance—that his resistance was his strength and not his weakness.

Even Frances, who believed that people never changed, did not realize that the grown-up Michael who didn't want to enlist was the same entity as the little Michael who hadn't wanted to go to the party, who had wanted to go on playing with himself, afraid of nothing so much as of forgetting "pieces of himself that he wanted to remember." He was Michael who refused to stay at school another term, and who talked about shooting himself because he had to go with his class and do what the other fellows were doing. He objected to being suddenly required to feel patriotic because other people were feeling patriotic, to think that Germany was in the wrong because other people thought that Germany was in the wrong, to fight because other people were fighting.

Why should he? He saw no earthly reason why.

He said to himself that it was the blasted cheek of the assumption that he resented. There was a peculiarly British hypocrisy and unfairness and tyranny about it all.

It wasn't—as they all seemed to think—that he was afraid to fight. He had wanted to go and fight for Ireland. He would fight any day in a cleaner cause. By a cleaner cause Michael meant a cause that had not been messed about so much by other people. Other people had not put pressure on him to fight for Ireland; in fact they had tried to stop him. Michael was also aware that in the matter of Ireland his emotions, though shared by considerable numbers of the Irish people, were not shared by his family or by many people whom he knew; to all intents and purposes he had them to himself.

It was no use trying to explain all this to his father and mother, for they wouldn't understand it. The more he explained the more he would seem to them to be a shirker.

He could see what they thought of him. He saw it in their stiff, reticent faces, in his mother's strained smile, in his sister's silence when he asked her what she had been doing all day. Their eyes—his mother's and his sister's eyes—pursued him with the unspoken question: "Why don't you go and get killed—for England—like other people?"

Still, he could bear these things, for they were visible, palpable; he knew where he was with them. What he could not stand was that empty spiritual space between him and Nicky. That hurt him where he was most vulnerable—in his imagination.

And again, his imagination healed the wound it made.

It was all very well, but if you happened to have a religion, and your religion was what mattered to you most; if you adored Beauty as the supreme form of Life; if you cared for nothing else; if you lived, impersonally, to make Beauty and to keep it alive; and for no other end, how could you consent to take part in this bloody business? That would be the last betrayal, the most cowardly surrender.

And you were all the more bound to faithfulness if you were one of the leaders of a forlorn hope, of the forlorn hope of all the world, of all the ages, the forlorn hope of God himself.

For Michael, even more than Ellis, had given himself up as lost.

And yet somehow they all felt curiously braced by the prospect. When the young men met in Lawrence Stephen's house they discussed it with a calm, high heroism. This was the supreme test: To go on, without pay, without praise, without any sort of recognition. Any fool could fight; but, if you were an artist, your honour bound you to ignore the material contest, to refuse, even to your country, the surrender of the highest that you knew. They believed with the utmost fervour and sincerity that they defied Germany more effectually, because more spiritually, by going on and producing fine things with imperturbability than if they went out against the German Armies with bayonets and machine-guns. Moreover they were restoring Beauty as fast as Germany destroyed it.

They told each other these things very seriously and earnestly, on Friday evenings as they lay about more or less at their ease (but rather less than more) in Stephen's study.

They had asked each other: "Are *you* going to fight for your country?"

And Ellis had said he was damned if he'd fight for his country; and Mitchell had said he hadn't got a country, so there was no point in his fighting, anyhow; and Monier-Owen that if you could show him a country that cared for the arts before anything he'd fight for it; but that England was very far from being that country.

And Michael had sat silent, thinking the same thoughts.

And Stephen had sat silent, thinking other thoughts, not listening to what was said.

And now people were whining about Louvain and Rheims Cathedral. Michael said to himself that he could stand these massed war emotions if they were sincere; but people whined about Louvain and Rheims Cathedral who had never cared a damn about either before the War.

Anthony looked up over the edge of his morning paper, inquired whether Michael could defend the destruction of Louvain and Rheims Cathedral?

Michael shrugged his shoulders. "Why bother," he said, "about Rheims Cathedral and Louvain? From your point of view it's all right. If Louvain and Rheims Cathedral get in the way of the enemy's artillery they've got to go. They didn't happen to be in the way of ours, that's all."

Michael's mind was showing certain symptoms, significant of its malady. He was inclined to disparage the military achievements of the Allies and to justify the acts of Germany.

"It's up to the French to defend Paris. And what have we got to do with Alsace-Lorraine? As if every intelligent Frenchman didn't know that Alsace-Lorraine is a sentimental stunt. No. I'm not pro-German. I simply see things as they are."

"I think," Frances would say placably, "we'd better not talk about the War."

He would remind them that it was not his subject.

And John laughed at him. "Poor old Mick hates the War because it's dished him. He knows his poems can't come out till it's over."

As it happened, his poems came out that autumn.

After all, the Germans had been held back from Paris. As Stephen pointed out to him, the Battle of the Marne had saved Michael. In magnificent defiance of the enemy, the "New Poems" of Michael Harrison, with illustrations by Austin Mitchell, were announced as forthcoming in October; and Morton Ellis's "Eccentricities," with illustrations by Austin Mitchell, were to appear the same month. Even Wadham's poems would come out some time, perhaps next spring.

Stephen said the advertisements should be offered to the War Office as posters, to strike terror into Germany and sustain the morale of the Allied Armies. "If England could afford to publish Michael—"

Michael's family made no comment on the appearance of his poems. The book lay about in the same place on the drawing-room table for weeks. When Nanna dusted she replaced it with religious care; none of his people had so much as taken it up to glance inside it, or hold it in their hands. It seemed to Michael that they were conscious of it all the time, and that they turned their faces away from it pointedly. They hated it. They hated him for having written it.

He remembered that it had been different when his first book had come out two years ago. They had read that; they had snatched at all the reviews of it and read it again, trying to see what it was that they had missed.

They had taken each other aside, and it had been:

"Anthony, do you understand Michael's poems?"

"Dorothy, do you understand Michael's poems?"

"Nicky, do *you* understand Michael's poems?"

He remembered his mother's apology for not understanding them: "Darling, I *do* see that they're very beautiful." He remembered how he had wished that they would give up the struggle and leave his poems alone. They were not written for them. He had been amused and irritated when he had seen his father holding the book doggedly in front of him, his poor old hands twitching with embarrassment whenever he thought Michael was looking at him.

And now he, who had been so indifferent and so contemptuous, was sensitive to the least quiver of his mother's upper lip.

Veronica's were the only eyes that were kind to him; that did not hunt him down with implacable suggestion and reminder.

Veronica had been rejected too. She was not strong enough to nurse in the hospitals. She was only strong enough to work from morning to night, packing and carrying large, heavy parcels for the Belgian soldiers. She wanted Michael to be sorry for her because she couldn't be a nurse. Rosalind Jervis was a nurse. But he was not sorry. He said he would very much rather she didn't do anything that Rosalind did.

"So would Nicky," he said.

And then: "Veronica, do *you* think I ought to enlist?"

The thought was beginning to obsess him.

"No," she said; "you're different.

"I know how you feel about it. Nicky's heart and soul are in the War. If he's killed it can only kill his body. *Your* soul isn't in it. It would kill your soul."

"It's killing it now, killing everything I care for."

"Killing everything we all care for, except the things it can't kill."

That was one Sunday evening in October. They were standing together on the long terrace under the house wall. Before them, a little to the right, on the edge of the lawn, the great ash-tree rose over the garden. The curved and dipping branches swayed and swung in a low wind that moved like quiet water.

"Michael," she said, "do look what's happening to that tree."

"I see," he said.

It made him sad to look at the tree; it made him sad to look at Veronica—because both the tree and Veronica were beautiful.

"When I was a little girl I used to sit and look and look at that tree till it changed and got all thin and queer and began to move towards me.

"I never knew whether it had really happened or not; I don't know now—or whether it was the tree or me. It was as if by looking and looking you could make the tree more real and more alive."

Michael remembered something.

"Dorothy says you saw Ferdie the night he died."

"So I did. But that's not the same thing. I didn't have to look and look.

I just saw him. I *sort of* saw Frank that last night—when the call came—only sort of—but I knew he was going to be killed.

"I didn't see him nearly so distinctly as I saw Nicky—"

"Nicky? You didn't see him—as you saw Ferdie?"

"No, no, no! it was ages ago—in Germany—before he married. I saw him with Desmond."

"Have you ever seen me?"

"Not yet.

"That's because you don't want me as they did."

"Don't I! Don't I!"

And she said again: "Not yet."

Nicky had had leave for Christmas. He had come and gone.

Frances and Anthony were depressed; they were beginning to be frightened.

For Nicky had finished his training. He might be sent out any day.

Nicky had had some moments of depression. Nothing had been heard of the Moving Fortress. Again, the War Office had given no sign of having received it. It was hard luck, he said, on Drayton.

And John was depressed after he had gone.

"They'd much better have taken me," he said.

"What's the good of sending the best brains in the Army to get pounded? There's Drayton. He ought to have been in the Ordnance. *He's* killed.

"And here's Nicky. Nicky ought to be in the engineers or the gunners or the Royal Flying Corps; but he's got to stand in the trenches and be pounded.

"Lot they care about anybody's brains. Drayton could have told Kitchener that we can't win this war without high-explosive shells. So could Nicky.

"You bet they've stuck all those plans and models in the sanitary dust-bin behind the War Office back door. It's enough to make Nicky blow his brains out."

"Nicky doesn't care, really," Veronica said. "He just leaves things—and goes on."

That night, after the others had gone to bed, Michael stayed behind with his father.

"It must look to you," he said, "as if I ought to have gone instead of Nicky."

"I don't say so, Michael. And I'm sure Nicky wouldn't."

"No, but you both think it. You see, if I went I shouldn't be any good at it. Not the same good as Nicky. He wants to go and I don't. Can't you see it's different?"

"Yes," said Anthony, "I see. I've seen it for some time."

And Michael remembered the night in August when his brother came to him in his room.

Beauty—the Forlorn Hope of God—if he cared for it supremely, why was he pursued and tormented by the thought of the space between him and Nicky?

XXII

Michael had gone to Stephen's house.

He was no longer at his ease there. It seemed to him that Lawrence's eyes followed him too; not with hatred, but with a curious meditative wonder.

To-night Stephen said to him, "Did you know that Réveillaud's killed?"

"Killed? Killed? I didn't even know he was fighting."

Lawrence laughed. "What did you suppose he was doing?"

"No—but how?"

"Out with the patrol and shot down. There you are—"

He shoved the *Times* to him, pointing to the extract from *Le Matin*: "It is with regret that we record the death of M. Jules Réveillaud, the brilliant young poet and critic—"

Michael stared at the first three lines; something in his mind prevented him from going on to the rest, as if he did not care to read about Réveillaud and know how he died.

"It is with regret that we record the death. It is with regret that we record—with regret—"

Then he read on, slowly and carefully, to the end. It was a long paragraph.

"To think," he said at last, "that this revolting thing should have happened to him."

"His death?"

"No—*this*. The *Matin* never mentioned Réveillaud before. None of the big papers, none of the big reviews noticed his existence except to sneer at him. He goes out and gets killed like any little bourgeois, and the swine plaster him all over with their filthy praise. He'd rather they'd spat on him."

He meditated fiercely. "Well—he couldn't help it. He was conscripted."

"You think he wouldn't have gone of his own accord?"

"I'm certain he wouldn't."

"And I'm certain he would."

"I wish to God we'd got conscription here. I'd rather the Government commandeered my body than stand this everlasting interference with my soul."

"Then," said Lawrence, "you'll not be surprised at my enlisting."

"You're not—"

"I am. I'd have been in the first week if I'd known what to do about Vera."

"But—it's—it's not sane."

"Perhaps not. But it's Irish."

"Irish? I can understand ordinary Irishmen rushing into a European row for the row's sake, just because they haven't got a civil war to mess about in. But you—of all Irishmen—why on earth should *you* be in it?"

"Because I want to be in it."

"I thought," said Michael, "you were to have been a thorn in England's side?"

"So I was. So I am. But not at this minute. My grandmother was a hard Ulster woman and I hated her. But I wouldn't be a thorn in my grandmother's side if the old lady was assaulted by a brutal voluptuary, and I saw her down and fighting for her honour.

"I've been a thorn in England's side all my life. But it's nothing to the thorn I'll be if I'm killed fighting for her."

"Why—why—if you want to fight in the civil war afterwards?"

"Why? Because I'm one of the few Irishmen who can reason straight. I was going into the civil war last year because it was a fight for freedom. I'm going into this War this year because it's a bigger fight for a bigger freedom.

"You can't have a free Ireland without a free England, any more than you can have religious liberty without political liberty. If the Orangemen understood anything at all about it they'd see it was the Nationalists and the Sinn Feiners that'll help them to put down Catholicism in Ireland."

"You think it matters to Ireland whether Germany licks us or we lick Germany?"

"I think it matters to the whole world."

"What's changed you?" said Michael.

He was angry with Lawrence. He thought: "He hasn't any excuse for failing us. *He* hasn't been conscripted."

"Nothing's changed me. But supposing it didn't matter to the whole world, or even to Europe, and supposing the Allies were beaten in the end, you and I shouldn't be beaten, once we'd stripped ourselves, stripped our souls clean, and gone in.

"Victory, Michael—victory is a state of mind."

The opportunist had seen his supreme opportunity.

He would have snatched at it in the first week of the War, as he had said, but that Vera had made it hard for him. She was not making it easy now. The dull, dark moth's wings of her eyes hovered about him, fluttering with anxiety.

When she heard that he was going to enlist she sent for Veronica.

Veronica said, "You must let him go."

"I can't let him go. And why should I? He'll do no good. He's over age. He's no more fit than I am."

"You'll have to, sooner or later."

"Later, then. Not one minute before I must. If they want him let them come and take him."

"It won't hurt so much if you let him go, gently, now. He'll tear at you if you keep him."

"He has torn at me. He tears at me every day. I don't mind his tearing. I mind his going—going and getting killed, wounded, paralysed, broken to pieces."

"You'll mind his hating you. You'll mind that awfully."

"I shan't. He's hated me before. He went away and left me once. But he came back. He can't really do without me."

"You don't know *how* he'll hate you if you come between him and what he wants most."

"*I* used to be what he wanted most."

"Well—it's his honour now."

"That's what they all say, Michael and Anthony, and Dorothy. They're men and they don't know. Dorothy's more a man than a woman.

"But you're different. I thought you might help me to keep him—they say you've got some tremendous secret. And this is the way you go on!"

"I wouldn't help you to keep him if I could. I wouldn't have kept Nicky for all the world. Aunt Frances wouldn't have kept him. She wants Michael to go."

"She doesn't. If she says she does she lies. All the women are lying. Either they don't care—they're just *lumps*, with no hearts and no nerves in them—or they lie.

"It's this rotten pose of patriotism. They get it from each other, like—like a skin disease. No wonder it makes Michael sick."

"Men going out—thousands and thousands and thousands—to be cut about and blown to bits, and their women safe at home, snuffling and sentimentalizing—

"Lying—lying—lying."

"Who wouldn't? Who wouldn't tell one big, thumping, sacred lie, if it sends them off happy?"

"But we're not lying. It's the most real thing that ever happened to us. I'm glad Nicky's going. I shall be glad all my life."

"It comes easy to you. You're a child. You've never grown up. You were a miserable little mummy when you were born. And now you look as if every drop of blood was drained out of your body in your teens. If *that's* your tremendous secret you can keep it yourself. It seems to be all you've got."

"If it wasn't for Aunt Frances and Uncle Anthony it *would* have been all I've got."

Vera looked at her daughter and saw her for the first time as she really was. The child was not a child any more. She was a woman, astonishingly and dangerously mature. Veronica's sorrowful, lucid eyes took her in; they neither weighed her nor measured her, but judged her, off-hand with perfect accuracy.

"Poor little Ronny. I've been a beastly mother to you. Still, you can thank my beastliness for Aunt Frances and Uncle Anthony."

Veronica thought: "How funny she is about it!" She said, "It's your beastliness to poor Larry that I mind. You know what you're keeping him for."

She knew; and Lawrence knew.

That night he told her that if he hadn't wanted to enlist he'd be driven to it to get away from her.

And she was frightened and held her tongue.

Then she got desperate. She did things. She intrigued behind his back to keep him; and he found her out.

He came to her, furious.

"You needn't lie about it," he said. "I know what you've done. You've been writing letters and getting at people. You've told the truth about my age and you've lied about my health. You've even gone round cadging for jobs for me in the Red Cross and the Press Bureau and the Intelligence Department, and God only knows whether I'm supposed to have put you up to it."

"I took care of that, Larry."

"You? You'd no right to interfere with my affairs."

"Hadn't I? Not after living with you seven years?"

"If you'd lived with me seven centuries you'd have had no right to try to keep a man back from the Army."

"I'm trying to keep a man's brain for my country."

"You lie. It's my body you're trying to keep for yourself. As you did when I was going to Ireland."

"Oh, then—I tried to stop you from being a traitor to England. They'd have hanged you, my dear, for that."

"Traitor? It's women like you that are the traitors. My God, if there was a Government in this country that could govern, you'd be strung up in a row, all of you, and hanged."

"No wonder you think you're cut out for a soldier. You're cruel enough."

"*You're* cruel. I'd rather be hanged than live with you a day longer after what you've done. A Frenchman shot his *wife* the other day for less than that."

"What was 'less than that'?" she said.

"She crawled after him to the camp, like a bitch.

"He sent her away and she came again and again. He *had* to shoot her."

"Was there nothing to be said for her?"

"There was. She knew it was a big risk and she took it. *You* knew you were safe while you slimed my honour."

"She loved him, and he shot her, and you think that's a fine thing. *How* she must have loved him!"

"Men don't want to be loved that way. That's the mistake you women will make."

"It's the way you've taught us. I should like to know what other way you ever want us to love you?"

"The way Veronica loves Nicky, and Dorothy loved Drayton and Frances loves Anthony."

"Dorothy? She ruined Drayton's life."

"Men's lives aren't ruined that way. And not all women's."

"Well, anyhow, if she'd loved him she'd have married him. And Frances loves her children better than Anthony, and Anthony knows it."

"Veronica, then."

"Veronica doesn't know what passion is. The poor child's anæmic."

"Another mistake. Veronica, and 'children' like Veronica have more passion in one eyelash than you have in your whole body."

"It's a pity," she said, "you can't have Veronica and her eyelashes instead of me. She's young and she's pretty."

He sighed with pain as her nerves lashed into his.

"That's what it all amounts to—your wanting to get out to the Front. It's what's the matter with half the men who go there and pose as heroes.

They want to get rid of the wives—and mistresses—they're tired of because the poor things aren't young or pretty any longer."

She dropped into the mourning voice that made him mad with her. "I'm old—old—old. And the War's making me older every day, and uglier. And I'm not married to you. Talk of keeping you! How *can* I keep you when I'm old and ugly?"

He looked at her and smiled with a hard pity. Compunction always worked in him at the sight of her haggard face, glazed and stained with crying.

"That's how—by getting older.

"I've never tired of you. You're more to me now than you were when I first knew you. It's when I see you looking old that I'm sure I love you."

She smiled, too, in her sad sexual wisdom.

"There may be women who'd believe you, Larry, or who'd say they believe you; but not me."

"It's the truth," he said. "If you were young and if you were married to me I should have enlisted months ago.

"Can't you see it's not you, it's this life we lead that I'm sick and tired of? I tell you I'd rather be hanged than go on with it. I'd rather be a prisoner in Germany than shut up in this house of yours."

"Poor little house. You used to like it. What's wrong with it now?"

"Everything. Those damned lime-trees all round it. And that damned white wall round the lime-trees. Shutting me in.

"And those curtains in your bed-room. Shutting me in.

"And your mind, trying to shut mine in.

"I come into this room and I find Phyllis Desmond in it and Orde-Jones, drinking tea and talking. I go upstairs for peace, and Michael and Ellis are sitting there—talking; trying to persuade themselves that funk's the divinest thing in God's universe.

"And over there's the one thing I've been looking for all my life—the one thing I've cared for. And you're keeping me from it."

They left it. But it began all over again the next day and the next. And Lawrence went on growing his moustache and trying to train it upwards in the way she hated.

One evening, towards dinner-time he turned up in khaki, the moustache stiff on his long upper lip, his lopping hair clipped. He was another man, a strange man, and she was not sure whether she hated him or not.

But she dried her eyes and dressed her hair, and put on her best gown to do honour to his khaki.

She said, "It'll be like living with another man."

"You won't have very long to live with him," said Lawrence.

And even then, sombrely, under the shadow of his destiny, her passion for him revived; his very strangeness quickened it to violence, to perversity.

And in the morning the Army took him from her; it held him out of her reach. He refused to let her go with him to the place where he was stationed.

"What would you do," she said, "if I followed you? Shoot me?"

"I might shoot *myself*. Anyhow, you'd never see me or hear from me again."

He went out to France three weeks before Nicholas.

She had worn herself out with wondering when he would be sent, till she, too, was in a hurry for him to go and end it. Now that he had gone she felt nothing but a clean and sane relief that was a sort of peace. She told herself that she would rather he were killed soon than that she should be tortured any longer with suspense.

"If I saw his name in the lists this morning I shouldn't mind. That would end it."

And she sent her servant to the stationer's to stop the papers for fear lest she should see his name in the lists.

But Lawrence spared her. He was wounded in his first engagement, and died of his wounds in a hospital at Dunkirk.

The Red Cross woman who nursed him wrote to Vera an hour before he died. She gave details and a message.

7.30. I'm writing now from his dictation. He says you're to forgive him and not to be too sorry, because it was what he thought it would be (he means the fighting) only much more so—all except this last bit.

He wants you to tell Michael and Dicky?—Nicky?—that. He says: 'It's odd I should be first when he got the start of me.'

(I think he means you're to forgive him for leaving you to go to the War.)

8.30. It is all over.

He was too weak to say anything more. But he sent you his love.

Vera said to herself: "He didn't. She made that up."

She hated the Red Cross woman who had been with Lawrence and had seen so much; who had dared to tell her what he meant and to make up messages.

XXIII

Nicholas had applied for a commission, and he had got it, and Frances was glad.

She had been proud of him because he had chosen the ranks instead of the Officers' Training Corps; but she persisted in the belief that, when it came to the trenches, second lieutenants stood a better chance. "For goodness' sake," Nicholas had said, "don't tell her that they're over the parapet first."

That was in December. In February he got a week's leave—sudden, unforeseen and special leave. It had to be broken to her this time that leave as special as that meant war-leave.

She said, "Well, if it does, I shall have him for six whole days." She had learned how to handle time, how to prolong the present, drawing it out minute by minute; thus her happiness, stretched to the snapping point, vibrated.

She had a sense of its vibration now, as she looked at Nicholas. It was the evening of the day he had come home, and they were all in the drawing-room together. He was standing before her, straight and tall, on the hearthrug, where he had lifted the Persian cat, Timmy, out of his sleep and was holding him against his breast. Timmy spread himself there, softly and heavily, hanging on to Nicky's shoulder by his claws; he butted Nicky's chin with his head, purring.

"I don't know how I'm to tear myself away from Timmy. I should like to wear him alive as a waistcoat. Or hanging on my shoulder like a cape, with his tail curled tight round my neck. He'd look uncommonly *chic* with all his khaki patches."

"Why don't you take him with you?" Anthony said.

"'Cos he's Ronny's cat."

"He isn't. I've given him to you," Veronica said.

"When?"

"Now, this minute. To sleep on your feet and keep you warm."

Frances listened and thought: "What children—what babies they are, after all." If only this minute could be stretched out farther.

"I mustn't," Nicky said. "I should spend hours in dalliance; and if a shell got him it would ruin my morale."

Timmy, unhooked from Nicky's shoulder, lay limp in his arms. He lay on his back, in ecstasy, his legs apart, showing the soft, cream-white fur of his stomach. Nicky rubbed his face against the soft, cream-white fur.

"I say, what a heavenly death it would be to die—smothered in Timmies."

"Nicky, you're a beastly sensualist. That's what's the matter with you," John said. And they all laughed.

The minute broke, stretched to its furthest.

Frances was making plans now for Nicky's week. There were things they could do, plays they could see, places they could go to. Anthony would let them have the big car as much as they wanted. For you could stretch time out by filling it; you could multiply the hours by what they held.

"Ronny and I are going to get married to-morrow," Nicky said. "We settled it that we would at once, if I got war-leave. It's the best thing to do."

"Of course," Frances said, "it's the best thing to do."

But she had not allowed for it, nor for the pain it gave her. That pain shocked her. It was awful to think that, after all her surrenders, Nicky's happiness could give her pain. It meant that she had never let go her secret hold. She had been a hypocrite to herself.

Nicky was talking on about it, excitedly, as he used to talk on about his pleasures when he was a child.

If Dad'll let us have the racing-car, we'll go down to Morfe. We can do it in a day."

"My dear boy," Anthony said, "don't you know I've lent the house to the Red Cross, and let the shooting?"

"I don't care. There's the little house in the village we can have. And Harker and his wife can look after us."

"Harker's gone to the War, and his wife's looking after his brother's children somewhere. And I've put two Belgian refugees into it."

"*They* can look after us," said Nicky. "We'll stay three days, run back, and have one day at home before I sail."

Frances gave up her play with time. She was beaten.

And still she thought: "At least I shall have him one whole day."

And then she looked across the room to Michael, as if Michael's face had signalled to her. His clear, sun-burnt skin showed blotches of white where the blood had left it. A light sweat was on his forehead. When their eyes met, he shifted his position to give himself an appearance of ease.

Michael had not reckoned on his brother's marriage, either. It was when he asked himself: "On what, then, *had* he been reckoning?" that the sweat broke out on his forehead.

He had not reckoned on anything. But the sudden realization of what he might have reckoned on made him sick. He couldn't bear to think of Ronny married. And yet again, he couldn't bear to think of Nicky not marrying her. If he had had a hold on her he would have let her go. In this he knew himself to be sincere. He had had no hold on her, and to talk about letting her go was idiotic; still, there was a violent pursuit and possession by the mind—and Michael's mind was innocent of jealousy, that psychic assault and outrage on the woman he loved. His spiritual surrender of her was so perfect that his very imagination gave her up to Nicky.

He was glad that they were going to be married to-morrow. Nothing could take their three days from them, even when the War had done its worst.

And then, with his mother's eyes on him, he thought: "Does she think I was reckoning on that?"

Nicholas and Veronica were married the next morning at Hampstead Town Hall, before the Registrar.

They spent the rest of the day in Anthony's racing-car, defying and circumventing time and space and the police, tearing, Nicky said, whole handfuls out of eternity by sheer speed. At intervals, with a clear run before him, he let out the racing-car to its top speed on the Great North Road. It snorted and purred and throbbed like some immense, nervous animal, but lightly and purely as if all its weight were purged from it by speed. It flew up and down the hills of Hertfordshire and Buckinghamshire and out on to the flat country round Peterborough and Grantham, a country of silver green and emerald green grass and purple fallow land and bright red houses; and so on to the great plain of York, and past Reyburn up towards the bare hill country netted with grey stone walls.

Nicholas slowed the car down for the winding of the road.

It went now between long straight ramparts of hills that showed enormous and dark against a sky cleared to twilight by the unrisen moon. Other hills, round-topped, darker still and more enormous, stood piled up in front of them, blocking the head of Rathdale.

Then the road went straight, and Nicholas was reckless. It was as if, ultimately, they must charge into the centre of that incredibly high, immense obstruction. They were thrilled, mysteriously, as before the image of monstrous and omnipotent disaster. Then the dale widened; it made way for them and saved them.

The lights of Morfe on its high platform made the pattern of a coronet and pendants on the darkness; the small, scattered lights of the village below, the village they were making for, showed as if dropped out of the pattern on the hill.

One larger light burned in the room that was their marriage chamber. Jean and Suzanne, the refugees, stood in the white porch to receive them, holding the lanterns that were their marriage torches. The old woman held her light low down, lighting the flagstone of the threshold. The old man lifted his high, showing the lintel of the door. It was so low that Nicholas had to stoop to go in.

❧

In the morning they read the date cut in the wall above the porch: 1665.

The house was old and bent and grey. Its windows were narrow slits in the stone mullions. It crouched under the dipping boughs of the ash-tree that sheltered it. Inside there was just room for Veronica to stand up. Nicholas had to stoop or knock his head against the beams. It had only four rooms, two for Nicholas and Veronica, and two for Jean and Suzanne. And it was rather dark.

But it pleased them. They said it was their apple-tree-house grown up because they were grown up, and keeping strict proportions. You had to crawl into it, and you were only really comfortable sitting or lying down. So they sat outside it, watching old Suzanne through the window as she moved about the house place, cooking Belgian food for them, and old Jean as he worked in the garden.

Veronica loved Jean and Suzanne. She had found out all about them the first morning.

"Only think, Nicky. They're from Termonde, and their house was burnt behind them as they left it. They saw horrors, and their son was killed in the War.

"Yet they're happy and at peace. Almost as if they'd forgotten. He'll plant flowers in his garden."

"They're old, Ronny. And perhaps they were tired already when it happened."

"Yes, that must be it. They're old and tired."

❧

And now it was the last adventure of their last day. They were walking on the slope of Renton Moor that looks over Rathdale towards Greffington Edge. The light from the west poured itself in vivid green down the valley below them, broke itself into purple on Karva Hill to the north above Morfe, and was beaten back in subtle blue and violet from the stone rampart of the Edge.

Nicholas had been developing, in fancy, the strategic resources of the country. Guns on Renton Moor, guns along Greffington Edge, on Sarrack Moor. The raking lines of the hills were straight as if they had been measured with a ruler and then planed.

"Ronny," he said at last, "we've licked 'em in the first round, you and I. The beastly Boche can't do us out of these three days."

"No. We've been absolutely happy. And we'll never forget it. Never."

"Perhaps it was a bit rough on Dad and Mummy, our carting ourselves up here, away from them. But, you see, they don't really mind. They're feeling about it now just as we feel about it. I knew they would."

There had been a letter from Frances saying she was glad they'd gone. She was so happy thinking how happy they were.

"They're angels, Nicky."

"Aren't they? Simply angels. That's the rotten part of it. I wish—

"I wish I could tell them what I think of them. But you can't, somehow. It sticks in your throat, that sort of thing."

"You needn't," she said; "they know all right."

She thought: "This is what he wants me to tell them about—afterwards."

"Yes, but—I must have hurt them—hurt them horribly—lots of times. I wish I hadn't.

"But" he went on, "they're funny, you know. Dad actually thought it idiotic of us to do this. He said it would only make it harder for us when I had to go. They don't see that it's just piling it on—going from one jolly adventure to another.

"I'm afraid, though, what he really meant was it was hard on you; because the rest of it's all my show."

"But it isn't all your show, Nicky darling. It's mine, and it's theirs—because we haven't grudged you your adventure."

"That's exactly how I want you to feel about it."

"And they're assuming that I shan't come back. Which, if you come to think of it, is pretty big cheek. They talk, and they think, as though nobody ever got through. Whereas I've every intention of getting through and of coming back. I'm the sort of chap who does get through, who does come back."

"And even if I wasn't, if they studied statistics they'd see that it's a thousand chances to one against the Boches getting me—just me out of all the other chaps. As if I was so jolly important.

"No; don't interrupt. Let's get this thing straight while we can. Supposing—just supposing I didn't get through—didn't come back—supposing I was unlike myself and got killed, I want you to think of *that*, not as a clumsy accident, but just another awfully interesting thing I'd done.

"Because, you see, you might be going to have a baby; and if you took the thing as a shock instead of—of what it probably really is, and went and got cut up about it, you might start the little beggar with a sort of fit, and shake its little nerves up, so that it would be jumpy all its life.

"It ought," said Nicky, "to sit in its little house all quiet and comfy till it's time for it to come out."

He was struck with a sudden, poignant realization of what might be, what probably would be, what ought to be, what he had wanted more than anything, next to Veronica.

"It shall, Nicky, it shall be quiet and comfy."

"If *that* came off all right," he said, "it would make it up to Mother no end."

"It wouldn't make it up to me."

"You don't know what it would do," he said.

She thought: "I don't want it. I don't want anything but you."

"That's why," he went on, "I'm giving Don as the next of kin—the one they'll wire to; because it won't take him that way; it'll only make him madder to get out and do for them. I'm afraid of you or Mummy or Dad, or Michael being told first."

"It doesn't matter a bit who's *told* first. I shall *know* first," she said. "And you needn't be afraid. It won't kill either me or the baby. If a shock could kill me I should have died long ago."

"When?"

"When you went to Desmond. Then, when I thought I couldn't bear it any longer, something happened."

"What?"

"I don't know. I don't know what it *is* now; I only know what it does. It always happens—always—when you want it awfully. And when you're quiet and give yourself up to it."

"It'll happen again."

He listened, frowning a little, not quite at ease, not quite interested; puzzled, as if he had lost her trail; put off, as if something had come between him and her.

"You can make it happen to other people," she was saying; "so that when things get too awful they can bear them. I wanted it to happen to Dorothy when she was in prison, and it did. She said she was absolutely happy there; and that all sorts of queer things came to her. And, Nicky, they were the same queer things that came to me. It was like something getting through to her."

"I say—did you ever do it to me?"

"Only once, when you wanted it awfully."

"When? When?"

Now he was interested; he was intrigued; he was on her trail.

"When Desmond did—that awful thing. I wanted you to see that it didn't matter, it wasn't the end."

"But that's just what I did see, what I kept on telling myself. It looks as if it worked, then?"

"It doesn't always. It comes and goes. But I think with *you* it would always come; because you're more *me* than other people; I mean I care more for you."

She closed and clinched it. "That's why you're not to bother about me, Nicky. If *the* most awful thing happened, and you didn't come back, It would come."

"I wish I knew what It was," he said.

"I don't know what it is. But it's so real that I think it's God."

"That's why *they're* so magnificently brave—Dorothy and Aunt Frances and all of them. They don't believe in it; they don't know it's there; even Michael doesn't know it's there—yet; and still they go on bearing and bearing; and they were glad to give you up."

"I know," he said; "lots of people *say* they're glad, but they really *are* glad."

He meditated.

"There's one thing. I can't think what you do, unless it's praying or something; and if you're going to turn it on to me, Ronny, I wish you'd be careful; because it seems to me that if there's anything in it at all, there might be hitches. I mean to say, you might work it just enough to keep me from being killed but not enough to keep my legs from being blown off. Or the Boches might get me fair enough and you might bring me back, all paralysed and idiotic.

"That's what I should funk. I should funk it most damnably, if I thought about it. Luckily one doesn't think."

"But, Nicky, I shouldn't try to keep you back then any more than I tried before."

"You wouldn't? Honour bright?"

"Of course I wouldn't. It wouldn't be playing the game. To begin with, I won't believe that you're not going to get through.

"But if you didn't—if you didn't come back—I still wouldn't believe you'd gone. I should say, 'He hasn't cared. He's gone on to something else. It doesn't end him.'"

He was silent. The long rampart of the hill, as he stared at it, made a pattern on his mind; a pattern that he paid no attention to.

Veronica followed the direction of his eyes. "Do you mind talking about it?" she said.

"Me? Rather not. It sort of interests me. I don't know whether I believe in your thing or not; but I've always had that feeling, that you go on. You don't stop; you can't stop. That's why I don't care. They used to think I was trying to be funny when I said I didn't care. But I really didn't. Things, most things, don't much matter, because there's always something else. You go on to it.

"I care for *you*. *You* matter most awfully; and my people; but most of all you. You always have mattered to me more than anything, since the first time I heard you calling out to me to come and sit on your bed because you were frightened. You always will matter.

"But Desmond didn't a little bit. You needn't have tried to make me *think* she didn't. She really didn't. I only married her because she was going to have a baby. And *that* was because I remembered you and the rotten time you'd had. I believe that would have kept me straight with women if nothing else did.

"Of course I was an idiot about it. I didn't think of marrying you till Vera told me I ought to have waited. Then it was too late.

"That's why I want you most awfully to have a baby."

"Yes, Nicky.

"I'll tell you what I'm going to do when I know it's coming. The cottage belongs to Uncle Anthony, doesn't it?"

"Yes."

"Well, I love it. Do you think he'd let me live in it?"

"I think he'd give it to you if you asked him."

"For my very own. Like the apple-tree house. Very well, he'll give it to me—I mean to both of us—and I shall come up here where it's all quiet and you'd never know there was a war at all—even the Belgians have forgotten it. And I shall sit out here and look at that hill, because it's straight and beautiful. I won't—I simply won't think of anything that isn't straight and beautiful. And I shall get strong. Then the baby will be straight and beautiful and strong, too.

"I shall try—I shall try hard, Nicky—to make him like you."

Frances's one Day was not a success. It was taken up with little things that had to be done for Nicky. Always they seemed, he and she, to be on the edge of something great, something satisfying and revealing. It was to come in a look or a word; and both would remember it afterwards for ever.

In the evening Grannie, and Auntie Louie, and Auntie Emmeline, and Auntie Edie, and Uncle Morrie, and Uncle Bartie came up to say good-bye. And in the morning Nicholas went off to France, excited and happy, as he had gone off on his wedding journey. And between Frances and her son the great thing remained unsaid.

Time itself was broken. All her minutes were scattered like fine sand.

February 27th, 1915.
B.E.F., FRANCE.

Dearest Mother and Dad,—I simply don't know how to thank you all for the fur coat. It's pronounced the rippingest, by a long way, that's been seen in these trenches. Did Ronny really choose it because it "looked as if it had been made out of Timmy's tummy?" It makes me feel as if I *was* Timmy. Timmy on his hind legs, rampant, clawing at the Boches. Just think of the effect if he got up over the parapet!

The other things came all right, too, thanks. When you can't think what else to send let Nanna make another cake. And those tubes of chutney are a good idea.

No; it's no earthly use worrying about Michael. If there was no English and no Allies and no Enthusiasm, and he had this War all to himself, you simply couldn't keep him out of it. I believe if old Mick could send himself out by himself against the whole German Army he'd manage to put in some first rate fancy work in the second or two before they got him. He'd be quite capable of going off and doing grisly things that would make me faint with funk, if he was by himself, with nothing but the eye of God to look at him. And *then* he'd rather God wasn't there. He always *was* afraid of having a crowd with him.

The pity is he's wasting time and missing such a lot. If I were you two, I should bank on Don. He's the sensiblest of us, though he is the youngest.

And don't worry about me. Do remember that even in the thickest curtain fire there *are* holes; there are more holes than there is stuff; and the chances are I shall be where a hole is.

Another thing, Don's shell, the shell you see making straight for you like an express train, isn't likely to be the shell that's going to get you; so that if you're hit you don't feel that pang of personal resentment which must be the worst part of the business. Bits of shells that have exploded I rank with bullets which we knew all about before and were prepared for. Really, if you're planted out in the open, the peculiar awfulness of big shell-fire—what is it more than the peculiar awfulness of being run over by express trains let loose about the sky? Tell Don that when shrapnel empties itself over your head like an old tin pail, you might feel injured, but the big shell has a most disarming air of not being able to help itself, of not looking for anybody in particular. It's so innocent of personal malice that I'd rather have it any day than fat German fingers squeezing my windpipe.

That's an answer to his question.

And Dorothy wanted to know what it feels like going into action. Well—there's a lot of it that perhaps she wouldn't believe in if I told her—it's the sort of thing she never has believed; but Stephen was absolutely right. You aren't sold. It's more than anything you could have imagined. I'm not speaking only for myself.

There's just one beastly sensation when you're half-way between your parapet and theirs—other fellows say they've felt it too—when you're afraid it (the feeling) should fizzle out before you get there. But it doesn't. It grows more and more so, simply swinging you on to them, and that swing makes up for all the rotten times put together. You needn't be sorry for us. It's waste of pity.

I know Don and Dorothy and Dad and Ronny aren't sorry for us. But I'm not so sure of Michael and Mother.—Always your loving,

NICKY.

May, 1915.

B.E.F., FRANCE

My Dear Mick,—It's awfully decent of you to write so often when you loathe writing, especially about things that bore you. But you needn't do that. We get the news from the other fronts in the papers more or less; and I honestly don't care a damn what Asquith is saying or what Lloyd George is doing or what Northcliffe's motives are. Personally, I should say he was simply trying, like most of us, to save his country. Looks like it. But you can tell him from me, if he gets them to send us enough shells out *in time* we shan't worry about his motives. Anyhow that sort of thing isn't in your line, old man, and Dad can do it much better than you, if you don't mind my saying so.

What I want to know is what Don and Dorothy are doing, and the last sweet thing Dad said to Mother—I'd give a day's rest in my billet for one of his *worst* jokes. And I like to hear about Morrie going on the bust again, too—it sounds so peaceful. Only if it really is anxiety about me that makes him do it, I wish he'd leave off thinking about me, poor old thing.

More than anything I want to know how Ronny is; how she's looking and what she's feeling; you'll be able to make out a lot, and she may tell you things she won't tell the others. That's why I'm glad you're there and not here.

And as for that—why go on worrying? I do know how you feel about it. I think I always did, in a way. I never thought you were a "putrid Pacifist." Your mind's all right. You say the War takes me like religion; perhaps it does; I don't know enough about religion to say, but it seems near enough for a first shot. And when you say it doesn't take you that way, that you haven't "got" it, I can see that that expresses a fairly understandable state of mind. Of course, I know it isn't funk. If you'd happened to think of the Ultimatum first, instead of the Government, you'd have been in at the start, before me.

Well—there's such a thing as conversion, isn't there? You never can tell what may happen to you, and the War isn't over yet. Those of us who are in it now aren't going to see the best of it by a long way. There's no doubt the very finest fighting'll be at the finish; so that the patriotic beggars who were in such a hurry to join up will be jolly well sold, poor devils. Take me, for instance. If I'd got what I wanted and been out in Flanders in 1914, ten to one I should have been in the retreat from Mons, like Frank, and never anywhere else. Then I'd have given my head to have gone to Gallipoli; but *now*, well, I'm just as glad I'm not mixed up in that affair.

Still, that's not the way to look at it, calculating the fun you can get out of it for yourself. And it's certainly not the way to win the War. At that rate one might go on saving oneself up for the Rhine, while all the other fellows were getting pounded to a splash on the way there. So if you're going to be converted let's hope you'll be converted quick.

If you are, my advice is, try to get your commission straight away. There are things you won't be able to stand if you're a Tommy. For instance, having to pig it on the floor with all your brother Tommies. I slept for three months next to a beastly blighter who used to come in drunk and tread on my face and be ill all over me.

Even now, when I look back on it, that seems worse than anything that's happened out here. But that's because at home your mind isn't adjusted to horrors. That chap came as a shock and a surprise to me every time. I *couldn't* get used to him. Whereas out here everything's shifted in the queerest way. Your mind shifts. You funk your first and your second sight, say, of a bad stretcher case; but when it comes to the third and the fourth you don't funk at all; you're not shocked, you're not a bit surprised. It's all in the picture, and you're in the picture too. There's a sort of horrible harmony. It's like a certain kind of beastly dream which doesn't frighten you because you're part of it, part of the beastliness.

No, the thing that got me, so far, more than anything was—what d'you think? A little dog, no bigger than a kitten, that was run over the other day in the street by a motor-cyclist—and a civilian at that. There were two or three women round it, crying and gesticulating. It looked as if they'd just lifted it out of a bath of blood. That made me sick. You see, the little dog wasn't in the picture. I hadn't bargained for him.

Yet the things Morrie saw in South Africa—do you remember how he *would* tell us about them?—weren't in it with the things that happened here. Pounding apart, the things that corpses can do, apparently on their own, are simply unbelievable—what the war correspondents call "fantastic postures." But I haven't got to the point when I can slap my thighs, and roar with laughter—if they happen to be Germans.

In between, the boredom is so awful that I've heard some of our men say they'd rather have things happening. And, of course, we're all hoping that when those shells come along there won't be quite so much "between."

Love to Ronny and Mother and all of them.—Your very affectionate,
NICHOLAS.

June 1st, 1915.
B.E.F., FRANCE.

My Darling Ronny,—Yes, I think all your letters must have come, because you've answered everything. You always tell me just what I want to know. When I see the fat envelopes coming I know they're going to be chock-full of the things I've happened to be thinking about. Don't let's ever forget to put the dates, because I make out that I've always dreamed about you, too, the nights you've written.

And so the Aunties are working in the War Hospital Supply Depôt? It's frightfully funny what Dorothy says about their enjoying the War and feeling so important. Don't let her grudge it them, though; it's all the enjoyment, or importance, they've ever had in their lives, poor dears. But I shall know, if a swab bursts in my inside, that it's Auntie Edie's. As for Auntie Emmeline's, I can't even imagine what they'd be like—monstrosities—or little babies injured at birth. Aunt Louie's would be well-shaped and firm, but erring a little on the hard side, don't you think?

That reminds me, I suppose I may tell you now since it's been in the papers, that we've actually got Moving Fortresses out here. I haven't seen them yet, but a fellow who has thinks they must be uncommonly like Drayton's and my thing. I suspect, from what he says, they're a bit better, though. We hadn't got the rocking-horse idea.

It's odd—this time last year I should have gone off my head with agony at the mere thought of anybody getting in before us; and now I don't care a bit. I do mind rather for Drayton's sake, though I don't suppose he cares, either. The great thing is that it's been done, and done better. Anyway we've been lucky. Supposing the Germans had got on to them, and trotted them out first, and one of our own guns had potted him or me, *that* would have been a jolly sell.

What makes you ask after Timmy? I hardly like to tell you the awful thing that's happened to him. He had to travel down to the base hospital on a poor chap who was shivering with shell-shock, and—*he never came back again.* It doesn't matter, because the weather's so warm now that I don't want him. But I'm sorry because you all gave him to me and it looks as if I hadn't cared for him. But I did. …

June 10th.

Sorry I couldn't finish this last week. Things developed rather suddenly. I wish I could tell you *what*, but we mustn't let on what happens, not even now, when it's done happening. Still, there are all the other things I couldn't say anything about at the time.

If you *must* know, I've been up "over the top" three times now since I came out in February. So, you see, one gets through all right.

Well—I tried ages ago to tell Dorothy what it was like. It's been like that every time (except that I've got over the queer funky feeling half-way through). It'll be like that again next time, I know. Because now I've tested it. And, Ronny—I couldn't tell Dorothy this, because she'd think it was all rot—but when you're up first out of the trench and stand alone on the parapet, it's absolute happiness. And the charge is—well, it's simply heaven. It's as if you'd never really lived till then; I certainly hadn't, not up to the top-notch, barring those three days we had together.

That's why—this part's mostly for Michael—there's something rotten about that poem he sent me that somebody wrote, making out that this gorgeous fight-feeling (which is what I suppose he's trying for) is nothing but a form of sex-madness. If he thinks that's all there is in it, he doesn't know much about war, or love either. Though I'm bound to say there's a clever chap in my battalion who thinks the same thing. He says he feels the ecstasy, or whatever it is, all right, just the same as I do; but that it's simply submerged savagery bobbing up to the top—a hidden lust for killing, and the hidden memory of having killed, he called it. He's always ashamed of it the next day, as if he had been drunk.

And my Sergeant-Major, bless him, says there's nothing in it but "a ration of rum." Can't be that in my case because I always give mine to a funny chap who *knows* he's going to have collywobbles as soon as he gets out into the open.

But that isn't a bit what I mean. They're all wrong about it, because they make it turn on killing, and not on your chance of being killed. *That*—when you realize it—well, it's like the thing you told me about that you said you thought must be God because it's so real. I didn't understand it then, but I do now. You're bang up against reality—you're going clean into it—and the sense of it's exquisite. Of course, while one half of you is feeling like that, the other half is fighting to kill and doing its best to keep on *this* side of reality. But I've been near enough to the other side to know.

And I wish Michael's friend would come out and see what it's like for himself. Or, better still, Mick. *He'd* write a poem about it that would make you sit up. It's a sin that I should be getting all this splendid stuff when I can't do anything with it.

Love to all of them and to your darling self.—Always your loving,

NICKY.

P.S.—I wish you'd try to get some notion of it into Dad and Dorothy and Mother. It would save them half the misery they're probably going through.

The gardener had gone to the War, and Veronica was in the garden, weeding the delphinium border.

It was Sunday afternoon and she was alone there. Anthony was digging in the kitchen garden, and Frances was with him, gathering green peas and fruit for the hospital. Every now and then she came through the open door on to the flagged path of the upper terrace with the piled-up baskets in her arms, and she smiled and nodded to Veronica.

It was quiet in the garden, so that, when her moment came, Veronica could time it by the striking of the clock heard through the open doorway of the house: four strokes; and the half-hour; and then, almost on the stroke, her rush of pure, mysterious happiness.

Up till then she had been only tranquil; and her tranquillity made each small act exquisite and delightful, as her fingers tugged at the weeds, and shook the earth from their weak roots, and the palms of her hand smoothed over the places where they had been. She thought of old Jean and Suzanne, planting flowers in the garden at Renton, and of that tranquillity of theirs that was the saddest thing she had ever seen.

And her happiness had come, almost on the stroke of the half-hour, not out of herself or out of her thoughts, but mysteriously and from somewhere a long way off.

She turned to nod and smile at Frances who was coming through the door with her basket, and it was then that she saw Nicholas.

He stood on something that looked like a low wall, raised between her and the ash-tree; he stood motionless, as if arrested in the act of looking back to see if she were following him. His eyes shone, vivid and blue, as they always shone when he was happy. He smiled at her, but with no movement of his mouth. He shouted to her, but with no sound.

Everything was still; her body and her soul were still; her heart was still; it beat steadily.

She had started forwards to go to him when the tree thrust itself between them, and he was gone.

And Frances was still coming through the door as Veronica had seen her when she turned. She was calling to her to come in out of the sun.

XXIV

The young men had gone—Morton Ellis, who had said he was damned if he'd fight for his country; and Austin Mitchell who had said he hadn't got a country; and Monier-Owen, who had said that England was not a country you could fight for. George Wadham had gone long ago. That, Michael said, was to be expected. Even a weak gust could sweep young Wadham off his feet—and he had been fairly carried away. He could no more resist the vortex of the War than he could resist the vortex of the arts.

Michael had two pitiful memories of the boy: one of young Wadham swaggering into Stephen's room in uniform (the first time he had it on), flushed and pleased with himself and talking excitedly about the "Great Game"; and one of young Wadham returned from the Front, mature and hard, not talking about the "Great Game" at all, and wincing palpably when other people talked; a young Wadham who, they said, ought to be arrested under the Defence of the Realm Act as a quencher of war-enthusiasms.

The others had gone later, one by one, each with his own gesture: Mitchell and Monier-Owen when Stephen went; Ellis the day after Stephen's death. It had taken Stephen's death to draw him.

Only Michael remained.

He told them they were mistaken if they thought their going would inspire him to follow them. It, and Stephen's death, merely intensified the bitterness he felt towards the War. He was more than ever determined to keep himself pure from it, consecrated to his Forlorn Hope. If they fell back, all the more reason why be should go on.

And, while he waited for the moment of vision, he continued Stephen's work on the *Green Review*. Stephen had left it to him when he went out. Michael tried to be faithful to the tradition he thus inherited; but gradually Stephen's spirit disappeared from the *Review* and its place was taken by the clear, hard, unbreakable thing that was Michael's mind.

And Michael knew that he was beginning to make himself felt.

But Stephen's staff, such as it was, and nearly all his contributors had gone to the War, one after another, and Michael found himself taking all their places. He began to feel a strain, which he took to be the strain of overwork, and he went down to Renton to recover.

That was on the Tuesday that followed Veronica's Sunday.

He thought that down there he would get away from everything that did him harm: from his father's and mother's eyes; from his sister's proud, cold face; and from his young brother's smile; and from Veronica's beauty that saddened him; and from the sense of Nicky's danger that brooded as a secret obsession over the house. He would fill up the awful empty space. He thought: "For a whole fortnight I shall get away from this infernal War."

But he did not get away from it. On every stage of the journey down he encountered soldiers going to the Front. He walked in the Park at Darlington between his trains, and wounded soldiers waited for him on every seat, shuffled towards him round every turning, hobbled after him on their crutches down every path. Their eyes looked at him with a shrewd hostility. He saw the young Yorkshire recruits drinking in the open spaces. Sergeants' eyes caught and measured him, appraising his physique. Behind and among them he saw Drayton's, and Réveillaud's, and Stephen's eyes; and young Wadham's eyes, strange and secretive and hard.

At Reyburn Michael's train was switched off to a side platform in the open. Before he left Darlington, a thin, light rain had begun to fall from a shred of blown cloud; and at Reyburn the burst mass was coming down. The place was full of the noise of rain. The drops tapped on the open platform and hissed as the wind drove them in a running stream. They drummed loudly on the station roof. But these sounds went out suddenly, covered by the trampling of feet.

A band of Highlanders with their bagpipes marched into the station. They lined up solemnly along the open platform with their backs to Michael's train and their faces to the naked rails on the other side. Higher up Michael could see the breast of an engine; it was backing, backing, towards the troop-train that waited under the cover of the roof. He could hear the clank of the coupling and the recoil. At that sound the band had their mouths to their bagpipes and their fingers ready on the stops. Two or three officers hurried down from the station doors and stood ready.

The train came on slowly, packed with men; men who thrust their heads and shoulders through the carriage windows, and knelt on the seats, and stood straining over each other's backs to look out; men whose faces were scarlet with excitement; men with open mouths shouting for joy.

The officers saluted as it passed. It halted at the open platform, and suddenly the pipers began to play.

Michael got out of his train and watched.

Solemnly, in the grey evening of the rain, with their faces set in a sort of stern ecstasy, the Highlanders played to their comrades. Michael did not know whether their tune was sad or gay. It poured itself into one mournful, savage, sacred cry of salutation and valediction. When it stopped the men shouted; there were voices that barked hoarsely and broke; voices that roared; young voices that screamed, strung up by the skirling of the bagpipes. The pipers played to them again.

And suddenly Michael was overcome. Pity shook him and grief and an intolerable yearning, and shame. For one instant his soul rose up above the music, and was made splendid and holy, the next he cowered under it, stripped and beaten. He clenched his fists, hating this emotion that stung him to tears and tore at his heart and at the hardness of his mind.

As the troop-train moved slowly out of the station the pipers, piping more and more shrilly, swung round and marched beside it to the end of the platform. The band ceased abruptly, and the men answered with shout after shout of violent joy; they reared up through the windows, straining for the last look—and were gone.

Michael turned to the porter who lifted his luggage from the rack. "What regiment are they?" he said.

"Camerons, sir. Going to the Front."

The clear, uncanny eyes of Veronica's father pursued him now.

At last he had got away from it.

In Rathdale, at any rate, there was peace. The hills and their pastures, and the flat river fields were at peace. And in the villages of Morfe and Renton there was peace; for as yet only a few men had gone from them. The rest were tied to the land, and they were more absorbed in the hay-harvest than in the War. Even the old Belgians in Veronica's cottage were at peace. They had forgotten.

For three days Michael himself had peace.

He went up to Veronica's hill and sat on it; and thought how for hundreds of miles, north, south, east and west of him, there was not a soul whom he knew. In all his life he had never been more by himself.

This solitude of his had a singular effect on Michael's mind. So far from having got away from the War he had never been more conscious of it than he was now. What he had got away from was other people's consciousness. From the beginning the thing that threatened him had been, not the War but this collective war-spirit, clamouring for his private soul.

For the first time since August, nineteen-fourteen, he found himself thinking, in perfect freedom and with perfect lucidity, about the War. He had really known, half the time, that it was the greatest War of Independence that had ever been. As for his old hatred of the British Empire, he had seen long ago that there was no such thing, in the continental sense of Empire; there was a unique thing, the rule, more good than bad, of an imperial people. He had seen that the strength of the Allies was in exact proportion to the strength and the enlightenment of their democracies. Reckoning by decades, there could be no deadlock in the struggle; the deadlock meant a ten years' armistice and another war. He could not help seeing these things. His objection to occupying his mind with them had been that they were too easy.

Now that he could look at it by himself he saw how the War might take hold of you like a religion. It was the Great War of Redemption. And redemption meant simply thousands and millions of men in troop-ships and troop-trains coming from the ends of the world to buy the freedom of the world with their bodies. It meant that the very fields he was looking over, and this beauty of the hills, those unused ramparts where no batteries were hid, and the small, silent villages, Morfe and Renton, were bought now with their bodies.

He wondered how at this moment any sane man could be a Pacifist. And, wondering, he felt a reminiscent sting of grief and yearning. But he refused, resolutely, to feel any shame.

His religion also was good; and, anyhow, you didn't choose your religion; it chose you.

And on Saturday the letters came: John's letter enclosing the wire from the War Office, and the letter that Nicky's Colonel had written to Anthony.

Nicky was killed.

Michael took in the fact, and the date (it was last Sunday). There were some official regrets, but they made no impression on him. John's letter made no impression on him. Last Sunday Nicky was killed.

He had not even unfolded the Colonel's letter yet. The close black lines showed through the thin paper. Their closeness repelled him. He did not want to know how his brother had died; at least not yet. He was afraid of the Colonel's letter. He felt that by simply not reading it he could put off the unbearable turn of the screw.

He was shivering with cold. He drew up his chair to the wide, open hearth-place where there was no fire; he held out his hands over it. The wind swept down the chimney and made him colder; and he felt sick.

He had been sitting there about an hour when Suzanne came in and asked him if he would like a little fire. He heard himself saying, "No, thank you," in a hard voice. The idea of warmth and comfort was disagreeable to him. Suzanne asked him then if he had had bad news? And he heard himself saying: "Yes," and Suzanne trying, trying very gently, to persuade him that it was perhaps only that Monsieur Nicky was wounded?

"No? *Then*," said the old woman, "he is killed." And she began to cry.

Michael couldn't stand that. He got up and opened the door into the outer room, and she passed through before him, sobbing and whimpering. Her voice came to him through the closed door in a sharp cry telling Jean that Monsieur Nicky was dead, and Jean's voice came, hushing her.

Then he heard the feet of the old man shuffling across the kitchen floor, and the outer door opening and shutting softly; and through the windows at the back of the room, he saw, without heeding, as the Belgians passed and went up into the fields together, weeping, leaving him alone.

They had remembered.

It was then that Michael read the Colonel's letter, and learned the manner of his brother's death: "… About a quarter past four o'clock in the afternoon his battalion was being pressed back, when he rallied his men and led them in as gallant an attack as was ever made by so small a number in this War. He was standing on the enemy's parapet when he was shot through the heart and fell. By a quarter to five the trench was stormed and taken, owing to his personal daring and impetus and to the affection and confidence he inspired. … We hear it continually said of our officers and men that 'they're all the same,' and I daresay as far as pluck goes they are. But, if I may say so, we all felt that your son had something that we haven't got. …"

Michael lay awake in the bed that had been his brother's marriage bed. The low white ceiling sagged and bulged above him. For three nights the room had been as if Nicky and Veronica had never gone from it. They had compelled him to think of them. They had lain where he lay, falling asleep in each other's arms.

The odd thing had been that his acute and vivid sense of them had in no way troubled him. It had been simply there like some exquisite atmosphere, intensifying his peace. He had had the same feeling he always had when Veronica was with him. He had liked to lie with his head on their pillow, to touch what they had touched, to look at the same things in the same room, to go in and out through the same doors over the same floors, remembering their hands and feet and eyes, and saying to himself: "They did this and this"; or, "That must have pleased them."

It ought to have been torture to him; and he could not imagine why it was not.

And now, on this fourth night, he had no longer that sense of Nicky and Veronica together. The room had emptied itself of its own memory and significance. He was aware of nothing but the bare, spiritual space between him and Nicky. He lay contemplating it steadily and without any horror.

He thought: "This ends it. Of course I shall go out now. I might have known that this would end it. *He* knew."

He remembered how Nicky had come to him in his room that night in August. He could see himself sitting on the side of his bed, half-dressed, and Nicky standing over him, talking.

Nicky had taken it for granted even then that he would go out some time. He remembered how he had said, "Not yet."

He thought: "Of course; this must have been what he meant."

And presently he fell asleep, exhausted and at the same time appeased.

It was morning.

Michael's sleep dragged him down; it drowned and choked him as he struggled to wake.

Something had happened. He would know what it was when he came clear out of this drowning.

Now he remembered. Nicky was killed. Last Sunday. He knew that. But that wasn't all of it. There was something else that followed on—

Suddenly his mind leaped on it. He was going out. He would be killed too. And because he was going out, and because he would be killed, he was not feeling Nicky's death so acutely as he should have thought he would have felt it. He had been let off that.

He lay still a moment, looking at the thing he was going to do, feeling a certain pleasure in its fitness. Drayton and Réveillaud and Lawrence had gone out, and they had been killed. Ellis and Mitchell and Monier-Owen were going out and they would certainly be killed. Wadham had gone out and young Vereker, and they also would be killed.

Last Sunday it was Nicky. Now it must be he.

His mind acknowledged the rightness of the sequence without concern. It was aware that his going depended on his own will. But never in all his life had he brought so little imagination to the act of willing.

He got up, bathed in the river, dressed, and ate his breakfast. He accepted each moment as it arrived, without imagination or concern.

Then his mother's letter came. Frances wrote, among other things: "I know how terribly you will be feeling it, because I know how you cared for him. I wish I could comfort you. We could not bear it, Michael, if we were not so proud of him."

He answered this letter at once. He wrote: "I couldn't bear it either, if I were not going out. But of course I'm going now."

As he signed himself, "Your loving Michael," he thought: "That settles it." Yet, if he had considered what he meant by settling it he would have told himself that he meant nothing; that last night had settled it; that his resolution had been absolutely self-determined and absolutely irrevocable then, and that his signature gave it no more sanctity or finality than it had already. If he was conscript, he was conscript to his own will.

He went out at once with his letter, though he knew that the post did not leave Renton for another five hours.

It was the sliding of this light thing and its fall into the letter-box that shook him into realization of what he had done and of what was before him. He knew now why he was in such a hurry to write that letter and to post it. By those two slight acts, not dreadful nor difficult in themselves, he had put it out of his power to withdraw from the one supremely difficult and dreadful act. A second ago, while the letter was still in his hands, he could have backed out, because he had not given any pledge.

Now he would have to go through with it. And he saw clearly for the first time what it was that he would have to go through.

He left the village and went up to Renton Moor and walked along the top for miles, without knowing or caring where he went, and seeing nothing before him but his own act and what must come afterwards. By to-morrow, or the next day at the latest, he would have enlisted; by six months, at the latest, three months if he had what they called "luck," he would be in the trenches, fighting and killing, not because he chose, but because he would be told to fight and kill. By the simple act of sending that letter to his mother he was committed to the whole ghastly business.

And he funked it. There was no use lying to himself and saying that he didn't funk it.

Even more than the actual fighting and killing, he funked looking on at fighting and killing; as for being killed, he didn't think he would really mind that so much. It would come—it must come—as a relief from the horrors he would have to see before it came. Nicky had said that they were unbelievable; he had seemed to think you couldn't imagine them if you hadn't seen them. But Michael could. He had only to think of them to see them now. He could make war-pictures for himself, in five minutes, every bit as terrifying as the things they said happened under fire. Any fool, if he chose to think about it, could see what must happen. Only people didn't think. They rushed into it without seeing anything; and then, if they were honest, they owned that they funked it, before and during and afterwards and all the time.

Nicky didn't. But that was only because Nicky had something that the others hadn't got; that he, Michael, hadn't. It was all very well to say, as he had said last night: "This ends it"; or, as their phrase was, "Everything goes in now." It was indeed, as far as he was concerned, the end of beauty and of the making of beauty, and of everything worth caring for; but it was also the beginning of a life that Michael dreaded more than fighting and killing and being killed: a life of boredom, of obscene ugliness, of revolting contacts, of intolerable subjection. For of course he was going into the ranks as Nicky had gone. And already he could feel the heat and pressure and vibration of male bodies packed beside and around him on the floor; he could hear their breathing; he could smell their fetid bedding, their dried sweat.

Of course he was going through with it; only—this was the thought his mind turned round and round on in horror at itself—he funked it. He funked it so badly that he would really rather die than go through with it. When he was actually killed that would be his second death; months before it could happen he would have known all about it; he would have been dead and buried and alive again in hell.

What shocked Michael was his discovering, not that he funked it now, which was natural, almost permissible, but that he had funked it all the time. He could see now that, since the War began, he had been struggling to keep out of it. His mind had fought every suggestion that he should go in. It had run to cover, like a mad, frightened animal before the thoughts that hunted it down. Funk, pure funk, had been at the bottom of all he had said and thought and done since August, nineteen-fourteen; his attitude to the War, his opinion of the Allies, and of the Government and of its conduct of the War, all his wretched criticisms and disparagements—what had they been but the very subterfuges of funk?

His mother had known it; his father had known it; and Dorothy and John. It was not conceivable that Nicky did not know it.

That was what had made the horror of the empty space that separated them.

Lawrence Stephen had certainly known it.

He could not understand his not knowing it himself, not seeing that he struggled. Yet he must have seen that Nicky's death would end it. Anyhow, it *was* ended; if not last night, then this morning when he posted the letter.

But he was no longer appeased by this certainty of his. He was going out all right. But merely going out was not enough. What counted was the state of mind in which you went. Lawrence had said, "Victory—Victory is a state of mind."

Well—it was a state that came naturally to Nicky, and did not come naturally to him. It was all very well for Nicky: he had wanted to go. He had gone out victorious before victory. Michael would go beaten before defeat.

He thought: "If this is volunteering, give me compulsion." All the same he was going.

All morning and afternoon, as he walked and walked, his thoughts went the same round. And in the evening they began again, but on a new track. He thought: "It's all very well to say I'm going; but how *can* I go?" He had Lawrence Stephen's work to do; Lawrence's Life and Letters were in his hands. How could he possibly go and leave Lawrence dead and forgotten? This view seemed to him to be sanity and common sense.

As his mind darted up this turning it was driven back. He saw Lawrence Stephen smiling at him as he had smiled at him when Réveillaud died. Lawrence would have wanted him to go more than anything. He would have chosen to be dead and forgotten rather than keep him.

At night these thoughts left him. He began to think of Nicky and of his people. His father and mother would never be happy again. Nicky had been more to them than he was, or even John. He had been more to Dorothy. It was hard on Dorothy to lose Nicky and Drayton too.

He thought of Nicky and Veronica. Poor little Ronny, what would she do without Nicky? He thought of Veronica, sitting silent in the train, and looking at him with her startling look of spiritual maturity. He thought of Veronica singing to him over and over again:

London Bridge is broken down—
Build it up with gold so fine—
Build it up with stones so strong—

He thought of Veronica running about the house and crying, "Where's Nicky? I want him."

Monday was like Sunday, except that he walked up Karva Hill in the morning and up Greffington Edge in the afternoon, instead of Renton Moor. Whichever way he went his thoughts went the same way as yesterday. The images were, if anything, more crowded and more horrible; but they had lost their hold. He was tired of looking at them.

About five o'clock he turned abruptly and went back to the village the same way by which he came.

And as he swung down the hill road in sight of Renton, suddenly there was a great clearance in his soul.

When he went into the cottage he found Veronica there waiting for him. She sat with her hands lying in her lap, and she had the same look he had seen when she was in the train.

"Ronny—"

She stood up to greet him, as if it had been she who was staying there and he who had incredibly arrived.

"They told me you wouldn't be long," she said.

"I? You haven't come because you were ill or anything?"

She smiled and shook her head. "No. Not for anything like that."

"I didn't write, Ronny. I couldn't."

"I know." Their eyes met, measuring each other's grief. "That's why I came. I couldn't bear to leave you to it."

"I'd have come before, Michael, if you'd wanted me."

They were sitting together now, on the settle by the hearth-place.

"I can't understand your being able to think of me," he said.

"Because of Nicky? If I haven't got Nicky it's all the more reason why I should think of his people."

He looked up. "I say—how are they? Mother and Father?"

"They're very brave.

"It's worse for them than it is for me," she said. "What they can't bear is your going."

"Mother got my letter, then?"

"Yes. This morning."

"What did she say?"

"She said: 'Oh, no. *Not* Michael.'

"It was a good thing you wrote, though. Your letter made her cry. It made even Dorothy cry. They hadn't been able to, before."

"I should have thought if they could stand Nicky's going—"

"That was different. They know it was different."

"Do you suppose *I* don't know how different it was? They mean I funked it and Nicky didn't."

"They mean that Nicky got what he wanted when he went, and that there was nothing else he could have done so well, except flying, or engineering."

"It comes to the same thing, Nicky simply wasn't afraid."

"Yes, Michael, he *was* afraid."

"What *of*?"

"He was most awfully afraid of seeing suffering."

"Well, so am I. And I'm afraid of suffering myself too. I'm afraid of the whole blessed thing from beginning to end."

"That's because you keep on seeing the whole blessed thing from beginning to end. Nicky only saw little bits of it. The bits he liked. Machine-guns working beautifully, and shells dropping in the right places, and trenches being taken.

"And then, remember—Nicky hadn't so much to give up."

"He had you."

"Oh, no. He knew that was the way to keep me."

"Ronny—if Nicky had been like me could he have kept you?"

She considered it.

"Yes—if he could have been himself too."

"He couldn't, you see. He never could have felt like that."

"I don't say he could."

"Well—the awful thing is 'feeling like that.'"

"And the magnificent thing is 'feeling like that,' and going all the same. Everybody knows that but you, Michael."

"Yes," he said. "I'm *going*. But I'm not going to lie about it and say I don't funk it. Because I do."

"You don't *really*."

"I own I didn't the first night—the night I knew Nicky was killed. Because I couldn't think of anything else *but* Nicky.

"It was after I'd written to Mother that it came on. Because I knew then I couldn't back out of it. That's what I can't get over—my having to do that—to clinch it—because I was afraid."

"My dear, my dear, thousands of men do that every day for the same reason, only they don't find themselves out; and if they did they wouldn't care. You're finding yourself out all the time, and killing yourself with caring."

"Of course I care. Can't you see it proves that I never meant to go at all?"

"It proves that you knew you'd have to go through hell first and you were determined that even hell shouldn't keep you back."

"Ronny—that's what it *has* been. Simply hell. It's been inconceivable. Nothing—absolutely nothing out there could be as bad. It went on all yesterday and to-day—till you came."

"I know, Michael. That's why I came."

"To get me out of it?"

"To get you out of it.

"It's all over," she said.

"It may come back—out there."

"It won't. Out there you'll be happy. I saw Nicky on Sunday—the minute before he was killed, Michael. And he was happy."

"He would be." He was silent for a long time.

"Ronny. Did Nicky know I funked it?"

"Never! He knew you wouldn't keep out. All he minded was your missing any of it."

She got up and put on her hat. "I must go. It's getting late. Will you walk up to Morfe with me? I'm sleeping there. In the hotel."

"No, I say—I'm not going to let you turn out for me. *I'll* sleep at the hotel."

She smiled at him with a sort of wonder, as if she thought: "Has he forgotten, so soon?" And he remembered.

"I can't stop here," she said. "That would be more than even *I* can bear."

He thought: "She's gone through hell herself, to get me out of it."

May, 1916.
B.E.F., FRANCE.

DEAREST MOTHER AND FATHER,—Yes, "Captain," please. (I can hardly believe it myself, but it is so.) It *was* thundering good luck getting into dear old Nicky's regiment. The whole thing's incredible. But promotion's nothing. Everybody's getting it like lightning now. You're no sooner striped than you're starred.

I'm glad I resisted the Adjutant and worked up from the ranks. I own it was a bit beastly at the time—quite as beastly as Nicky said it would be; but it was worth while going through with it, especially living in the trenches as a Tommy. There's nothing like it for making you know your men. You can tell exactly what's going to bother them, and what isn't. You've got your finger on the pulse of their morale—not that it's jumpier than yours; it isn't—and their knowing that they haven't got to stand anything that you haven't stood gives you no end of a pull. Honestly, I don't believe I could have faced them if it wasn't for that. So that *your* morale's the better for it as well as theirs. You know, if you're shot down this minute it won't matter. The weediest Tommy in your Company can "carry on."

We're a funny crowd in my billet all risen from the ranks except my Senior. John would love us. There's a chap who writes short stories and goes out very earnestly among the corpses to find copy; and there's another who was in the publishing business and harks back to it, now and then, in a dreamy nostalgic way, and rather as if he wanted to rub it into us writing chaps what he *could* do for us, only he wouldn't; and there's a tailor who swears he could tell a mile off where my tunic came from; and a lawyer's clerk who sticks his cigarette behind his ear. (We used to wonder what he'd do with his revolver till we saw what he did with it.) They all love thinking of what they've been and telling you about it. I almost wish I'd gone into Daddy's business. Then perhaps I'd know what it feels like to go straight out of a shop or an office into the most glorious Army in history.

I forgot the Jew pawnbroker at least we *think* he's a pawnbroker—who's always inventing things; stupendous and impossible things. His last idea was machine-howitzers fourteen feet high, that take in shells exactly as a machine-gun takes in bullets. He says, "You'll see them in the next War." When you ask him how he's going to transport and emplace and hide his machine-howitzers, he looks dejected, and says, "I never thought of *that*," and has another idea at once, even more impossible.

That reminds me. I've seen the "Tanks" (Nicky's Moving Fortresses) in action. I'd give my promotion if only he could have seen them too. We mustn't call them Fortresses any more—they're most violently for attack. As far as I can make out Nicky's and Drayton's thing was something between these and the French ones; otherwise one might have wondered whether their plans and models really did go where John says they did! I wish I could believe that Nicky and Drayton really *had* had a hand in it.

I'm most awfully grieved to hear that young Vereker's reported missing. Do you remember how excited he used to be dashing about the lawn at tennis, and how Alice Lathom used to sit and look at him, and jump if you brought her her tea too suddenly? Let's hope we'll have finished up this damned War before they get little Norris.

Love to Dorothy and Don and Ronny.—Your loving, MICK.

When Frances read that letter she said, "I wonder if he really is all right. He says very little about himself."

And Anthony said, "Then you may be sure he is."

May 31st, 1916.
B.E.F., FRANCE.

MY DEAR RONNY,—I'm glad Mummy and Father have got all my letters. They won't mind my writing to you this time. It really *is* your turn now. Thanks for Wadham's "Poems" (I wish they'd been Ellis's). It's a shame to laugh at Waddy—but—he *has* spread himself over Flanders, hasn't he? Like the inundations round Ypres.

I'm most awfully touched at Dad and Mummy wanting to publish mine. Here they all are—just as I wrote them, in our billet, at night or in the early morning, when the others were sleeping and I wasn't. I don't know whether they're bad or good; I haven't had time to think about them. It all seems so incredibly far away. Even last week seems far away. You go on so fast here.

I'd like Ellis and Monier-Owen to see them and to weed out the bad ones. But you mustn't ask them to do anything. They haven't time, either. I think you and Dorothy and Dad will manage it all right among you. If you don't I shan't much care.

Of course I'm glad that they've taken you on at the Hampstead Hospital, if it makes you happier to nurse. And I'm glad Dad put his foot down on your going to Vera. She gave you up to my people and she can't take you back now. I'm sorry for her though; so is he.

Have I had any adventures "by myself"? Only two. (I've given up what Mother calls my "not wanting to go to the party.") One came off in "No Man's Land" the other night. I went out with a "party" and came back by myself—unless you count a damaged Tommy hanging on to me. It began in pleasurable excitement and ended in some perturbation, for I had to get him in under cover somehow, and my responsibility weighed on me—so did he. The other was ages ago in a German trench. I was by myself, because I'd gone in too quick, and the "party" behind me took the wrong turning. I did manage to squeeze a chilly excitement out of going on alone. Then I bumped up against a fat German officer and his revolver. That really was an exquisite moment, and I was beast enough to be glad I had it all to myself. It meant a bag of fifteen prisoners—all my own. But that was nothing; they'd have surrendered to a mouse. There was no reason why they shouldn't, because I'd fired first and there was no more officer to play up to.

But the things you don't do by yourself are a long way the best. Nothing—not even poetry—can beat an infantry charge when you're leading it. That's because of your men. It feels as if you were drawing them all up after you. Of course you aren't. They're coming on their own, and you're simply nothing, only a little unimportant part of them—even when you're feeling as if you were God Almighty.

I'm afraid it *does* look awfully as if young Vereker were killed. They may hear, you know, in some roundabout way—through the Red Cross, or some of his men. I've written to them.

Love to everybody. Certainly you may kiss Nanna for me, if she'd like it. I wish I liked Waddy more—when you've given him to me.—Always your affectionate,

MICHAEL.

P.S.—I don't sound pleased about the publication; but I am. I can't get over their wanting to do it. I thought they didn't care.

Ronny—I've been such a beast to them—when Father tried to read my stuff—bless him!—and couldn't, I used to wish to God he'd leave it alone. And now I'd give anything to see his dear old paws hanging on to it and twitching with fright, and his eyes slewing round to see if I'm looking at him.

June 14th, 1916.
B.E.F., FRANCE.

MY DEAR RONNY,—I'm glad you like them, and I'm glad Father thinks he "understands Michael's poems" this time, and I'm glad they've made Mother and Dorothy feel happier about me—BUT—they must get it out of their heads that they're my "message," or any putrescent thing of that sort. The bare idea of writing a message, or of being supposed to write a message, makes me sick. I know it's beastly of me, but, really I'd rather they weren't published at all, if there's the smallest chance of their being taken that way.

But if Ellis is doing the introduction there isn't the smallest chance. Thank God for Ellis.

There—I've let off all my beastliness.

And now I'll try to answer your letter. Yes; the "ecstasy" in the last two poems *is* Nicky's ecstasy. And as Ellis says it strikes him as absolutely real, I take it that some of Nicky's "reality" has got through. It's hard on Ellis that he has to take *his* ecstasy from me, instead of coming out and getting it for himself.

But you and Nicky and Lawrence are right. It *is* absolutely real. I mean it has to do with absolute reality. With God. It hasn't anything to do with having courage, or not having courage; it's another state of mind altogether. It isn't what Nicky's man said it was—you're not ashamed of it the next day. It isn't excitement; you're not excited. It isn't a tingling of your nerves; they don't tingle. It's all curiously quiet and steady. You remember when you saw Nicky—how everything stood still? And how two times were going on, and you and Nicky were in one time, and Mother was in the other? Well—it's like that. Your body and its nerves aren't in it at all. Your body may be moving violently, with other bodies moving violently round it; but *you*'re still.

But suppose it is your nerves. Why should they tingle at just that particular moment, the moment that makes *animals* afraid? Why should you be so extraordinarily happy? Why should the moment of extreme danger be always the "exquisite" moment? Why not the moment of safety?

Doesn't it look as if danger were the point of contact with reality, and death the closest point? You're through. Actually you lay hold on eternal life, and you know it.

Another thing—it always comes with that little shock of recognition. It's happened before, and when you get near to it again you know what it is. You keep on wanting to get near it, wanting it to happen again. You may lose it the next minute, but you know. Lawrence knew what it was. Nicky knew.

June 19th.

I'm coming back to it—after that interruption—because I want to get the thing clear. I have to put it down as I feel it; there's no other way. But they mustn't think it's something that only Lawrence and Nicky and I feel. The men feel it too, even when they don't know what it is. And some of them *do* know.

Of course we shall be accused of glorifying War and telling lies about it. Well—there's a Frenchman who has told the truth, piling up all the horrors, faithfully, remorselessly, magnificently. But he seems to think people oughtn't to write about this War at all unless they show up the infamy of it, as a deterrent, so that no Government can ever start another one. It's a sort of literary "frightfulness." But who is he trying to frighten? Does he imagine that France, or England, or Russia or Belgium, or Serbia, will want to start another war when this is over? And does he suppose that Germany—if we don't beat her—will be deterred by his frightfulness? Germany's arrogance will be satisfied when she knows she's made a Frenchman feel like that about it.

He's got his truth all right. As Morrie would say: "That's War." But a peaceful earthquake can do much the same thing. And if *our* truth—what *we*'ve seen—isn't War, at any rate it's what we've got out of it, it's our "glory," our spiritual compensation for the physical torture, and there would be a sort of infamy in trying to take it from us. It isn't the French Government, or the British that's fighting Germany; it's we—all of us. To insist on the world remembering nothing but these horrors is as if men up to their knees in the filth they're clearing away should complain of each other for standing in it and splashing it about.

The filth of War—and the physical torture—Good God! As if the world was likely to forget it. Any more than we're likely to forget what *we* know.

You remember because you've known it before and it all hangs together. It's not as if danger were the only point of contact with reality. You get the same ecstasy, the same shock of recognition, and the same utter satisfaction when you see a beautiful thing. At least to me it's like that. You know what Nicky thought it was like. You know what it was like when you used to sit looking and looking at Mother's "tree of Heaven."

It's odd, Ronny, to have gone all your life trying to get reality, trying to get new beauty, trying to get utter satisfaction; to have funked coming out here because you thought it was all obscene ugliness and waste and frustration, and then to come out, and to find what you wanted.

June 25th.

I wrote all that, while I could, because I want to make them see it. It's horrible that Dorothy should think that Drayton's dead and that Mother should think that Nicky's dead, when they wouldn't, if they really knew. If they don't believe Lawrence or me, can't they believe Nicky? I'm only saying what he said. But I can't write to them about it because they make me shy, and I'm afraid they'll think I'm only gassing, or "making poetry"—as if poetry wasn't the most real thing there is!

If anybody can make them see it, you can.—Always your affectionate,
MICHAEL.

XXV

Anthony was going into the house to take back the key of the workshop.

He had locked the door of the workshop a year ago, after Nicky's death, and had not opened it again until to-day. This afternoon in the orchard he had seen that the props of the old apple-tree were broken and he had thought that he would like to make new ones, and the wood was in the workshop.

Everything in there was as it had been when Nicky finished with his Moving Fortress. The brass and steel filings lay in a heap under the lathe, the handle was tilted at the point where he had left it; pits in the sawdust showed where his feet had stood. His overalls hung over the bench where he had slipped them off.

Anthony had sat down on the bench and had looked at these things with remembrance and foreboding. He thought of Nicky and of Nicky's pleasure and excitement over the unpacking of his first lathe—the one he had begged for for his birthday—and of his own pleasure and excitement as he watched his boy handling it and showing him so cleverly how it worked. It stood there still in the corner. Nicky had given it to Veronica. He had taught her how to use it. And Anthony thought of Veronica when she was little; he saw Nicky taking care of her, teaching her to run and ride and play games. And he remembered what Veronica's mother had said to him and Frances: "Wait till Nicky has children of his own."

He thought of John. John had volunteered three times and had been three times rejected. And now conscription had got him. He had to appear before the Board of Examiners that afternoon. He might be rejected again. But the standard was not so exacting as it had been—John might be taken.

He thought of his business—John's business and his, and Bartie's. Those big Government contracts had more than saved them. They were making tons of money out of the War. Even when the Government cut down their profits; even when they had given more than half they made to the War funds, the fact remained that they were living on the War. Bartie, without a wife or children, was appallingly rich.

If John were taken. If John were killed—

If Michael died—

Michael had been reported seriously wounded.

He had thought then of Michael. And he had not been able to bear thinking any more. He had got up and left the workshop, locking the door behind him, forgetting what he had gone in for; and he had taken the key back to the house. He kept it in what his children used to call the secret drawer of his bureau. It lay there with Nicky's last letter of June, 1915, and a slab of coromandel wood.

It was when he was going into the house with the key that John met him.

"Have they taken you?"

"Yes."

John's face was hard and white. They went together into Anthony's room.

"It's what you wanted," Anthony said.

"Of course it's what I wanted. I want it more than ever now.

"The wire's come, Father. Mother opened it."

It was five days now since they had heard that Michael had died of his wounds. Frances was in Michael's room. She was waiting for Dorothea and Veronica to help her to find his papers. It was eight o'clock in the evening, and they had to be sorted and laid out ready for Morton Ellis to look over them to-morrow. To-morrow Morton Ellis would come, and he would take them away.

The doors of Michael's and of Nicky's rooms were always kept shut;

Frances knew that, if she were to open the door on the other side of the corridor and look in, everything in Nicky's room would welcome her with tenderness even while it inflicted its unique and separate wound. But Michael's room was bare and silent. He had cleared everything away out of her sight last year before he went. The very books on the shelves repudiated her; reminded her that she had never understood him, that he had always escaped her. His room kept his secret, and she felt afraid and abashed in it, knowing herself an intruder. Presently all that was most precious in it would be taken from her and given over to a stranger whom he had never liked.

Her mind turned and fastened on one object—the stiff, naked wooden chair standing in its place before the oak table by the window. She remembered how she had come to Michael there and found him writing at his table, and how she had talked to him as though he had been a shirker and a coward.

She had borne Nicky's death. But she could not bear Michael's. She stood there in his room, staring, hypnotized by her memory. She heard Dorothea come in and go out again. And then Veronica came in.

She turned to Veronica to help her.

She clung to Veronica and was jealous of her. Veronica had not come between her and Nicky as long as he was alive, but now that he was dead she came between them. She came between her and Michael too. Michael's mind had always been beyond her; she could only reach it through Veronica and through Veronica's secret. Her mind clutched at Veronica's secret, and flung it away as useless, and returned, clutching at it again.

It was as if Veronica held the souls of Michael and Nicholas in her hands. She offered her the souls of her dead sons. She was the mediator between her and their souls.

"I could bear it, Veronica, if I hadn't made him go. I came to him, here, in this room, and bullied him till he went. I said horrible things to him—that he must have remembered.

"He wasn't like Nicky—it was infinitely worse for him. And I was cruel to him. I had no pity. I drove him out—to be killed.

"And I simply cannot bear it."

"But—he didn't go then. He waited till—till he was free. If anybody could have made him, Nicky could. But it wasn't even Nicky. It was himself."

"If he'd been killed as Nicky was—but to die like that, in the hospital—of those horrible wounds."

"He was leading a charge, just as Nicky was. And you know he was happy, just as Nicky was. Every line he's written shows that he was happy."

"It only shows that they were both full of life, that they loved their life and wanted to live.

"It's no use, Ronny, your saying you know they're there. I don't. I'd give anything to believe it. And yet it wouldn't be a bit of good if I did. I don't *want* them all changed into something spiritual that I shouldn't know if it was there. I want their bodies with me just as they used to be. I want to hear them and touch them, and see them come in in their old clothes.

"To see Nicky standing on the hearthrug with Timmy in his arms. I want things like that, Ronny. Even if you're right, it's all clean gone."

Her lips tightened.

"I'm talking as if I was the only one. But I know it's worse for you, Ronny. I *had* them all those years. And I've got Anthony. You've had nothing but your poor three days."

Veronica thought: "How can I tell her that I've got more than she thinks? It's awful that I should have what she hasn't." She was ashamed and beaten before this irreparable, mortal grief.

"And it's worse," Frances said, "for the wretched mothers whose sons haven't fought."

For her pride rose in her again—the pride that uplifted her supernaturally when Nicky died.

"You mustn't think I grudge them. I don't. I don't even grudge John."

The silence of Michael's room sank into them, it weighed on their hearts and they were afraid of each other's voices. Frances was glad when Dorothy came and they could begin their work there.

But Michael had not left them much to do. They found his papers all in one drawer of his writing-table, sorted and packed and labelled, ready for Morton Ellis to take away. One sealed envelope lay in a place by itself. Frances thought: "He didn't want any of us to touch his things."

Then she saw Veronica's name on the sealed envelope. She was glad when Veronica left them and went to her hospital.

And when she was gone she wanted her back again.

"I wish I hadn't spoken that way to Veronica," she said.

"She won't mind. She knows you couldn't help it."

"I could, Dorothy, if I wasn't jealous of her. I mean I'm jealous of her certainty. If I had it, too, I shouldn't be jealous."

"She wants you to have it. She's trying to give it you.

"Mother—how do we know she isn't right? Nicky said she was. And Michael said Nicky was right.

"If it had been only Nicky—*he* might have got it from Veronica. But Michael never got things from anybody. And you *do* know things in queer ways. Even I do. At least I did once—when I was in prison. I knew something tremendous was going to happen. I saw it, or felt it, or something. I won't swear I knew it was the War. I don't suppose I did. But I knew Frank was all mixed up with it. And it was the most awfully real thing. You couldn't go back on it, or get behind it. It was as if I'd seen that he and Lawrence and Nicky and Michael and all of them would die in it to save the whole world. Like Christ, only that they really *did* die and the whole world *was* saved. There was nothing futile about it."

"Well—?"

"Well, *they* might see their real thing the same way—in a flash. Aren't they a thousand times more likely to know than we are? What right have we—sitting here safe—to say it isn't when they say it is?"

"But—if there's anything in it—why can't I see it as well as you and Veronica? After all, I'm their mother."

"Perhaps that's why it takes you longer, Mummy. You think of their bodies more than we do, because they were part of your body. Their souls, or whatever it is, aren't as real to you just at first."

"I see," said Frances, bitterly. "You've only got to be a mother, and give your children your flesh and blood, to be sure of their souls going from you and somebody else getting them."

"That's the price you pay for being mothers."

"Was Frank's soul ever more real to *you*, Dorothy?"

"Yes. It was once—for just one minute. The night he went away. That's another queer thing that happened."

"It didn't satisfy you, darling, did it?"

"Of course it didn't satisfy me. I want more and more of it. Not just flashes."

"You say it's the price we pay for being mothers. Yet if Veronica had had a child—"

"You needn't be so sorry for Veronica."

"I'm not. It's you I'm sorriest for. You've had nothing. From beginning to end you had nothing.

"I might at least have seen that you had it in the beginning."

"*You*, Mummy?"

"Yes. Me. You *shall* have it now. Unless you want to leave me."

"I wouldn't leave you for the world, Mummy ducky. Only you must let me work always and all the time."

"Let you? I'll let you do what you like, my dear."

"You always have let me, haven't you?"

"It was the least I could do."

"Poor Mummy, did you think you had to make up because you cared for them more than me?"

"I wonder," said Frances, thoughtfully, "if I did."

"Of course. Of course you did. Who wouldn't?"

"I never meant you to know it, Dorothy."

"Of course I knew it. I must have known it ever since Michael was born. I knew you couldn't help it. You had to. Even when I was a tiresome kid I knew you had to. It was natural."

"Natural or unnatural, many girls have hated their mothers for less. You've been very big and generous.

"Perhaps—if you'd been little and weak—but you were always such an independent thing. I used to think you didn't want me."

"I wanted you a lot more than you thought. But, you see, I've learned to do without."

She thought: "It's better she should have it straight."

"If you'd think less about me, Mother," she said, "and more about Father—"

"Father?"

"Yes. Father isn't independent—though he looks it. He wants you awfully. He always has wanted you. And he hasn't learned to do without."

"Where is he?"

"He's sitting out there in the garden, all by himself, in the dark, under the tree."

Frances went to him there.

"I wondered whether you would come to me," he said.

"I was doing something for Michael."

"Is it done?"

"Yes. It's done."

Five months passed. It was November now.

In the lane by the side door, Anthony was waiting in his car. Rain was falling, hanging from the trees and falling. Every now and then he looked at his watch.

He had still a quarter of an hour before he need start. But he was not going back into the house. They were all in there saying good-bye to John: old Mrs. Fleming, and Louie and Emmeline and Edith. And Maurice. And his brother Bartie.

The door in the garden wall opened and they came out: the four women in black—the black they still wore for Michael—and the two men.

They all walked slowly up the lane. Anthony could see Bartie's shoulders hunched irritably against the rain. He could see Morrie carrying his sodden, quivering body with care and an exaggerated sobriety. He saw Grannie, going slowly, under the umbrella, very upright and conscious of herself as wonderful and outlasting.

He got down and cranked up his engine.

Then he sat sternly in his car and waited, with his hands on the steering-wheel, ready.

The engine throbbed, impatient for the start.

John came out very quickly and took his seat beside his father. And the car went slowly towards the high road.

Uncle Morrie stood waiting for it by the gate at the top of the lane. As it passed through he straightened himself and put up his hand in a crapulous salute.

The young man smiled at him, saluted, and was gone

Afterword

It's perhaps unsurprising, for a novel published in late 1917, that all roads lead to war. The action of the novel starts in the last years of the Victorian period, but the decisions and activities of the Harrison family are made and undertaken with a clear novelistic eye on the First World War – whether that be Frances's brother's experience of the Boer War, Michael's aesthetic anti-nationalism, or Dorothea's ventures as a suffragette.

May Sinclair weaves many threads through *The Tree of Heaven*, with each of the Harrison children (Dorothea or Dorothy, Michael, Nicholas or Nicky, and John) experiencing the 1910s in a manner that could hardly have taken place much earlier or much later. She looks back on the political questions of the time with the ironic eye that comes from hindsight – perhaps most evident when Anthony plays up his role of the father of the familiar, certain that 'things did not change; they endured; they went on'. But the aspect that is probably most relevant for a series looking at women's lives in the first half of the twentieth century is Dorothy's involvement with the suffrage movement.

When *The Tree of Heaven* was published in 1917, women still did not have the vote in the UK. A few months later, the Representation of the People Act 1918 enfranchised women over 30 who met the minimum property qualifications (and, incidentally, almost all men who had not previously had the vote). Ten years later, this was extended to give the vote to women on equal terms with men.

Sinclair was passionately in favour of women's enfranchisement, and accordingly there is little in *The Tree of Heaven* about whether or not women should have the vote – either in the narrative or in the stock

❧ ❧ ❧

character of the period, the stubborn anti-suffrage male. Rather, the main question in Dorothy's plotline is *how* the vote should best be won.

Dorothy's first proper encounter with the Women's Franchise Union isn't especially promising. 'They might have been children whose behaviour amused her', we are told. There are impassioned, vibrant speeches – but these are quickly interrupted by an argument about whether they should restrict themselves to 'every constitutional means' or whether they should 'oppose the Government that refuses us the vote, whatever Government it may be, regardless of party, by *every means in our power*'.

For Dorothy, on the other hand, the question is really about safeguarding her independence – and not being called upon to agree to slavish obedience. She doesn't question the cause, or even rule out taking extreme steps for the cause (though she is not keen); she rules out only 'blind, unquestioning obedience'.

This is part of *The Tree of Heaven*'s central theme – which forms the central of the three parts of the novel. These are named 'Peace', 'The Vortex', and 'Victory'. The meaning of 'The Vortex' is initially a little unclear, and it is applied differently to different characters. In each case, it is the set of society's expectations that blunt individualism and prize the usual against the exceptional. This might be patriotism, war, marriage or the school spirit. For Dorothy, it is 'the Feminist Vortex':

> For Dorothy was afraid of the Feminist Vortex [...] She was afraid of the herded women. She disliked the excited faces, and the high voices skirling their battle-cries, and the silly business of committees, and the platform slang. She was sick and shy before the tremor and the surge of collective feeling; she loathed the gestures and the movements of the collective soul, the swaying and heaving and rushing forward of the many as one. She would not be carried away by it; she would keep the clearness and hardness of her soul.

The Vortices that Sinclair suggests are often not inherently bad – it is the lack of individualism within their more fervent manifestations that she is against. Was Sinclair a feminist? By any reasonable definition, yes – and, indeed, she wrote the 1912 pamphlet *Feminism*. This was largely in reply to a letter in the *Times* from Sir Almroth Wright, a Professor of Experimental Pathology at the University of London who alleged that 'mental disorder' and 'sexual bitterness' were at the heart of the suffrage movement. Sinclair's response was that 'the element of hysteria is either absent or negligible' among both militant and non-militant suffragettes. And yet she adds in the same pamphlet that she is 'not an ultra-Feminist'; that is, she does not hate men. This caveat should be needless, and yet it is far from the last time that a cry for equality would be wilfully misinterpreted. She concludes admiringly with the 'new sociological factor – the solidarity of women'.

Later in *The Tree of Heaven*, despite her reservations, Dorothy does show this solidarity and joins in protests that lead to her spending a short time in prison. She is much feted by the Women's Franchise Union but their partnership is relatively short lived. A couple of years later, the novel describes the Women's Franchise Union as being 'in the full whirl of its revolution':

> Under the inspiring leadership of the Blathwaites it ran riot up and down the country. It smashed windows; it hurled stone ginger-beer bottles into the motor cars of Cabinet Ministers; it poured treacle into pillar-boxes; it invaded the House of Commons by the water-way, in barges, from which women, armed with megaphones, demanded the vote from infamous legislators drinking tea on the Terrace; it went up in balloons and showered down propaganda on the City; now and then, just to show what violence it could accomplish if it liked, it burned down a house or two in a pure and consecrated ecstasy of Feminism. It was bringing to perfection its last great tactical manoeuvre, the massed raid followed by the hunger-strike in prison. And it was considering seriously the very painful but possible necessity of interfering with British sport – say the Eton and Harrow Match at

Lord's – in some drastic and terrifying way that would bring the men of England to their senses.

But by now Dorothy has more or less parted ways with them, working instead for the Social Reform Union. She later regrets that she spent 'all those years – like a fool – over that silly suffrage'. It's not entirely clear, to me at least, how the reader is intended to react to these words. We can hardly be expected to dismiss 'silly suffrage', but this list of crimes and actions – some little more than pranks; some much more damaging – is clearly not held in high esteem by the narrator. There is no admiration in the depiction of 'a pure and consecrated ecstasy of Feminism', where a faux-sacred tone seems to undermine the work of the Women's Franchise Union. (This 'ecstasy' might even be considered orgasmic – though Sinclair's *Feminism* argues strongly against Sir Almoth Wright's idea that suffragettes were drawn largely from unmarried, 'frustrated' women, 'in whom instincts long supressed have in the end broken into flame'.) And yet the dry narrative voice is equally scornful of those who consider the disruption of a cricket match to be 'drastic and terrifying'. The novelist Stella Benson framed something similar in her 1915 novel *I Pose*, where the prospect of suffragettes burning down buildings is satirically compared to killing in war: 'One may virtuously destroy life in a good cause, but to destroy property is a heinous crime, whatever its motive.'

It is worth mentioning that the Women's Franchise Union did not exist as a body under that name, but a glance towards its prominent fictional figures reveals who Sinclair was depicting with a paper-thin disguise. The leaders of the Union are Mrs Palmerston-Swete, Mrs Blathwaite, and Miss Angela Blathwaite. They do not appear on the page as much as they create influential noises off, but it doesn't take a very vivid imagination to see Emmeline Pankhurst (who had co-founded the similarly named Women's Franchise League in 1889) and Christabel Pankhurst in the Blathwaites – and thus the Women's Franchise Union as the Women's Social and Political Union, or WSPU.

This militant suffrage organisation was founded in 1903 and had the motto 'deeds, not words'. WSPU members were described by the *Daily Mail* as 'suffragettes' in 1906, and they adopted the name.

The catalogue of incidents described above certainly reflects the methods of the WSPU. The 'deeds' of their motto started with tax resistance, and moved to publicly disruptive acts such as heckling speakers. Militancy escalated at the turn of the decade and, by 1912, included arson and bombing of private property – though many suffragettes who considered themselves militant went no further than disruptive, rather than violent, protest.

While Sinclair recognised that there was a spectrum of suffragists and suffragettes, it is only her version of the WSPU which features prominently in *The Tree of Heaven*. We see the others chiefly represented in the form of their colours at a banquet: 'purple and blue, sky-blue and sapphire blue and royal blue, black, white and gold, vivid green, pure gold, pure white, dead-black, orange and scarlet and magenta'. The Women's Franchise Union uses the nationalistic red, white and blue – a parallel of the purple, white and green of the WSPU. The editor of the newspaper *Votes For Women*, Emmeline Pethick-Lawrence, wrote that purple was 'the royal colour' and stood for 'freedom and dignity', white stood for purity, and green for hope. It has also been suggested that the first letters of green, white and violet were intended to echo those of 'give women the vote'.

Sinclair herself seems to have had increasing reservations towards militant women's movements. She was briefly a member of the Women's Freedom League, founded in 1907 by 77 members of the WSPU who opposed violent forms of protest. She was also a member, and eventually a vice-president, of the Women Writers Suffrage League (WWSL). It was this organisation that published *Feminism*, in which she writes, 'I am not going to justify or to defend Militancy, still less do I condemn the women who have been driven to it. The end – *if it indeed can only be accomplished through violence* – will justify it'. By the time *The Tree of Heaven* was written, she appears to have decided that it was not the only means. Dorothy rails against a speaker who suggests that 'Fighting women, not talkers – not writers – not thinkers are what we want!' – a version of 'deeds, not words' – saying that 'our tongues' and 'our brains' are the weapons needed.

Perhaps the change in Sinclair's views had to do with the War. Certainly, both in the novel and in reality, the War changed the movement's activities drastically:

> The gates of Holloway were opened, and Mrs Blathwaite and her followers received a free pardon on their pledge to abstain from violence during the period of the War. And instantly, in the first week of war, the Suffrage Union and Leagues and Societies (already organised and disciplined by seven years' methodical resistance) presented their late enemy, the Government, with an instrument of national service made to its hand and none the worse because originally devised for its torture and embarrassment.
>
> The little vortex of the Woman's Movement was swept without a sound into the immense vortex of the War. The women rose up all over England and went into uniform.

Dorothy's is only one of the stories in *The Tree of Heaven*, and all of them lead, from different directions, to the all-subsuming War. For Nicholas and Michael, the stories end there. Naturally, in 1917 Sinclair couldn't reflect on either the end of the First World War or the next developments in the fight for female suffrage. Perhaps if the novel had been written a few years later, it would have shown a broader spectrum of women's franchise movements, and been able to tell of their eventual victory. As it is, *The Tree of Heaven* is an excellent snapshot of the views and experiences of a representative family in the face of great uncertainty.

Simon Thomas
Series Consultant